Three Fortunes in One Cookie

Three Fortunes in One Cookie

By Cochrane Lambert

Celebrating Twenty-Five Years

All characters in this book are fictitious. Any resemblance to real individuals—either living or dead—is strictly coincidental.

Manufactured in the United States of America.

This trade paperback original is published by Alyson Books,
P.O. Box 4371, Los Angeles, California 90078-4371.
Distribution in the United Kingdom by Turnaround Publisher Services Ltd.,
Unit 3, Olympia Trading Estate, Coburg Road, Wood Green,
London N22 6TZ England.

First edition: August 2005

05 06 07 08 09 a 10 9 8 7 6 5 4 3 2 1

ISBN 1-55583-910-X
ISBN-13 978-1-55583-910-9

Library of Congress Cataloging-in-Publication Data
Lambert, Cochrane.
Three fortunes in one cookie / by Cochrane Lambert.—1st ed.
ISBN 1-55583-910-X; ISBN-13 978-1-55583-910-9 (pbk.)
1. Gay men—Fiction. 2. Fortune cookies—Fiction. 3. New York (N.Y.)—Fiction. I. Title.
PS3612.A5464 T47 2005
813'.6—dc22 2005048055

Credits
Cover photography by Davies & Starr/Stone Collection/Getty Images.
Cover design by Matt Sams.

For Timothy:

A truly rich life contains love and art in abundance.

For Becky:

Your dreams are worth your best efforts to achieve them.

Acknowledgments

Continuing gratitude for their help and guidance to Alison Picard, Nick Street, all the people at Alyson who make this happen, and Tom Wocken.

Thanks to the Biloxi and Ocean Springs Visitors Centers, the Harbor View Café in Pass Christian, and the hospitable patrons of Just Us and Barcode in Biloxi. Thank you to the booksellers who helped in the past, including Cullen at Borders and Marlon at Hollywood Café and Books in Houston, and to all the readers who got in touch.

Especially to friends and family for encouragement and support, including Dorothy Cochrane, Lynne Demarest, James McCain Sr., D-C Tregant, Bazzer in Liverpool, Som246, Fraetor(Flange Monkey), Changeling, and all the lads at OUTeverywhere.com.

And three muses: U2, R.E.M., and Mark Rothko.

Your secret desire to completely change your life will manifest.

Chapter 1

The day was full of more omens than a Hitchcock movie, although Phillip failed to see even one of them. The phone rang at eight, jarring him from a dream about Aerosmith guitarist Joe Perry. Phillip had been about to remove Joe's leather pants, so he whimpered in frustration as he listened to the voice talking to his answering machine.

"Phillip, it's Renata." Phillip's landlady had the gravelly voice of a nicotine addict—although she never hesitated to tell him, usually just after he lit a cigarette, that she'd stopped smoking fifteen years ago. He was suspicious of this claim, since he'd rented from her for five years and her line never changed: "It was a Thursday, fifteen years ago, cold turkey. Anyone with character can do it."

Phillip pulled the covers over his lack of character while she went on.

"You told me three weeks ago, when you paid half a month, that you'd have the rest in two weeks. How many days are in your week, Phillip? Oh, look out your window. It rained earlier. There's a rainbow over the whole damned island." The answering machine clicked—she'd hung up. It was one of her milder calls.

Four months earlier, Phillip's best friend and roommate, Alyssa, had abandoned him to move with her boyfriend to Eugene, Oregon, where they planned to grow and harvest their own oregano. Not only did he desperately miss her—they'd lived together the entire five years that Phillip had been in Manhattan—but it had become a struggle to come up with his rent money on time. He didn't make much in his lowly position as a sales associate at Barnes & Noble. Plus, a boy had to eat sometimes. There wasn't much else in his larder besides pasta and single-serving oatmeal packets.

He could either pay the rest of his rent or the phone bill. If he didn't pay the phone bill, Renata would have no way to harass him. She certainly never came to the building and walked up the seven flights to his Midtown apartment. Then again, if he paid rent, Renata would have no reason to call him.

He pondered that as he stumbled to the window to look for the rainbow. All he saw were a few gray clouds and a woman shaking out a dust mop on the fire escape across the street. Rolling his eyes, he turned to his efficiency kitchen to make a pot of coffee, spilling half the grounds in the sink. After he went to the bathroom, he came back, poured himself a cup, and stepped from the cracked linoleum into his dingy living room.

When he lifted the coffee to his mouth, he found himself with only a handle. His Teenage Mutant Ninja Turtles cup crashed at his feet. Fortunately, the hot liquid splattered away from him, adding to the array of stains already covering the mustard-colored carpet. It looked like a bad Jackson Pollock imitation. As he stood gaping from the ceramic handle to the mess on the floor, the phone rang again.

"It's Eddie," Phillip's sort-of boyfriend informed the machine. "You told me not to let you be late for work again. So get the hell up and get moving. Before you do, check out the incredible rainbow in the sky. It's, like, a double one. I've never seen anything like it. And don't forget: We're meeting Bryant and Stefan at Lo Ching tonight. I'll treat. You need to pay rent. You know, if you'd give up that stupid slave-labor job at Barnes—"

The machine cut Eddie off—the first good thing that had happened all morning. The day didn't improve. Phillip had no hot water, so he took a brief, frantic shower and opted not to shave. The zipper broke in his favorite black pants. He took a deep breath and dressed in a pair of brown jeans that he found in the back of the closet—probably a remnant of some former boyfriend of Alyssa's. He couldn't afford to do his laundry and was down to castoffs from the early Nirvana era. He found a brown shirt that almost matched the pants. After he dressed, he folded a tie and stuck it in his backpack before leaving the apartment. He looked like a UPS man.

He was waiting to cross the street when he heard a child's voice say, "Mommy, is that man homeless?"

He looked around to see whom the kid was talking about, then glanced down to realize that she was staring up at him. Her mother smiled apologetically and let Phillip stride ahead of them when the light changed.

The absence of color on the canvas of his life became even more dismaying when he got to work to find that Stewart was the assistant manager during his shift. Phillip wondered why he hadn't just called in dead while he still had phone service.

"Phillip," Stewart purred, "so glad you could join the rest of us today."

"I'm not late," Phillip said defensively. "In fact, I'm early."

"Indeed you are early. For your shift. We had a mandatory store meeting this morning, dear."

"Fuck," Phillip said under his breath.

"Susannah wrote up the reprimand for your file before she left. Clock in, sign here, and grab a bin. There are books to be shelved, customers to be helped, ties to be put on."

Phillip tossed Stewart a scathing look, pulled his backpack from the locker where he'd stowed it, and retrieved his tie. Instead of grabbing the bin of self-help books that Stewart had indicated, he shoved a cart of art books from the stockroom onto the floor. No one shopped for art first thing in the morning, and it was Phillip's favorite section, where he could daydream about the future coffee-table book titled *Greatest Paintings of Phillip Powell.*

"Hello, un-morning person," Anna whispered into his ear. He jumped, banging his shoulder on a shelf.

"*Shitpissdamnhell,*" he said, rubbing his shoulder. "Did you have to sneak up on me?"

"Too much coffee?" she asked, reaching over to caress his arm—the last thing he wanted from her.

"No coffee at all," he said, sliding away from her grasp. He'd told her a hundred times that he was gay, a fact that neither offended nor deterred her.

"Did you see that rainbow a while ago?" Anna asked. "The whole staff went out and looked at it. Susannah said it was almost a religious experience for her. She gave each of us a gift certificate. Too bad you weren't here."

"I forgot about the meeting," he confessed. He picked up a stack of books and pointedly added, "I hope I don't spend the whole day trying to catch up. I hate days like that."

"I have tickets tonight to the Warhol—"

"I have plans," he said. "With Eddie. My *boyfriend,* Eddie."

"Sweet," she said, wrinkling her nose at him—an affectation that had probably been cute the first time she did it when she was two years old.

"Anna, you've been paged to the register three times," Carlos said, stepping over from the next aisle.

"Think about Warhol," Anna said as she hurried off.

"Does she have some kind of learning disability?" Phillip asked, scowling at her departing back. "I have used the word *homosexual* and every variation thereof since the first time she ran her hands over my chest six months ago. What the hell is her problem?"

"I don't know," Carlos said with a shrug. "It's not even a particularly impressive chest."

"Comments like that make me doubt that you're straight," Phillip said.

"Straight men notice other men's bodies too."

"Yes, but they don't insult inferior ones."

"Let me make it up to you. I figured you woke up late when you missed the store meeting. Business section, right next to *Macintosh for Dummies.* Starbucks."

"You're a saint," Phillip said. "If you ever switch teams—"

"We'll take the first train to Vermont," Carlos promised.

The day lasted several decades. Phillip screwed up two returns and lost a customer's hold books. During his break, he rushed to Renata's stuffy, overdecorated apartment and gave her cash for the rest of his rent. He sneezed violently as her Yorkie used his lap as a trampoline.

"Munchkin, stop that," Renata rasped. The dog ignored her, but it didn't matter. Renata had her own agenda. "Phillip, you're like a son to me. The one who never calls, never writes, takes and takes, never gives."

"I'm sorry I'm late again. Since Alyssa moved out—"

"I'm not running a charity here. Either we need to find another roommate or another apartment, hmm?"

"Yes, ma'am," he said.

"You're so adorable when you use that Southern accent. I can't bank adorable, Phillip. I mean it, Munchkin. No yummies if you don't settle down."

"I have to get back to work," Phillip said.

More than anything in the world, after he finally clocked out and dragged himself home, Phillip wanted to leap from his seventh-floor window. As far as he knew, there'd never been a jumper in the neighborhood. It might make *Greatest Paintings of Phillip Powell* sell faster—if, of course, the paintings had actually existed. Phillip stared guiltily at the box of canvases and oil paints that Alyssa had sent from Eugene the week before and fought another wave of loneliness. Nothing sucked like having a soul mate move across the continent.

He found some reasonably clean jeans and a decent shirt. The hot water was back, so he took a real shower and shaved, then spent an inordinate amount of time on his hair. He wasn't sure why. He certainly had no reason to try to impress Eddie's friend Bryant, who either had the worst adenoids in New York or a cocaine habit. Stefan he'd met only two weeks before, and he immediately cottoned to the fact that he was after Eddie.

Phillip wasn't sure how he felt about that. He wasn't madly in love with Eddie, but he'd gotten comfortable with him after eight months of dating. Plus, Eddie never spent the night or asked Phillip to spend the night with him. Phillip liked a man who was good in bed and eager to part company after sex. And even though he bitched about Phillip's job, Eddie was always happy to pay Phillip's way. The only thing he'd ever asked for in return was a painting. He'd seen pictures of the ones stored in Mississippi, and like Alyssa, he was full of praise for Phillip's work. Phillip figured if they made it to a year, he'd give Eddie a painting for their anniversary.

But as his dinner companions scrutinized their menus at Lo Ching, Phillip didn't need to read the leaves in the bottom of his teacup to see the future. The electricity between Eddie and Stefan could have lit the Eastern Seaboard. His sort-of boyfriend was about to become his ex-boyfriend.

As if he sensed the dull misery creeping over Phillip, Eddie gave him a brilliant smile and said, "I've been priming Stefan all week—"

I'll bet, Phillip thought.

"To hear stories about your family."

"I love a Southern accent," Stefan said. "It's like *yaaaawwwl* came from another country, isn't it?" Phillip's flesh crawled as Stefan spoke.

"Y'all is plural," Phillip said. "It means 'you all.' We never use it to mean one person. And I rarely use it at all. I've lived in New York for five years."

"Your mother is from Alabama, right?" Eddie asked.

"*Her* mother was from Alabama," Phillip replied.

"See, he's getting it all wrong," Bryant said. "You tell the story."

"My grandfather, Exton Godbee—" Phillip began.

"One of those old Southern names!" Stefan said with delight.

"Was from New Hampshire," Phillip continued, trying not to look smug. "He met my Grandmother Lorraine while he was visiting investors in Montgomery, Alabama. She never forgave him for moving her to Mississippi after their marriage, even though he made good with his oil and gas business. In Alabama, they have a phrase: 'Thank God for Mississippi.' It's the only state that consistently ranks lower than Alabama in everything. Lorraine got her revenge by popping out four daughters in quick succession. Exton wanted sons. She added insult to injury by naming the girls after cities in her beloved home state: Andalusia, Eufala, Florence, and Selma."

"The aunts," Eddie said in a tone one might use to say *the lunatics.*

Phillip pretended to concentrate on his food while he considered the possibility of describing his aunts. Andi, the perfectionist. Fala, the genius. Florence, the beauty. Selma, the pragmatist. Any of them would hate the notion of being a dinner topic. He backed away from his mental image of their disapproving faces and said, "When Lorraine got pregnant again, she told her faithful maid, Odell—"

"This gets more *Gone With The Wind* every minute," Bryant remarked between sniffs.

"That she was sure her fifth child was a boy. She planned to name him Montgomery, after Alabama's capital, which was, incidentally, also the first Confederate capital. She even embroidered all the baby blankets and clothes with elaborate M's. Unfortunately, she hemorrhaged to death in childbirth before she could be told that the baby was another girl. Thus it was left to my grandfather to pick my mother's name. Odell insisted that she still should be Montgomery, but Papa was adamant that no daughter of his was going to be named for a bunch of secessionist hoodlums. He pulled out a map and found another Alabama *M* name: McClellan. Odell didn't feel that was much of a girl's name. Papa pointed out that they could shorten it to Ellan. Thus the baby was duly christened McClellan, and Papa had the last laugh. Fort McClellan was named for Major General George B. McClellan, a Union general. Odell still doesn't know that part."

"Good grief, you grew up with a *mammy*?" Stefan asked in a horrified tone.

"She was our housekeeper," Phillip said. "She raised my mother, and she's the only grandmother I've ever known. She owns the house next to my grandfather's. She married a welder named Vernie. My grandfather put their two sons through college. One got a degree in engineering, the other in geology. They both have executive positions and seats on the board at Godbee Energy."

"That is the most politically incorrect story I've ever heard," Bryant said.

"My grandfather is a *Yankee*," Phillip reminded them. "And a curmudgeon. Then again, he has reason to be a little bitter. Not only did his wife die and leave him with five daughters, but they were a headstrong lot. They all married well, except for Selma, who runs her own landscaping business. So they don't need his money, which means they can do as they damn well please. Only my mother, Ellan, married to suit him. My father fell from an oil rig in the Gulf and drowned when I was three. After that, Mama and I moved in with Papa. I became his next great disappointment by refusing to go to college and fleeing to Manhattan right out of high school."

"Where you live in near poverty while that old bastard sits on billions," Eddie said.

Phillip had the uneasy feeling that Eddie had been researching his grandfather's company online. He quickly said, "It's not billions—but whatever, it's his money. I don't want anything from him. If anyone deserves it, Odell's sons do. They're the ones who've put up with him all these years."

Phillip took a fortune cookie from the plate the waitress brought and cracked it open. Three slips of paper fluttered to the table in front of him. Everyone else was busy with their own cookies—or at least Bryant was. Stefan and Eddie were covertly exchanging smoldering glances while they thought Phillip was distracted.

Phillip snatched his three fortunes from the table, jammed them in his jacket pocket, and said, "Eddie, I can't thank you enough for offering to pay for my goodbye dinner."

"Are you going somewhere?" Eddie asked with a blank look.

"No, but I think you are. *Y'all* have a great night."

It started to rain again as Phillip trudged home, and he ducked under an awning to smoke a cigarette. When he reached for his lighter, he felt the slips of paper. He pulled them out and read them in the light from the street.

Your secret desire to completely change your life will manifest.

"I guess I'm getting fired tomorrow too," he muttered bitterly.

You may be hungry soon: Order takeout now.

Phillip laughed. Maybe he should go back and ask Eddie to buy him one more meal for the lonely, impoverished road ahead. On the tail end of that thought, the next fortune made him shiver.

One must know there is a path at the end of the road.

"That's just creepy," Phillip said.

While he smoked and hoped for the rain to stop, he replayed the conversation at Lo Ching. He couldn't understand how he'd been goaded into sharing details of his life that he rarely allowed himself to think about.

Mama and I moved in with Papa. I became his next great disappointment by refusing to go to college and fleeing to Manhattan right out of high school.

It was an unemotional summary of an ugly event, and it had been raining that night too. Phillip's mother had dashed around the house in her nightgown, slamming down windows while Phillip fought with his grandfather. Phillip kept glancing her way, feeling that he should be helping her, especially when she bumped against a table as she hurried to close the French doors. A Waterford egg was jostled from its silver stand. When she caught it as it rolled off the table, she shot Phillip a triumphant look and he smiled at her.

"You think this is funny? Texas A&M has one of the best engineering programs in the country. You've already been accepted. Of course you're going!" Papa roared.

"No, I'm not. I don't care about engineering or running Godbee Energy."

"Godbee Energy put food on your table and clothes on your back all your life, boy. You owe it everything. You'll do as I say!"

"My father paid my way!" Phillip yelled, finally matching his voice to his grandfather's. His mother stopped and turned hurt eyes Phillip's way. "He died working for your fucking company, and I don't owe you a fucking thing."

Papa's face turned purple, as much from Phillip's language as his defiance. When Papa lunged for him, Ellan grabbed her father's arm and said, "Phillip, go upstairs."

"I'm not afraid of him," Phillip said, lowering his voice when he saw how upset she was. "He can't make me be the son he never had."

Papa's fury died and his eyes went cold. "Get out," he said. "See what it's like out there without having all these advantages forced on you. Go on, get out."

Phillip stared at him, sure he didn't mean it. The Gulf Coast was being drenched by near-hurricane weather, and he had no means of getting anywhere.

"Go to Odell's," Ellan begged, tears streaming down her face.

"Don't go to Odell's," Papa said. "Get off my property."

Phillip had tried to convey his remorse to his mother, but she'd turned away. He watched, horrified, as she hurled the Waterford egg at the fireplace. His grandfather's head whipped around when he heard it shatter. Phillip left the house without another word, walking several miles in the torrential rain to his Aunt Florence's house in Long Beach.

Florence was the middle of the five Godbee girls and the only one who'd ever lived away from Mississippi. A former fashion model, she'd worked in New York for years, until she met Sam Garrett on a trip to Biloxi. Sam was the heir to a retail dynasty; his family's stores spread from Atlanta to Dallas, including an anchor store at Biloxi's Edgewater Mall. Florence had married Sam the summer before Phillip's senior year and moved back home, and as he'd begun to know her better, he recognized a kindred spirit. The most logical person for Phillip to run to, she took him in that night without a word of reproach.

The phone lines between the four sisters and his mother had hummed for days. The end result was that he was given an airline ticket, the names of some of Florence's contacts in New York, and a check for a thousand dollars. He hadn't been back to Mississippi in five years.

Phillip tossed his second cigarette into the street, turned up his jacket collar against the drizzle, and thought about the miserable joke his New York adventure had become as he traversed the damp blocks home. He dragged himself up the stairs and came to a horrified stop at the last sight he expected to see outside his door. His grandfather, Exton Godbee, glowered at him from beneath unruly eyebrows. The mountain had come to Manhattan.

Chapter 2

When he was a little boy, Phillip woke up every Saturday and raced downstairs full of excitement and anticipation. Cartoons weren't what got him into an uproar; it was breakfast. All week long he'd eat a bowl of the same cold cereal every morning and yearn for the weekend. A day without school was great, but it was the grab-bag lottery payoff of his mother's Saturday-morning breakfasts that was the reward for suffering through a week of boring classes and soggy corn flakes.

Sometimes she'd make pancakes, pouring batter on the griddle in different shapes and sizes and serving up a heaping plate of Rorschach batter-blots with butter and syrup. Waffles were a rare treat, and Phillip would burn his fingers trying to nip the batter runoff from the sides of the waffle iron. Eggs were served often and in many forms. Poached on toast, boiled, sunny-side up, over easy, and many other varieties, all served with fried potatoes, sausage or bacon, and toast. Or sometimes, if he was really lucky, Odell would have brought over a batch of biscuits or a bowl of grits, neither of which his mother cooked.

He was craving his mother's breakfasts when he woke up the Saturday after his grandfather's surprise visit. He fixed two pieces of toast and tried to decide what he wanted to do on his day off. He stood in the middle of his tiny apartment and stared at the stack of empty canvases leaning against a barren wall in his living room. They looked like rebellious youths, challenging Phillip to touch them. He frowned, measuring the creativity inside himself as he nibbled on a piece of toast, and finally decided that he wasn't awake enough to paint. The pigeons outside his window were cooing loudly and eyeing the toast in his hands as they paced back and forth on the ledge. He flipped on his radio—a war hero of a boom box from his youth that was cracked, missing several knobs, and spattered with paint—and drowned out the sound of the pigeons with R.E.M.'s music.

The smell of coffee brewing lured him back into the kitchen. With the greed and impatience of a seasoned addict, he yanked the empty carafe from the brewer and held a mug under the thin stream as it burbled and dripped out of Mr. Coffee. Just then the phone rang. He turned to glare angrily at the nuisance, then he realized that the phone was off its base and lost somewhere in his cluttered apartment. He frowned, alternating between digging around for the phone and tending to the coffeemaker, trying to decide which was more important. Like an attentive secretary, the answering machine made the decision for him.

"Phillip? Hello? This is Stewart. I don't suppose you're there, listening?" Phillip was relieved that he hadn't picked up the phone and stuck out his tongue at his answering machine like an insolent six-year-old. After a moment, Stewart sighed heavily and said, "I guess you're not there. If you get this message relatively soon, please return my call. Several people called in sick and now we're short-handed. I figured you'd appreciate the extra hours. Thank you."

Phillip took up a new internal debate. As much as he hated to admit it, Stewart was right; Phillip needed the extra hours. It was the first of the month again, and he had less than half his rent money. He barely went out, skipped meals, and put off bills, but no matter how he juggled, he still came up short. He could have consoled himself with the theory that he was suffering for his art, but unlike van Gogh or Rembrandt, his body of work was as meager as his bank account.

However, Stewart's words galled him. Stewart's life's mission seemed to be making Phillip's days at Barnes & Noble a living hell, yet there he was leaving an almost conciliatory message. Phillip couldn't blame his coworkers for calling in sick. The sun was shining outside, and Stewart was a bastard. No contest. Going to work would be like doing Stewart a favor.

No sooner had he made up his mind than the phone rang again. "What is this, ICM?" he asked aloud as he waited for the machine to pick up again.

"Phillip? Are you home?" a male voice with an Irish accent inquired. Phillip put the mug down, sloshing coffee all over the counter, then jammed the carafe back into the coffeemaker. "Phillip? Pick up the phone, mate." Phillip ran into the living room and searched frantically for the phone. "I guess you're out. Don't blame you. The sun's shining, shaping up for a grand day. I'm on the ockie, and thought you might like to pop over for a fry. That is, if you remember where I live. Right. I'll stop rabbiting on and wasting tape on your machine."

Phillip finally found the phone under a pile of dirty clothes and yelped, "Kieran! Please, don't hang up."

"Phillip? 'Bout ye, mate?"

"Yes. I mean, what?" Phillip stammered, suddenly nervous. "I don't know what the heck you're saying. Speak English."

He heard Kieran laugh, which made him relax enough to breathe, then Kieran said, "Sorry. I get going and forget which country I'm in. I'll try again. How are you?"

He spoke with such deliberation that it made Phillip laugh. "I'm all right. What were you saying on my machine? What are you on?"

"On the ockie. It means I've rung work, lied, and said I'm sick."

"Oh, good. I thought it was some drug I didn't know about. There's a lot of that going around today."

"Drug abuse?"

"No. People calling in sick," Phillip explained. "My assistant manager just called me to ask if I'd come in to work, since half the staff called in sick."

"Manager? I thought you told me you're an artist."

"Um, yeah," Phillip replied, feeling guilty for the complete absence of paintings in his apartment.

"But how can you be on the dole if you're working?" Kieran asked. "This must be one of those language barriers. You're makin' me feel awful thick, mate."

"On the what?" Phillip went back into the kitchen to clean up the mess he'd made. Unfortunately, he'd put the carafe in wrong, and coffee was running all over the counter, dripping onto the floor. "Aw, crap," he said.

"Problems?"

"I'm making a mess," Phillip groaned, grabbing for a sponge. "You were saying?"

"Ah, I wasn't. But I was wondering if you'd eaten? Would you fancy a fry?"

"A fry?"

"Eggs, sausage, and the like. Or we could just have flakes. It's up to you."

Phillip's stomach rumbled at the thought of real food, so he said, "Yeah, sure. Sounds great."

"Brilliant! I've got to pop out for me messages, but—"

Just then the phone died, R.E.M. stopped playing, the coffeemaker sputtered and went silent, and the answering machine clicked erratically. It was a short symphony of death. Phillip stormed into his living room, riffled through a pile of old mail, and found the power bill. He tore the pages from the envelope and leafed through them until he found the turnoff date.

"Damn it all to hell," he muttered, realizing he was a month past due. Before he knew what was happening, he was crying. "Oh, great," he moaned. "Twenty-three years old and I'm acting like a child."

He wasn't sure if he meant that he was acting childish because he was crying or because of his inability to handle his finances. It was quite possible that he was more worried about his eyes being red and puffy for his breakfast with Kieran. He couldn't help it. He needed comfort, and the arms of a handsome Irishman sounded very appealing at that moment.

Unfortunately, Kieran's and Phillip's unlucky karma seemed to go hand in hand. Not only had they met on the night that Phillip walked out on his sort-of boyfriend Eddie, but it had happened while Phillip was having a deep discussion with his grandfather about his future.

Exton Godbee had stood at his door that night demanding to be heard; there was nothing for Phillip to do but follow his grandfather to the nearest bar.

"Uh, Papa? Are you sure you want to go here?" he asked, stopping him before they entered Posh, a gay bar in the middle of Phillip's block. "There's a great Italian restaurant up the street. We could have a drink and get some food, if you're hungry."

"This place has beer?" Exton asked.

"Yeah."

"That's good enough for me," he said and held open the door.

Phillip hesitated for a second, then realized that if he balked he would call more attention to their situation. He walked inside the dimly lit bar and through the crowd lining the walls and tables. He needn't have worried, as Posh drew a mixed clientele. His grandfather followed him inside, staying close behind and squinting at the bottles behind the bar.

Without asking what Phillip wanted, his grandfather ordered two bottles of Bud and commandeered a table. The music was loud, so Phillip had to lean in as his grandfather opened with a guilt trip and commented on Phillip's physical changes since they'd last seen each other. Then he moved on to news from home—mostly about his business and how it had grown, how busy he was, and the amount of time it took away from the family.

As his grandfather started to harp on the importance of family—a familiar yarn of family folklore—Phillip allowed himself a few glances around the room and noticed several attractive faces. He'd had many chances to practice his cruising techniques in crowded clubs and bars, but it never failed to amaze him how quickly gay men could reject or accept a person within a few seconds of eye contact. He noticed that a few men were already casting curious glances toward him, then turning away the moment he looked up. He realized it was useless to try to cruise while he was with his grandfather, since most of the guys at Posh probably assumed the old man had hired Phillip for the evening or that Phillip was a gold digger. Both thoughts made him slightly ill.

While his grandfather went to the bar to order another round, Phillip noticed several people crowded around a table across the room. They were laughing and contributing greatly to the din of the bar. The mixed group of men and women were all about his age, and their hands never left their drinks as they talked. They looked happy, as if they were having fun, and he longed to be with them instead of listening to his grandfather as he disparaged Phillip's hand-to-mouth existence in Manhattan. Papa returned and handed him another Bud, and Phillip tried to concentrate as his grandfather picked up his monologue where he'd left off.

Soon Phillip's concentration lagged, and he found himself looking around the room again. Which was when he caught one of the guys from the crowded table watching him. The man was taking a long pull from his bottle of Guinness as he stared. His hair was long and black and contrasted with his green eyes and pale skin, which glowed in the dark room. He tucked his hair behind his ear, exposing his sharp cheekbones and handsome jaw. He swallowed, then rested his elbows on his denim-clad knees and held the bottle between them. He smiled at Phillip when he noticed his interest.

"Boy, pay attention when I'm talking to you," Papa barked. Phillip quickly did as he was told. "I'm not here to listen to myself speak, which is damned near impossible with all this racket. How can you live like this?"

"I like it here, Papa," Phillip said. "If I'm going to be a serious artist, Manhattan's the place to do it."

"Serious artist," Papa repeated in a mocking tone. "You can't live on dreams, boy."

His grandfather launched into another diatribe about how Phillip needed to wake up and take life more seriously. Phillip covertly turned his head and found Emerald Eyes looking at him again. Making sure his grandfather was distracted, Phillip mouthed the word, *Stop.*

Emerald Eyes smiled broadly, shook his head, and mouthed back, *No.*

Phillip grinned and returned his attention to his grandfather. He spent another hour getting nowhere in his efforts to convince the old man that he knew what was best for his own life. Finally, after extracting a promise that Phillip would meet him at his hotel before he flew out the next day, Papa left.

Minutes after his grandfather left Posh, a group of people walked toward the door. Some of them stared at Phillip and grinned slyly, and he realized that they were Emerald Eyes's friends. Noticing that he wasn't with them when they left, Phillip looked back at his table and saw him sitting alone, still gazing at Phillip. Emerald Eyes smiled mischievously, crossed a leg over his knee, and gestured to an empty chair opposite him. Phillip pretended to consider the offer, then left his seat. He stopped by the bar to order another beer, as if he was in no hurry to join his admirer, then finally reached his table.

"Hallo," the man said, standing to greet Phillip before he could sit down. "I'm Kieran McClosky."

Phillip was immediately charmed by his politeness, which seemed a little at odds with his previous flirtatiousness. Kieran's demeanor reminded Phillip of his aunts' tales of Southern gentleman callers. Phillip told Kieran his name and asked, "Are you Scottish or Irish?"

"Irish," Kieran replied, holding up his bottle of Guinness as proof. "Did I steal you away from your date?"

"My date? Hell, no! That was my grandfather."

"Smashing, then," Kieran said. "I'm not usually such a bold boy, but I thought you're a fine bit of stuff. I couldn't help flirtin' but."

Between the loud music and Kieran's rapid-fire slang, Phillip could barely understand him. But the message was conveyed in the way he moved his chair closer to Phillip's and leaned in and smiled when he spoke. He was very forward and happy, making Phillip forget all about his unpleasant evening.

Kieran mentioned his friends, who'd left to go to another bar. They worked together—all programmers for a software company, all from Ireland. They regularly put in ten hours at work, sometimes longer, then hit the bars.

"I know what you're thinking. We're all a bunch of gee-eyed cafflers," Kieran said.

"I don't even know what that means," Phillip said.

"Drunken idiots," Kieran said with a grin. "We just like a bit o' craic now and then. You got to let off steam, you know? I do other stuff—museums, concerts, cinema. You like theater?"

"Sure. But I can hardly ever afford to go," Phillip said. Kieran tucked his hair behind his ear after it fell over his eyes again, then stared at Phillip for what seemed like an eternity. Phillip felt his face flush and said, "What?"

"You got a fella?" Kieran asked.

Phillip thought of Eddie, who was probably in bed with Stefan by then. He replied, "No."

"When are you gonna shift me, mate?" When Phillip gave him a blank look, Kieran moved in closer, took Phillip's bottle of Bud, and set it next to his Guinness on the table. Just when Phillip thought he was going to demonstrate his meaning with the bottles, Kieran put his hand on Phillip's shoulder and leaned in to kiss him. Their lips met, and Phillip felt a shiver run up his spine. Kieran's kiss was soft and gentle, unlike his rough and boisterous outward appearance.

He made love the same way, gently caressing Phillip and making sure he was comfortable with him in his bed. He was passionate, sensitive, and curious as he explored every inch of Phillip's body. He kept talking too, telling Phillip how he liked his eyes, his lips, his hands. He whispered in Phillip's ear to tell him how excited he was. Kieran fell asleep afterward with his head on Phillip's chest. Phillip stared at his profile, tracing his jaw and lips lightly with a fingertip and burning the image in his memory so he could recreate it later in a sketch.

In the morning Kieran was back to his energetic self, racing back and forth from the kitchen to the bathroom as he simultaneously cooked breakfast and got ready to leave for work. Phillip remained in bed. Watching Kieran was exhausting, and Phillip rubbed his bleary eyes. When Kieran brought him a bowl of Irish oatmeal, Phillip stared at it distrustfully, since he was slightly hungover.

"It's good for you, Phillip. Here's your cha, mate," he said, passing Phillip a steaming mug.

"What is this, tea? You don't have any coffee?"

"Never touch the stuff," Kieran said as he walked back to the bathroom. "It's bad for you."

"And all that booze you drank last night was good for you?" Phillip called after him. "There's really no coffee?"

Kieran didn't answer, but Phillip heard him laughing as he turned on the shower. Before he closed the door, he said, "Don't give me any guff. Eat up."

Phillip ate. The oatmeal was thick and calmed his uneasy stomach. The tea seemed almost as thick as the oatmeal. It was black and strong, forcing Phillip to leave the bed to forage for sugar. He found some in a small bowl on the kitchen counter. He sipped at the tea and looked around Kieran's apartment. It was stark and modern—it could've been photographed for an IKEA catalog. There were no photographs or pictures anywhere, though his bookshelves were piled with books, CDs, wooden boxes. and other small objects. Everything was in its place: magazines stacked neatly on a coffee table, cushions angled at either end of a leather sofa, dishes stacked carefully on metal shelving in the kitchen.

Phillip thought of his own apartment and felt out of place; he worried that his bed-head violated an appearance clause. He put down the mug of tea and picked up Kieran's toaster, looking at his reflection in the chrome and smoothing down his hair. Satisfied, he returned the toaster to its proper place and picked up the mug again.

Kieran came out of the bathroom with a towel wrapped around his waist and asked, "How's about ya?"

"I'm okay," Phillip answered. Kieran leaned over, and Phillip ran his free hand over Kieran's naked back as Kieran kissed him. "Thanks for breakfast. Aren't you having any?"

"No time," Kieran said. He noticed Phillip's empty oatmeal bowl in the sink. As he washed it, he said, "I have to get to work. You can stay, if you want."

"No; thank you, though. I have to meet my grandfather at his hotel in a couple of hours," Phillip answered. After Kieran put the bowl in a drying rack and went to his closet to dress, Phillip washed his mug. "I had fun last night. It was nice. You're nice."

Phillip felt awkward. Kieran pulled a black sweater over his head, and his smooth, flat stomach disappeared from view. Phillip watched Kieran slip into a pair of jeans before he gathered his own clothes so he could get dressed too. Kieran put on a pair of boots and topped off his outfit with a black leather blazer. After he tied back his hair, he made the bed, arranged the pillows, and smoothed the covers as if he were hoping to pass a military inspection.

Kieran walked Phillip out, and Phillip gave him his number when they were on the sidewalk. Kieran pulled Phillip to him, gave him a lingering kiss, then flashed another of his mischievous grins before he hailed a cab and disappeared. Phillip walked the fourteen blocks from the Upper West Side to his apartment on 51st Street, all the while replaying the night in his head.

He hadn't seen Kieran since that morning. He'd gone to Posh a few times, hoping to run into him and his friends on a bar crawl, but to no avail. Barnes & Noble was a few blocks from Kieran's apartment building, and Phillip would look for his face in the crowds on his walks to work, or hope that he might run into Kieran on his lunch hour. He couldn't stop thinking about the Irishman. So when he actually called and invited Phillip to breakfast, it was as if Phillip had been given a new lease on life. And when his phone died in mid conversation, it was if his lease had suddenly been revoked.

He tossed the dead phone aside in disgust, hastily got dressed, then ran down seven flights of stairs to the street below. He couldn't afford a cab, so he alternated between jogging and walking to the high-rise on 65th Street where Kieran lived. He was out of breath by the time he got there, and the doorman could barely understand him when he wheezed Kieran's name.

"Mr. McClosky isn't answering," the doorman said after calling up to Kieran's apartment.

"Are you sure? Can you try again?" Phillip begged.

The doorman tried again, but Kieran still wasn't answering. Feeling chagrined, Phillip thanked the doorman and walked back outside into the brisk February air. He leaned against the wall and lit a cigarette, taking a moment to think of what to do next.

"He thinks I hung up on him," Phillip said aloud. He slid down the wall and sat on the sidewalk while he smoked. "He thinks I'm rude. He's polite and charming, and I'm a rude bastard."

"Away in the head, perhaps, but I wouldn't say you're a bastard," a voice said next to Phillip. He looked up and saw Kieran holding several plastic D'Agostino's bags filled with groceries. Kieran grinned and asked, "What are ya at, Phillip?"

"Nothing. I'm fine," Phillip said, flustered and a bit embarrassed as he flicked his cigarette into the street and stood up. He searched his pockets for a mint while he sheepishly said, "Hi."

"Hi," Kieran said. He motioned Phillip closer with his head, so Phillip took a few steps forward and Kieran gave him a chaste kiss. "Marlboros?"

"Lights," Phillip confirmed.

"Smashing. I ran out of fags last night. Part of the reason I had to go to the store."

"You smoke? I had no idea," Phillip said, feeling as if he'd just won a prize.

"Aye. Ready for breakfast? Or would you rather stand out here and have a chinwag in the cold?"

"Lay on, Macduff," Phillip said happily.

"Macbeth was Scottish, ya dolt."

Phillip followed him upstairs and sat on a chair at the kitchen counter, watching Kieran while he cooked. He told Phillip about a project he'd been working on, sometimes through the night, writing code for a computer program that would eventually be used for tax preparation. The deadline was tight, so he and his friends had been too busy to do anything other than work, which was why he hadn't called. He lit a cigarette off the stove and told Phillip about growing up in Belfast and how he'd hated to leave a year ago but couldn't resist the idea of working in America with his friends. As he cooked, smoked, and talked, Phillip watched the end of his cigarette, waiting to see if the ash would fall into the skillet, which never happened. It was as if Kieran was an actor playing a part he'd rehearsed over and over, performing a monologue for Phillip: cooking, smoking, and talking. Phillip wondered if Kieran knew how to juggle too.

When he was finished cooking, Kieran pulled out a chair for Phillip at a small dining table with a glass top. When Phillip sat down, Kieran placed a plate of eggs, fried potatoes, sausage, bacon, and scones in front of him.

"What are you trying to do, give me a heart attack?" Phillip asked. Then he quickly said, "I'm kidding. It looks fantastic."

"Good answer," Kieran said. He put a mug of tea next to Phillip's plate, then sat down to eat. After they'd chewed several bites in silence, Kieran gestured to the food with his knife and asked, "Any use?"

"This is so good. Thank you. It reminds me of Saturday mornings," Phillip said. He told Kieran about his affinity for his mother's breakfasts.

"What about Sunday?" Kieran asked.

"Sunday was oatmeal, church, and chores. Somehow they went hand in hand. Sitting through mass while digesting oatmeal was like a prelude to penance."

"You're Catholic?"

"Somehow I was raised Catholic," Phillip said. "I'm not sure why. My family's not, but my mother decided I shouldn't be raised Baptist, which my family was. None of them are religious freaks or anything, but I think it was a community thing. They liked feeling as if they belonged to something." Kieran nodded as he chewed. "My grandfather wasn't happy about me being raised Catholic. He doesn't seem that happy with a lot of the things I do. Anyway, I think he even blames Catholicism for my mother's…" Phillip broke off, not wanting to talk about his mother. Kieran looked at him expectantly. Phillip threw caution to the wind and finally said, "Craziness."

"Craziness?" Kieran asked. For a moment Phillip wondered if the word didn't translate, then Kieran said, "As in off her nut, or just silly?"

"Either. Both. Whatever," Phillip said. "Half the reason I'm so nostalgic about my mother's Saturday morning breakfasts is that she stopped making them when I was seven. We were doing an elementary school play, acting out a bunch of nursery rhymes. I was playing Humpty Dumpty. I had an egg costume; I fell off a wall, the whole gambit. My mother came to see my performance, and when I fell off the wall and cracked, so did she. She became hysterical and rushed the stage to hold me, screaming the whole time for an ambulance. It was like she didn't understand that it was just a play."

"Stop the lights! Are you serious?"

"It's all true. We never had eggs again after that. She couldn't look at an egg for the longest time without weeping uncontrollably. They did call an ambulance that day. For her. They kept her overnight and then sent her home, prescribing bed rest and aspirin. I don't think they quite understood the gravity of her situation. She did seem okay for a while after she slept for a couple of days."

"Jaysus," Kieran said in awe.

"Of course, she couldn't read stories to me after that. She'd read *Little Red Riding Hood* to me and weep when the grandmother was eaten. If a pig's house was blown down by a wolf, that would set her to crying—anything like that. Finally, I begged her not to read to me and asked her to make up stories, thinking that might be safer."

"Did it work?" Kieran asked.

"It worked out all right for her," Phillip stated, "but not for me. I'll give you an example. She told me one story about a schizophrenic axe murderer who hid in a little boy's and girl's closet for a whole week, because the schizophrenic could only kill the children when it was dark. He was thwarted because the children were afraid of the dark and wouldn't turn out their light. So the schizophrenic axe murderer starved to death. The end!"

"You must've been feckin' scared to bits," Kieran said, laughing.

"I couldn't sleep without the lights on for years. It infuriated my mother, because I'd missed the whole moral of her story. Which apparently was that I should overcome my fears so others wouldn't be put off by them."

"Poor axe murderer," Kieran said sadly.

"We lived with my grandfather, who was concerned about her health by then. Other folks in the family, being Southern and taking great pride in crazy people, convinced him that my mother—McClellan," Phillip said, adding his mother's name, which made Kieran smile, "was fine and he should let her be. Ever since my grandfather's housekeeper, Odell, became too old to watch over Mother, he's hired a slew of nurses, all disguised as maids. She's usually not a problem; she doesn't want to leave the house or cause any harm. She just wants to go about her business—being crazy."

"I don't know what to say, Phillip. I'm sorry," Kieran said.

"It's all right. Sometimes it was fun having a crazy mother. Everyone in school knew, so nobody gave me any grief in case I went psycho on them," Phillip said, laughing. Kieran smiled politely, but his face grew concerned when Phillip started crying.

Kieran got up and led Phillip to his bed, where they lay down and Kieran held him. Phillip cried against his chest, feeling comforted as Kieran softly stroked his back. After a while Phillip stopped crying but didn't move. He felt like time had stood still, and he didn't want to go forward. When Kieran kissed the top of his head, Phillip moved so he could look at him.

"How's about ya?" Kieran asked, wiping his thumb across Phillip's cheek.

"Smashing," Phillip said, trying to sound Irish. "I don't know what came over me; I'm sorry."

"Don't sweat it," Kieran said gently.

"Hey, that was very American of you," Phillip said. Kieran playfully chucked Phillip's chin. "There's been a lot of crap going on for me lately. I want to paint but can't because I feel so uninspired. I want to be an artist, but I have to work a miserable job at Barnes & Noble. My roommate moved out, and I'm always behind on the rent because I haven't found anyone to live with me. My electricity was turned off because I couldn't afford to pay the bill. And now I'm embarrassed for telling you all this, and for having a meltdown after you cooked me that amazing breakfast. You probably think I'm crazy too."

"Naw, I don't," Kieran said. "You're human, Phillip. Happens to the best of us. I think you're brilliant."

"Thanks," Phillip said bashfully. "But I haven't told you the worst of it. The reason my grandfather was here last week is because he wants me to move back home."

"Aw, crap," Kieran said.

"You're telling me. He has to work in China for six months and doesn't trust his current nurse with Mother. Or rather, he doesn't trust Mother with the nurse. He's never been gone so long, and he doesn't want to risk my mother having an emotional breakdown."

"He's probably right. A family member should be there," Kieran said reluctantly.

"I got a huge speech about family responsibility from my grandfather," Phillip said. "I didn't give him an answer yet."

"When would you have to go?" Kieran asked, taking Phillip's hand and holding it against his stomach.

"The end of the month," Phillip said.

"Stop the lights!"

"ConEd already did," Phillip reminded him, and Kieran laughed. "But I'm here now."

Chapter 3

Although Phillip's grandfather wouldn't give him money, sure that he'd squander it, once Phillip agreed to go to Mississippi, he paid his grandson's rent and utility bills, enabling Phillip to quit his job and use his last paycheck however he wanted. A born procrastinator, Phillip put off packing his apartment by attempting to paint. He was upset with the idea of leaving Manhattan and thought he'd channel his emotions into his art. Each morning, he studied postcards of John Marin's watercolors of New York, agreeing with Marin's belief that an artist needed to truly know a place before he could paint it. But whenever he picked up his brush, trying to capture his unique perspective of the city, he painted nothing. The blank canvases said more about him than his artistic abilities possibly could, so he decided to start packing.

After he'd filled the first box with his canvases and art supplies and sealed it, he went for a walk. The city always vibrated with noise during the week, as if Manhattan and her inhabitants were having a long and boisterous quarrel, but when Phillip stepped outside he greeted a relatively calm Sunday afternoon. The only automobiles soaring down Ninth Avenue were taxi cabs, and pedestrians moved at a lazy pace, mostly in pairs. Phillip heard someone laughing across the street.

The sun felt warm on his face, although the air was crisp and chilly. Phillip could practically smell spring in the air, as if it was lurking somewhere on 46th Street having an early dinner on Restaurant Row. He had a sudden craving for Goldfish crackers, so he walked to Tenth Avenue to Xth Ave. Lounge, where he put his scarf and coat on a stool at the bar, staked claim to a dish of Goldfish, and ordered a beer.

The door to the bar opened, and Phillip cringed as cold air rushed past his neck. He cringed again when a voice said, "Hey, Phillip! Did that pesky rash of yours clear up?"

"Funny, Bunny. Very funny," Phillip replied.

Bernard "Bunny" Wallace was one of Phillip's friends from the neighborhood. Bunny, a recent Fordham University graduate, worked for a travel agency, a menial job that irked his Fortune 500 family. However, Mr. and Mrs. Bunny were reluctant to include their son in their respective companies—a brokerage firm and a baked-goods industry—because of Bunny's fey yet boisterous demeanor.

"I'll have a pink lady," Bunny said as he slipped onto a barstool.

The bartender, a lesbian named Darla, replied, "You *are* a pink lady," before she sauntered to the other end of the bar.

"Takes one to eat one!" Bunny called after her. He turned to Phillip and smiled brightly. "I booked another affair today," he said. "It's so funny how cheap adulterous men are. He paid with a platinum card, but the trip was brass, brass, brass! Economy class, two-star hotel adjacent to the beach, no view. Tacky. Why do women put up with that kind of crap?"

"Where are they going?" Phillip asked.

"Besides hell? Ibiza."

"How fabulous. I'm jealous," Phillip said.

"Don't be. If I went to Ibiza, it would be four stars all the way," Bunny announced. "You and I should go sometime."

"Okay," Phillip agreed in a tone that suggested Bunny had just offered to sell him a bridge.

"I'm serious," Bunny insisted. "That's what's wrong with you, Phillip. You don't dream big. You think you're fated to live in Hans Christian, Mississippi, forever."

"*Pass* Christian," Phillip said, giving Christian the proper pronunciation of *Chris-chee-ann*. "And you're wrong."

"Thank you," Bunny said to Darla as he accepted his pink lady. He took a dainty sip, then said, "If I'm wrong, why haven't you painted anything since you moved here? You knew you'd go back home, so you never even bothered. One might say you *willed* it all to happen. Or not to happen, as the case may be."

"One might also say that you're a bitchy queen with a big mouth," Darla observed.

"Shut the fuck up, please," Bunny said politely. Darla laughed and left to fill another drink order. "What have you been up to today?"

"Packing," Phillip said sullenly. "I even failed at that. I only packed my art supplies. Don't say it."

"Say what? I wasn't going to say anything," Bunny insisted. There was a pause. "It's not like you were going to use them anyway."

"Thanks for not saying anything," Phillip said. "I'm going to see if Carlos is home. Want to come?"

Bunny sighed and stared at the wall behind the bar as if he were consulting an imaginary appointment book and finally nodded. He knocked back the rest of his pink lady and said, "Sure. Whatever."

Carlos lived in an apartment on 38th Street off Tenth Avenue. It was a short walk, but by the time they got there, Bunny was complaining of frostbite.

"Would you shut up? It's not that cold," Phillip said.

"It's *freezing*," Bunny insisted. "My skin is very sensitive. I wouldn't expect a troglodyte like you to understand or relate. And this is a horrible part of town. I wouldn't be surprised if we got mugged—or worse."

"We're not going to get mugged," Phillip said. He was beginning to wish he hadn't invited Bunny along.

"Oh! We're not? I wasn't aware I was traveling with Madame Sousatzka, clairvoyant extraordinaire."

They phoned from the corner, and Carlos tossed the keys to his building down to Phillip, since the buzzer system was broken. Inside, Carlos greeted them with hugs and cold bottles of Budweiser.

Phillip watched Bunny eye Carlos with his usual expression of lust. Phillip didn't blame him. Carlos's ruddy skin and black hair emphasized his gold-flecked brown eyes. His sweater seemed too small, not only because it strained over his biceps and pecs, but when he moved, it inched up and provided a tantalizing peek at his stomach. But Carlos's sexiest feature was that he seemed totally comfortable with himself.

"When are they going to fix that intercom system?" Phillip asked.

Carlos shrugged. "I have no idea. Nobody else in the building seems to care, and I can't exactly complain about it."

Carlos's building was a run-down tenement tagged with graffiti and marred by a few boarded-up windows. It was the kind of place where Phillip expected drug dealers to buy guns while their prostitute girlfriends turned tricks in the basement. Carlos had been illegally subletting his apartment from a friend since he'd been dumped by his last girlfriend.

"I don't know how you can stand to live here. This place is disgusting," Bunny said.

"The rent is four hundred a month," Carlos replied.

"You get what you pay for," Bunny said. He removed his leather blazer, draped it over a chair that had been rescued from the streets of New York, and gingerly sat down.

"We miss you at the store," Carlos said to Phillip, purposely bumping into him with his shoulder as he moved to a beat-up sofa. He dropped onto it and pointed to the PlayStation that Bunny had been eyeing since their arrival. "It's already on. Ready to go. All you have to do is turn on the television."

"Blade?" Bunny asked, biting a hangnail. When Carlos nodded, Bunny squealed with glee and lunged for the television. Jubilation suddenly turned into shrieks of terror, and he jumped on the sofa. "Something ran over my foot!"

Trying to appear nonchalant, Phillip stepped onto a chair and crouched down as he peered across the room. "Where? I don't see anything."

"It was probably a mouse," Carlos said, drinking his beer as if nothing had happened. "The buildings on either side of this one are empty. They're just passing through. It's no big deal."

"That was no mouse!" Bunny wailed. "I swear on my mother's eyes it was a rat. It ran behind the bookcase. Oh, it was disgusting." Bunny looked at Carlos with narrowed eyes. "That's it! You have to move out of here."

"Rats or mice, it is kind of nasty," Phillip agreed. "Not to mention the locals that hang out on the corner all night."

"Phillip, how much is your rent?" Bunny asked. "Eight? Nine hundred?"

"Eight hundred and fifty. Why?"

"You should sublet your place to Carlos. Legally," he added, staring pointedly at Carlos. "Have you terminated your lease?"

"Not yet. Renata's out of town. Instead, I could ask her about a sublet."

"It's a nice idea, but no go, guys," Carlos said. "There's no way I can come up with that much rent."

"Fine. Phillip, you and I will visit your landlady together. I'll sublet your apartment from you, but Carlos will actually live there. Illegal, but why break tradition? You can pay me four hundred, Carlos, and I'll pay the rest."

"No way, man," Carlos said. "Again. Nice idea but—"

"Oh, please," Bunny interjected. "Don't give me any of your macho bullshit and just do it. Get out of this hellhole. This may be my last act of good will. Do you really want to pass it up?"

Phillip, amused, watched as Carlos rubbed his jaw thoughtfully while Bunny sat on the arm of the sofa and examined his cuticles in frustration. He knew that for Bunny, a trust-fund baby, the money was a drop in the bucket, and he was making a genuine offer to a friend in need.

"Fine," Carlos said.

"Fantastic," Bunny said, heaving a sigh of relief. "I refuse to play PlayStation in this pit any longer."

"You could always get your own," Phillip pointed out.

"Are you kidding? I'd rather spend my money on something more worthwhile."

"Like buying your own Latin love slave?"

"Ooh, you're catching on."

"Hey!" Carlos exclaimed.

"Besides," Bunny continued, "if this move back to the bayou doesn't work out for you, you can always come home."

"It's the coast, not the bayou," Phillip said. He wistfully added, "I'm not sure where home is anymore."

"Oh, Dorothy," Carlos chided.

Phillip grabbed one of Carlos's sneakers from the floor and lobbed it at his head. Carlos deflected the shot and sent the sneaker flying across the room. It crashed into the bookshelf, causing something behind it to hiss and screech.

Bunny slammed his beer bottle on the coffee table like a judge with a gavel and said, "That's it. I'm out of here."

"I have to go too," Phillip said. "Kieran is cooking me dinner tonight. Let's share a cab. Carlos, I'll call you about the sublet, okay?"

Carlos, who'd been eyeing the bookcase with trepidation, said, "Yeah, sure. Uh, can I stay at your place tonight?"

Kieran cooked another elaborate meal for Phillip, which left him feeling sleepy and happy. They sat together on Kieran's sofa afterward, drinking wine and filling each other in on the day's events. Phillip almost told Kieran about Bunny's idea to sublet his apartment, but decided against it at the last minute. He didn't want to offer Kieran—or himself—false hope that he'd return to Manhattan. Instead, he told Kieran about Bunny and Rabid Rodent, the squatting tenant behind Carlos's bookcase.

Kieran smiled and said, "It's said that the Irish have a sure way to get rid of a rat."

"How?"

"We rhyme them to death."

"So I should take it as a good sign that you didn't read me poetry on Valentine's Day?" Phillip asked.

"I think you already know the answer to that one, mate." Kieran finished his wine, set down the glass, and stood up, offering his hand to Phillip. "May I have this dance?"

"There's no music."

"You can't hear it? It's louder than thunder, lad. Just listen." Phillip sat frozen in place on the sofa, staring at Kieran and wondering which of them was the crazy one. Kieran laughed and beckoned to him, saying, "Come on then. Come closer."

Phillip set down his glass, took Kieran's hand, and allowed himself to be led to the center of the room. Kieran put an arm around Phillip's waist and guided Phillip's head to his chest.

"Can you hear it now?" Kieran asked.

Phillip heard Kieran's heart beating and said, "Yes. It's my favorite song in the whole world." They swayed together and moved in slow circles. Kieran hummed a tune that sounded familiar to Phillip, but he couldn't place it. All he knew was that he didn't have a care in the world; he wished time would stop so he could live in that moment forever. He raised his head, closed his eyes, and felt Kieran's lips cover his. *Now I know why people in musicals sing,* he thought. Kieran playfully bit his neck, causing Phillip to yelp in giddy surprise. He pulled off his shirt, allowing Kieran easy access to nibble wherever he pleased.

"What did I do to deserve this?" Kieran asked.

"You must've been a very good boy," Phillip replied as he unbuttoned Kieran's jeans.

"I don't feel like being a good boy," Kieran cautioned.

"That's fine too."

Hours later, Phillip stared at the lights of New York City through Kieran's bedroom window. He thought about the millions of people on the other side of the glass and wondered if they were half as content as he was at that moment. He lay back on the pillow and closed his eyes, trying to form a picture of Pass Christian in his mind—of the beach, his grandfather's house, anything. But nothing appeared.

"What about your da?" Kieran asked.

Phillip had thought Kieran was already asleep, so the question startled him. "What?"

Kieran lit a cigarette for them to share and said, "Your father."

"I got what you meant, but what do you want to know? He died when I was three," Phillip said.

"Do you remember him?"

Phillip considered the question a moment. The picture of home became clearer in his mind. The oak trees, the roads, Odell's roses. "I don't know. Sometimes I think I have memories, but I'm not sure if they're real or just what I made up out of what I was told." He laughed. "Although if I relied on what I was told, I'd have a contradictory picture. Papa only ever said he was a good hand. That's oil field code for someone who works hard and can be counted on. Aunt Selma said much the same thing. That he was a hard worker. Aunt Andi thought Mama married beneath her—my father didn't go to college. His mother died after a long illness when he was fifteen. He went to work to help his father pay the medical bills. He dropped out of school, got his GED—"

"What's that?" Kieran asked.

"If you pass a test, you get a certificate that's the same as a high school diploma," Phillip explained. "You need it to get a job or get into college if you didn't finish high school. Anyway, his father died a few years later, so Mama and I were all he had. Probably the person who would describe him the most accurately is Aunt Florence, but she was already living in New York when Mama met and married him. My grandfather had an apartment in the Garden District in New Orleans, and he set up my parents in a small house near his place."

"So you were born there then?"

"Oh, no. My mother spent the last few weeks of her pregnancy in my grandfather's house in Pass Christian. She said she wasn't having a baby without Odell. She took me back to New Orleans when I was a few weeks old."

Phillip struggled to remember any impressions of their life in New Orleans, but as usual, only one came to mind. "I think I remember him coming home. He would spend several weeks at a time working offshore, so I guess having him in the house was different enough to stick in my head. To me, he was big, loud, and fun. He'd pick me up and put me on his shoulders while he hugged my mother. Actually, he wasn't a large man to anyone but a little kid. He wasn't much taller than my mother. Probably the same as me: five foot ten or so. At least I think I remember that. There aren't many pictures of him, except wedding pictures, but my mother has one in her bedroom of me on his shoulders. He wasn't built like me. He was more solid, sturdy, like you'd expect of someone who worked on an oil rig."

"Do you remember when he died?"

"I only know what Aunt Fala told me. My mother put me down for an afternoon nap and fell asleep on the couch. A summer storm blew up. That's common on the coast. Apparently my mother was startled awake by thunder, and she jumped up, feeling like something was wrong. She was in my room, making sure I was okay, when my grandfather and some other Godbee employees got there. I read the fatality report a long time ago, but basically, a crew was using a crane to put something on the top platform of their rig. They did something wrong, and three of the guys ended up falling to the lower platform. They were injured but okay. A fourth guy was thrown into the Gulf in ninety feet of water. That was my father. It took them two weeks to find his body."

"That's terrible," Kieran said. "How old was he?"

"Same as my mother: twenty-three. Aunt Fala said my mother couldn't stop crying. They took us back to Pass Christian because they didn't think she was in any shape to take care of me. And we never left."

"Twenty-three," Kieran mused.

Phillip smiled and said, "Don't think that hasn't occurred to me. In fact, my grandfather even mentioned it. Something about how every year after this is one my father didn't have, so I shouldn't waste them. I'm not a superstitious person; I don't attach any particular significance to my age. Anyway, Aunt Fala contends that my mother's heart was broken, and she never got over it."

"Do you think so?"

"She never said that—my mother, I mean. I can remember things she said when I was growing up. For example, my father liked to draw. She said he always had a pad and pencil with him, but he mostly used it for working out ways to fix things. I don't know if I started drawing because she told me that, or vice versa. But she always made sure I had sketch pads, pencils, chalk, then watercolors, inks, and paint. Either I was born an artist or she turned me into one, but drawing always made me feel connected to my father. His name was Mike. Michael Powell."

Kieran stubbed out his cigarette and lit another. "What else?" he asked.

"She says that when I'm thinking, I walk like him. I clasp my hands behind my back and sort of push forward with my head. I remember walking on the beach like that when I was mad or upset about something. My grandfather's house is separated from the water by a busy road that parallels the beach. It's the longest man-made beach in the world. The true Gulf of Mexico is several miles out from the shore."

"So you grew up at your grandfather's house?"

"He would say I haven't grown up yet," Phillip said. "But yes. He wasn't there much. He still keeps a place in New Orleans. When I lived there, Pass Christian was where he came to rest or take a vacation. These days, he goes there mostly to check on my mother."

"And now that he has to go to China—"

"Right. He expects me to be the man of the house." Phillip was quiet for a while. He needed to lighten the mood. "One day when I was fourteen, Mama took me out back, which…I don't know how to describe this. The land behind Papa's house isn't a typical backyard. It's really deep—about the length of a football field."

"American football or *real* football?" Kieran teased.

Phillip pretended not to hear him and said, "There are several live oaks on the property. Live oaks are a big deal in the South."

"How so?" Kieran asked.

"They get names."

"You name your trees?"

Phillip laughed and said, "There's a Live Oak Society. Over four thousand trees from all over the South are members. There's only one human member at a time, who oversees things. Some trees are named for people. Others have names like Faith, Hope, Charity, Friendship, and Patriarch. If something happens to them, the cause of death is listed in the Live Oak Society records."

"Like what?" Kieran asked, genuinely fascinated.

"Lightning, hurricane, or construction too near the tree roots. Some of the trees are hundreds, even a thousand years old, and although their membership continues after death, they can get in trouble with the society for breaking its rules."

"You're coddin' me."

"No! I'm serious. Wearing whitewash is an infraction. So is wearing signs. Although admittedly the members have no control over this. Oh, and there was a scandal when a water oak sneaked in. Big Bertha is still listed, but she isn't a legal member of the society."

Kieran couldn't stop laughing, until he finally said, "And you say your mother's mad?"

"I'm not making this up," Phillip said solemnly.

"No, it's brilliant," Kieran replied. "Trees are significant in Celtic legends. The oak—*duir*—is the most sacred tree of all. It's the strongest of the trees, the doorway to the Otherworld. They carry messages to the beyond and offer blessings. Go for a walk in the woods in Ireland and you'll see trees with ribbons and messages tied to them from people asking for safety, prosperity, love. So I'm not one to be laughin' at your trees with their rules and regulations. I didn't mean to get you off track."

"There's one tree behind the house that's my favorite. It's over thirty feet tall, but the branches sweep the ground, so it's good for climbing. Mama took me out back once, and we sat in the tree to have a little talk about my father. She told me that even though she'd loved him a lot she didn't want me to romanticize the past. They had their problems. She'd had a tough time as a new bride because she hadn't learned to manage a household. And he was used to being on his own. Stuff like that.

"Like any couple," Kieran said.

"I suppose. She mostly felt sad that I'd never know him, but she said, 'My heart's not in his grave.' I'd always been careful not to talk about him or ask questions, but after that I didn't worry about it so much. After all, she gave me plenty of other things to worry about." Phillip reached across Kieran, took a cigarette from the pack, and lit it. "What about your family?"

"They give me plenty to worry about too," Kieran replied cryptically. When Phillip frowned, Kieran smiled and said, "I'll tell you all about them, I promise. But I have to sleep. I'm going to close my eyes and dream of trees."

"Good night," Phillip said softly.

He turned to the window again as he smoked his cigarette, wishing he could take Kieran with him to Mississippi. While he contemplated that, he recognized the song playing through his mind as the one Kieran had hummed while they danced in the living room: U2's "I Still Haven't Found What I'm Looking For."

Chapter 4

Phillip adapted quickly to being a man of leisure in Manhattan. He enjoyed being able to go anywhere and do anything on a whim. He visited museums and galleries. He went out at night with Bunny, sometimes staying at clubs until dawn and then sleeping all the next day. He met Kieran for breakfast when everyone else was having dinner. He felt reckless, but his wild abandon came with an expiration date.

Phillip's creativity emerged from hibernation. His paints and brushes remained packed away, but he carried a sketchbook and pencils on his jaunts. He filled its pages with thin-lined impressions of Central Park vistas, buildings that struck his fancy, and people in cafés. He treated his sketchbook like a journal, preserving memories and visions for future reflection on the inevitable days when he'd be bored and lonely back home in Mississippi.

Every other page seemed to contain an image of Kieran. Kieran laughing while holding a cup of tea at a bistro in the village. Kieran sleeping with his hand over his chest. Kieran standing on the bridge that led to the Ramble in Central Park. Kieran not only dominated Phillip's sketchbook but also his time. Even though Kieran and his associates were busy with several important projects at work, he was generous with what little free time he had. Kieran and Phillip wanted to spend as many hours together as they could before Phillip left, so they traded copies of their apartment keys, which made things a lot easier.

The only complication was that neither of them wanted to talk about the fact that their time together was fleeting. February 28, Phillip's last day in New York, became the elephant that followed them all over Manhattan and usually insisted on being noticed at the worst possible moments.

"I couldn't get it up last night," Phillip told Bunny while they waited on the stoop of Renata's building for her to return from an errand so they could finalize the sublet.

Bunny yelped and covered his ears. "What makes you think I want to know about that? Now I'm picturing your flaccid penis in my head."

Phillip ignored him and continued. "We were fooling around, and Kieran said something about wanting to remember all the details about me: the mole on my neck, the small of my back—all the little things."

Bunny snorted.

"He's working tonight, so it was our last night together. It made me sad," Phillip said wistfully. "I've been memorizing him the same way. I don't want to go. I have to. Whatever. But neither of us is talking about it. It's becoming a problem."

"If it's affecting your—" Bunny broke off and cringed, making strange hand gestures as if he were reaching for a word he didn't want to pick up.

"Performance," Phillip offered.

"Thank you. Yes, that. If it's affecting *that*, then it's a problem." Bunny readjusted his sunglasses and sipped noisily from a Starbucks cup. "Whatever, Phillip. You're going. It's the eleventh hour, pumpkin. Have you asked Kieran to go with you?"

"No."

"Are you going to ask him for a commitment? To remain faithful?"

"I don't see how I can."

"Are you going to have a long-distance relationship?"

"Doubtful."

"Okay then. Enough said. There's no reason for you to worry yourself into a state of flaccidity over this any longer. I don't want to hear any more about it."

"If you'd meet him, you'd see how wonderful he is," Phillip said. He'd tried several times to invite Bunny to dinner with Kieran, to the movies with them, or to join them on pub crawls with Kieran and his friends. Bunny always begged off, citing an important party he had to go to or prior commitments, which bothered Phillip. It seemed rude of Bunny, as if he thought Phillip's relationship with Kieran was trivial and not worth his time. Phillip added, "But if it's not important for you to meet my boyfriend—"

"Drama," Bunny cautioned. "I'm not Meryl Streep. I don't do drama. Why is everything in life so tragic to young people?"

"You're a year older than me."

Bunny waved his hand dismissively as he sipped his coffee.

"Is that Phillip on my stoop? Of course it is. He doesn't owe me money," Renata said, wheezing slightly as she pushed past them and hoisted herself up the steps. "Come in, boys, and we'll sign those papers. If my heart doesn't give out on the stairs. Watch out for Munchkin. He gets under foot. If you smoosh him, I'll have you killed."

Renata was irritable, having just returned from a trip to Israel. She'd been there for three weeks—long enough to be reminded how much she loved her family but also how necessary it was to live in a different hemisphere from them.

"I feel for you, Phillip. I really do," she said. "They drove me crazy! I love them, but my God, a woman can take only so much. Every day they insist I come back to live with them. Why do I run these apartment buildings if it gives me so much grief? Why do I only go home a few times a year? Why do I live so far when my mama could go at any day?" Renata spit on her fingers and threw her hands in the air, exasperated. "They make me want to put my head in the oven. But I love each and every one of them, Phillip. That's what family is. That's why you have to go take care of your mama. Now, who is this?"

"This is Bunny," Phillip said.

As she shook Bunny's hand, Renata said, "I expected a woman. But don't worry. I love the gays. I had a gay boy in another one of my buildings. He was such a wonderful boy. Always visiting with me, bringing me food, telling stories—a talented man. He died. Let's sign the papers."

She produced a new lease for them to sign, going over each line in great detail and explaining a litany of rules, codes, and laws. The entire process, which could have been simple and brief, took nearly two hours, not only because of Renata's vast knowledge of real estate law, but her need to elaborate each section of the lease with a story.

"Phillip knows this already, but there will be no pets," she decreed. "One time, in a seven-story walk-up I own in Flatbush, there was a man who left town for a month. I'll never forget him. Bad man. Lived in 3R."

"Renata, we really need to—"

"He left behind a beautiful Siamese cat," Renata said, ignoring Phillip, "for a whole month. In August. The food and water ran out. I don't understand how people can be so cruel to one of God's creatures! No food! No water! Can you believe it? It's terrible. Now we have laws to protect our animals and lock up monsters like that bad man from 3R. But this happened in 1985. When he left, the other tenants kept complaining about an awful noise. Then an awful smell. To make a long story short—"

"Too late," Bunny muttered.

"The poor kitty died. I felt like an accessory! To murder!" Renata's hand fluttered to her chest, her eyes bulged, and she grabbed a tissue, dabbing at her eyes. "From then on, no pets. I couldn't take it if something bad like that happened again."

"What about Latin boys? Are they allowed?" Bunny asked. Phillip slapped his leg and glared at him. "What? I'm serious!" He leaned toward Renata and said, "I consider mine a pet."

Renata said, "I have a building in Spanish Harlem. I'm a Jew! I'm not a racist. Now, on to page two. Oh, my eyes. I forgot my glasses."

Afterward, Phillip and Bunny toasted the finalized sublet over champagne in Phillip's kitchen. "When she launched into that story about her brother the architect in Israel, I wanted to puncture my ear drums with my pen," Bunny moaned.

"She's not that bad," Phillip protested. "She just takes a little getting used to."

"No, thanks. I want as little contact as possible with Jabba the Landlady."

"Besides, she started telling us about him after she found out that you're gay. I think she wanted to fix you guys up."

Bunny appeared to think it over and said, "That might not be such a bad idea. It could really irk my parents. If it's not a WASP, they can't be bothered."

"If it's not a woman," Phillip added, having heard horror stories of Bunny's parents before. "Anyway, I'm glad that's over. And I'm glad it's you and Carlos who are holding on to this place for me. I like the idea of having a safety net." Bunny regarded him thoughtfully but said nothing. Phillip smiled and lifted his cup. "At the least, now you'll be forced to stay in contact with me."

"Why wouldn't I?" Bunny asked. He walked out of the kitchen, saying, "You've been a good friend to me, Phillip. I'm so glad I took the time to get to know you, and I—what is that?"

Phillip followed him into the living room, where Bunny was staring at a large mural. Phillip had delved into his box of art supplies for his charcoal sticks and worked on a mural that occupied most of his nights. It was of Kieran, inspired by one of the rough outlines in his sketchbook.

"There's a nude in my apartment," Bunny stated.

"My apartment," Phillip said.

"Not entirely, pumpkin. I hope Carlos doesn't mind," Bunny said. "Is this your Irishman?"

Phillip nodded and regarded his handiwork. He stepped forward and rubbed at the charcoal, improving the shading on the sheet that fell off the bed to drape the floor.

"You know, there are only two places my clients vacation that they never complain about when they come home," Bunny mused. "Alaska and Ireland. Is that anatomically correct?"

"As if I'd answer," Phillip said.

"If it is, I understand your obsession now," Bunny said. He looked at his watch and said, "I met this guy at XL the other night. He's throwing a party at his place, and I thought I'd go. Do you want to come?"

"Why not? Kieran's working all night. I might as well," Phillip said, staring at the mural.

"Don't I feel second-rate?" Bunny downed his champagne and said, "Let's go. I'm loaning you clothes because all of yours are wrong."

Later, in borrowed designer jeans, a D&G shirt, and a suit jacket, Phillip found himself following Bunny up 15th Street. "Do you see any house numbers?" Bunny asked, consulting a bar napkin with an address scribbled on it.

"Here it is," Phillip said, stopping short and causing Bunny to run into him. They stared at a cinder-block building, which looked bland in comparison to the town houses on either side of it. "Are you sure you read the napkin right?"

"Yes," Bunny said impatiently. "This has to be it. He made it sound like a fabulous apartment building. Not a bomb shelter. Maybe it's nicer on the inside."

"I used to think that about people too," Phillip muttered.

They heard the dull thumping of a house beat when they got off the elevator on the sixth floor. They followed the sound down a hallway, until a door on the right burst open and a girl grabbed Phillip's arms for balance.

"Excuse me," Phillip said politely. "Are you okay?"

She looked up and nodded, then lurched to the right and threw up in a potted plant.

"Lovely," Bunny said. "This must be the place."

Inside, the apartment was stark except for the crowd of people crammed into a space no larger than Phillip's apartment. The walls were bare, save for a few posters and a dartboard. As they pushed their way through people, Phillip scanned the crowd for a familiar face but didn't see anybody he knew.

"It's like NYU in here," Bunny said. "This isn't the scene I was promised. I expected guys in shirts and ties snorting coke and making deals, not guys in baggy jeans and girls with backpacks."

"I thought backpacks were out," Phillip said.

"That's what I'm saying!" Bunny shrieked.

"Where's our host?" Phillip asked. "What's his name?"

"Theodore? Trevor?" Bunny guessed before consulting his bar napkin. "Thor."

"You're kidding, right?"

Bunny shook his head and said, "Nope. It's short for Thorsten, apparently. I don't know what to believe anymore. I think I'm the victim of a snow job."

"Was it good for you?" Phillip asked. Bunny just glared at him. "Where did Thor say he worked?"

"I don't remember. Some firm with three names."

"Beavis, Butthead & Jackass?" Phillip offered.

"Lickem, Dickem & Stickem."

"Findem, Fuckem & Forgetem," Phillip suggested. "Let's find the kitchen. I'm guessing that's where the alcohol is. There's no sense in being here sober."

"Are you guys talking about Thor?" a guy next to them asked. His head was shaved and he wore a blue hoodie. Phillip looked at Bunny, who nodded in answer. "Sorry. I couldn't help but overhear. He likes to pretend he's a big shot when he meets people, but he's really a glorified secretary."

"I knew it!" Bunny exclaimed.

"Snow job," Phillip agreed.

Bunny turned to Blue Hoodie and said, "He gave my friend VD."

"Hey!" Phillip exclaimed when Bunny pointed at him. Blue Hoodie took a step backward.

"Come on, Phillip," Bunny said. "Let's go."

"I don't have VD!" Phillip exclaimed in the hall. "I can't believe you said that."

"What's the difference? You're leaving anyway," Bunny said. "It's not like you'll ever see these people again."

The next address that Bunny rattled off to a cab driver took them to a refurbished warehouse in Tribeca. "Tell me this isn't another guy you met in a bar," Phillip pleaded.

"Stop being such a prude," Bunny said. "Besides, that's how I met you. This party will be fabulous."

Phillip followed Bunny inside the building to a service elevator. As the doors closed like jaws swallowing them whole, Phillip asked, "Whose party is this?"

"An old friend, Ernst Gerhardt," Bunny said, preoccupied by his reflection in the chrome elevator walls. He fussed with his hair. "He owns a couple of restaurants in Chelsea. And a gallery in the East Village."

Phillip's eyes bulged. "A gallery? You know someone who owns a gallery? Why didn't you ever tell me that?"

"Why? You never paint, darling." The elevator ground to a halt, and Bunny hoisted open the doors. "Here we are."

Instead of a thumping bass line, Phillip heard the sound of a piano competing with laughter and chatter as they stepped into a spacious loft. It was the sort of apartment Phillip had seen only in magazines: vast open spaces, expensive art on the walls, sculpture, and furniture constructed for form rather than function. Phillip immediately felt intimidated but walked in with his head up instead of following his natural instinct to retreat.

Bunny seemed to glide as he took in the scene, picked up two flutes of champagne from a passing server, and nodded a greeting to another guest all in one fluid motion. He handed a flute to Phillip and said, "Cristal?"

"Thanks," Phillip said. He didn't bother scanning the crowd, since he doubted he'd see anyone he knew. "How do you know these people?"

"I don't know all of them," Bunny said. "Ernst and I had a thing a few years ago. I met him at Tunnel, and before I knew it, I was back at his place and he was snorting coke off my back."

"How lovely," Phillip said drily.

"He was trying to impress me. Maybe he was trying to feel young again.

I don't know. It didn't last long, but we remained friends," Bunny said. "I'll find him so I can introduce you. I'll be back."

"Oh, don't, really," Phillip said, but Bunny had disappeared into the crowd of well-heeled strangers. Phillip stood nervously in place, scanning the people around him. Nobody seemed to be smoking, so he decided to find an open window or a bathroom. As he wandered through the loft, he heard snippets of conversations, none of which interested him.

"…insists things will improve, but I'm really worried my portfolio is on life support…"

"…fired the maid, and now I have to take the kids to school before Pilates…"

"…jeté, jeté, grand jeté, piqué, piqué…"

"…drug test. Does drinking vinegar beforehand really work?"

"…software is out of date, but if we upgraded to a newer server…"

In the back of the loft, Phillip found an open door that led to a small balcony. In spite of the cold, several people were standing outside and smoking. Phillip lit a Marlboro and leaned against a wrought-iron railing, willing it to give way so he'd plunge over the side and escape all the superficial conversation and pettiness of the party.

"Got a light?" He looked up and saw a girl his age extending a cigarette. As he lit it, he studied her blue hair, the fur-trimmed collar of her jacket, the labret pierced into her lower lip, and wondered how she fit in to the scene around him. She exhaled and said, "Thanks. Is this where the cool people are hanging out?"

"If I see any, I'll let you know," Phillip said, pleased that he made her laugh. "Who do you know here?"

"My girlfriend is showing at Ernst's gallery. Supposedly, I'm here for moral support, but I haven't seen her for, like, an hour. I assume she's networking. This is so typical. I'm always dragged to these things, then I get pushed aside or left behind. That's what I get for falling in love. How about you?"

"What about me?" Phillip asked.

"Is your significant other here?" She was standing with her arms folded, smoking almost violently. She'd inhale languorously, then exhale suddenly, her arm darting over the edge of the balcony to tap off the ash. She was shorter than Phillip, which caused her to look up at him, her chin jutting out accusingly. Everything about her seemed aggressive, especially the way she kept inching toward him, encroaching on his personal space.

"I have no idea where he is," Phillip said, casually taking a step back. "He's a programmer. He works long hours."

"I know how that is," she said. She made a snorting noise and smoke blew out of her nose. She made Phillip think of a cartoon bull. "What do you do? Are you an artist?"

"I don't paint," Phillip replied. When she looked at him quizzically, he added,

"I'd like to think I'm an artist, but I haven't painted anything in ages."

"That's what's wrong with you. When someone asks if you're an artist, you have to emphatically say, 'Yes. I'm an artist.' If you don't believe it, you're not going to be it. Know what I mean?"

Easy for you to say, Phillip thought. He imagined the girl breaking into a song from *Rent*—or, better yet, *The Rocky Horror Picture Show*—until he picked her up and threw her over the railing. Everyone else on the balcony would applaud, and he'd be the toast of the party. Ernst would offer to show his work, and he wouldn't have to move to Mississippi.

Instead of launching the girl from the balcony, Phillip crushed out his cigarette and said, "You're right. I'll keep that in mind. Excuse me; I think I see someone I know."

He went back inside and looked around but couldn't spot Bunny anywhere. He was suddenly aware of how mentally and physically drained he felt, as if the loft and its occupants were feeding on the last of his energy. He wished he could transport himself into his bed so he could sleep until Kieran came to wake him up.

He meandered through groups of strangers, shutting out one inane conversation after another as he scrutinized the art on the walls. Ernst's gallery was probably a huge success because his taste was excellent. The paintings provoked a mixture of jealousy and admiration in Phillip. As he backed away from a large canvas to get a better perspective on its swirl of colors, he bumped into a table. He turned around and looked down at the hors d'oeuvres nobody was touching. It was the kind of party where no one wanted to be caught eating. The food could have been plastic or ambrosial and no one would've noticed.

He saw Bunny approaching the table with a man in tow. Phillip scrutinized the dimple in the man's chin, his ice-blue eyes, and his expensively cut hair, which was graying at the temples. As they reached him, the man looked at Phillip and said, "Didn't you blow me at—"

"Ew! No!" Phillip exclaimed. Before Bunny could introduce them, Phillip said, "I think I'm taking off. I'm tired."

"Don't be such a slug, Phillip," Bunny said. "It's your last night in New York. Enjoy the party."

"No," Phillip said, glancing around. "It's all so phony. Everyone in their fancy clothes, talking about the most boring crap that nobody cares about. You can tell they're all just here so they can say they were. It's all crap. Pointless. Pointless crap."

Bunny's friend looked at him and said, "That's rather odd coming from someone in Helmut Lang denim trousers."

"It's all borrowed," Phillip said. "At midnight I turn into a pumpkin."

"In what time zone?" the man asked. "I think it's half past a pumpkin now."

The man's accent reminded Phillip of Kieran, and he asked, "Where are you from?"

"No place special. A town that's like the New Jersey of England."

At least he's honest, Phillip thought. He turned wearily to Bunny and said, "Sorry, Bunny, but this isn't my New York."

"*Your* New York?" Bunny asked, his eyebrows arched. "I guess you'd have been more comfortable at the other party, with all those Bohemians pretending to be misunderstood geniuses, so beyond all this crass commercialism. Ironic, considering that your grandfather could buy and sell everyone here ten times over."

It was exactly the kind of remark that got under Phillip's skin, and he glared at Bunny before turning to his companion to say, "Sorry, Ernst, but these people bore the shit out of me. They'll only know they've been at a good party when they see themselves photographed in *W* magazine. Nor will they appreciate the paintings hanging on your walls until some art critic tells them they're supposed to. They're shallow, superficial, and—" He broke off, suddenly aware that the music had stopped and his loud insults had attracted the stares of all the people around them. Like a herd of wild animals, they assessed him with blank faces until, determining that he wasn't worth goring or being insulted by, they turned back to their conversations.

Bunny, however, was glowering at him. But before Bunny could speak, Ernst said, "You're a cheeky one, aren't you? Sadly, however, your judgments are wasted on me. I'm not Ernst. My name's Bazzer."

"I'm out of here," Phillip said.

He got lost trying to find his way back to the elevator, which was in use when he found it. When he finally got to the street, he walked to the corner to hail a cab. Unfortunately, he'd forgotten what a ghost town Tribeca could be and ended up walking ten blocks before he found an available taxi.

He chastised himself on the ride uptown. Bunny had always been a good friend to him, and Phillip knew he'd behaved badly. What made it even worse was that instead of being able to meet Bunny for a drink the next day and let an apology ease them into laughing about the night, Phillip would be on a plane to Mississippi. He hated leaving Bunny on a sour note.

Inside his apartment, Phillip went directly to the bathroom to brush his teeth. After spitting and rinsing, he flipped off the light and started removing his clothes while he walked. He tossed everything into a corner, set the alarm, and slid into bed. When his leg grazed against someone else, he screamed and leaped out of bed.

He flipped on the light, and Carlos said, "Sorry I scared you. Are you okay?"

"I'm fine," Phillip said, panting. "I'm nice and relaxed now, thank you. You scared the bejesus out of me."

"You said I could hang with you tonight, remember?"

"Right," Phillip said.

"I was waiting up for you, but I guess I fell asleep," Carlos said sheepishly. "Sorry."

"Don't worry about it. Besides, I think I'm sober now."

"Did you and Bunny have fun?" When Phillip just groaned and buried his face in his hands, Carlos patted the bed and said, "Come here and tell Daddy all about it."

"Since you put it that way," Phillip said and jumped onto the bed. He told Carlos everything and said, "The whole day was sucky, like a bad movie."

"We're friends, right?"

"Yes. But that statement usually precedes something I don't want to hear."

"Your life is always like a movie, Phillip. For the past month, you've been in Meg Ryan's New York. Why are you frowning?"

"Does it have to be Meg Ryan?"

Carlos sighed and said, "You're not casting this. You're only the actor. But okay. You've been in Sandra Bullock's New York, saying a sentimental goodbye to the city with a beautiful, wonderful man. Today, it became Parker Posey's New York: a quirky but harmless cast of people and randomly wild parties."

"Who's writing this?" Phillip asked. They stared at each other a minute, then simultaneously said, "Who cares?" When they stopped laughing, Phillip said, "It wasn't wild. Wild is doing tequila shots at a dive bar and licking the salt off a hot guy's chest before you hook up with someone else and bring them both back home."

"Not that you've ever thought about doing that," Carlos said, grinning.

"Oh, no. Never," Phillip said. "You're right. The whole night was random. Not my idea of fun. And Bunny—I don't know what that's all about. It's like I never realized how different we are."

"Anybody could see that. Do you remember when we first met him? He sat next to us at that bar in the East Village for an hour, obviously eavesdropping, and only introduced himself once he heard that your family's in oil."

Phillip laughed and said, "I hate that phrase: 'My family's in oil.' Mix in a little vinegar and they make a great dressing. But I know what you're saying—Bunny can be superficial. But he's been a decent friend, and I don't have a lot of those. Look what he's doing for you, helping you with the sublet and all."

"Yeah, yeah," Carlos said. "I wouldn't worry about it. Put it out of your head. Speaking of head, where's Kieran? Why are you in bed with me and not him?"

"His team has some important project they have to finish. He's coming by in the morning to go with me to the airport." Phillip sighed and said, "Carlos, I don't want to go. I came to New York for a reason, and I feel like I'm going back a nobody. I've squandered all my time here. I've done nothing. Do you think it's too late to back out and stay?"

"That's your call," Carlos said. He began rubbing Phillip's back soothingly. "What I can say is that you're not a nobody. You're my friend. You made working at Barnes & Noble bearable. We've had a lot of fun. I'm bummed that you're going, but I know it's not the end of our friendship. As far as doing nothing, you've been soaking up experience to use later. You'll do big things, Phillip. You'll go far."

"All the way to Mississippi," Phillip said.

"For now. Your family needs you. But once that's settled, the world is your oyster."

"What a weird expression," Phillip said. "What does it mean?"

"I have no idea," Carlos admitted. "Don't worry. Everything is happening exactly as it should. I think you'd better get some sleep."

"Thanks, Carlos."

"Come here." Carlos pulled Phillip back and wrapped his arms around him from behind. They fell asleep spooning, and Phillip dreamed that he and Carlos were in Tribeca trying to sell a shipment of stolen oysters to a giant slug with an Irish accent. The slug pried apart an oyster, found a dead rabbit, and started screaming.

"What the bloody hell is this? What's going on here?"

Phillip woke up and realized the lights were on. He squinted, rubbed his eyes, and saw an angry Kieran staring at him with his arms folded across his chest.

"Kieran? What time is it? I didn't hear the alarm," Phillip said groggily.

"It's early. I thought I'd come by and surprise you. Seems I got the surprise instead," Kieran said.

"Who's yelling?" Carlos moaned.

"Oh, fuck," Phillip said.

Kieran began vehemently twisting his key ring, threw Phillip's apartment keys at him, and said, "You know what to do with these. Have a good flight. Bastard."

As Kieran stormed out of the apartment, Phillip said, "I don't believe this."

"I think someone's trying to tell you something," Carlos said. "This just isn't your day."

Phillip jumped out of bed and yanked on Bunny's fancy loaner jeans. "I've got to go after him!"

"Go!" Carlos said. "It's time for the whimsical chase scene in your movie."

There was nobody to chase once Phillip reached the sidewalk. It was still dark outside, and there was barely anybody on the streets. Phillip ran to Eighth Avenue and frantically flagged down a cab. Minutes later, he was on the corner of 65th Street. He threw money at the cab driver and ran to the door of Kieran's building, only to be stopped in his tracks by the doorman.

"I'm here to see Kieran McClosky," Phillip said.

"Do you know what time it is?" the doorman asked.

"Uh, yeah. The little hand is on the five—"

"Perhaps you could return at a more suitable hour."

"This is an emergency," Phillip insisted. "I really need to see him."

"I'm sorry," the doorman said. "I'm afraid I can't disturb him."

"But—"

"Perhaps I'm not making myself clear. I can't call up. He specifically told me not to—"

"Okay!" Phillip interrupted. "I got it."

He turned around and went outside, taking a few steps down the sidewalk before stopping to lean against the side of the building. A few weeks earlier, when he'd found himself in the same place, Kieran had come along with food, humor, and an invitation to breakfast.

Phillip sank to the sidewalk and started to cry. After a few minutes he dried his face on his sleeve and lit a cigarette. He looked up and saw the pink light of dawn peering through the skyscrapers of Manhattan.

"Mississippi, here I come," Phillip softly said, "right back where I started from."

Chapter 5

Phillip had planned to spend his flight mentally compiling his favorite memories of New York as a sort of buffer against the challenges he'd be facing in Mississippi. Instead, he found himself gathering evidence of the Boyfriend Curse. He'd always been careful about using the word *boyfriend.* He preferred to call his series of relationships sort-of boyfriends, semi-boyfriends, faux boyfriends, potential boyfriends, and most frequently, ex-boyfriends—as if they only earned the boyfriend title after a CD they'd bought together or an extra toothbrush ended up in the trash.

He should have known from the moment that he started calling Kieran his boyfriend and breaking his rule about sleepovers that he'd brought on the Boyfriend Curse. He just wasn't meant to be half of a couple, unless it was a couple of friends. Although the parallel direction his relationships with Bunny and Kieran had taken the night before made him wonder if there might not also be a Friendship Curse.

Carlos had gone with him to the airport and stood by in silent support when Phillip repeatedly called Kieran's home and office numbers. Since Kieran didn't answer at either place, Phillip could only leave messages trying to explain that Kieran had misunderstood what he'd seen. But Phillip wasn't sure it even mattered. He'd be in Mississippi. Kieran was in New York, and eventually he'd go home to Ireland. Phillip had always known they were moving in separate directions.

His feeling that he was living under a black cloud grew stronger when the pilot announced that it was storming in New Orleans. In any case, his grandfather had left nothing to chance. He'd arranged for one of his New Orleans employees to pick up Phillip and drive him the eighty or so miles to Pass Christian.

The man grunted a name at Phillip from behind a wad of chewing tobacco—either Bud or Bug; Phillip couldn't be sure—then hefted Phillip's bags into the back of his pickup and covered them with a tarp. As soon as he cranked the truck, they were rolling to the sound of men who'd lost their women or loved their country. The music effectively cut off any possibility of conversation, which was fine with Phillip, except he started getting a headache. When he asked if he could smoke, Bud/Bug said, "Shore thang," and Phillip cracked the window, staring longingly at New Orleans as they drove past it. No one could ever mistake the skyline for Manhattan's, but it was comfortingly urban with its smog and traffic. Once they were beyond it and there was nothing to look at but the tall pines lining the interstate, Phillip felt like he'd gone back in time. Nothing had changed. He wanted the landscape to feel welcoming, but it seemed foreign, as if he hadn't spent his first eighteen years there.

By the time they went south to Bay St. Louis and crossed the bridge to Pass Christian, the skies had cleared, and Phillip's spirits lifted when he got his first sight of the Gulf and its white beaches. He turned his attention to the beautiful houses lining the coast, feeling a mixture of dread and excitement at the prospect of returning to the one he'd grown up in.

When Bud/Bug slowed his truck, Phillip said, "You don't have to pull in. I'll walk from the road."

Bud/Bug gave him a funny look and said, "Wull, ah-ite." In spite of the fact that Phillip was coming home under duress, the man's accent made him feel better. At least it was easier to decipher than Kieran's.

Phillip thanked him, stepped from the truck, took his bags, and trudged down Godbee Lane, which was really just a driveway that ended at two houses: his grandfather's and Odell's. His grandfather's mansion seemed to loom protectively over its dominion. It was three stories of white brick, with black shutters and four stately white columns—a pair on either side of the beveled-glass double doors that offered a glimpse at the imposing two-story foyer. The chimneys on opposite ends of the house rose defiantly above the majestic live oaks. The house was as intimidating as his grandfather, and Phillip's eyes automatically shifted to the left. Vernie's and Odell's single-level cottage was as comforting as ever. The hedges that divided the two yards were thick, but Phillip knew that if he walked along them, he'd find an open iron gate. He chose that route so he could enter his boyhood home through the less daunting kitchen.

Once inside, he dropped his duffel bag and backpack on the floor and stopped to listen. His grandfather had left for China the week before, which was a good thing, because he would never have tolerated the strange music that reverberated through the house. It sounded New Age; maybe his mother had abandoned Catholicism and the Baptist church for a more trendy religion. Bewildered, Phillip followed the sound through several downstairs rooms, pausing at the French doors that led to the sunroom to take in the scene before him.

His four aunts were sitting around a table, iced-tea glasses sweating next to them, locked in silence as they concentrated on a card game. The music had muffled any sound he might have made, so he had all the time in the world to consider the memories the sight of them evoked. Not of his adolescence—they'd only occasionally let him play cards with them—but of his first summer in New York.

He was strolling back to his apartment after the Pride parade and checking out a man walking in front of him. The man had shucked his T-shirt and tucked it into the waist of his jeans. Although that cheated Phillip out of the sight of the man's ass, he was mesmerized by the beauty of his back. A glistening valley ran down between his well-developed trap and lat muscles, and Phillip fell into step behind him. Phillip was so enraptured that it wasn't until the man turned to walk up a stoop that Phillip realized they were at his own building. Phillip followed him through the door, and after the first flight of stairs, the man turned around with a frown.

"Seventh floor," Phillip explained.

"Fourth," the man answered. They paused on the stairs. "Were you at the parade?" When Phillip nodded, he said, "Happy Pride. You want to join me for a beer?"

Phillip nodded again, although he wasn't much of a drinker back then. It didn't matter that he was underage; it was ridiculously easy for anyone to drink in New York. But in his few weeks there, he'd been too drunk on the city itself—not to mention his freedom from his grandfather's domination and his mother's neuroses—to need alcohol.

The man's name was Claude, and he was the laziest person Phillip had ever met. Claude loved nothing more than lolling naked in bed all day, which worked out well for Phillip. It wasn't just the sex—although Claude was a good lover. He was a master at lying still for hours, and Phillip filled sketchbooks with images of Claude's body. Although he was sometimes baffled that someone who never seemed to do anything had such well-defined musculature, Phillip learned his best lessons in anatomy from Claude.

For two years they wore a path to each other's door between other lovers, boyfriends, and tricks. Phillip never got tired of looking at Claude, who thoroughly enjoyed being looked at.

One night Phillip went down the three flights to find Claude with two other friends. They were thrilled when Phillip showed up, because they wanted four at their card game of Shanghai. As they taught him the rules, Phillip realized it was a variation of the game his aunts called Progressive Rummy. He also learned why his aunts had rarely let him play; they'd obviously made up their own rules because they were all unrepentant cheaters. The game as Claude and his friends played it was just as lively, and it became a weekly ritual.

His aunts presented an equally companionable picture, and he regarded them with a fresh perspective. The eldest, Andi, was the archetype of a society matron. Her husband, Gregory Beasley, was a surgeon, and Andi served on countless committees of one type or another. They often threw elaborate soirees in their Gulfport home. Odell had always called Andi a "silver polisher," which meant she had too much time on her hands. Phillip had never been close to the Beasleys or to their three children, who he was sure were all off doing something productive and noteworthy with their lives, unlike him.

Andi was as immaculately groomed as ever, and her spine was straight. Phillip had never seen her back receive the full embrace of a chair. He stared at her profile, with its high forehead and aquiline nose, and realized that except for a few streaks of gray in her dark hair, she looked exactly as she had when he was a child: stern and unapproachable.

"I want to buy that card," Andi said, breaking the silence that had been filled with ethereal synthesized music.

"You've already made three buys," Selma said.

"Two," Andi replied firmly.

"Three."

"Two."

"You sound like children," Fala said. "Count your cards, Andi."

"I'm not counting my cards. I know perfectly well how many I've bought."

"You bought Fala's six of spades, my queen of diamonds, and my queen of clubs," Selma said.

"How do you do that?" Florence asked admiringly. "I can barely remember what cards I have in my hand, much less everyone else's."

Fala noted Andi's miffed expression and said, "It's your turn to draw, Florence."

Fala was next in age to Andi. She was a linguistics professor married to a poetry professor, both of them in the English department at the University of Southern Mississippi, located more than an hour away. Although Doctors Harold and Fala Breyer were childless, their Hattiesburg home was a popular gathering spot for graduate students. Phillip had fallen asleep on one of their cozy overstuffed sofas many times while debates about deconstructionism and postmodernism raged around him. He hadn't learned a thing.

Fala seemed to inhabit a realm that hovered somewhere above everyone else, and he'd always liked her. She had a tendency to burn meals, lose her glasses, and stumble over things—a pleasing counterpoint to Andi's determined perfection. Fala's red hair wasn't as bright as he remembered, and she had it pulled up in a black scrunchie, but he was sure it still fell past her shoulders. Andi was forever scolding her to get it cut. In Andi's world, women of a certain age were supposed to have short hair.

As Fala toyed with her ponytail and considered her cards, Andi said, "Do you have any idea how many germs are in human hair? From your hair to your hand to the cards we're all playing with."

"We've been swapping germs for decades," Florence said. "I'm sure we're all immune to each other by now." She had her back to Phillip, but even sitting down, she looked like a giant next to her sisters. She was nearly six feet tall, with a willowy figure. He noticed that she'd changed her hairstyle since he last saw her. Not only was it cut in subtle layers that just reached her shoulders, but it had been artfully streaked with golds and reds. When she'd first come back to Mississippi from Manhattan, Phillip had spent many hours looking through scrapbooks that were jammed full of photos from her modeling career and her happy times in New York.

Florence's and Sam's children were born after Phillip left Mississippi, but he knew them because of the twice-yearly visits the Garrett family made to Manhattan. He would share a couple of meals with them and sometimes tag along on family excursions. Sam and Florence were generous with their money and their approval; neither of them had ever reproached him for staying away. He even liked their children. Samantha was four; Susan was two. They were both happy little girls who knew how to behave around adults.

His gaze moved to his Aunt Selma, who sat opposite Andi. Selma was wearing denim leggings and an oversize white shirt that did nothing to hide her stocky figure. Her brown hair was cut short, and her skin was dark from working outdoors. Although she looked a little weathered, she was the youngest of his aunts. If Phillip's relationship with Andi was distant; with Fala, respectful; and with Florence, affectionate, what he and Selma shared could best be described as contention. Like his grandfather, Selma could be autocratic and liberal with disapproval. When he'd refused to come home during his first Christmas in New York, telling Florence about an imaginary boyfriend who wouldn't be welcome, Selma had called him and without preamble said, "You're being a self-righteous ass. If I never made this a problem, why are you?"

Phillip had no idea whether Selma had girlfriends or even a partner. Their shared proclivity to same-sex relationships hadn't caused them to bond. Once he made himself an outcast from his family, Selma treated him like one. Florence never discussed her sisters' personalities with Phillip, nor did his mother's vague letters ever divulge anything more than how successful Selma's landscaping business was.

His gaze was drawn back to Fala when the cards she'd been shuffling suddenly skittered like sand crabs in all directions, and she gasped, "Phillip?"

Four faces turned to gape at him.

"Good God!" Selma exclaimed.

Fala's hands were over her heart as she said, "Land's sakes, you scared the fire out of me. I thought Daddy's house had finally gotten a ghost."

Florence jumped up and crossed the room to throw her arms around him. "Phillip!" she cried. "Why didn't you tell us?" She barraged him with questions, never pausing to let him answer any of them.

Fala and Selma continued to watch him while Andi gathered the scattered cards into a neat stack. When she finished, she looked at Phillip as if a particularly large moth had flown into the room and asked, "Now what?"

"Where's my mother?" Phillip asked.

"She's at the doctor," Fala said. She noticed his wary expression and added, "Just an allergist. She's not crazy."

"That's not what I heard," Phillip said. When the four sisters exchanged suspicious glances, he added, "From Papa."

Florence's eyebrows shot up and she said, "You talked to Daddy? Maybe we'd better sit down and start at the beginning."

As they moved in a group toward the living room, Andi asked, "How did you get here?"

"Bug?"

They looked at him perplexedly. Florence said, "You bought one of those new Volkswagens?"

"Oh, those are so precious," Fala said.

"No. Someone from Godbee drove me. Bug? Bud?"

"Spud," Selma corrected him.

"That word has an interesting origin," Fala said. "It actually comes from the tool used to uproot potatoes, but there's a popular misconception that—"

"Fala, who cares?" Andi snapped, then looked at Phillip. "Are you hungry? Thirsty?"

"I can fix myself a glass of tea," Phillip said. He was already feeling exhausted by them and wanted a few minutes alone in the kitchen.

"I'll get it," Fala said. "We don't sweeten it anymore. Do you want me to—"

"Unsweetened is fine," Phillip said.

A pall of silence descended briefly as Fala left the room. Selma broke the spell, giving him a critical look and saying, "You're nothing but skin and bones. You're not on drugs, are you?"

"Selma, for goodness sake—"

"No," he cut Florence off. "I'm not on drugs. I'm not sick. And I'm not out on bail. I'm just...home."

"Without a word of warning," Andi said.

"Warning?" Fala asked, handing Phillip his iced tea. "He doesn't have to stand on ceremony in his own home. I think it's a wonderful surprise."

He took a swallow of tea, and before he could even look for one, Andi put a crystal coaster on the table next to his chair and said, "Don't let that drip on the upholstery."

"Oh, who cares?" Selma said. "Daddy's gone, and Ellan wouldn't notice the furniture if it was upside down on the Bermuda grass."

After this unfortunate but honest remark, the aunts were quiet again, until Florence said, "I can't believe you're here! I didn't realize that you and Daddy had been talking again."

"We're not really talking," Phillip said. "He gives orders, and I take them. Just like old times."

"Your timing couldn't be worse," Selma said. "You should have called one of us before coming for a visit."

"I assumed Papa had told everyone," he said. "And I don't know if you can call it a visit. I'm not here for a few days. Papa said I have to stay here while he's in China—because Mother needs me."

Florence rolled her eyes and looked at Fala, who shook her head as if defeated.

"Isn't that just like him?" Andi asked. "To force the issue?"

"What issue?" Phillip asked. When no one answered, he went on. "He said she needs a family member living with her while he's gone. And that I could use the third floor to paint. He even threw in an allowance for art supplies."

"The third floor," Selma said with a laugh. "Aren't you afraid you'll trip over the chains when we lock Ellan up there?"

"Hush," Florence said. "It's obvious that Phillip doesn't know what we've been arguing about."

"He certainly doesn't," Phillip agreed.

"Considering her latest escapade, Selma and I think that your mother needs help," Andi said quickly.

"What escapade?" Phillip asked. His aunts looked at one another, each of them reluctant to explain. "Just tell me."

"Your mother started leaving in one of the cars in the mornings, not coming back until late afternoon. She hadn't driven a car in years. She was between nurses, and Odell didn't tell us. Andi found out by accident," Fala said.

"She wouldn't tell me what she was up to, so I followed her," Andi said. "She was going to a trailer park every day." Andi paused.

"Why?" Phillip asked. He hoped she wasn't about to tell him that his mother was having a fling with someone who lived in a trailer.

"Who knows?" Andi replied. "She was interviewing those people like she was from the census bureau. She even had a clipboard and a questionnaire, asking them all kinds of questions about the size of their families and how much money they made."

"Why would she do that?"

"Because she's nuttier than a pecan pie," Selma said.

"Your mother needs help," Andi repeated. "If she got it, she'd stop acting like the Madman of Alcatraz."

"I think that was Birdman," Fala interjected.

"It's all the same," Andi said. "We decided to put an end to this kind of nonsense while Daddy's out of the country. We took all the car keys. That's when she started breaking dishes."

"Which dishes?" Phillip asked nervously, thinking of his grandmother's antique Meissen dinnerware.

"It was one glass," Florence said, rolling her eyes.

"She threw it at Odell," Selma countered.

"It was an accident," Florence said. "Nobody would throw stemware at a seventy-year-old woman."

Nobody sane, Phillip thought, but kept his mouth shut. As did his aunts, creating another uncomfortable silence.

"Phillip, I don't mean to be critical," Fala finally said, "but you've been away for a long time. I don't blame you. I know you had some difficulties here when you were growing up."

"Difficulties," Selma repeated, with another of her scornful laughs.

"You're not helping," Fala scolded. "We all decided that while Daddy's gone, we'll settle this once and for all. Florence and I don't agree that Ellan's out of her mind. She's got some bad habits that need to be broken."

"Like that glass she threw at Odell," Selma needled.

Florence sighed and said, "Fala and I think if she could just be left to her own devices, she'd be fine. Oh, we weren't going to abandon her," she added hastily when she saw Phillip's appalled reaction. "Just let her have some breathing room. She doesn't need a nurse disguised as a housekeeper to run things around here."

"She needs more than a nurse," Andi said. "And there's nothing you can do to help her. You just get right back on a plane to New York."

"I gave my word to Papa," Phillip replied. "I didn't want to come home, but he insisted."

"I'm sure," Selma said acidly. Phillip didn't know if her tone conveyed a judgment of him or his grandfather.

"She might do better if she has to take care of Phillip too," Florence said thoughtfully.

"But she won't take care of him," Fala said. "Phillip will end up stuck here playing nursemaid."

"That's probably true," Florence admitted. "Daddy is trying to control everyone from thousands of miles away—even Phillip. I won't have it."

"What are we going to do about it?" Andi asked briskly.

"The first thing we have to do is get *him*," Selma pointed at Phillip, "out of here. Before Ellan knows he's back."

"Now just a minute," he protested.

"No, Selma's probably right about that," Florence said. "Did you bring luggage with you?"

"It's in the kitchen," Fala said helpfully.

"I am not leaving without seeing my mother," Phillip insisted.

"It's for the best," Fala said. "Until we can figure all this out."

"You can stay with me," Florence said. "Phillip, your mother won't like it if she believes that you were forced to come home. I don't know how she'll react. But she did *not* throw that glass at Odell. She treats her like a queen. When Odell was bedridden last year, Ellan was tireless in taking care of her."

"Is Odell sick?" Phillip asked.

Florence's face softened at his worried tone, and she said, "She's just old, honey. She had pneumonia, and that's not good for someone her age."

"We're wasting time," Andi warned.

"Please, Phillip. At least for tonight. The girls will be so happy to see you."

"All right," he said, relenting. He placed his glass in its coaster, started to stand up, and stopped mid rise when he noticed the Rothko painting over the fireplace. "Isn't that…"

"Yes, it's upside down," Fala said. "Ellan said she was sure Mark Rothko meant for it to be that way."

"He clearly didn't," Phillip said, outraged. "She *is* crazy."

"She's not crazy," Florence said. "She's playful."

"Look, I'll go home with you. I'll stay away from my mother. For now. But I'm not leaving this house with a painting worth more than all your houses put together hanging upside down. That's horrible."

Selma stared at the Rothko with wonder and said, "How much do you think it's worth?"

"Millions," Phillip stated. When she gaped at him, he said, "I'm not joking. His paintings sell at auction for truckloads of money."

"And to think of what Daddy paid for it forty years ago," Andi said with admiration.

"He's not the crazy one," Selma said, trying to turn her head to look at the painting from the correct angle.

"We've been pretending not to notice it," Fala said helplessly.

"Then you're *all* crazy," Phillip said.

"If we promise to fix it, will you leave?" Selma asked, jerking her head back up. "Now?"

Phillip went to the kitchen to get his bags, feeling sulky and wronged. By the time he was in her minivan, Florence was clearly in a penitent mood. "I'm really sorry your homecoming turned out this way, Phillip," she said. "They'll rehang the painting."

"It's not just the painting," he replied. "I feel like an idiot for giving in to that manipulative old man. I had a life, you know. It might not be successful in Aunt Andi's eyes. Okay, maybe not even in my eyes. But at least it was *my* life. Now I feel like the pathetic little kid I used to be—giving in to him, waiting for the next bizarre thing she does, feeling useless to make things right."

Florence smiled and said, "If you want to curl up in the back with a juice box, I can let you watch one of the kids' DVDs on the TV screen."

"No, thanks," Phillip said.

"You were not pathetic. You were a darling child—precocious. As tough as your boyhood might have been, you did find a way to make things right: in your art. That's the world you can control, and you do it beautifully. I think that's the reason I'm angriest at Daddy. Promising you the third floor so you could paint, knowing all the while that you'd be too preoccupied with your mother. She doesn't want that, Phillip. And I won't allow it."

Her chin jutted out, and he had to laugh. When she gave him a sideways look, he said, "You know you're the only one who understands me at all."

"That isn't true," Florence said. "She let you go, Phillip. And she never tried to pull you back. Remember the egg?"

"Which one?" he asked.

She darted a confused look his way and said, "When you played Humpty Dumpty, and she got so upset. I can't say I understood it at the time, but I have children of my own now. It was horrible for her to let her baby go. She knew you'd be falling off a lot of walls. She did it for you—to let you become your own person."

They were greeted at the door of her house by a squall of girls and golden retrievers. By the time he made it to the guest room with his bags, he felt thoroughly nudged, tasted, and sniffed, and he wasn't sure which human or hound had done what. He was worried about his mother and Odell and homesick for his dreadful apartment. Most of all, he missed Kieran's high spirits and reasonable way of viewing the world. His own world felt more upside down than his grandfather's Rothko. After weeks of preparing himself, nothing had gone as he'd envisioned, either in New York or Mississippi.

Phillip knew that Florence, unlike her sisters, didn't have a housekeeper. Instead, she'd hired a series of au pairs, usually young USM students from other countries. But it was just family at dinner that night. Since his young cousins dominated the table, he found his eyes traveling to the recessed shelves that took up two walls of the dining room. Florence had a compulsion for collecting odd things in silver, and he examined the assortment of antique serving pieces scattered among groupings of thimbles, hat pins, cigarette holders and cases, compacts, napkin rings, and items whose function he couldn't identify. Her walls held a small fortune, and as far as he knew, she didn't even have an alarm system. That underscored his belief that Southerners had a bizarre tendency to respect property more than people.

After dinner, he intercepted a look between Florence and Sam. They'd obviously discussed his dilemma and reached some conclusion. Sam was the relief pitcher, and he led Phillip into his study to give him the game plan.

Phillip watched him with a wariness tinged with admiration. Sam was in his late forties, but he was still lean and handsome. He was the same height as his wife—around six feet—but he seemed larger. The strength and confidence he'd always exuded were only enhanced by the touch of gray in his dark hair, and his blue eyes seemed to survey the world with undauntable humor. He looked like one of the models in his department store's display ads, and Phillip admired Florence for managing to marry a man who was as strong as her father without being domineering.

"Go ahead and smoke," Sam said, leaning against his desk and noticing Phillip's restlessness. "We know you do. It's okay in here. Not in your bedroom, though."

"Thank you," Phillip said, lighting up his Marlboro as if he had money on the losing team in the bottom of the ninth. He wasn't sure what that meant, but it went with the baseball metaphor that he'd started in his head. He almost expected Sam to throw him a curve ball.

"Which, now that I think of it, perfectly illustrates why you shouldn't stay with us," Sam said, staring at Phillip's cigarette. "You're a grown man. You need to be where you can do your thing without feeling like we're laying down rules. You need your own space, for whatever you want to do in it."

"So you think I should stay?" Phillip asked. "Instead of going back to New York?"

"It's up to you," Sam said. "Honestly, I think it would be great for your mother to have you around, but only if she thinks it's your choice to be here. Florence and I have talked it over. If you want to stay, we're willing to help you find a place of your own—get you set up, pay your rent if you want to paint."

"I can't accept that," Phillip said hastily.

Sam grinned and said, "You're afraid there might be strings attached, right? I'm not your grandfather, Phillip. You don't have to do what I want to get my help, not that I want anything. Don't worry; I'm not offering you a job at my store. I've heard the Barnes & Noble stories, remember?"

"Oh, yeah," Phillip said and focused on his cigarette, wondering what terrible things he'd unwittingly revealed about his character to this captain of retail. So much for the baseball metaphor.

"Why don't you stay with us while you make up your mind? We'll get one of your grandfather's cars for you to use."

"Won't my mother notice it's missing?" Phillip asked. When Sam didn't answer, Phillip said, "Never mind."

"Find yourself a decent place where you can live and work comfortably. They've built a lot of new apartments in Biloxi since you moved away."

"I could always live in Florence's minivan," Phillip said. "It's apparently stocked with groceries and entertainment."

"Don't make that suggestion to her," Sam said with a grin. "She might take you up on it. She hated giving up her Saab for a more kid-friendly vehicle. If you want to get a job and pay your own way, you could always work at one of the casinos. By the time Exton gets back, maybe you'll be in a position to return to Manhattan. Be honest. How much painting were you doing in New York?"

"None," Phillip admitted.

"So you see, you can turn all this to your advantage. Don't be afraid to accept help. We're family."

"I'm sure you didn't know what you were marrying into," Phillip said.

Sam shrugged dramatically—a boyish gesture that heightened his handsomeness. "All families are a little crazy. Think how boring it would be otherwise. That said, I'm glad I married the sister I did. Anyway, your aunts mean well. They do love your mother. And you."

When Phillip lay in bed that night, twitching from a lack of nicotine and noise, he decided Sam was right. He should see his journey home as an opportunity.

Your secret desire to completely change your life will manifest.

It was uncanny how that fortune was forcing him to look at his life differently. Maybe he had been keeping his desire for real change a secret from himself. Things had been so easy when Alyssa was in New York with him. They'd commiserated over unpaid bills, bad boyfriends, and the failure of the world to recognize their talents. But they'd also had fun, and Phillip had missed that. Mostly he missed the comfort of feeling like someone knew him—his habits, his flaws, his better qualities. Someone who cared if he'd had a bad day. Someone who knew not to talk to him before he had his coffee in the morning. Someone who disliked Stewart at the bookstore on his behalf.

They'd been like an old married couple, so comfortable with each other that they'd stopped looking for adventure elsewhere. When Alyssa fell in love with Eric, it had taken them both by surprise. She'd done the right thing by moving away with him. It was hard to make changes, and if she'd stayed, Phillip would have been a safety net if they started having problems. *When* they started having problems, because all couples did. Phillip had tried really hard not to be needy and childish when she made her decision to move to Oregon. Maybe that had been his better nature instinctively kicking in.

She let you go, Phillip. And she never tried to pull you back.

After September 11, Alyssa's mother had called from Minnesota several times a week to insist that she move away from New York. It worked Alyssa's nerves, but Phillip had been envious. His own mother had never brought up the attacks in her letters or their occasional phone calls. Sometimes he doubted that she even knew what had happened, which reinforced his suspicion that she was out of touch with reality.

I think it would be great for your mother to have you around.

Phillip couldn't stop thinking of Sam's words, or the confusing accounts of his mother that his aunts had presented. The least he could do was stay in Mississippi long enough to see her again and judge for himself. If she was okay, he could go back to New York—maybe even repair his relationship with Kieran.

He shuddered as he remembered the inverted Rothko. *Playful, my ass*, he thought. The woman was certifiable. And if he'd started depending on fortune cookies for insight and guidance, he wasn't far behind her.

Chapter 6

Almost every room in Aunt Florence's house had a bookshelf, and Phillip blindly pulled a book down each morning and read straight through the day. He'd migrate through the house, cracking open the book during breakfast, eventually relocating to a chaise on the patio behind the house, back to the kitchen for lunch, then to Sam's study where he could smoke. He was a fast reader, usually finishing a book a day so he could discuss it during dinner. His aunt was delighted to have the opportunity for adult conversation at home. His cousins, however, weren't. Samantha grew bored and a little jealous, often interrupting Phillip with stories from her day at preschool. Susan was less subtle and threw food at him from her plate. The dogs stayed at his feet for the payoff.

He wasn't avoiding the goals he'd set for himself, or the promise of independence he'd made to Sam. Instead, he was trying to acknowledge his fate. It took him a while to accept that he wasn't living in New York anymore. He hadn't had the easiest childhood, and he wasn't thrilled to be reminded of it on a daily basis.

He finally gathered enough courage to leave Aunt Florence's house. He wasn't ready to move out, but after a few days of having peas and carrots thrown at him, he thought it might be nice to have a child-free dinner alone. He drove his grandfather's Volvo for the first time since he'd arrived, finally ready to revisit an uneasy old acquaintance: the South.

He thought he'd go to Smith's Diner, his favorite greasy spoon near the private high school he'd attended. He'd often hang out there after school, ordering a side of onion rings and coffee, smoking cigarettes, and doing his homework. He'd wait until the last moment before he absolutely had to go home. Other kids from his school would hang out at Smith's too, but nobody ever bothered him there. It was like a safety zone, a place where he could draw in his sketchbook for hours undisturbed.

Unfortunately, he discovered that Smith's had been replaced by a mail services outlet. It was the same in a lot of the places he drove by. Many of his old haunts had been wiped out by generic chain stores, strip malls, and parking lots that had sprung up since the casinos had begun pumping money into the area's economy. It was disappointing, and he felt as though he'd let down monuments of his past, like a babysitter who'd lost his charge.

Phillip explored all the little coastal towns on the twenty-odd-mile stretch between Bay St. Louis and Ocean Springs. Pass Christian hadn't changed much, but there was something new or different nearly everywhere else—especially Gulfport and Biloxi, where he stopped at a pancake house.

The restaurant was packed, and he had to wait a while but finally got a seat and ordered a turkey club sandwich and fries. The place was noisy, which was comforting. Apparently it was a gathering place for the under-twenty-one crowd on Friday nights before they found other places to go. Phillip wasn't sure what clubs were in the area, but based on some of the conversations he overheard, wrist bands were used so that those not of drinking age could mingle with their older counterparts. Even though the majority of the diners were only a few years younger than Phillip, he felt old and out of place, on the edge looking in.

"Is this seat taken?" Phillip looked up to see a man at least fifteen years older than him standing next to his booth. He was wearing a leather jacket, jeans, and black cowboy boots. His handlebar mustache was as dark as his closely cropped hair, but his eyes were light blue and kind, so Phillip shrugged and gestured for him to sit down. "Thanks. I appreciate it. This place is packed with you young'uns. I'd be waiting up there all night if you hadn't let me join you."

"No problem. I could use the company. I was starting to feel like a leper sitting here on my own," Phillip said.

After ordering a patty melt and a Coke, the man introduced himself as Dash. Phillip told him about his journey that evening, visiting history gone horribly wrong. Dash said, "I guess there have been a lot of changes over the past few years. They're not as noticeable when you see them happen gradually."

"It still doesn't seem like there's a lot to do if..." Phillip trailed off, remembering he was in Mississippi. He'd have to learn again to guard his tongue. "What I mean is, what does a guy do if he's looking for a little companionship?"

Dash stared at him a minute, then he grinned. "I thought so. You are gay, right?"

"Uh-huh," Phillip answered, relieved that his initial assessment of Dash had been accurate.

"There's a dance club the younger folks go to. Mixed. And a couple of gay bars. Neither is very big. One is sort of comfortable. Lesbians and gays. The other's an S&M bar."

"Really?" Phillip asked, surprised. Things *had* changed since he'd left.

"Stand and model," Dash explained.

"Who knew that acronym had made its way down South?" Phillip mused aloud. "I thought you meant the old-fashioned kind."

"Biloxi hasn't changed that much," Dash said with a laugh. "Actually, I'm a leatherman myself, but that's not exactly something that's done in the open—not because of where we are. Believe it or not, our gay brothers frown upon it. We have a few...I guess what you'd call social clubs, private parties for whatever scene you're into. Give me your number; I'll be glad to introduce you to some of my friends."

"Leather's not really my thing," Phillip said.

Dash smiled and said, "We'll go easy on you. You don't get the collar until the second party. Then you have to grovel your way up to the sling." When Phillip blushed, Dash laughed again. "I'm kidding. We do other things. You never know who you might meet and find you have something in common with. Or you could just drive around listlessly night after night, mourning the loss of your life in Manhattan."

Phillip apologized and said, "I didn't mean to snub your offer." He wrote Florence's number on a napkin and pushed it across the table toward Dash. "That's my aunt's number in Long Beach. I'm looking for my own place, though, so it might change."

"Here's my card," Dash said.

Phillip took it and said, "You're a lawyer?"

"Yep," Dash said. "I'm in practice by myself, so you don't have to hesitate to call me there. My assistant is family too."

They talked a while longer, and Dash explained that if Phillip wanted intimate encounters of a more transitory kind, the casinos offered a bounty of possibilities. After Dash paid his check and left, Phillip ordered dessert. He watched the kids around him laughing and talking loudly, and listened in on a few conversations. They were mostly gossiping, which bored him, but one boy grabbed his attention. He was quieter than his friends, with ash-brown hair, light-blue eyes, and a gentle smile. He moved slowly and deliberately, seeming timid as he dipped his Buffalo wings into barbecue sauce. He was almost bird-like as he stared thoughtfully at his friends, sometimes tilting his head when he asked questions.

He was nondescript, especially among his friends, who were dressed just like him. He wore baggy jeans with frayed bottoms that draped over his ratty sneakers, and a blue plaid button-down shirt with short sleeves. A couple of leather thong necklaces with colorful stones hung around his neck. Phillip wanted to draw him, especially his hands.

He hadn't realized how long he'd been staring until he got caught. He'd been gazing with his fork halfway into his mouth, which could have been interpreted wrong. The boy smiled, and Phillip broke eye contact and finished his cake without another glance in his direction.

While Phillip drove back to his aunt's house, he tried to remember as much as he could about the boy, hoping to do some sketching before he went to bed. Unfortunately, Florence and Sam were still awake when he got home, and Phillip recounted his evening for them. Once again, he found himself censoring his words. Although they'd never shown any discomfort with Phillip's sexuality, they hadn't had to deal with it in their own backyard. Or their guest room. When Phillip went upstairs, he grabbed the paper to start checking the classifieds for jobs. The boy with the beautiful hands faded from his memory.

A few days later, he was reading the Sunday comics while sitting on the back steps and smoking when Florence came outside and sat down beside him. He quickly crushed out his cigarette.

"You didn't have to do that," she said.

"Yeah, I did. You're sitting downwind," he replied.

"I came out to ask if you wanted to join us in a game of Monopoly," Florence explained. "Please say no."

"Um, okay, rude lady. No."

"Phillip, you're twenty-three years old. You shouldn't be cooped up in this house with two old fuddy-duddies and their little kids. Why don't you call one of your old friends and enjoy this beautiful day?"

"In theory, that sounds great. But I never had that many friends here. Or any, for that matter," Phillip explained. "Can I be the shoe?"

"What about that boy you were always with? Maury? Maurice? Morris?"

"Chad?"

"Yes! That's the one. You should call him," she urged.

"I don't even know if he still lives around here. The places I used to hang out are all gone. He probably is too," Phillip complained.

"His mother lives where she always did. Chad must live around here somewhere. Call her and ask."

"Okay, I give up. I'll call Mrs. Cunningham and try to get in touch with Chad. Happy?"

"Ecstatic," his aunt said. She grinned, slapped her hands on her knees, and stood up.

"This is unlike you," Phillip said, following her inside. "You're never this forceful."

"Maybe your Aunt Selma is rubbing off on me," she suggested. They both looked thoughtful for a moment and then laughed. "Perhaps not. Selma doesn't rub off. She grates. I just want to see you happy. Your old friend made you happy once. Why not reconnect?"

When Phillip called Chad's mother, she told him that Chad shared a house with two friends in an old neighborhood in Biloxi. They often played tennis on Sunday afternoons in a nearby park. Phillip thanked her, promised to visit her soon, then hung up and called the number she'd given him. Chad didn't answer. Phillip assumed he must be playing tennis and decided to drive by and find out.

He found the park after a few wrong turns. Though it occupied an entire block, it was small and easy to miss. He slowly circled it, observing children playing on a jungle gym and swings while their parents talked on nearby benches. A few people walked their dogs on the path that cut through the middle of a green lawn. There were beds of flowers along one side shaded by tall oak trees. The community center and tennis court were on the opposite side of the park from the playground. The court was a few yards from the street, so he parked the car but didn't get out, preferring to observe Chad from the safety of the Volvo's tinted windows.

Chad was every bit as attractive as Phillip remembered. He was ruggedly handsome, even in Nike shorts and an Ole Miss T-shirt. His short brown hair was disheveled, standing out in haphazard tufts from his head. Phillip couldn't tell if it was purposely styled that way, but it looked good on him. His jaw was set in grim determination as he served, his hazel eyes never leaving the ball for a second. Phillip watched the muscles in Chad's legs ripple as he raced to his left to connect ball to racket, sending it back to his opponent with a resounding whack. Though he looked rough and solid, he moved with the swiftness and grace of a horse being put through its paces in the ring.

Even when they were kids, Chad had had an untamed look in his eye, as if he was waiting for a chance to break free and run. He was new to their elementary school when they first met, and Phillip was assigned to be his buddy to help him fit in, which was ironic, since Phillip had no friends and the other kids assumed he was as crazy as his mother. But Phillip and Chad hit it off because of the similarities in their lives. Chad was from New Mexico, and his mother had moved to Pass Christian, where she had a couple of old friends, to make a fresh start after Chad's father left them. There were many rumors as to why he'd left. Chad never bothered to explain or correct the wild stories circulating around the playground; his favorite was that his father was in prison, convicted of murder.

Phillip and Chad stayed friends through high school, even though their interests pulled them in different directions at their separate schools. Phillip remained a loner, but Chad had other friends. He joined his school's tennis team but shunned the jock label by participating in chorus and school plays. He was an editor on the school paper, a member of student council, and runner-up for prom king. Phillip confined his interests to his school's art room, contributed drawings to the yearbook, and was eventually voted "Most Artistic" in his class. He and Chad worked at the same bookstore after school and hung out together at Smith's Diner sometimes, either doing their homework or sharing a pack of cigarettes and a plate of fries as they talked.

Chad's friend leaped over the net and they began to gather up their belongings, which Phillip took as a sign that they were done with their match. If he was going to reconnect with Chad, it was now or never, so he got out of the car. He walked to the chain-link fence that surrounded the court and stood by the entrance. When they approached, he held out an imaginary microphone and said, "Chad Cunningham, you've just won the Wimbledon cup. What are you going to do now?"

"I'm going to get loaded!" Chad exclaimed. He threw down his gym bag and pulled Phillip into a bear hug. "How the hell are you? Man, it's good to see you! I thought you were in New York. What are you doing here?"

"I'm back," Phillip said simply. "For good, I guess."

"Why the hell would you move back here?" When Phillip just shrugged, Chad turned to his friend and said, "This is Pete. One of my roommates."

Phillip and Pete shook hands, then Phillip offered to give them a lift home. Pete laughed, but Chad said, "That would be great. Thanks."

They piled into the Volvo, and as Phillip pulled away from the curb, Chad said, "Take a left here. Okay, now another left. Cool. You can park right there."

They were on the other side of the park from where they'd started. Phillip parked the car and said, "You could've just told me you live on this block."

"Yeah, but that wouldn't have been any fun," Chad replied.

Pete lightly smacked the back of Phillip's head and said, "Come on, sport. Let's grab a beer."

They were renting a red-brick one-story house, which looked like a smaller version of Chad's childhood home. However, the inside was a stereotypical bachelor pad. Every available surface was covered with clothes, magazines, and used glasses, all lightly coated with dust. The furniture was mismatched and looked as if it might have been rescued from a curb on trash day. Pete passed around opened bottles of Corona, then left the room after grunting something about showering before a date.

"Roger, my other roommate, is at work. He's a chef," Chad explained.

"What does Pete do? I'm guessing he's not a maid."

"He's a doctor."

"No, really. What does he do?" Phillip repeated.

"He's in pediatrics. He graduated at the top of his class. Why is that so hard to believe?" Chad asked.

"The man took a beer with him into the shower," Phillip stated. "Do you think he's using it for conditioner?"

"What's wrong with you?" Chad asked.

"Nothing," Phillip said. Chad didn't look convinced. "It's just strange to see you after all this time, and to make matters worse, you're living like this."

"Like what?" Chad asked, sounding offended. He pointed to the window and said, "They used to sell crack in that park. But it's gotten better around here. Now they only sell pot. This is a great house, and property values in this neighborhood have gone way up."

"Whoever came up with those figures has obviously never been in here," Phillip said. "This place is a mess. How do you live like this? I pictured you in some fabulous new apartment complex, not drinking beer on a ratty sofa with the bubba twins."

"You haven't even met Roger, and I think you're being awfully rude. Jesus Christ, Phillip, you sound like a fag," Chad said bluntly.

"I can't believe you just said that." Phillip stared at him, wondering what had happened to his old friend. Which one of them had changed? Phillip didn't really know what Chad had gone through during the past five years, but it occurred to him how he was different. "I *am* a fag, Chad."

Pete had walked into the room with wet hair and a towel around his waist. Since he had an empty bottle in his hand, Phillip assumed he was on his way to the kitchen for another beer. But when Phillip made his announcement, Pete quickly turned around, went back into the bathroom, and shut the door.

Phillip turned back to Chad, who was staring at him slack-jawed, and said, "It was great seeing you again, Chad. We'll have to do this again sometime."

As he unlocked the Volvo and opened the door, he heard Chad yell, "Phillip, stop!" Phillip paused, weighing his options, then turned to face Chad, who said, "I suck."

"Hey, then we have something in common," Phillip said, lightly punching his arm.

"That's not what I meant," Chad said, laughing nervously. "You surprised me. I didn't mean to offend you."

Phillip shrugged and said, "I understand. You're right. I guess I was being rude."

"Not to mention showing up out of the blue after five years," Chad continued. "Why did you drop off the face of the earth? Don't they have phones in New York?"

"I guess I was hoping to avoid an awkward situation," Phillip said. "I can't imagine why I thought that. This has been a swell time."

"Let's grab a cup of coffee somewhere and talk," Chad offered. "I just need to change."

"No, really, you can be yourself," Phillip joked.

Chad rolled his eyes and said, "My clothes."

He came back five minutes later looking like a living J. Crew ad in jeans and a crew-neck sweater. They went to a nearby coffeehouse. Once they were armed with two large cups of coffee, Chad said, "Side patio. It's not as noisy." Chad led them outside and chose a table. After a few moments of awkward silence, Chad said, "I'm guessing from what you said before that it was your new lifestyle that made you cut your ties to the past?"

Phillip cringed at the word "lifestyle" and said, "Yes. I was too busy building my own fashion label, snorting cocaine off hot men's abs, and spending my enormous disposable income—in between hounding the Supreme Court about sodomy laws. You have no idea how exhausting it is to be gay these days." He heard a snicker from the next table, but he kept his eyes glued to Chad.

"Defensive, much?" Chad asked.

"Offensive, much?" Phillip replied.

"Okay," Chad said. "This is the point when we either bitterly agree to part ways, or I suggest we start over."

"Your call," Phillip said.

"The coffee's not cheap here. I'd hate to waste it. What *have* you been doing the last five years?"

"I went to New York, eked out an existence thanks to Barnes & Noble—"

"Hey, you put our high school experience to work for you."

"And made a bunch of friends. Most of whom moved to other places one by one. My best friend, Alyssa, was the last to go. That's when the money ran out, and I decided to come home for a while, nudged by my grandfather."

"Friends? But no..." Chad trailed off.

"Boyfriend?" Phillip asked and thought of Kieran. "Almost. It didn't work out." Chad's slight look of discomfort made Phillip feel defiant. "Lots of sex, though. My friend Claude helped me understand who I am and what I wanted."

"What kind of name is Claude?" Chad muttered. Phillip just stared at him. "Did Claude move away too?"

"Yes. A friend got him a job as a caretaker at a cemetery in Maine."

"Hasn't he ever read a Stephen King novel?" Chad asked.

Phillip grinned and said, "Claude's lazy. All that lying around makes it the perfect place for him. What about you?"

"I went to UT and majored in journalism. I hated leaving Austin, but the *Sun Herald* was the only paper that offered me a job. So I moved back last year. Now I cover the local scene, get a few bylines here and there, and dream of writing my own column."

"Any girlfriends?"

"A couple in college. Now I'm too busy with my job. What about you?"

"I thought we cleared that up already."

"I meant what about your art? Were you painting in New York? Did you ever have a show?"

"A show? Yeah, it opened off Broadway. It was called *Okrahomo*. I won a Tony."

"Ha," Chad said, rolling his eyes.

"No, I never had a showing. I have sketchbooks full of ideas and starts but no new paintings." Phillip frowned as an annoying rendition of "Take Me Out to the Ball Game" assaulted his ears.

"Crap," Chad said. He pulled a flip phone from his pocket and opened it, saying, "I know it's rude, but I have to take this."

Phillip waved with understanding, and Chad opened the phone as he got up and drifted to a corner without patrons. Bored, Phillip let his attention wander to the next table, which had been the source of that earlier snicker. A girl was facing him but looking down at the table, so Phillip studied her. She was pale, with a round face lightly dusted with freckles and red hair that looked natural. She was biting her lip and frowning in concentration.

Since her companion had his back to Phillip, all he could see was long black hair—not natural—pulled into a ponytail that stopped a few inches below his neck. Both of his ears had several piercings with an array of silver loops and dangling stones. He looked like he'd be really tall if he stood up.

"Something is going to happen to the throat of someone you know," Phillip heard him say. "Maybe a choking incident. Or maybe he's choking back his words. No, wait. I think he's a singer, and he's going to lose his voice. It's not permanent."

"Uh-huh," the girl said, and her eyes flickered up and gave him a skeptical look. "Go on."

Phillip craned his neck to see what the man was doing and spotted what he assumed were tarot cards spread on the table. Phillip had met people who read cards, including one of his sort-of boyfriends, and he'd never heard such a load of crap.

"The throat thing is coming up again," the man said. "Only this time it's someone much closer to you. He's not telling you something important. I see a large, empty room."

I see a large, empty head, Phillip thought and leaned forward to get a better look, which was when he noticed a round, murky stone in front of the man, apparently his crystal ball.

"You know, Mitch," the girl said, "it occurs to me the reason you don't make much money at this is because you're really depressing. People don't want to hear about throat cancer and stuff."

"I didn't say throat cancer," Mitch said. "I'm just telling you what I see."

"Your presentation could use a little work," she said.

"You're such a fucking Aries," he said. "How would you do it, Miss Cleo?"

She narrowed her eyes at him, reached over to pull the quartz globe toward herself, and said in a hushed voice, "You're about to have an amazing opportunity. There's someone in your life who needs you. I see a singer who's having voice problems. Your relationship will be stronger when your support through this difficult time helps him regain his voice."

"Whatever," Mitch muttered.

"I see something else," she said with a gasp. "Another person in your life is keeping something from you. When you find out, you have a choice. See yourself as a large room. You can continue to let it be cluttered by people you can't trust, or you can empty it and open it wide to the fresh winds of change." Mitch groaned. "I'm getting another vision," she said excitedly. "A man has a growing stain on his shirt. Is it blood? Oh, no. It's only coffee that he's leaning into while he eavesdrops."

Phillip glanced down at his shirt with alarm, but it was dry, and when he turned his frown the girl's way, her green eyes were narrowed at him. Phillip blushed and was grateful when Chad chose that moment to return to the table.

"Sorry," Chad said. "Where were we?"

"You were being taken out to the ball game, and I was being put in my place," Phillip said, refusing to look at the girl again as she burst out laughing.

Chapter 7

The morning after his reunion with Chad, Phillip woke up determined not to obsess over it. They'd parted cordially enough, but nothing had been mentioned about meeting again. Phillip felt like he'd done his part; the ball was in Chad's court. If Chad didn't stay in touch, Phillip could go back to doing what he had the past five years, shoving Chad from his thoughts.

He hadn't wanted to think about him the night before either, after leaving the coffeehouse. Remembering his conversation with Dash the lawyer, Phillip had stopped at one of the casinos with a halfhearted plan to hook up with someone. Not only had he not seen even one likely prospect, but the casino depressed him. The gamblers looked old, tired, and pallid, as if the flashing lights and constant din of the slot machines were draining the life from them. The casino itself had none of the glitz and intrigue that movies set in Las Vegas had led Phillip to expect. He didn't have enough money to gamble, so he bought a beer, smoked too much, and compounded his misery by reliving his last night in New York before finally driving back to his aunt's.

Facing another idle day, he tried to force himself out of bed with guilt about needing to find a job, but so far nothing had been promising. Apparently the only jobs available for someone of his limited skills were in retail or restaurants. Neither prospect appealed to him, and after the night before, Sam's suggestion that he could work in one of the casinos seemed equally unattractive.

He turned over when he heard his bedroom door open, and Florence stuck her head in and said, "You awake?"

"Kind of."

"Fala called to find out if your boxes have gotten here yet."

"Have they?" Phillip asked, wondering if his aunts' conspiracy to intercept his belongings before his mother could see them had been successful.

"No. But I told Odell that you were shipping some stuff for storage and to let me know when it gets here. Maybe that'll work. If not, we'll deal with it then. Fala wanted me to remind you that she still has some of your old sketchbooks at her place, if you want them. I'll be out most of the day. Do you need anything?"

"No, thank you," Phillip said.

"Don't forget to wear green."

"What?"

"It's St. Patrick's Day," she said before closing the door.

He had no intention of lying in bed and torturing himself with fantasies of spending this night with Kieran in New York. He was going to Hattiesburg. It might be interesting to look through his sketches and see what kinds of things he'd drawn when he was a teenager. He could hang out on campus and possibly stick around to eat dinner with Fala and his Uncle Harold. Maybe fate would be kind to him and some of their graduate students would show up, including a gay literary god who'd sweep him off his feet, or at least into the kitchen pantry for a hot grope and make-out session.

He showered and went downstairs. While he was eating his oatmeal, he heard the thunk of mail falling through the slot and went to the front door to pick it up, grinning when there was actually an envelope postmarked from Maine and addressed in Claude's familiar scrawl.

Greetings, my little magnolia blossom,

Thanks for sending your address. How are things back home? I'm so tired of snow and cold weather that I briefly considered leaving the dead to take care of themselves and hitchhiking my way down South. I'd relish lying in a hammock with you and sucking on a mint julep, not to mention your sexy throat. Then I realized how much work that would be—the hitchhiking, not seducing you, as I well recall how easy you are. So I added a few logs to the fire and brought my tablet to bed to write you instead.

Have you acclimated yourself? Bought a pickup truck and a shotgun? A coonhound? My advice is to forego the first two and get yourself a dog. Last fall, a stray showed up at my door, and we've been keeping company since. I named him Bisquick because his coat looks like he ran through a barrel of flour on his way here. You'll be pleased to know that he has a great deal more energy than I do and actually coerces me to take walks with him. Our conversations remind me a bit of you, except that he answers with a Maine accent. "Ready for a walk, Bisquick?" "Ayuh."

"Time to eat, Bisquick?" "Ayuh." "Does Phillip still have a hard time saying no to a pretty boy?" "Ayuh."

Does Bisquick lie? Are you indulging yourself in a little Southern comfort? Or are you still dwelling on a certain Irishman that you were annoyingly vague about in your letter? Details, son. I need fantasies to get me through these cold nights.

If it gets too hot in old Mississippi, bring your butt...sorry, I had to pause for a memory there...to Maine to party with me and the ghosts. They don't drink much, and you'll feel right at home with the crazy stories they tell.

Fondly,
Claude, Keeper of Spirits

Phillip folded the letter and put it in his backpack, then spent the hour's drive to Hattiesburg composing an answer in his head. It wouldn't be difficult to describe Kieran in greater detail, but thinking about him not only made the knot of misery return to Phillip's stomach, it didn't exactly alleviate his desire for male physical contact.

He drove to the Breyers' rambling white Victorian house on Short Bay Street without having to pause to remember the directions. He parked and stared at the house. It was the least ostentatious of all his aunts' houses, and his favorite. Fala had never allowed Selma anywhere near the yard, so it had a random, almost wild beauty beyond the black iron fence. Two tall oaks stood between the yard and the street, and two gliders still sat invitingly on the porch that traversed the entire front of the house. The only thing different was the American flag hanging from one of the slender white columns. Flags used to be brought out on holidays or special occasions, but now they flew from most houses every day.

Although his aunt and uncle were probably on the USM campus, he knew the front door would be unlocked and Persia would be busy inside. The Breyers' housekeeper had lived in a small apartment behind the kitchen for as long as Phillip could remember. Uncle Harold teasingly called her "Inertia," claiming she sat in the kitchen all day listening to preachers on the radio. Phillip knew better, although there was only so much Persia could do to the house. Harold and Fala were pack rats, and there were books, magazines, and newspaper clippings piled everywhere in a system understood only by them.

Since Persia wasn't allowed to move anything, she dusted, mopped, or vacuumed around it all. But Phillip knew any of the three bathrooms would be immaculate, just like the kitchen. The bedrooms stayed ready for an unexpected guest, with fresh flowers on the bureaus and crisp linens on the beds. And there would always be something wonderful cooking or warming on the stove. Persia recoiled in horror if Fala did anything in the kitchen. Which was understandable since, in Phillip's memory, Fala had caught it on fire three times. Fortunately,

Persia kept several fire extinguishers handy, but Florence had once observed that the fires always managed to coincide with Persia's hankering for a new countertop, coat of paint, or larger appliance.

"Persia!" he yelled as he went through the front door.

She came through the dining room from the kitchen, her ear-to-ear grin turning into a scowl as she looked him over, saying, "Look at you! Thin as a rail. Get in here, boy. I got biscuits and gravy left over, or maybe I'd better fry up some eggs— "

"No, thank you," Phillip said, bending for her hug. "I already ate breakfast."

"What'd you have?" she asked suspiciously.

"Oatmeal," he said. "Sticks to your ribs."

"You need something on those ribs. How come nobody told me you were home for a visit?"

He followed her into the kitchen and said, "It's a secret. Even my mother doesn't know yet."

She looked back at him, rolling her eyes, and before he could stop her, she pushed him into a chair at the kitchen table and started filling a plate for him. He resigned himself to being taken care of and managed to eat one of the biscuits with some honey before he reached over and grabbed a handful of peas to shell. She pushed the colander between them and asked him a dozen questions about New York, his trip home, and what his plans were.

"I don't know," he said. "I'm still trying to get used to being back."

"You gonna stay?" He shrugged, and she took his dishes and rinsed them off before putting them in the dishwasher. "You not staying at your mama's?"

"I'm at Aunt Florence's right now."

"Hmph," she said to make it clear that Florence was probably the reason he was starving to death.

"Aunt Fala said I could pick up my old sketchbooks," Phillip said. "Do you mind if I look around?"

"It's your house too," Persia said. "You ought to be staying with us. That Florence is too busy with her girls to take care of you."

"I can take care of myself," Phillip said, grinning as he stood up. When Persia looked him up and down and shook her head, he said, "I might stay tonight, though. After I find my sketchbooks, I'm going to the school to see Fala and ask her."

"You want the blue room or the yellow room?" Persia asked, having already made the decision for him.

Phillip just laughed and left the kitchen, going to a cabinet in the study. As he'd expected, the sketchbooks and his drawing pencils were on the bottom shelf. He took them out, but instead of looking through them, he walked around the room, thinking how little it had changed, except the stacks of books were taller. He stopped in front of the fireplace and stared gratefully at the three small paintings that still hung above it. He'd done them when he was thirteen and had stumbled across an article at Fala's house about the artist Arshile Gorky, who had learned how to paint by studying other artists. In turn, Phillip imitated three of Gorky's works. Uncle Harold had loved the paintings and written three poems inspired by them. The poems had been printed, matted, framed, and hung next to the paintings.

Phillip could still remember how choked with happiness he'd been the night Uncle Harold surprised him by reading the poems aloud to a group of his writing students. Everyone had been full of predictions about what a brilliant future Phillip had as an artist. Looking at the paintings now, Phillip realized they were being overly kind, but it was still one of the best moments of his teenage years.

Toting the sketchbooks, he said goodbye to Persia, then drove to the USM campus, parking at the nearby Walgreen's so he wouldn't have to get a visitor's permit. He took a sketchbook with him, but instead of crossing the campus, he went to tiny Lake Byron and sat next to a tree while he looked through his drawings.

He'd done several of the sketches in the same spot where he now sat. Coming to Hattiesburg for a few weeks had been a part of all his summer vacations, and he'd never felt lonely, although he had no friends there. He'd loved wandering around the campus, fooling himself into believing that people thought he was old enough to be a college student. Even in the summer, there'd always been exhibits, concerts, or other events that appealed to his artistic sensibilities. He'd looked forward to going to college there, never dreaming that his grandfather had an entirely different course mapped out for him. It was strange to realize that if he'd stuck with his plan, he'd have graduated the year before. There was no way of knowing how different his life might have been.

He impatiently flipped past the drawings of various spots around campus, then stopped to stare at a sketch of Chad. He had no memory of the sketch. He'd obviously done it from his imagination, as Chad was standing on the bridge at Lake Byron. Chad had never come to Hattiesburg with him. It was a good likeness, especially of Chad's crooked nose and muscular legs, but it left Phillip feeling unsettled. He'd existed in a fog of confusion and misunderstanding about himself in those days, but the sketch's detail was tangible evidence that his hands had understood what his mind couldn't grasp.

He closed the sketchbook and stared at the little island on the other side of the bridge, trying not to stir up long-forgotten memories. He watched as a man crossed the bridge toward him, noting how his faded jeans and T-shirt hugged his body. Phillip wished he'd brought his pencils with him.

The man's eyes met his, lingered, then moved on. As he walked toward an area of denser foliage, he looked back. Phillip wasn't as naïve as he'd once been. He glanced around to make sure there were no students passing by or sitting on the scattered concrete benches. After a minute, he followed the man. Thick shrubbery separated them from Hardy Street, and live oak branches blocked the view from the upper windows of Southern Hall.

It was sexual gratification at its most efficient. No muddying the event with conversation, explanation, or emotion. Tricking might lack a certain kind of intimacy, but it offered the comfort of human touch. It was stripped of guilt and meaningless promises, an opportunity to exchange pleasure before hurling oneself back into the world.

And sometimes, like today, it left Phillip feeling like an enormous pressure had been released. Once the man left him alone, after the two of them shared satisfied, conspiratorial grins, Phillip tapped the edge of the sketchbook against his forehead. He pondered how many similar opportunities he must have missed when he was an adolescent boy roaming USM's campus. He was sure that learning to read the desire of men wasn't a lesson that would earn his grandfather's approval.

He paused to admire the rose gardens, then crossed the campus to the College of Arts and Letters, where he was directed to Fala's office. She gave him a welcoming hug, insisted that he stay for dinner, and graciously agreed that he should spend the night. While they talked, she managed to pull the clasp out of her hair, twist it back up into a sloppy knot, and knock over a cup, which fortunately was empty. It was comforting to know that some things never changed.

He experienced that feeling again when they sat around the table that night, eating Persia's feast of fried chicken, mashed potatoes and gravy, the peas he'd helped shell, and rolls that melted in his mouth. His uncle was a little balder and a little rounder, but his eyes still twinkled as he baited a few of his students with questions about politics. Phillip was glad he hadn't counted on the appearance of the literary god of his fantasies, since all their dinner guests were females who obviously doted on Harold and Fala. Just like the boy he'd once been, he stayed quiet, content to let conversation flow around him.

Later, he was sitting on the front porch when his uncle joined him. "Do you still smoke?" Phillip asked, offering his pack of Marlboro Lights.

"Your aunt would skin me alive," Harold said, looking regretful. "Ever since I quit, I've been packing on the pounds. I remember when pretty coeds used to flirt with me. Now they ask me to play Santa Claus at their sorority parties."

"At least they sit on your lap, right?" Phillip asked.

"And chuck me under the chin like the doddering old fool I am," Harold said.

"You don't deceive me. I ordered your latest collection of poetry when I worked at Barnes & Noble. Brilliant, as usual."

"I owe it all to Mississippi," Harold said. "We don't turn out bad writers. How's the Magnolia State treating you?"

"I'm surviving," Phillip said, lighting another cigarette.

"If Florence and the girls are too rough on you, you know you can come stay with us," Harold said.

"Thanks." They fell into a comfortable silence broken only by the sound of crickets, until Phillip said, "Do you think my mother's nuts?"

His uncle waited a long time before he answered. Phillip knew he wasn't wishing he could dodge the question, but choosing his words with the precision of a poet. "That's an easy label for someone whose behavior we don't always understand," Harold finally said. "I'm no psychologist, but I think Ellan has developed her own set of survival skills."

"What does she have to survive? It's a pretty easy life she's living, with everyone taking care of her."

Harold's intelligent eyes held Phillip's, and he said, "If it's so easy, why did you leave?"

"I was only eighteen. I didn't want Papa to run my life."

"Have you changed your mind? Are you ready to let him be in control now?"

"Of course not," Phillip said. "But it's different. I'm—"

"A man?" Harold asked. "His grandson, not his child? More independent or better able to take care of yourself?"

"I know I can take care of myself in a way that she's never had to," Phillip said, wondering if that was true, considering how ineptly he'd managed his life in Manhattan.

Harold smiled gently and said, "Ellan was the age you are now when she came home. Only she'd just suffered a terrible loss, and she had a young child to take care of. Maybe she could have done things differently. Maybe she just did the best she could."

"I'm grown up. What's her reason now?"

"You'd have to ask Ellan," Harold said. "I understand your grandfather better than I understand her. Exton is too proud and stubborn to apologize for the past, but I believe he feels a lot of regret. You proved you didn't need his money or approval to survive. You would never have obeyed a direct order to come home."

"So he managed to scare me here by using my mother," Phillip said. "I already know that."

"The question is, *when* did you know it?" Harold asked.

"Probably as soon as he brought it up," Phillip said.

"Yet you came home," Harold said, managing not to sound too sage, although Phillip got his point.

Lying in bed later, Phillip found himself wishing he'd left those stupid fortunes on the table at Lo Ching along with his broken romance. Maybe he was as proud and stubborn as his grandfather. Maybe he had latched on to his mother's condition because it gave him a plausible excuse for coming back. But what was the point? What was he trying to prove to himself? Or to anyone else?

He turned over on his stomach and buried his face in the thick pillow, redirecting his thoughts toward Claude, then his afternoon's trick, and finally to Kieran. He gave up on the idea of sleep and turned on the light, taking the first sketchbook his hand found.

He studied the drawings of people at Smith's Diner with the comforting sense that he hadn't lost one of the haunts of his youth after all. He'd committed it to paper. Once again, the truth of who he'd been was glaringly evident. The girls he'd drawn were sometimes indistinguishable from one another. But the boys were depicted down to the most subtle details of what made them appealing to him.

If nothing else, he was discovering that his work had always contained an innate honesty that he sometimes wasn't willing to face. He refused to dwell on what that implied about his inability to paint. Instead, he picked up a pencil, found a blank page, and began drawing Kieran.

Chapter 8

Phillip waited at the Harbor View Café in Pass Christian until he saw Florence's minivan drive by. Since she didn't turn in, he knew she'd been successful. Somehow she'd managed to get his mother, Odell, and Vernie away from the house. She'd seemed to enjoy the idea of pulling a fast one on them.

Within five minutes, he was inside the house, hurrying to his old studio on the third floor. As much as he wanted to stop and look at the paintings stacked against the wall, he stayed focused, Aunt Florence's warning ringing in his ears. He had less than two hours.

Everything was just as he'd left it five years before, so he found the mat cutter without any problem. It took a while to mat the charcoal sketch of Kieran lying in bed with him that he was sending to Alyssa. In the drawing, Phillip was asleep on his stomach, sheets covering the lower half of his torso, and his arm was stretched over Kieran's chest. Kieran was awake and looking at Phillip. Phillip had deliberated a long time about whether to partially drape Kieran with the sheet. He finally stayed true to his original vision, leaving Kieran uncovered. Alyssa would love the honesty of the sketch.

He finished framing the picture and put everything back the way he'd found it, then after another look at his watch, he crossed the room to the paintings. They covered the span of his teenage years, and most of them were of his grandfather's house, all in different styles of whatever painter he'd been studying as he did each one. The Dali house made him smile. Live oaks were flat and folding down over the house with a smothering effect. His Braque imitation had been a cubist effort at viewing the house through his perception of his mother's fractured personality. The Seurat house was a little more cheerful, with its soft divisions of colored dots. He flipped through a few more, finally stopping at the Cézanne house. It was better than he'd remembered and made him feel hopeful that his talent was still lying dormant inside him. He pulled it out and took it to the window to study it in better light. He was tempted to take it with him but decided not to. It gave him more incentive to get a job and a place of his own. Once his mother knew he was in Mississippi, he could take all the paintings if he wanted to.

It was a perfect April day on the Gulf Coast: breezy, moderate temperature, no humidity. The only clouds in the sky were so white they almost hurt his eyes. With a pang, he thought of what he might do on a day like this in Manhattan—probably walk around Central Park, which would be full of people smiling, lying on the grass, and enjoying the first days of spring. He and Alyssa had often greeted the warm weather with impromptu picnics on days neither of them had to work. She'd have her long blond hair pulled back in a braid, playing with the tuft of hair on the end while they people-watched. Those were their times; no other friends or boyfriends were invited. It seemed there was always music playing somewhere in the background, like a sound track for their running commentary on which men were hot, or at least doable.

He was so lost in memories that he kept driving, passing up every opportunity to stop at a post office, until he realized he was on the bridge going into Ocean Springs. He turned off Bienville Boulevard into the post office, parking so he could assemble his package. He'd put a box, tape, and bubble wrap in the car before he left Florence's house. He carefully wrapped the framed sketch, taped his letter to it, and finally sealed and addressed the box.

There was a line in the post office, and Phillip shook his head when he saw that almost everyone in it was talking on a cell phone. Even in Mississippi, it seemed people never spoke to one another anymore unless something was attached to their ears. A couple of people ahead of him, a girl with red hair was trying to juggle her phone, several envelopes, and a package. When the line moved forward, she took a step and everything she was holding slid to the floor.

"I can't talk right now," Phillip heard her say as he stepped forward and bent to retrieve her stack of mail. Snapping her phone shut, she half bent too, and as he stood up, they almost bumped heads. She laughed and said, "Thank you."

"I know you," Phillip said, trying to place her.

"No, you don't," she disagreed.

Phillip suddenly realized that her red hair and skin color reminded him of Gustav Klimt's painting *Danae,* which depicted a woman's face at the moment of orgasm. "Sorry," he muttered, paralyzed with embarrassment.

"Are you trying to break into the line, young man?" an older gentleman behind her asked.

"No, sir," Phillip said, returning to his place and looking at everything but the girl, feeling like he'd just invaded her bedroom.

Her phone rang again, and she answered with an exasperated, "What? I told you I'm busy."

Phillip would have continued eavesdropping, but not only did she lower her voice, the man behind her turned around to speak to him, perhaps because they seemed to be the only two without cell phones. "Good weather, huh?"

"It is," Phillip agreed.

"Whereabouts you from?"

"Manhattan," Phillip said, hoping that his accent hadn't marked him as a Southerner.

"I've got no use for New York," the man said.

"Have you been there?" Phillip asked.

"I was on leave there in '64," the man said.

Behind Phillip, a woman asked, "Where did you serve?"

The man looked past Phillip and said, "Da Nang."

"Ah," she said. "My husband was in Saigon."

The two of them continued talking around Phillip, sharing information about their pasts. It was determined that the man lived in Ocean Springs and the woman in Gautier, and they were both widowed. When Phillip saw a gleam in the man's eyes, he turned to the woman to say, "Would you like to go in front of me?"

"Thank you," she said, stepping around him so the two could continue their conversation.

Phillip decided he was having an epiphany. He was some kind of relationship portal: *All those who pass through Phillip's life will find love.* He couldn't count the number of sort-of boyfriends who'd moved from him into passionate relationships; Eddie and Stefan had just been the most recent. No doubt Kieran had also found a replacement. Alyssa had found Eric. Now he was doing the same for senior citizens. He'd had no idea what power he held.

The redhead gave him a glance as she stepped away from the counter and walked with purpose toward the door.

Beware, he thought. *The next man you meet is your true love.*

When he got to his aunt's house, he went to his bedroom and locked the door, hoping to replace the erotic image from his post office trip with something a little more masculine. It wasn't often that no one was home, and he'd discovered that it was impossible to masturbate with an aunt or a couple of young cousins nearby. After a few minutes, he found that it was also impossible to masturbate when the phone wouldn't stop ringing. He finally gave up and answered.

"What are you doing?" Aunt Selma barked.

He sat up guiltily and said, "I'm just...uh...I'm just lying here. *Sitting* here."

"I don't mean right this minute," Selma said. "Have you found a job?"

"Not yet," Phillip said, hating the way she made him feel like an indolent teenager.

"I managed to get your worldly goods from Pass Christian without too many questions being asked. It's all stored in one of my toolsheds," Selma said.

"Thank you."

"If you want to earn some money," she went on, her tone making it sound like she expected him to mooch off his family indefinitely, "I'm putting together a crew for a big job. Of course, it'll be hard work."

Phillip stifled his impulse to hang up on her implied insult and said, "I don't mind hard work. What do I have to do?"

"Be at the nursery at six in the morning so you can fill out paperwork. You'll need your Social Security card and driver's license. The crew leaves for the job site at seven. Wear jeans. Buy some work gloves. I'll give you a shirt. Bring sunscreen and a lunch. Any questions?"

He figured digging in the dirt and moving plants around couldn't be any worse than retail. "No," he said, then added again, "Thank you."

In spite of the early mornings, physical labor, heat, and mosquitoes, Phillip found that he actually liked the job. Maybe he had more of his father's blue-collar tendencies than he'd realized.

A couple from New Orleans had bought a decaying antebellum mansion deep in the country north of Biloxi with an eye toward getting it on one of the popular home tours. Because the house was still under renovation, the first phase of landscaping was on the more remote areas of the grounds and mostly involved clearing out underbrush and an overgrowth of small pine trees and other invasive saplings. Phillip and the all-male crew were generally out of their Godbee's Gulf Coast Nursery shirts well before noon, and his starter tan was marred by scratches from tree limbs, vines, and brush.

His coworkers were an assortment of ages and races; he was the only white boy. No one gave him any crap about being related to Selma, but they ribbed him every time he put on sunscreen. By the third day, his nickname of "Coppertone" underwent one of those permutations that would mystify an outsider, becoming simply "Cop," and he knew he'd been accepted.

Although they worked hard, there was a relaxed camaraderie among the men, and Phillip enjoyed feeling like one of them. The crew's manager, Roy, was a huge black man of so few words that Phillip at first thought he was mute. He wished that Stewart at Barnes & Noble had been similarly afflicted.

Roy was an improvement over Stewart in many ways. He treated Phillip respectfully but showed him no favoritism as Selma's nephew, and Phillip knew this was one reason why the others accepted him. Roy's hulking presence was everywhere; he worked as hard as any of his men. He also saw everything. If

Phillip tried to do something that was beyond his physical strength, Roy was always there to lend a shoulder, but he did that for all the men, some of whom were no larger than Phillip.

Phillip was intrigued by Roy's silence. He devised questions that he thought would force answers, but Roy always managed to thwart him with grunts, facial expressions, nods, and other gestures. One day they were gathered around a barrel-size water cooler in the back of a pickup truck when Roy walked over.

"So how long do you think this job will last?" Phillip asked Roy, who shrugged. "Are we landscaping all the property? Do you know how many acres it is?"

Roy shrugged again, finished his water, and walked away. The small Cuban man standing next to Phillip laughed and said, "Mr. Roy gonna swat you like a gnat, you don't stop pestering him."

Phillip shifted his curiosity to his companion and said, "How come they call you Rafter?"

Rafter rolled his eyes and said, "'Cause I'm Cuban." When Phillip looked blank, he went on. "Like I'm one of the boat people."

"Oh," Phillip said. "Are you?"

"No. I was born in Gainesville."

Everyone had a nickname. Phillip's favorite person to team up with was a sturdy Mexican who smiled all the time and was called Evita. Each morning, they'd put on gloves and start hacking away at something, and before long, Evita would be singing, off-key and in Spanish, any of several Madonna songs. This usually provoked some kind of response from a pair of black twins, about twenty years old, who had amazing bodies that Phillip was careful not to get caught ogling. They were indistinguishable, except that Goldie had a gold-capped front tooth. Unless they smiled, Phillip was never sure whom he was talking to, but from his first morning, a pattern was set.

"Damn, it's hot," Goldie had muttered.

Evita warbled a line in Spanish as Phillip tried to figure out what melody he was attempting.

"Stop that shit," Booty complained. "That skinny white bitch is old."

Evita's only answer was another line of off-key Spanish.

"He gonna start singing Slutney Spears if you don't shut up," Goldie warned.

"Or Christine Aguiwhora," Booty said.

Roy walked up and grunted, handing Phillip a machete so he'd stop ineffectively assaulting kudzu with his spade.

"Thanks, Roy. How'd you get the name Booty?" Phillip asked.

"Name's Lucian," Booty answered. "Cheech kept fucking it up with Lucius. That turned into Licious. Like booty-licious."

Yet another dissonant line came from Evita.

"You lucky they don't call you Beyoncé," Goldie said.

Evita capped it off with a big, inharmonious finish, making Phillip feel like he was working among a group of sweating drag divas.

By the end of his second week, he'd noticed a grudging respect in Selma's eyes when he came back to the nursery each evening. He was determined to stick out the grunt work and looked forward to actually planting things based on the diagrams Selma gave Roy.

What he didn't look forward to was the possibility of his grandfather coming home and seeing the condition of his Volvo. The carpet was clumped with dirt from his work boots, and the car was littered with plastic water bottles and junk food wrappers. Before he drove back to Florence's house on a Friday night, he stopped at a self-service car wash and vacuumed and washed the Volvo. He put his work boots in the trunk and drove home in his sock feet, undressing as usual in the laundry room and heading for the shower in his boxer briefs. He always felt weird going through the house half-naked, but he wasn't about to track dirt over Florence's lush carpets.

He was getting out of the shower when Florence tapped on the bathroom door. "Are you decent?"

"Not yet," he said.

"I just wanted to let you know that—what the hell's his name?"

Phillip grinned as he ran the towel over his wet hair and called out, "Chad."

"Right. Chad called. He said to call him back."

"Thanks," Phillip said.

He saw it as a good sign that Chad had called. As soon as he was dressed, he found his number.

"Hey," Chad said. "You got anything going on tonight?"

"No," Phillip said.

"I have a date, but she doesn't get off work until nine. I thought you might want to meet at the usual place for coffee."

Phillip smiled at the idea that they had a "usual place" after a one-time meeting, but he said, "Sure."

Chad was already on the patio when Phillip got there. He ordered an iced mocha and joined his friend, who greeted him with a half smile and said, "I'd have called you sooner, but I got sent to Florida to profile some race-car drivers. Remember that February we drove down to Daytona for race week?"

"Yes," Phillip said, trying not to visibly wince. "That was out of control."

"Like you remember any of it," Chad said. "From the time we were invited into the first RV on the infield, you were drunk."

"All I remember is the noise," Phillip said.

"And Tent City," Chad reminded him. "Those two girls…" He broke off, looking uncomfortable.

"If I only knew then what I know now," Phillip said. "I think men outnumbered women ten to one."

"Straight men," Chad said, as if to defend the masculinity of the world's NASCAR bubbas.

"Just keep telling yourself that," Phillip said. His gaze drifted across the room and he felt a click of recognition. The redhead he'd seen in the post office a couple of weeks before, and hadn't recognized out of context, was sitting at a table with her pseudopsychic friend.

He looked back at Chad, who motioned with his head and asked, "Friend of yours?"

"Not so much," Phillip said.

"Too bad," Chad said, giving the redhead a quick, appraising glance. "Her ass is bangin'."

"Bangin'?" Phillip repeated. "I can't believe you just said that. Do you plan on writing like that? I can see it now. One day, I'll open the newspaper and read: 'The First Lady said her main concerns were education and literacy programs. She leaned down to hug one of the children after reading to them, displaying an ass that was totally bangin'.'"

"Yeah, right!" Chad exclaimed, grabbing packets of sugar from the table and throwing them at Phillip. "Like I'd say that about her butt. And stop talking about my vocabulary. You sound like my mother."

"How is Taryn?"

"She's great," Chad said brightly. "I mean, she's pretty much given up on photography these days. She still takes pictures, but her main concern is the restaurant."

"The what?" Phillip said in surprise.

"I keep forgetting how out of the loop you are. Yeah, she and this friend of hers, Georganne, opened a place in Pass Christian: the Burning Phoenix. It's really fancy. I couldn't afford to eat there if I wasn't related. That's where Roger, my roommate the chef, works."

"Well, good for her," Phillip said. "I had no idea."

"Yeah. She's totally into it too. I'm glad she has something that's hers. I mean, her photography is great, but this is something that doesn't require brokers, galleries, and all that dependency." Chad drank his coffee while Phillip nodded, then he tentatively asked, "How's your mom doing?"

"Still crazy after all these years," Phillip joked.

Chad rolled his eyes and said, "That's so wrong."

"No, it isn't. The aunts claim she's making progress, and they're worried that she'll regress with me being back. I haven't seen her yet, so I don't know what to think. But my grandfather dragged me here to look after her while he's out of the country because he says she's unstable."

"I'm sorry," Chad offered.

"Hey," Phillip said, waving his hand dismissively. "Psycho mother, *qu'est que c'est?*"

Chad recognized the Talking Heads parody and laughed. He said, "Run, run away, huh? Well, that's just what you did."

"Yeah, I guess," Phillip said quietly.

Chad flipped open his phone and looked at the display. "Speaking of running away, I've got to pick up Glee at the mall. Are we cool?"

"You tell me," Phillip said.

"I don't know. I mean, can you handle the fact that I'm straight? I know it's really unorthodox."

"Heathen!" Phillip exclaimed. He sighed and said, "I guess I can learn to accept it."

"Do you want me to hug you or something?" Chad asked. "To prove that I accept you too?"

"Just go," Phillip said, shielding his face with one hand. "People are staring."

Chad laughed. After he left, Phillip went to the counter to get a stirrer for his coffee, since all the chocolate was settling on the bottom. When he turned back to his table, he gave a surprised look at the redhead, who was sitting in the seat Chad had vacated. She wiggled her fingers and said, "Hi."

"Uh, hi," Phillip said.

"Would you like a tarot reading?"

"No, I'm good. Thanks."

"Wow. I guess that's the way it was meant to be," she said. "They're Mitch's cards, and he's gone now. So if you wanted a reading, I couldn't do it."

"Oh," Phillip said, unsure of an appropriate response and trying to think of a good exit line.

"I really don't know anything about tarot cards anyway," she said and laughed. "I would've been making it up, and that's no good. But sit down. I know how to read palms."

"Oh, that's too bad," Phillip said. "You can't read my palm in Mississippi. It's on the banned list. Sorry."

"Your palm is dirty, huh?" she said, arching an eyebrow. "That's okay. I don't mind."

"Do you have a twin sister?" Phillip asked, finally sitting down.

"No. Why?"

"Because a woman who looks just like you snubbed me in the post office in Ocean Springs."

"I didn't snub you," she disagreed. "I didn't know who you were, and you acted like you knew me."

"I saw you the first time I was here, but I didn't remember that. I was just trying to place you. It wasn't a lame attempt to come on to you."

"Right, because you're the gay one," she said. She gestured toward Chad's empty cup. "Is your friend learning to live with that?"

"Apparently. I'm Phillip Powell."

"Shanon Lamarre," she said, extending a hand. "Your palm doesn't seem so dirty to me."

"You should have seen it a couple of hours ago," he said. "I work for a landscaping company."

"Do you live in Ocean Springs?" she asked.

"I'm between homes," he said. "Right now, I'm staying with my aunt in Long Beach. As soon as I get my next paycheck, I'm looking for an apartment."

"Really?" she asked, her expression thoughtful. "Where?"

"Biloxi, I guess," Phillip said. "The nursery I work for is here."

She studied him a minute, then said, "You want to take a ride? I know a place that might interest you." She laughed when he just stared at her. "I'm not kidnapping you. What the hell would I do with a gay man? Force you to fix my hair?"

"It's so nice that you're comfortable with stereotypes," Phillip said.

She narrowed her eyes and said, "Your hands are clean, but you have a big ol' chip on your shoulder. I have gay friends. Do you need references? Or do you think you can manage to stop seeing bad intentions when someone's trying to do you a favor?"

Phillip dropped his gaze to his coffee cup, feeling ashamed of himself. Five years ago, he'd gratefully accepted the kindness of another stranger and ended up with his best friend. Had he gotten so cynical living in the Northeast that he didn't recognize a nice person when he met one? Alyssa would have smacked him down for being obstinate and rude.

He looked back at Shanon and extended his hand again. "Hi. I'm Phillip Powell, and I'm not always an asshole."

"Nice to meet you, Phillip," she said. "Let's go."

Chapter 9

Phillip spent the next weekend moving his belongings from a shed at Godbee's Nursery to the third floor of a Victorian house in Ocean Springs. Or rather, the attic that had been converted into a third floor. Shanon had been honest during their drive that night, telling him all of the house's bad features.

"It's over one hundred twenty years old and was falling apart when the current owner bought it. The foundation had to be repaired first. Then it was repainted inside and out. Lowell, who used to live in the attic," she paused to roll her eyes, "insisted that his part of the house get fixed first. Stairs were constructed on the outside of the house behind the garden room so he'd have his own entrance. They took out the east wall and put in floor-to-ceiling windows and an outside deck on top of the garden room. Lowell is an artist. He wanted more light so he could paint. Then a bathroom was put on that floor. Other than that, it's a big, open room. There's a tiny refrigerator and stove that Lowell never used, because he was always downstairs in the kitchen plundering my groceries or trying to get Julianna to cook for him."

"Who's Julianna?"

"My other roommate. Well, she would be, if she was ever home. She's almost always at Jess's house. Julianna is in serious lust. She keeps this address so her family won't know she's screwing her brains out somewhere else seven nights a week. Anyway, Lowell moved out in the dead of night about a week ago."

"Mitch warned you," Phillip said.

Her eyes widened and she said, "You're right, Mr. Eavesdropper. Mitch did tell me that someone close to me was hiding something, and he saw a big empty room. Lowell's such a flake—artists, you know."

"Uh-huh," Phillip said warily. "Do you mind if I smoke in your car?"

"Go ahead. Eventually the place will get central heat and air, but for now, the attic can sometimes feel like an oven. There are fans up there, but Lowell used to sneak down to Julianna's bed. Since she wasn't in it, and there's a window-unit air conditioner in her room that wheezes and drips all over the place."

"I'm guessing you're not a real estate agent," Phillip said.

"I just don't want you to get any surprises. I don't like surprises."

"We have something in common," Phillip said. "I don't like surprises either."

"*Thank* you," Shanon said. "Isn't it the worst when someone makes a big gesture or buys you something that you didn't expect? I hate that."

"Or when someone reveals some facet of his character that you hadn't suspected," Phillip said. She glanced at him, her eyebrows arched. "I should tell you before Mitch sees it in his crystal ball; I'm an artist too."

"God," she moaned.

"I'm also a lousy housekeeper. I was always behind on my rent and utility bills in my last apartment. My phone was constantly being turned off."

"There's no phone in the house," Shanon said, as if trying to top his list of reasons for not moving in. "Julianna and I use our cell phones."

"I had a love-hate relationship with my landlady. I'm moody, and half of my family should be locked up."

"It's a match made in hell," Shanon said, pulling into a bricked driveway.

Phillip barely had time to regret all the weeds and grass growing up from between the bricks because he took one look at the gray Victorian with its elaborate white wood trim and fell in love. "A Stick-Eastlake," he said. "I can't believe I never noticed it before."

"It used to be hidden by tree limbs and eight thousand vines. How did you know it's a Stick House?" Shanon asked.

"My Aunt Andi's house in Gulfport is the same style. Hers is in pristine condition. She wouldn't have it any other way. But I like the faded elegance of this one."

"Does faded elegance mean the same thing as termite damage?" Shanon asked, unlocking the door. "I thought you said your aunt lived in Long Beach."

"Different aunt," Phillip said. "Long Beach is the Greek Revival." He gaped at the high ceilings, the molding, and the parquet floors that were in dire need of refinishing. "On the plus side, I do have a job that I'm not likely to get fired from. I've been artistically blocked for years, so you may never have to endure the smell of turpentine or oil paint. I don't own a stereo; the walls won't vibrate with house or trance music at all hours of the day and night. I'm great at givin straight women relationship advice because I slept with all the worst New York. And I'll never steal your food."

"I don't date men," Shanon said.

"Women? Rottweilers?"

"I don't date at all."

Phillip filed that comment away, saying only, "This is great," as she led him through the downstairs. "I love the fireplace—"

"It doesn't work."

"And the built-in bookshelves. Is the molding original?"

"Yes."

"Are all these antiques yours?"

"Uh-huh." She pulled him to the kitchen, saying, "This is the next project, now that all the bathrooms are done."

"I hope they won't change it too much."

"Actually, Julianna's love slave, Jess, is doing the work. Jess is a fervent believer in keeping as many of the house's original features as possible."

Phillip admired the renovated bathroom. A shower had been added, but a claw-foot tub was still there, as was the original floor with its octagonal tile. They moved to the second floor, where Shanon allowed him only a cursory look at her bedroom. His impressions were of buttery yellow walls, a sleigh bed, and plantation blinds before she closed the door.

Apparently, she had no scruples about Julianna's right to privacy because she walked into her absent roommate's bedroom and turned on the lights. Phillip's eyes bugged out as he looked at the pictures, ribbons, and trophies that dominated the room.

"Pageant girl, huh?" he asked.

"I think she won every title in the state except Miss Mississippi before she threw it all away for love," Shanon said.

He stared at the pictures and said, "That's her? She's gorgeous. Glamorous even."

"She's got a little different look now," Shanon said. "You'll see. If you move in, I mean."

Each girl had her own bathroom, and these had undergone refurbishing much like the one downstairs. Phillip continued to make admiring noises as Shanon walked him to what looked like a closet. When she opened the door, he saw a narrow staircase.

"I *love* these houses," he said, following her up the stairs. It took him five seconds of looking around for his brain to scream, *You want this space!* "How much is the rent?"

"Um..." She looked vague for a moment, then said, "Your share would be two hundred a month."

"I may do menial labor, but I'm not poor. How much is the rent, really?"

"Two hundred a month will cover it. I honestly just want somebody here.

I work weird hours sometimes, and I don't like to leave the house empty."

"What do you do?" Phillip asked.

The vague expression returned, and she said, "I'm a consultant." She walked away from him and opened the French doors, allowing a breeze into the stuffy room. "Come look at the deck. And the stairs. You can entertain guests whenever you want, and I'll never know anyone is here. It's private."

Like you, Phillip thought, recognizing an evasion when he saw one. If there was anything he understood, it was reluctance to delve into one's private history for a stranger. It still baffled him that he'd told Kieran so much about his background, and he promised himself that if Shanon ever decided to be more forthcoming, he'd listen to her with the same nonjudgmental interest that Kieran had shown him—because Phillip definitely intended to share the house with her. He could already picture where he would set up his easel. He could get his paintings from his grandfather's. He felt like this house could be his muse.

"A lot of these old houses have names," he said. "Does this one?"

Shanon smiled and said, "I've heard it called Belfast House."

Phillip whipped around to look at her and said, "Why?"

"I think the family who had it built was from Ireland," she said. "You could probably find out more at the Visitors' Center."

Hearing that the house was named for Kieran's home city settled the matter for Phillip, and he said, "If you're sure you trust me not to flake on you—"

"One more thing," Shanon interrupted. "I keep my telescope up here. I like to set it up on the new deck sometimes. It's heavy. I really don't wait to haul it up and down the stairs."

"I don't mind," Phillip said. "My former roommate Alyssa [...]d I didn't have anywhere near this much space in Manhattan, and we ma[...] not to get on each other's nerves."

[...]boxes of things that evoked

Phillip thought about Alyssa while he e[...]stifled his feelings of guilt over memories of their life together in New Y[...] to pay to have a phone installed. the low rent by reminding himself th[...]os, and he had to be accessible to his He wanted to be able to call Alyssa[...]gh he never wanted to enslave himself aunts and, presumably, his m[...]ell phone, he'd already decided to buy a to the information age by[...]one line. It would be a lot easier to keep in computer, which would[...]-mail.

touch with his frien[...]d looked around. It was amazing how little he [...]e garbage bags of stuff before he left New York. Even

He finished [...] space than he needed, he felt no regret for the things owned. He'd [...]acked his empty canvases and paints from Alyssa in the though h[...]tended to set up his easel. He could also retrieve his art he'd l[...] co[...]

supplies from Pass Christian. His stomach felt hollow when he thought of seeing his mother. As if the house was sympathizing, he heard what sounded like pots and pans crashing downstairs. Shanon's Jetta hadn't been in the driveway when he got there, but she must have come home while he was unpacking.

He clattered noisily down the stairs so he wouldn't startle her, but when he got to the kitchen, a strange woman was poised with an iron skillet, ready to strike.

"You're not Shanon," he said.

"Neither are you."

They assessed each other. She had brown eyes and dark hair pulled into a ponytail. Even if she'd been wearing makeup, he knew that the blond, blue-eyed beauty pageant contestant couldn't have changed this much. "You're not Julianna either."

"Why don't you tell me who you are, genius?" she asked, still holding the skillet aloft.

"Shanon's new roommate. I just moved into the attic."

"Oy," she said, smacking her head and putting the skillet on the counter. "I totally forgot that Shanon told us you were moving in."

Phillip had an impulse to hug her. He wasn't sure if it was provoked by her bravery with a skillet or because of her exclamation, which took him right back to Manhattan. "Are you from New York?"

"Long Island," she said. "I'm Jess."

Startled, he said, "I thought Jess—are you the one who's renovating the place?"

"That's me. Julianna's girlfriend."

"I'm so happy!" Phillip exclaimed.

"Thanks. ·t it's not like you know us."

"I grew up h· but I've been in Manhattan for the last five years. Coming back has been a cu· shock. You're my first out Sapphic sister south of the Mason-Dixon Line."

She looked him up a·

He laughed, held out hi·wn and said, "You are one boyish lesbian."

Her handshake was firm, a·and said, "Phillip. It's nice to meet you."

his urge to cling to her. She said,·seemed to understand that he was fighting Probably taking a nap. Whenever ·auty queen is around here somewhere. curled up on the nearest soft surface. ·work to be done, you can find her

"What are you doing?" he asked.

"Emptying cabinets. I'm going to start s·

"I'll help," he volunteered. "Do you need ·m tomorrow."

"Sure," she said. "Thanks."

After he got the boxes, Phillip discovered th·ot several upstairs." who sounded more efficient than bossy when sh· e of those people worked well together, talking while they packed. ·at to do. They

"What do you miss most about New York?" she asked.

"Variety," Phillip said. "You've got a thousand choices, and they're all within walking distance."

"Oh, I know," Jess said. "I remember when I moved down here and found out how hard things are without a car. And how surprised I was the first time I saw the help wanted section of the paper and kept asking, 'Where's the rest of it?' Or discovering that not everything was open twenty-four hours. Then there were movies I wanted to see that never came here—and an appalling lack of pro sports teams."

"There are infinite choices in the city—of jobs, movies, theaters, clubs, and men." Phillip grinned. "Actually, I complain, but of all those? I mostly took advantage of the vast selection of men. I was too broke to go out much, and I had the same job for five years."

"I'm the opposite of you," Jess said. "I only had one girlfriend, but more jobs than I can count. Or want to. After losing the last one, my girlfriend and I came down here because she had a friend who promised us jobs at a casino. The girlfriend didn't last. The job did. I'm a blackjack dealer at Singing River Casino."

Jess pulled something plastic from a cabinet and held it out with a confused look. Phillip smiled, flipped over a tray inside it, and said, "Deviled egg keeper."

"Nobody's ever made deviled eggs here."

"Doesn't matter. No Southern kitchen is without a deviled egg plate of some kind. Do you like working at the casino?" Phillip asked, picking up the thread of their conversation and thinking of his one dreary casino excursion.

"I do. Have you been to Singing River?"

"No."

"It's not upscale like Beau Rivage, or like the one Hard Rock plans to open. I know the money's better at the nicer casinos, but Singing River has a kind of downtrodden appeal for me. I'm comfortable there. Plus my managers don't give me any shit about being a dyke." Her eyes went past Phillip and she said, "Julianna works there too. She's a cocktail waitress."

Phillip turned and saw Julianna standing in the doorway, staring at them with sleepy eyes. Although she was quite different from the girl in the photos in her bedroom, she still had the face of an angel. But she was missing the tousled blond curls and the artful makeup. Her face was scrubbed clean, and her hair had been shorn into an undercut bowl, shaved on the bottom and a couple of inches long on the top. She was wearing a tiny T-shirt and low-riding cutoffs that exposed most of her taut midriff. She seemed too young to be the girlfriend of Jess, whose age he'd estimated at around thirty.

Without a word to either of them, Julianna wended her way through the boxes they'd packed and found a spoon and a jar of peanut butter. She scooped out a spoonful and stuck it in her mouth, looking like a little girl with a lollipop.

Jess kept working, and Phillip moved around Julianna to pull out drawers and stack them on the table. He was startled when Julianna reached out and ran her fingers over his upper arm.

"Good muscles for a slender man," she said after taking the spoon from her mouth. "Ever thought about modeling?"

"I'm not pretty enough," Phillip said, trying not to be too obvious as he moved away from her. He felt invaded.

Julianna clicked the spoon against her tongue piercing and said, "You've got a good look." As if her announcement was the final word on the subject, she turned to Jess. "When are we leaving? I'm starving."

"I want everything to be ready tonight so I can get right to work tomorrow," Jess said. "Why don't you go pick up some barbecue?"

Julianna sighed as if she'd been asked to track, kill, and prepare their meal over an open fire, then abruptly turned back to Phillip saying, "Don't expect me to cook for you like Lowell did."

Goaded, Phillip said, "I don't, but you will clean my room and do my laundry, right?"

Julianna gave him a look that let him know she was done with him before she ambled out of the kitchen, presumably to get food.

"She's not always like this," Jess said apologetically. "She doesn't wake up well."

Phillip let his grunt as he picked up a heavy box serve as his only answer. Jess went back to work, and he pondered how Julianna had managed to become friends, or at least a roommate, with a good-humored person like Shanon, much less the girlfriend of someone who seemed as sensible and down-to-earth as Jess.

When Jess suddenly let out a bark of laughter, Phillip gave her a curious look, and she said, "I'd better warn you. Somehow, Shanon, Julianna, and I have ended up on the same cycle. For one week a month, you might want to stay in the attic."

"Maybe I'll get synchronized," Phillip said. "I can be daunting when I'm having cramps."

"I'll buy Midol in bulk," Jess said, helping him restore their convivial mood.

Chapter 10

Although Phillip's phone was installed by the end of his first week in Belfast House, he decided not to tell his aunts. They could always reach him at the nursery through Selma, and he knew that the ban on seeing his mother was due to be lifted anytime since he had a job and a place to live. He didn't think another week or so would make a difference, and he was enjoying the novelty of time without family responsibilities or the demands of Florence's daughters, though he did miss walking the dogs. He liked putting in a hard day of work at Whittier Plantation and then coming home to make his own decisions about what he wanted to eat and when, or how he wanted to spend his evenings. He was sure that Florence and Sam were equally relieved by the return of routine and privacy to their household.

It had been great to reconnect with his friends by phone. His first call was a four-hour conversation with Alyssa so they could catch up. Stories about his aunts, roommates, and coworkers became funnier when she was his audience, but it also made him feel good to help her laugh at her own tales of woe. She and Eric had mostly adjusted to living together, with a few skirmishes about their individual bad habits. Because of the success of their first crop, they'd been given a small business loan and had already lined up several new buyers for the organic herbs their farm produced. They even had their own Web site.

"Did you ever think we'd both end up making a living by playing in dirt?" Phillip asked.

"Isn't that weird?" Alyssa asked. "Two cosmopolitan gals like us. If Bunny could see us now."

"I think he'd approve of the physical effects," Phillip said. "I'm getting muscles—and a tan. I look almost healthy."

"I want pictures," Alyssa said. "Are you painting?"

"Not yet. But I'm not beating myself up about it."

"Gardening can be healing," Alyssa said. "It'll happen, Phillip."

It had been just as good to talk to Carlos, whose life also sounded like it was on an upward turn. Carlos's inherent honesty had compelled him to visit Renata and explain the arrangement he'd made with Bunny and Phillip about the apartment. Renata, apparently delighted by timely rent payments, hadn't cared. In fact, she was so dazzled by Munchkin's fondness for Carlos that she'd had her handyman do some greatly needed repairs in the apartment.

Carlos didn't mention Bunny, and Phillip hadn't tried to call him. In a gesture of reconciliation, he'd picked up brochures about the tourist appeal of the coast and used them to make a funny little travel guide, complete with sketches titled "Men of Mississippi," that he mailed to Bunny.

He considered leaving his number on Kieran's office voice mail but decided not to. It was more productive to focus on his new life—rebuilding his friendship with Chad and making new friends, including his roommates, who kept him engaged. At least Shanon did. She was proof it wasn't true that a bad temper necessarily went with red hair. Nothing seemed to ruffle her, including the complete disarray of their kitchen.

He rarely saw Jess, who worked on the kitchen during the day before putting in her shift at the casino. Every night he checked on her progress, and sometimes Shanon was there maneuvering around the mess as she made herself a meal. She always offered to share with Phillip. He always declined, but he would make a pot of coffee and keep her company while she ate.

He maintained a running narrative of his work crew or told her things about his Manhattan friends, but he never discussed his family, which was easy, because she never said anything about her family. Nor did she talk about her job, which was still a mystery to him. He couldn't even determine what hours she kept. Sometimes she seemed to have been out all day; others, she was gone until late at night. She told him stories about his predecessor, Lowell, or talked about Mitch and his metaphysical interests.

He'd only seen Julianna a couple of times, and she'd been sugary sweet, nothing like the night he met her. He was wary of anyone whose moods shifted for no discernible reason, so whenever he saw her car parked in front of the house, he took the outside entrance to his apartment.

Which was the case when he got home late on a Friday afternoon after an unusually bad day. The humidity had been suffocating, and he'd been stung on the shoulder by a hornet, which hurt like hell when it happened and was still throbbing hours later. He went right to his apartment and swallowed a Benadryl and some aspirin before taking a long, cool shower. It wasn't quite as exotic as Booty's cure, which had been to chew tobacco from one of Phillip's Marlboros until it was a moist glob, then gently plaster it against the sting.

He'd just slid into a clean pair of jeans when he heard the door to the staircase open and Julianna call out, "Can I come up?"

"Sure."

She walked up the stairs and looked around, saying, "Wow, it's so clean. Lowell was a pig."

"What's up?" Phillip asked, hoping she didn't plan to linger. Since she was wearing nothing but an oversize T-shirt, she obviously didn't have to work.

"Your boss came by this afternoon. She said she wasn't going back to work in time to catch you before you left, so she gave me a note for you," Julianna said, holding it out. "I told her that she could have called, but I guess she doesn't have your phone number."

Fuck, he thought, taking the note and opening it.

> *It's time for a meeting with your aunts. Tonight, please, at seven. We'll be at Landry's at Gateway and Beach Boulevard. Don't be late.*

"Okay, thanks," he said with a sinking feeling. Julianna showed no sign of leaving and stared at him curiously, which made him ask, "What?"

"Selma Godbee is your aunt, huh?"

He looked back at the note, which wasn't signed, and assumed Selma had introduced herself to Julianna. "Yeah."

"I know her. I mean, I don't *know* her. But she comes into Singing River now and then. She's what my boss calls an 'IL.'"

"What's that?"

"Influential local."

"I'm not surprised. She's run a successful business in Biloxi for a long time."

Julianna laughed and said, "Oh, come on, Phillip. Everyone knows who the Godbee family is. I've served your grandfather and his business associates plenty of cocktails in Faulkner's Library."

"Faulkner's Library?" he repeated blankly.

"It's the bar where I work at the casino. Your grandfather is a lousy tipper, by the way. A lot of rich people are."

"I'm sorry to hear that," Phillip said, growing weary of the conversation. "I need to get ready."

"I guess Shanon doesn't know that this poor-boy thing is an act," Julianna said.

"I support myself," Phillip said. "My grandfather is the one with money. Besides, I never told Shanon that I'm poor. How much rent do you pay?"

"Are you kidding? Jess is doing all this work on the house for practically nothing, and I'm hardly ever here. I pay the power bill and that's it."

"Then what's the problem?"

Julianna tapped her tongue stud against her teeth and finally said, "Shanon's a really generous person, and she's good about accepting people for who they are. You might want to be careful about misleading her. Nobody likes a liar." With that she turned and daintily descended the stairs.

"I haven't lied to her," Phillip said. He made a face at her departing back and then looked at the note with frustration. There was no getting around the meeting, and he wasn't going to make it worse by showing up late.

His aunts had arrived early, however, and were seated and having drinks when he got to Landry's. He sat down, ordered iced tea, and endured their comments about his appearance.

"You should get some new clothes," Andi said with a critical look at the plaid short-sleeved shirt that wasn't tucked into his jeans.

"I think he looks great," Florence said. "You're really filling out, Phillip. Your skin looks so healthy. You're being careful about sunscreen, aren't you?"

"Yes, ma'am," he said, taking a piece of bread and buttering it.

"He's dressed like everyone his age," Fala said. "At least the waist of his pants isn't down around his derriere."

Phillip laughed and said, "I could never get away with that look."

"Roy says you're a hard worker," Selma remarked. "Now that you have a job and a place to live, it's time to let the cat out of the bag."

She was distracted by the waiter, giving Phillip the opportunity to turn to Fala and say, "What's the origin of that cliché? Do you know?"

"It's an eighteenth-century phrase arising from a practice that began in the 1500s," Fala said. Andi sighed audibly, but Fala gamely continued. "Farmers used to buy and sell suckling pigs tied up in sacks."

"A pig in a poke?" Florence asked.

"Yes. Poke is another word for sack. By the eighteenth century, a practice arose of sealing the sacks. When the buyer arrived home and opened it—"

"He'd been cheated because a cat jumped out," Phillip guessed.

"Do you think you could ever eat cat?" Florence asked.

"Ew—no," Phillip said.

"You could eat anything the good Lord provided if you were starving," Andi stated as she gestured toward the waiter, who was poised to take Phillip's order.

Once he was gone, Selma got to the point. "How do you want to handle this?"

"I don't know," Phillip said. "How is she? Have you seen the improvements you hoped for with Papa out of the way?"

"She seems okay to me," Florence said.

"Oh, really?" Selma asked. "When I went by there earlier today, she asked me where she could buy lawn statuary."

When Selma paused, the rest of them watched her with dread, until Andi weakly asked, "What does she have in mind?"

"She thinks it will be *cute* to have a family of deer on the front lawn," Selma said with a grimace.

"That's not crazy; it's tacky," Andi said. Phillip knew that in her estimation, tackiness was the graver of the two.

"She's just yanking your chain," Florence said. "It would be like asking me where she could get spandex leggings and blue eye shadow."

"Or asking me if I have any Jacqueline Susann novels she can borrow," Fala chimed in.

"Do you?" Phillip asked both aunts in a hopeful tone, and Florence swatted at his arm. He dodged her and said, "Maybe when I see her, she'll ask where she can get a print of those dogs playing poker. She can replace the Rothko with it."

"They might look better upside down," Fala said.

"Can we get back on topic?" Selma asked.

"What does your gut tell you to do?" Florence asked Phillip.

"To show up at the house and tell her the truth," Phillip said. "Papa wanted me nearby, and I waited to see her until after I settled in."

"I wish you'd leave Daddy out of it," Andi said.

"I think Phillip's right," Florence interjected. "Why not be honest?"

"That would be a new approach," Selma said. "This family's always been full of cross-questions and crooked answers."

Phillip choked on his tea and met Fala's eyes, sending her into a giggling fit. The other aunts stared at the two of them, and Fala finally said, "Ignore me. I'm sorry." She gave Phillip a stern look.

He didn't need the warning. He wasn't about to tell the others their inside joke. He'd been about fifteen years old, playing Scrabble in the sunroom with Fala, while Selma, his mother, and Andi bickered about something in the living room. Selma had used that same line: "This family is full of cross-questions and crooked answers." Phillip had looked at Fala and said, "Did she just say our family is full of cross-dressers?"

"And crooked antlers!" Fala had answered. It had become a running joke between them.

"I'll handle it," Phillip said, forcing his attention back to the matter at hand. "I'll let her think the rest of you were keeping my secret because I wanted to surprise her."

"She doesn't react well to surprises," Andi said.

Phillip didn't relish hearing that he and his mother shared a trait, as if that doomed him to middle age in a nightgown, rattling his family and weeping over fairy tales.

After the subject of what he should do was more picked over than the crab legs and lobster they ordered, he was happy to escape. When he got home, all the downstairs lights were blazing, and Shanon's Jetta was tucked between Julianna's Civic and Jess's beat-up Jeep Cherokee. Since all three of them were home, Phillip decided to use the front door and see what they were up to, although he wasn't sure why he was willing to endure yet another all-female group after the ordeal with his aunts.

He found them in the middle of a margarita party and was in the door less than a minute when Shanon shoved a drink in his hand with the exhortation to catch up. "Why?" he asked warily.

"Because we're buzzed to the point of spilling secrets. It's not fair if you're the only sober one among us."

"I don't have any secrets," Phillip said, taking a sip. It was surprisingly good, and he gave Shanon an appreciative look.

"Riiiiight," Julianna drawled.

He frowned, wondering if she intended to tell them that Phillip Powell was the grandson of Godbee Energy. He sat on the floor across from Shanon and, in an effort to head off Julianna, said, "I used to fantasize about Joe Perry from Aerosmith."

"So did I!" Shanon said. She and Phillip exchanged high-fives.

"Sometimes I still do," Phillip admitted.

"So do I!" Shanon exclaimed again.

"I never have," Jess said. "Well, maybe *being* him. All those chicks."

"He's, like, a hundred years old," Julianna said, wrinkling her nose.

"He's still hot," Shanon said.

"What's your secret?" Phillip asked Julianna. "What scandal drove you away from pageants?"

"There are no skeletons in my closet," Julianna insisted. He stared at her, waiting, and she sighed. "I was a good Lutheran girl from Laurel when I started on the Little Miss circuit. I was barely out of diapers when I won Miss Baby Boll Weevil, Paint Horse Petite Princess, Little Delta Duchess, Bayou Belle, Field Pea Princess, Little Miss Levee, Miss Pontotoc Ridge, Cotton Countess—I don't remember them all. When other little girls packed away their crowns, I kept going. No matter what they say about prize money or scholarships, families sink fortunes into the pageant circuit, so it's really not that. It's competing. No, it's *winning.* It's an addiction. I was a pageant junkie. I didn't have time for friends. Girls were my competition. And no boy ever set my pulse racing like the sight of a tiara resting on a satin pillow."

Julianna was in full performance mode, walking around the living room while she talked, and Phillip could see her inner contestant emerging. He looked at Jess, who watched her girlfriend with knowing amusement, and Shanon, who grinned at him.

"Three years ago, when I was nineteen, I met my nemesis," Julianna said, her eyes glittering with a mixture of anger and admiration. "Eveline Roby was from Louisiana, and everyone said she was my strongest competition for Miss Yazoo River. She was raven-haired, with big green eyes and the flattest stomach I ever saw in my life. You could feel the hostility crackle in the air between us, and I guess it was someone's idea of a joke to make us room together at the Edison Walthall Hotel in Jackson.

"Eveline was the devil. She flashed her teeth at me and said, 'I read in your bio that you want to model. But, Julianna, you have *beeeeutiful* breasts, honey. Models are so flat-chested. You have the breasts of a country singer.' The next morning I snuck in the bathroom and taped my breasts flatter because I can't carry a tune. Or, 'Julianna, you always look so confident with that long-legged stride,' and the next time I had to rehearse my runway walk, I looked like a foot-binding victim. 'Julianna, sugar, your swimming suit is so wholesome, like a Miss America finalist in the 1950s!' I wasn't sure why I let her get under my skin; no one else ever had.

"We were being shuttled to the fairgrounds, and Eveline stopped glossing her lips and said, 'Girls, y'all don't get shaken up by those protesters outside the Coliseum. They're just a bunch of bitter ol' lesbians.' I'd seen protesters before, so I didn't think much about it. But then she fixed her gaze on me with this smug smile that I didn't understand."

Julianna stopped to take a sip of her margarita. When she realized that her glass was empty, she went to the kitchen. The silence was unbroken except for the noise of Julianna's spoon scraping the rest of the mixture into her glass before she returned and picked up her story.

"I looked at the little group of women as we rode by them. I don't know what I expected bitter old lesbians to look like, but the only one I really had time to focus on was this slip of a girl who looked like a young Blythe Danner. She was holding a sign that said EDUCATION, NOT EXPLOITATION! I put that—and Eveline—out of my mind. I knew that one of the Miss Yazoo River judges owned a modeling agency in Atlanta, and this was my big chance to strut my stuff."

Julianna paused again to take a Marlboro from Phillip's pack. He lit it automatically, like the Southern gentleman Odell had raised.

"I took my first walk down the runway, Vaseline smeared over my teeth, and checked out the judges to see how many men were on the panel. Only for the first time ever, in any pageant, I faltered. The woman who owned the modeling agency was looking up at me, and I saw something in her eyes that I'd never seen from another woman. When I walked off the stage, I just kept going—in swimming suit, sash, and high heels—right out the door of the Coliseum. I walked up to young Blythe and said, 'Are you a bitter old lesbian?'

She said, 'I'm not bitter. And I'm not old.' I spent the next two weeks between the sheets with her, and I never went back. I got a haircut, my first pair of Doc Martens, and a pierced tongue. That's how a pageant princess becomes a baby dyke."

Phillip suppressed his urge to applaud and said, "What was your talent?"

"Tap," Julianna said. She did a few dance steps to prove it, although she was a little wobbly from the margaritas. "I'm drunk. Who else?"

"I think we're all a little drunk except Phillip," Jess said.

"That's not what I meant," Julianna said, fixing her eyes on Phillip. "Everybody has to tell something the rest of us don't know."

He glanced at Shanon, who didn't look any more willing than he was to be in the spotlight. "Jess is right; I'm not drunk. I'll make the next pitcher," he said, fleeing to the kitchen and taking his time in the faint hope that Julianna would forget her request or pass out.

Unfortunately, she seemed to be a girl who could hold her tequila. Her eyes were bright with expectation when he returned to the living room.

"Fine," he said. He had no intention of spending every day waiting for her to expose his background; he might as well get it over with. "Please don't quadruple my rent, Shanon. Even though I come from a wealthy family, none of the money is mine."

"How wealthy?" Shanon asked, looking a little surprised.

"Fortune 500 wealthy," he said.

"Hmm," she said. "Which fifth are you in? Where's my calculator?"

"The only fifth I'm in is that bottle of tequila in the kitchen," Phillip insisted.

"You could have pleaded the fifth," Jess said.

"That's helpful, after the fact," Phillip said.

"Would I recognize the family name?" Shanon asked.

"It's Godbee."

"Like the sugar plantation?"

"That was the Godchaux family. From Louisiana. You know, theirs is an interesting story—"

"A feeble effort. What's Godbee?" Shanon persisted, as Julianna's gaze went back and forth between them.

"Godbee Energy," Phillip said. "Also based in Louisiana."

"Are you the black sheep of the family?"

"More like the pink one. I didn't show any interest in the company, and I fought with my grandfather about it. He rewards hard work and enthusiasm, and I offered him neither."

"But your parents have money, right?" Julianna asked.

"My father's dead," Phillip said. "My grandfather has five daughters, and I doubt he'll leave my mother in charge of any substantial part of his company or his money because she's not competent to manage it. Satisfied? I'm an impoverished artist who ekes his living from the soil, and I'm practically an orphan."

"You make it sound like you're selling your homegrown tomatoes at Courtney Farms," Shanon said. "And you are not an orphan. *I'm* an orphan."

"Both your parents are dead?" Phillip asked sympathetically, happy to shift the attention away from himself.

"I have no idea. I meant it literally. I'm an orphan. I need another margarita." She went to the kitchen.

Phillip exchanged nervous glances with Jess and Julianna, and Jess hissed, "See what you started?"

"How was I supposed to know?" Julianna asked. "Her whole life's a secret. I don't even know where she works."

"I've told you a million times that I'm a consultant," Shanon said as she came back. "My office is wherever I am. I'm self-employed. You can all stop looking so stricken. It doesn't bother me that I'm an orphan. It just sounds silly to say it—very Dickens."

"If you don't know whether your parents are dead, how can you be an orphan?" Julianna asked.

"I grew up in an orphanage. They don't really call it that. It's in Clinton, South Carolina: the Thornwell Home and School for Children. I lived in a cottage with several other children and three adults." She stopped to stare at their sympathetic faces and insisted, "I had a great childhood. We had a farm, beautiful rose gardens, tennis courts, swimming pool, gym, and our school. I was placed there by the state when I was eight weeks old; it's the only home and family I ever knew. My records are sealed, so I have no idea why I was there. I don't really care. It's no big deal."

"How did you end up here?" Jess asked.

"This will sound silly," Shanon said, "but it's the truth. Thornwell gets kids from South Carolina, Georgia, and Florida. I wanted to stay in the South, and I wanted to be on a coast, but it's kind of weird to think you might end up sleeping with a relative. Know what I mean? When I turned eighteen and could be on my own, I closed my eyes and pointed at a map. My finger landed on Louisiana. So I chose Mississippi."

Phillip laughed and said, "Good choice."

"It's been fine for the last five years," Shanon agreed.

"You're the same age as me," Phillip said. "That means you came here the year I left."

"You're all babies," Jess said. She pointed at Julianna, who'd passed out on the sofa. "I'll clean up the kitchen."

"I'll help," Phillip said.

"I'm going to look through my telescope," Shanon said. "Kick me off the deck when you're ready to go to bed, Phillip."

After they washed the dishes, Phillip helped Jess get Julianna upstairs, then he went up to the attic. The doors to the deck were open, but Shanon was curled up on his bed, sound asleep. He didn't have the heart to wake her, so he tiptoed outside, lit a cigarette, and stared at the sky, where the clouds formed a strange pattern, as if coarse pinkish gauze had been dropped over the starry heavens of Matisse or van Gogh. No wonder she'd given up stargazing.

He smoked and contemplated the things he and his roommates had revealed about themselves. Although he already knew a lot about Jess's past, it was interesting that she hadn't had to endure her moment under the microscope.

Or the telescope, he thought, his eyes resting on the black metal. It wasn't pointed at the sky, so he bent to look through it, seeing only darkness. He nudged it until he saw a lit window, which was when he realized that it was pointed at the Villa Maria, a high-rise apartment building for senior citizens. It was eerie how well he could see into the apartments, but he decided the telescope's placement was random. No one would spy on a bunch of elderly people.

He turned to go inside, then stopped, looking back at the telescope. He examined it, noting the tension on the adjustment knob, and changed his mind. The telescope had deliberately been positioned to look at something much closer to home than the stars. He peered through the lens again, turning it to the left and right with the realization that if so many homes didn't have their lights turned off, he'd be able to see into a lot of windows.

He understood. As a kid, there'd been plenty of nights when he'd left Chad's house later than he was supposed to, traversing streets with more houses than his own, checking out their windows as he walked home. He'd been looking for signs of a normalcy that didn't exist inside the walls of his grandfather's house. Or even at Chad's, with his single mother and dinners in front of the TV. When he'd moved to New York, he'd been surprised to discover how many private lives became window displays for anyone who bothered to look. It wasn't strange that Shanon might also feel like an outsider searching for clues about how "normal" families lived.

He took the telescope inside, turned on the fans, and stared at Shanon, wondering if he should wake her. Or if he could, since he had no idea how many rounds of margaritas had been consumed before he got home. He finally turned off the lights and lay on the bed, fully dressed. After a few minutes, he was sure he heard a sniff.

"Are you awake?" he whispered. When she didn't answer, he said, "Are you crying?"

That did it; the floodgates opened, and Phillip scooted over and put his arms around her while she sobbed. He wasn't sure whether they were all really on the same cycle, or she was less nonchalant about her past than she'd seemed, or if she was just a crying drunk. It didn't matter. He had a feeling that when he woke up, Shanon would be gone, and they'd both act like it hadn't happened. In the meantime, he couldn't give her everything Kieran had given him, but no one deserved to cry alone.

Chapter 11

Phillip fully intended to sleep in on the second Sunday in May, but he woke up at dawn. It was a new habit, acquired from the routine of working in the landscaping business. He tried to go back to sleep but couldn't, so he quietly slipped out of bed and put on a T-shirt and a pair of old, worn jeans.

He glanced at his bed, making sure that he hadn't disturbed Shanon. She'd fallen asleep there again, the third time in two weeks. There was little chance of anything sexual happening between them, so Phillip thought it odd but somewhat comforting, since it was obvious that Shanon trusted him.

He resisted the urge to start sketching her, knowing it could be startling to wake up and find someone staring at you and committing your vulnerability to paper. Instead, he pulled the sheet over her, stole softly from the room, and went outside.

The weeds growing through the cracks of the brick driveway taunted Phillip every morning when he went to work; he felt it was his duty to pull them and restore the driveway to its former glory. As he worked, he thought about planting violets and alyssum between the shrubs in front of the house. The project grew in his mind; he mentally reformed the beds, adding curves to them instead of the traditional rectangular shapes.

The front door opened and Shanon plodded down the steps, squinting and frowning. The hand she used to shield her eyes from the sun held Phillip's phone. "You have a call," she said, holding out the receiver. "I would've taken a message, but it's a friend of yours from New York—Bunny—so I figured you'd want to talk to her."

"Thanks, Shanon." Phillip laughed. Not bothering to correct her, he took the phone and said, "Bunny, old girl, how are you?"

"I'd forgotten why I wasn't speaking to you. Thank you for reminding me," Bunny snapped. "You always were a ballsy little thing. Call me old again and we're through."

"I've missed you, your voice, and all the bile and venom that comes with it," Phillip teased. Shanon looked at Phillip strangely, then went back inside the house. "You didn't answer my question. How are you? What's that racket?"

"I'm hailing a cab. I just left Arc. Or was I at Roxy? Whatever. I thought I'd torture you by waking you up at an ungodly hour, but it seems I miscalculated time zones. Or else Mississippi is ungodly country. Instead, I woke up—who was that who answered, your wife? Are you married now?"

"That was my roommate Shanon. I'm subletting part of the house she lives in."

"That reminds me. I wish someone had bothered to tell me that Carlos had gone to Jabba the Landlady and told her that he was living in the apartment. When I paid rent, she mentioned our boy in conversation. I feigned ignorance, and she played me like a violin, letting me get deeper and deeper into this elaborate story about how Carlos is my half-brother, the black sheep of the family. She finally confessed and had a good laugh at my expense."

"Sorry," Phillip said. He could hear Bunny give his address to a cab driver, which made him miss Manhattan. He looked at the trees and green grass around him and felt a million miles away from his former life.

"That's what I get for coming to the aid of you two shysters. Apparently the lease is being reworked yet again to add Carlos. I thought I'd find out if you still want to be on it."

Phillip thought it over. It was good to have a safety net, a refuge, an escape plan. If his impending visit with his mother didn't go well, he could take off to New York again. His aunts had made it abundantly clear when he returned to Pass Christian that they could take care of his mother until his grandfather returned. He was tempted to give up, admit defeat to his aunts, and go back to Hell's Kitchen.

But back to what? To paying rent he could barely afford? He had no job there. He'd be starting over. New York or Mississippi: Either way, Phillip felt as if he was being given a choice to correct mistakes he'd made.

"Are you still there? Did I lose you?" Bunny asked. "Hello?"

"I'm still here," Phillip said. "Would you change the past, if you could?"

"What kind of stupid question is that?" Bunny asked. "I stand by every choice I've ever made. What's it going to be with the lease, Phillip?"

"Keep me on it," Phillip said. "I'm staying here for now, but just in case, can you send me a copy to sign?"

"Of course," Bunny said. "I'm mailing you some things anyway."

"What things?"

"Old clothes. I cleaned out my closet the other day. I detest the idea of some stranger wearing my stuff, and you were the first person I thought of, since your clothes are so terrible and you're my size."

"Gee, thanks," Phillip said. He decided to gingerly approach the subject of their last fight. "How's your friend Bazzer?"

"He wasn't just a friend. However, we broke up. Men suck."

"I had no idea you were dating anyone. What's the story?"

"I dated Ernst a few years ago. Bazzer's one of his business partners. Out of the blue, I hooked up with Ernst several months ago. It was just one of those things, you know? We were stoned and horny, and then there was the familiarity, the connection. It was all still there. However, Bazzer was there too, and the three of us had a good time."

"Wow," Phillip said.

"Yeah. It happened a few times, but I was more interested in Bazzer than in a rerun with Ernst. We started dating, keeping it on the DL so Ernst wouldn't find out. That's why you didn't know," Bunny explained before breaking off to instruct the cabbie. "Far-right corner. Anyway," he went on, "Bazzer was a tart. I don't know why I expected him to take me seriously and not screw around."

"Why not? You deserve love," Phillip said.

"Oh, Phillip," Bunny sighed, "always the dreamer. Get real. Listen, I'm home now. I'm going to take a bath, put on my robe, smoke some opium, and pass out. Be on the watch for a package on your doorstep."

"I'm trying to think of a package joke," Phillip said.

"You try too hard," Bunny said. "Bye."

"I miss you," Phillip said, then heard nothing but a dial tone.

He finished pulling the rest of the weeds, then went inside the house, following the smell of freshly brewed coffee to the kitchen, where Shanon was rinsing out a coffee mug. Julianna was perched on a stool, eating cereal and staring at the floor with a glazed expression. Shanon was dressed in a suit. Her hair was swept back into a twist, and she was wearing a smart pair of eyeglasses. "You're working on Sunday?"

"Uh-huh." She picked up an attaché from a chair, then motioned to the coffeemaker. "There's coffee, if you want. By the way, you don't have to do yard work around here."

"I know," Phillip said.

"It's like taking your work home with you," Shanon said, wrinkling her nose. "But, hey, it's your life. If you want to spend your day off playing in the dirt, who am I to stop you?"

"I'm thinking about seeing my mother today," Phillip said. He hadn't planned on actually going through with it but was vocalizing the thought to see how it made him feel. The idea appealed to him, even though it made him nervous.

"I wasn't going to work today, then I realized that Jess is coming by later. Whoever's within ten yards of her is going to be put to work, so I figured I'd git while the gittin's good. I suggest you do the same."

"We'll see," Phillip called as she walked out. He looked at Julianna and said, "What's with her?"

Julianna glanced up from the floor and frowned, looking like she smelled something foul. "You are so fucking insensitive. It's Mother's Day. At least you have a mother to visit."

Phillip's mouth dropped open, but he couldn't think of anything to say. He hadn't meant to offend anyone. He hadn't really thought about Mother's Day in years. When he was a little boy, he presented his mother with shoddily crafted clay ashtrays or runny watercolor pictures that he'd made in art class, which she'd accept haphazardly. One year she might stare at them dully, the next she'd coo with appreciation and place the gift on the mantel. He'd always handled Mother's Day with kid gloves and given it the same respect he would a ticking time bomb.

When Julianna resumed her staring contest with the floor, he went upstairs and showered. Then, without thinking too much about it, he packed his painting supplies and a canvas into the Volvo and started driving. Although he tried to drive without purpose or a specific destination, he soon found himself at his job site at Whittier Plantation. The work was nearly completed on the grounds. The undergrowth had been cleared and all the trees had been pruned; the walkways were rebuilt with dark red brick; new flower beds were raised using old railroad ties, stones, and other salvaged materials. The rolling lawns were trimmed and fertilized. Phillip had replaced the sod in many areas himself—a task he'd found arduous. But now that he could see the results from a distance, he was pleased and proud of his work.

The shoulder of the road in front of the house was wide, so he parked and leaned the canvas against an old horse tie at the base of the drive. He stared at the blank canvas and felt the daunting weight of all the artists he admired. He thought of his grandfather's Rothko and the absence of light. He let his mind skim memories as he looked at the colors surrounding the house, thinking of the French painters Caillebotte and Bazille. He wanted to capture the light and color of the environment, but also the house. He reflected upon Mississippi's history, its pre–Civil War slavery and post–Civil War poverty. He thought of the specters of Rodrigue's Acadian paintings and knew he wanted the house to be more than a ghost, but still almost ephemeral among its surroundings. What might have been easy with watercolors he felt desperate to show in oils: that what remained was better than what had been. He wiped his mind clear of everything but the house and began to paint, pausing only to light an occasional cigarette and compare the house to the image on the canvas.

When a drop of rain hit one of the upstairs windows on the painting, Phillip lifted his head to see a dark cloud moving overhead. His neck was stiff and he glanced at his watch; five hours had passed. He hurriedly packed his supplies. He worried about the canvas, hoping it would somehow fit in the car without getting ruined, but discovered that it could lie in the trunk without shifting. Just as he slammed the car door, the rain started to fall.

"Damn," he said and turned the ignition.

He intended to return to Belfast House, but before he could go that way, a phrase repeated itself in his brain. *What remained was better than what had been.* He drove in the opposite direction, alongside the beach to Pass Christian, where the sun was still shining. Instead of turning into Godbee Lane, he parked in a beach lot. After opening the trunk to make sure the painting was unharmed, he took off his Puma sneakers and walked onto the sand. His feet sank; the granules moved through his toes like warm sugar. There were a few people lying on towels. Others were jogging, flinging Frisbees, or wandering across the sand as the wind blew in from the Gulf and whipped through their hair. He didn't see anyone he recognized; they were probably all tourists. This particular beach usually attracted an older, more sedate crowd, most of whom would eventually succumb to the lure of the homes across from the beach.

Plenty of times when he was young, people brazenly walked onto their property. His family never got more Southern than when they felt invaded. "The carpetbaggers are back," Odell would call from some window, and his mother would flit from room to room, spying on the trespassers who looked at the flower beds and the azalea bushes, or just circled the house, examining its architectural details. He couldn't count the number of times one of his aunts, watching children tromp through flower beds, would mutter some phrase like, "They're worse than Sherman in Vicksburg," or, "They're pillaging the roses like Grant at Beauvoir." Ellan delighted in reminding her sisters that they were half Yankee themselves, but they paid her no mind.

Phillip had often worried that his mother might run outside like Scarlett defending Tara, but it was another of Vivian Leigh's characters that she'd finally emulated to make sport of the tourists. He blamed himself. One night he stayed up late to see *A Streetcar Named Desire.* He'd been aware that his mother was sitting on the stairs, watching the movie from a distance, but he ignored her. The next day, she spotted a group of pale-legged tourists snapping pictures of themselves in front of the house. She drifted outside in a white cotton nightgown, doing her best Blanche DuBois as she babbled about tender feelings, kitchen candles, and kind strangers. That was the summer his grandfather hired someone to install the iron fence. Phillip was never sure if it was meant to keep tourists out or his mother in.

As he stood on the beach, he could just make out the façade of his grandfather's house through the branches of the live oaks on the front lawn. He shielded his eyes from the sun and scanned the windows, wondering if he'd spot the lone figure of his mother as she moved from room to room. Of course, he saw nothing. He almost wished he'd borrowed Shanon's telescope so he could see what he was about to get himself into.

He put on his shoes and dashed across the road, careful of the cars that sped up and down Beach Boulevard. A few pedestrians walking on Scenic Drive greeted him pleasantly, which made Phillip think of the people in New York who stared straight ahead with steely resolve.

He felt a little like a trespasser as he walked up the lane to the Godbee house. He went in the back entrance, shut the door softly, and moved quietly through the kitchen. He noticed a coffee cup on the counter next to a half-eaten sandwich on a plate. He put his fingers on the mug. It was still warm.

"Mother?" he called out. The word sounded formal; Phillip could hardly remember what he used to call her—Mama, when he was younger, then Mom? Certainly not Mommy, and never by her first name. Although he often thought of her as Ellan and was accustomed to Chad referring to his own mother by her first name, Phillip's mother would've rebuked him for being disrespectful.

He wandered through the dining room and into the front parlor. The ticking of a grandfather clock filled the silent room. He stepped into the entry hall and peered through the beveled windows on either side of the door, scanning the front yard.

There was nobody outside. The trees were bigger, but otherwise the lawn looked exactly as it had when he was a boy. He'd stare through the same windows for hours, wishing he was out there with friends, playing.

A staccato note on the piano in the parlor made his head turn. He glanced inside and noticed one of the long white curtains fluttering back into place. He retraced his steps into the dining room and saw the kitchen door swinging. He dashed through it and ran smack into Selma.

"Sake's alive!" she exclaimed.

"I'm sorry, Aunt Selma," Phillip said, backing away from her. "Did you see—"

"What are you two doing, playing tag?"

"You saw her?" Phillip asked. "Which way did she go?"

Selma pointed over her shoulder and said, "Library." She picked up the sandwich and added, "Let me know how it turns out."

Phillip went into the library, but his mother wasn't there. He walked into the living room and saw a flash of blue nightgown in the front hall.

"Mom, stop!" he called, racing after her. At the foot of the stairs, he held the banister for support and yelled, "Would you just stop?"

Ellan stopped on the landing and turned around. She was thinner than when he'd last seen her, and her brown hair was dirty and unkempt. Her pale skin accentuated the sudden flush of red on her cheeks, and her eyes scorched him as she opened her arms and said, "Welcome to Elavil. Population—one." She stepped to the side as if looking back at herself and said, "Two." Then she looked at him again. "Three. Some residents get same results with sugar pill."

After a bewildered pause, Phillip said more quietly, "Can't you even pretend you're glad I'm home?"

"Sometimes I feel like a nut; sometimes I don't." When he just stared at her, she leaned over the railing on the landing and asked, "What are you doing here, Phillip?"

"I came to see you," he answered feebly. He watched her run a hand through her messy hair. Her eyes seemed to roll a little, as if searching for something to focus on. Phillip was worried she might fall over the railing or, worse, jump. But something about the way her knuckles gripped the rail and the tension in her biceps told him that she was stronger and steadier than she appeared.

"Nothin' says lovin' like my head in the oven," she said. "You saw me. Now be a good boy and go back to New York."

"I can't," he said. "Get used to seeing me, because I moved back."

"You what?" She turned her head to the side. "Tired? Stressed? Big-city living got you down? Enjoy a break from reality at Ellan's Bedlam and Breakfast."

"Mom?" Phillip said tentatively.

Ellan pointed her finger at him, reminding Phillip of a painting he'd once seen of Pontius Pilate standing on a balcony and pointing his finger at Jesus. "We agreed that you'd be better off away from here. Now go."

"But I—"

"Go!" she screamed, holding her hands over her ears and repeating the word, like a child having a tantrum.

"What's going on out here?" Selma asked as she came from the kitchen. She saw Ellan bent over and screaming and said, "I knew this would happen. You'd better leave."

Phillip ran. Once he'd cleared the kitchen door and raced across the backyard, the tears started. He kept running, his feet pounding grass, gravel, then pavement as he ran down the road. The route was familiar. He'd done it when he was nine, twelve, fourteen—the last time when he was seventeen—and many times while he was crying.

He was gasping for breath when he stopped in front of the brick bungalow. He leaned over and rested his hands on his knees, gulping in air, worried that he might throw up. He checked the mailbox and was comforted to see CUNNINGHAM printed in black letters on a white background. He walked down the driveway, passed an unfamiliar red Honda, and stepped tentatively onto the porch. He knocked on the front door and wiped his eyes.

Taryn Cunningham looked momentarily surprised when she opened the door.

But she visibly softened and stepped forward, taking Phillip's face in her hands and saying, "Look at you. Come here."

Phillip allowed himself to be pulled forward and wrapped his arms around her, burying his face in the crook of her neck while he cried. Her hand moved through his hair as she murmured something soothing. Eventually her words dissolved into humming a tune that she'd made up years ago, perhaps when he was nine, or twelve, maybe fourteen.

Later, they sat at her kitchen table, sipping herbal tea sweetened with honey as she let him talk. Phillip finally laughed and said, "Tell me to shut up. I can't believe I'm chattering like this. I sound like a squirrel in a tree talking to a jaybird."

"Stop that. I love hearing your New York stories. It's the tones of home that worry me," she said, chastising him lightly. "I've missed hearing your voice around here, Phillip."

"That's nice. Thank you. Chad told me about your restaurant. Congratulations."

Taryn smiled broadly; the lines around her bright blue eyes crinkled. "You have to come by for dinner. On the house, of course."

"I'll do that," Phillip said. "Who's this new partner of yours?" When Taryn's shoulders tensed, he added, "At the restaurant? Chad said something about a business partner."

"Georganne," Taryn said. "She helped me go from caterer to restaurateur. She's special." She glanced up at the ceiling and laughed. "Oh, what the hell? She's my dearest friend, but she used to be my girlfriend."

Phillip smiled. "Really?"

"Uh-huh," Taryn said. "You don't mind?"

"Mind? Who am I to say anything?" Phillip asked. "I think it's great."

"I'm relieved," Taryn said. "There are so many uptight people around here who don't share your opinion. I almost moved back west when Chad went away to school, but then I met Georganne."

"I am too, you know," Phillip said quietly.

Taryn smiled, put her hand over Phillip's, squeezing gently, and said, "Oh, honey. I know."

"You do?" Phillip said. "What tipped you off? It's not like a Gucci handbag falls out every time I open my mouth."

"A mother knows these things about her boys," Taryn said. Phillip noted the plural and felt his eyebrows jump. Taryn laughed and said, "Just you, hon. All I meant was that I know you boys like I know myself. Does Chad know?"

Phillip shifted uncomfortably and said, "Yeah. I'm still not sure how okay he is with it."

Taryn nodded, stared into her teacup, then asked, "Does he know about me?"

"He doesn't? I mean, I don't know. He didn't say anything about it. I'm kind of surprised. I thought you two shared everything with each other."

Taryn sighed and stood up, bringing the kettle from the stove to refill her cup. "You like to think you prepare your kid for everything he'll encounter when he goes out into the world," she said. She refilled Phillip's cup and put the kettle back on the stove. She stared through the window over the sink; the light caught her ash-blond hair, causing it to glow warmly. "But more and more, I wonder if I did enough for him. Sometimes he says certain things and I wonder, *Where did he get that from?* Or he does something stupid and I get defensive, thinking, *Must be from his father's side.* Maybe that's it. Maybe I should've stayed with him so Chad would have a father figure in his life." She turned back to Phillip and added, "But look at you. You didn't have a father, and you turned out all right."

"The jury's still out on that one," Phillip said.

"You're fine." Taryn blew on her tea, her lips hovering at the rim of the cup. Phillip froze the image in his mind, saving it for his sketchbook. "Children never turn out the way you think they will. You look at them when they're babies, and you imagine their future. You can map out a million different scenarios, but they'll always surprise you."

"You don't think he can handle a lesbian mother?"

"Do you?" Taryn asked pointedly.

"No," Phillip said. When Taryn's face clouded, he amended, "Maybe. I don't know."

"That's exactly how I feel about it," she said, smiling. "I hate to be rude, honey, but I have to go. If I don't get to the restaurant soon, Georganne will send out the cavalry."

As he went back to the beach to get his car, carefully avoiding walking too near the Godbee house, Phillip felt infinitely better. He was still shaken by his visit with his mother and slightly annoyed by his Aunt Selma. How had she known he'd be there, and why were his aunts always interfering? He hadn't expected the encounter to be pleasant, however, so he comforted himself with the fact that his mother hadn't thrown anything.

The sun was beginning to set as he drove, so he parked the car again at the Long Beach pier. He walked halfway down the wooden planks, then sat with his feet dangling high over the lapping waves. He looked toward the end of the pier, crowded with people casting lines in the water, hoping to catch mackerel, red snapper, and other fish that populated the shallow waters near the shore. He watched the sky turn brilliant orange and slowly fade to a dusty rose as the day drew to a close. He thought back to sunsets in New York City and could hardly believe it was the same sky. He felt like he was on another planet.

"Is this seat taken?"

Phillip looked up and saw Chad standing next to him, leaning against the pier's wooden railing. "What are you doing here?" he asked.

"Taryn called me," he said, sitting down next to Phillip. "She said you could use a friend."

"How'd you know I'd be here?" He knew the answer, but he wanted to hear it anyway.

"This is where we always ended up after things got intense with your mother," Chad said. Out of the corner of his eye, Phillip could see Chad smiling slightly. It made him smile too. "You'd be all upset and we'd start walking down the beach, talking, sometimes drinking, if we could get someone to buy for us. Then we'd end up here, sitting on the end of the pier late at night."

"It was so dark and quiet. I always felt like I was floating in a Joan Miró painting of the stars," Phillip said.

"Must've been the pot," Chad said, leaning over and bumping his shoulder into Phillip's.

"That too," Phillip agreed. "I don't suppose you have any?"

"What kind of juvenile delinquent do you take me for?" Chad asked. He reached into his pocket and handed Phillip a tightly rolled joint. "Here. Wait until it's a bit darker, or until some of those people at the end of the pier clear out." Phillip tucked the joint behind his ear, still staring into the water. "So you saw your mom?"

"Yeah," Phillip said. "She's doing commercials now."

"Huh?" Chad asked.

"She expresses her…thoughts…in advertising jingles."

"At least she's innovative. Old Mr. Brighton still goes to the post office every day at noon and orders a soft serve vanilla with sprinkles," Chad said.

"That's not crazy. That's eccentric. There's a difference," Phillip said.

"The funny thing is, there's an ice cream place nearby," Chad said, ignoring him. "So now, five minutes before he arrives, someone runs out, gets him a vanilla cone with sprinkles, and gives it to him when he comes in. He tips his hat, plunks down a quarter, and leaves happy."

"Is there a moral to this tall tale?" Phillip asked testily.

"No moral. I'm just talkin' is all," Chad said. Phillip stared at him, then started laughing. Before he knew what was happening, he was crying again and Chad was holding him, rocking him gently. "Oh, Phillip. I'm sorry."

"She told me to go back to New York," Phillip said, his voice breaking. "She doesn't want me here. I knew she didn't. I don't know why I came back."

"Sometimes it's easier to plow around a stump," Chad said.

"What?" Phillip pulled away. "When did you get so fucking Southern?"

"A lot can happen in five years," Chad replied. He leaned forward and brushed away one of Phillip's tears. When Phillip flinched, he said, "What?"

"Nothing," Phillip answered. Random images flashed through his head: girls laughing, Chad having sex, a dark motel room. He put his hands over his eyes, trying to block them out. "Just don't."

"I'm sorry," Chad stammered. "I wasn't—I didn't—"

"Yeah, you never do," Phillip said. He stood up and walked away.

You may be hungry soon:
Order takeout now.

Chapter 12

Phillip followed the directions Dash had given him over the phone and parked his Volvo in front of a brick home in one of Biloxi's older neighborhoods. The house was one story, on a double lot. A walkway leading from the side of the house to the land next door was covered by a vine-laden arbor, and he could hear, behind privacy shrubs, music, voices, and the unmistakable sound of people in a swimming pool. Dash had told him to bring something to swim in, but Phillip had conveniently forgotten. He had no intention of getting undressed without seeing the lay of the land at what Dash called the Men-Only Spring Garden Party.

He let himself blend in with a group of five men who were walking from the house to the pool, then moved inconspicuously among groups of guests to gauge the mood of the party. He lit a cigarette in an effort to fend off dozens of competing product odors and colognes.

The pool had attracted mostly people around his age, who were talking, horsing around, or posing as the potential centerpiece of male scrutiny. The men who stood in groups near the pool were of every variety, from early twenties to sixties, dressed in shorts, jeans, or khaki pants, T-shirts, polo shirts, and button-downs, sleeves short or rolled up. They ranged from slender to gym-built, average to paunchy. No one was in leather regalia, Dash's proclivities notwithstanding.

They all had one thing in common: Everyone knew someone. Phillip felt like the lone stranger. Although the men's eyes were constantly scanning, assessing, and moving on, it was easy not to attract attention as long as he didn't make eye contact or any other kind of connection. It was his preferred way of entering a bar or a party. He was glad he didn't see Dash so that he could keep flying under the radar until he was ready to become social.

A gym clone wearing nothing but leather square-cuts, work boots, and a barbed-wire tattoo around his upper arm was acting as bartender, and Phillip asked for a gin and tonic. While the bartender made the drink, he continued his conversation with a fifty-ish man who was practically drooling over all those exposed biceps, abs, and pecs. It didn't bother Phillip, who figured the bartender was no fool when it came to soliciting tips. He got his drink and moved slowly through the crowd, catching little pieces of conversation, oddly comforted by the familiar Southern cadence of their voices.

"We haven't had good sex since the last hurricane."

"I guess fear of imminent death can make you cling to each other."

"Fear had nothing to do with it. With no *CSI*, no Xbox, and no computer, we were desperate to do anything but talk."

"…can't go wrong buying when the interest rates are this low. Come into my office and we can…"

"So then I said, 'Honey, you're not Cher. Lay off the Botox.'"

"…biggest bunch of thugs since Nixon was in the White House…"

"If I have to hear about their trip to Greece one more time, I'm going postal."

"Didn't one of them come back with crabs?"

"I'm sure if he did, it's documented on videotape."

"With a sound track."

"…Bay Reader Society, which is weird because he hasn't cracked a book in the ten years I've known him."

"There's a reason it's known as the *Gay* Reader Society, hon. They're not reading to each other at those meetings."

"…how can anyone not know the difference between iceberg and loose-leaf? Cretin."

"Or do you mean crouton?"

"…has the biggest porn collection…"

"So this year he is *not* going with us to Southern Decadence."

"…get off that cell phone? He'll be here when he gets here."

"It's not like him to be so late."

"What are you talking about? He's always late."

"…whether that many condoms means it's been a long time or that he's promiscuous?"

"So basically, if your mutual funds were in—"

"Phillip! You came."

"Hi, Dash," Phillip said, relieved that Dash found him first, since he wasn't sure he'd have recognized him from their one meeting. There were at least ten men at the party who looked too much like him, except for the regrettable handlebar mustache, which Phillip had almost forgotten.

"I see you found the bar. Have you met anyone? Shall I introduce you around? Or do you want to lurk and mingle?"

"Actually, I was wondering if I could use your bathroom."

"The one in the cabana is always occupied, so you might want to go to the house. There are three. Feel free to wander around."

"May I look in the medicine cabinet?"

"Of course. I already hid the Viagra and Propecia so that you won't discover any of my dirty little secrets."

"Sly," Phillip said, walking away as Dash laughed.

The house practically screamed, *No women or children live here!* The furnishings were masculine, though there were plenty of tchotchkes that he'd have to peruse later. Dash was either very neat or had a good housekeeper, because everything was spotless. What he assumed was a bathroom was in use, so he kept going toward the bedrooms. He stuck his head into a room so generic that it had to be a guest room and spied an open door in the far corner.

He crossed the room and stepped into the bathroom, then froze before he could turn on the light. Beyond him was another bedroom, and in the shadows, he could see a man wearing Navy dress whites, his arm propped against a door while his free hand seemed to caress a companion. The wall blocked Phillip's view of the second man, but Navy Guy was the stuff of fantasies. The gold buttons of his tunic were undone, and his tight T-shirt made the most of a great torso. He had short dark hair; even in the dimness, Phillip could see that his face was cinematic.

"C'mon, Jay," Navy Guy murmured. "Why are you torturing me?"

"I'm not," Phillip heard a panicked response. "I have to get out there. He's waiting for me."

"He doesn't know you're here yet. We could leave, and nobody would know. I'll get us a room at the beach." His voice dropped to a whisper, presumably to describe all the things he'd like to do to Jay. It must have been effective, because Phillip could see the mysterious Jay's hands creep around Navy Guy's back, under his tunic. Navy Guy leaned forward.

The unmistakable sound of a kiss was broken as Jay gasped, "Dennis, stop! I can't."

Phillip heard the door open. When Navy Guy—Dennis—stepped backward with an expression full of frustrated longing, Phillip knew he was probably about to be spotted, so he said, "I can."

Dennis whirled around and reached in to turn on the bathroom light. "Who the hell are you?" he snapped.

"I didn't mean to catch you in the act, so to speak. I just wanted to use the bathroom. I'm Phillip."

"Mind your own business," Dennis said as he closed the door between them.

Phillip grimaced and said, "I guess you told me." He used the bathroom, washed his hands, and hurried back outside, wondering if he could figure out which of the men was the frustratingly faithful Jay.

Unfortunately, several new arrivals were scattered among the guests. He got another gin and tonic and waited for Dennis to show up. But Dennis didn't appear, in or out of uniform, so Phillip began his circuit again, filtering out the random conversations until one stopped him.

"But I called you at least five times," Cell Phone Guy was saying to a man whose back was to Phillip. "Why didn't you answer? Or return my calls?"

"I guess my phone's off."

Bingo, Phillip thought, recognizing Jay's soft drawl.

"Why were you so late?"

"I got off work late. Traffic sucked. I don't know. Can we drop it, Travis? I'm here now."

"I don't get it. If you knew you were going to be late—"

Jaysus, Phillip thought in Kieran's voice, *give it a rest, mate.* He found himself wishing Dennis would stride in and sweep Jay away like they were in the final scene of *An Officer and a Gentleman.* Although he'd yet to determine if Jay would look cute wearing Dennis's white hat. He maneuvered past them and walked a few steps before casually turning around to check out Jay.

His eyes widened. He knew him, or he thought he did. Sweet face. Sensitive eyes. Pale and slender. Around Phillip's age. He tried to remember if Jay was someone he'd gone to school with but didn't think he'd forget a classmate. Still, Phillip was sure he knew him. He stared, puzzled, until he saw a leather necklace with two stones, then he placed him. He'd wanted to draw him. He'd seen him at the pancake house on the same night he met Dash. The boy—Jay—had caught Phillip staring at him.

In a bizarre repeat of that night, Jay was looking back at him now. When Phillip smiled, Jay smiled shyly back. Travis turned around to see who Jay was looking at, and Phillip smiled at him too, hoping to head off another inquisition.

"Hi, I'm Phillip. I'm sorry I'm staring, but I noticed your stones. What are they?" he asked quickly.

"I'm Travis. This is my boyfriend, Jay," Travis said, taking a stance that was obviously meant to be a barrier between Phillip and Jay.

"Nice to meet you," Jay said, and Phillip nodded his agreement. "Black onyx and jasper."

Phillip knew he shouldn't, but Travis was goading him against all reason, and he leaned forward and lifted the stones from Jay's chest, saying, "They're nice. Do they have any particular meaning?"

He could feel Travis glowering at him, but Jay merely said, "Black onyx is for grounding, and jasper is for courage and protection."

Phillip gently lowered the stones back to Jay's chest and said, "Cool. I don't know much about that stuff. Do you?"

"I work in a gem and crystal shop in Ocean Springs," Jay said. "Stone Love."

"Really? I live in Ocean Springs. I'll have to come in and let you help find the right stone for me."

Travis had obviously reached his limit and said, "Phillip, could you excuse us? Jay and I need to talk to some friends that we're going out with later."

"I'll look forward to seeing you at the shop," Jay said as Travis nudged him away. "We're not open on Sunday. I'm there every day but Thursday."

Phillip nodded and kept his face pleasant, although he was even more inclined to wish Dennis would put in an appearance. Men like Travis annoyed the crap out of him. He turned and scanned the crowd until he saw Dash talking to a somewhat intimidating bear of a man. After a pause, he walked around the pool and joined them. Dash introduced the bear as Larry Tanner.

"I had no idea there were this many gay men in Biloxi," Phillip said, looking around. "What keeps them here?"

Dash stared at him a minute, then said, "Not everyone can move to Manhattan or San Francisco."

"It's home," Larry said with a shrug. "Good weather, low cost of living, laid-back lifestyle. Besides, New Orleans is just down the road. What's gayer than New Orleans?"

"I guess," Phillip said. He was having a hard time not watching Travis and Jay, who appeared to be arguing.

"Who's caught your eye, young'un?" Dash asked.

Phillip blushed and said, "Nobody, really. I was watching that couple over there. They look like they're fighting."

Dash and Larry looked, and Dash said, "Oh. Travis White. I guess that's his boyfriend. I've never met him."

"It is," Larry said. "I think his name's Jasper or Jason—something like that."

"Is Travis an attorney too?" Phillip asked.

"Insurance claims adjuster," Dash said. "I've known him for years, but he's not one of my favorite people."

Larry laughed and said, "That's an understatement." He looked at Phillip. "Dash and Travis have butted heads in court a few times."

"He's a weasel," Dash said.

"Why'd you invite him to your party?"

"Hell if I know," Dash said. "Did you bring your suit? Do you want to swim?"

"I'm having my period," Phillip said, and Larry roared with laughter.

Phillip surrendered himself to Dash, who took him around and introduced him to men whose names he'd never remember. He wasn't sure when Jay and Travis left, and part of him wanted to do likewise, but he kept trying to think of a plausible way to bring up Dennis and find out what his story was.

As the crowd dwindled, he let himself be talked into putting on a Speedo and getting into the water with Dash, who had a good body for a man closing in on middle age. A few more gin and tonics lulled Phillip into lassitude, which only got worse when everyone was finally gone and he shared a joint with Dash while they dangled their feet in the pool. After a while, Dash kissed him. When Phillip didn't resist, Dash kissed him more deeply. When they came up for air, Dash got to his feet and extended a hand. "Let's go inside," he said. "I think my neighbors have taken about all the gay they can stand for one day."

Phillip followed Dash to his bedroom. He slid out of the wet Speedo and lay down for some more kissing. When Dash propped himself up and opened a drawer in his headboard to take out lube and a condom, Phillip said, "Nuh-uh."

"Sorry, young'un, I don't fuck without a rubber," Dash said.

"I wouldn't either, but I meant no fucking," Phillip said.

"No? I'll be gentle." When Phillip shook his head, Dash didn't argue and put everything back before resuming their kisses.

Phillip was uncharacteristically passive when Dash's mouth moved down his body. He wasn't sure if it was the gin, the pot, or Dash's prowess, but he rated it as some of the best head he'd ever gotten. When he came, he heard himself crying out as if from a distance.

Dash moved back up to kiss him again before saying, "I'm glad you enjoyed it, but I'm not Dennis."

Phillip was horrified and said, "Oh, my God, did I—"

"You did," Dash interrupted, but he laughed. "Who's Dennis?"

Phillip embarrassed himself further by giggling and said, "A seaman."

"Ah," Dash said with comprehension. "Actually, he's a chief petty officer. He's also my little brother."

"I'm dying here," Phillip said. "Call the coroner to take my body away."

Dash laughed again and said, "It's okay. Even if he's my brother, I get that he's hot."

"How Southern," Phillip said. He couldn't tell Dash that he'd been fantasizing about his brother without explaining that he'd actually been visualizing Dennis with Jay. He wasn't going to divulge the details of the aborted rendezvous he'd witnessed.

Dash ruffled his hair and said, "You're something else."

"You too," Phillip said. He gently pushed Dash into the pillows so he could prove that he wasn't a selfish bedmate.

They finally dozed for a while. When Phillip sat up, Dash said, "Is there anyone you need to call? I'll be glad to get you a cab, or you can stay, but I can't let you drive. I don't want you to have to retain me as your attorney."

"Didn't you just violate the lawyer-client relationship?" Phillip asked.

"Not quite the way I hoped," Dash said with a grin.

Dash was a gentleman, however, and even though they spent the next morning in bed, he was perfectly willing to keep things at Phillip's comfort level. While Phillip showered, Dash retrieved his clothes from the cabana and left them tidily folded on the bathroom counter.

After grooming himself as best he could, Phillip padded down the hall, stopping when he heard Dash in the kitchen softly saying, "I don't know why you think it would be an issue. None of my friends would cause any problems for you."

"There were just a couple of people I didn't want to see."

Brother Dennis, Phillip thought and stepped into the kitchen to say, "Morning."

Dennis quickly covered up his scowl when Dash introduced them. Dash claimed his turn at the master bathroom and urged Phillip to make himself at home, pointing to the coffeepot and ashtray.

Dennis's silence was oppressive. After Phillip poured a cup of coffee, he turned around and said, "Not that it matters, but I think Travis is an asshole."

"You know Jay and Travis?" Dennis asked, looking surprised.

"No. But I saw enough of them yesterday to form an opinion."

Dennis sighed and ran his hands over the stubble on his chin, looking so much like a model in an ad that Phillip was baffled by Jay's ability to resist him. "You're right. He is an asshole. And it doesn't matter because Jay doesn't see it that way."

"You really care about him, don't you?" Phillip asked.

Dennis stared at him a few seconds before apparently deciding he was all right, then said, "I'm crazy about him."

"How long has he been with Travis?"

"Two fucking years. He acts like it's twenty."

"I think he's nuts," Phillip said.

"He's not nuts. He's just loyal and faithful. And you are *not* coming on to me after sleeping with my brother, are you?"

"No! Although it would be kind of like scoring with half the Village People. The leather guy. The sailor." That elicited a faint grin from Dennis. "I was never a fan of disco, though, so I'll pass."

"I guess I was rude to you yesterday."

"I took you by surprise," Phillip said forgivingly.

"True, but I'm still sorry. Now if you'll apologize for eavesdropping—"

"I'm sorry," Phillip said. "Does that make us even?"

"Yeah. We're good. I was just about to make myself some breakfast. You hungry?"

"Usually, I only let a hot man make me breakfast after a night in bed."

"Now listen," Dennis said, then stopped, realizing that Phillip was kidding him. "You have to help."

Phillip scrambled eggs while Dennis fried bacon and made toast. He set a place for Dash, who joined them just as they sat down.

"I'm the trick who never leaves," Phillip explained.

"I'm not complaining," Dash said. "It'd be a great Sunday on the water. You two want to take the boat out to the barrier islands? Do some dolphin watching?"

"No, thanks," Phillip said. "I have a sort of love-hate relationship with the water."

"Me too," Dennis said.

Phillip's fork paused halfway to his mouth, and he said, "You're in the Navy."

"Yeah. You spend a few months on a nuclear sub worrying that more than a hundred men under your command might find out you're gay, and see how much you like it."

"No, thanks," Phillip said again. "When do you go back?"

"I don't. I'm pushing papers around a desk for three more weeks before my discharge."

"Then he can be gay outside these walls," Dash said. "Why do you hate the water?" When Phillip only shrugged, Dash didn't pursue it.

Dennis left after breakfast to run errands before returning to base. While Dash and Phillip washed dishes, Phillip said, "You have a nice home."

"Thanks," Dash said. "It belonged to my parents. They bought the lot next door because my father didn't like feeling closed in. Ironic, since he and my mother now live in a condo in Sand Key, Florida. They thought if they sold me the house, Dennis could build one next door when he decided to settle down. Instead, I put the pool in. Dennis and I have never wanted to live on top of each other. Where'd you end up after you left your aunt's house?"

"I'm renting with some friends in Ocean Springs," Phillip said. "Isn't chief petty officer a pretty high rating? How long has Dennis been in the Navy?"

Dash thought a minute and said, "Fourteen years."

"Couldn't he retire in a few years? How come he's getting out?"

"I don't know. Maybe he's disgusted with the Iraq situation. You'd have to ask him."

Phillip thought it over and said, "I guess that whole 'don't ask, don't tell' thing must suck."

"He handles it. You know, you remind me of Dennis."

"Yeah, I get that a lot: 'Weren't you in the last Calvin Klein ad?' But I think I'm more Abercrombie & Fitch."

Dash swatted him with the dish towel and said, "Not physically. You're careful with what you tell about yourself."

"I've been known to waylay strangers in the subway to describe my last failed romance," Phillip countered. "The first time I met you, I whined your ear off about coming back here from Manhattan."

"It's easy to talk to strangers," Dash said. "Maybe that's why you keep people at a distance."

Later, lying on a float in the pool while Dash made phone calls, Phillip considered Dash's assessment. Wasn't there a limit to what one should disclose to acquaintances? Was he socially inept or just private? Was it really necessary to say over breakfast, *I don't like the water because my father died there?* Or, *I don't talk about my background because when people like Eddie or even Bunny find out about the money, they treat me differently.* Or, *Your mother lives in Sand Key? Mine should live in Sand Hill Mental Hospital.* Or how about, *I can't give you access to my ass because, like my heart, it still hasn't forgotten an Irishman in New York who's not speaking to me.* Or there was, *I don't trust people easily because once upon a time my best friend betrayed me in a way that still fucks with my head.*

He closed his eyes, enjoying the sun beating down on him and the cool water lapping at his feet and arms around the edges of the float. Anyway, it wasn't true. There were people in his life he trusted. Claude. Alyssa. Carlos. Even if it sometimes felt like the first two had abandoned him. And he'd had no trouble spilling the most intimate secrets of his life to Kieran. Something about Kieran, whether the perfect order of his home or his air of stability, had allowed Phillip to relinquish his usual control over his emotions. Kieran had made him feel safe enough to believe that if he went to that place where he shared himself without masking truth in sarcasm or jokes, he wouldn't get lost there, as his mother had.

And look how that turned out.

He rolled off the float and swam across the bottom of the pool to the deep end before surfacing for air. His breathing sucked. Too much smoking.

Dash's words continued to needle him over the following days, making him question himself. Sometimes he wished life came with a guidebook so he'd know who he was and where he was going.

One must know there is a path at the end of the road.

Phillip had forgotten his three fortunes. The first one definitely came true. His life had changed. He'd left his apartment, his job, his city, his friends, Eddie, and Kieran.

He struggled to remember the second one. Something about being hungry. Which might not literally be hunger, so he speculated about what else he'd been hungry for. Artistic satisfaction. Closure with his mother and grandfather. Maybe seeing Chad again and being honest. Sex. Money.

He was sure Dash would continue taking care of his sexual hunger if that was what Phillip wanted. He was painting again, so he felt more satisfied creatively. And his job for Selma, along with his low cost of living, was helping him with the money issue. As for his other hungers, maybe if he found some way to satisfy those, he could make the last fortune come true. His road was Mississippi, but the path out of there led to New York, where he still had an apartment in his name and Carlos as a roommate to make it affordable.

He'd cracked the code. He had to live where he could be himself, which was New York. In Mississippi, except for a few safe homes like Fala's, Florence's, Dash's, and Shanon's, he had to be straight—especially at work, which was a lot more exhausting than physical labor. He wondered what would happen if he responded honestly to his work crew's good-natured ribbing about how his new muscles could help him score with the ladies. Would they be uncomfortable? Stop bragging about their own conquests? Refuse to work next to him? Stop taking off their shirts or give him sidelong glances to see if he was looking at them when they did?

The funny thing was, they didn't use the insulting language he would have expected. If someone wasn't strong enough to do some job by himself, no one called him a fag. They didn't throw around words like homo or queer. Even in Manhattan at Barnes & Noble, which should have been a more liberal environment, he'd had coworkers who'd said stupid, insensitive things. And he'd endured attention from Anna, whose feeble brain couldn't seem to wrap itself around the truth of his sexuality.

Maybe if any of the men on his crew had tossed out those loaded words, he'd have been emboldened to speak up. But they had a live-and-let-live attitude, so he let it lie. It wasn't like straight people went around saying, *Hi, my name is Whatever and I'm straight.* If anyone asked him, he'd tell the truth. He wasn't in Dennis's "don't ask, don't tell" world. Besides, his aunt owned the company that was paying them. She was a lesbian, whether or not her employees knew it. It wasn't like she would fire him for being gay. Although knowing her, she might pull him off the job if he made everyone else uncomfortable.

On the Thursday after Dash's party, Phillip got an unexpected break when it started raining and Roy sent the crew home early. He drove to Ocean Springs hoping that his new computer had arrived, but it hadn't. He spent the evening writing Claude. The next morning, it was still raining, and Selma called to let him know they weren't working. He lay in bed, too accustomed to his new schedule to go back to sleep but too lazy to get up. He loved the sound of the rain and daydreamed about spending the morning in bed with a lover. Or, more exactly, with Kieran. He was beginning to think he was obsessed.

When the phone rang at noon, he finally dragged himself out of bed to answer it.

"It's Andi. What are you doing this Sunday?"

"Going to mass," he lied. This was greeted by stone silence. "I don't know. Maybe going to the Pass."

"That's not a good idea," Andi said. "Wasn't one reunion with your mother enough?"

He had no intention of discussing his mother with Andi and said, "Why'd you ask about Sunday?"

"Geoffrey and I are hosting an afternoon barbecue. There will be lots of young people here. Since your mother knows you're back, you may as well be more social, with an appropriate group of friends."

Phillip indulged himself in a brief fantasy of describing Dash's Garden Party, then frowned and improvised. "I'm not sure I can make it. My roommates and I have tentative plans."

"You're free to bring them with you."

Oh, God, he thought, imagining Julianna sharing the story of her lesbian epiphany with Andi's guests. Or Jess checking out the Beasleys' house for soundness while his aunt kept a close eye on the silver.

"I might bring Shanon," he said.

"Shanon? Is that a boy or a girl?"

"She's a woman," Phillip said. "One of my roommates." More silence, so he added, "Just a roommate."

"The more the merrier," Andi said, sounding anything but merry. "Dress nicely."

"Yes, ma'am," Phillip said, suddenly twelve years old.

"Three-ish."

"I'll try."

He couldn't think of anything less appealing than a Sunday afternoon at Andi's, although he was a little intrigued by her choice of days. According to Florence, Andi had gotten angry at her Baptist minister and moved her membership to a church more to her liking—some nondenominational sect called Redemption Center, which had made him think of turning in cans for recycling. Florence said that Andi had the zeal of a new convert and was always pressuring her to enroll Susan and Samantha in their day-care program.

He showered and dressed, then stared disconsolately at the rain. He could paint, but the light sucked. He rejected the idea of driving to Pass Christian to try again with his mother. Shanon wasn't home, and Jess was apparently taking a rain day too. He watched the driveway, willing the UPS man to show up with his computer, but apparently UPS wasn't cooperating.

Stone Love, he thought and his mood lifted. He had something to do after all.

He loved the little historic section of Ocean Springs with its art galleries and quirky shops. He found Stone Love tucked between a florist and a crafts dealer and dashed inside.

The rain was apparently keeping customers at bay; Jay was working alone. He smiled warmly at Phillip and said, "You remembered."

"I need a stone that wards off evil spirits," Phillip said.

"Do you live in a house with a ghost?" Jay asked.

"No. I'm going to a party at my aunt's this weekend."

Jay looked confused and said, "Is your aunt evil?"

"Completely."

"Then why are you going?"

"Because I trust you to protect me," Phillip said. Jay blushed and dropped his eyes, which was so becoming that Phillip decided to keep flirting. "You *could* go with me. Then I know I'd be safe."

"Not from Travis," Jay said.

"That's an inconvenient detail."

"The truth is in the details," Jay said.

"The truth will set you free."

"The truth is out there?" Jay ventured.

"The naked truth," Phillip said in a salacious tone.

"Here you go," Jay said, reaching into a display case. "Obsidian. The stone of truth."

"I bow to your superior wisdom," Phillip said, taking the stone from Jay and looking it over. "Will it also ward off evil spirits?"

"It protects and invigorates," Jay said. "It helps you see your negative qualities so you can change them."

"You think I have negative qualities?" Phillip asked with a mock gasp. When Jay blushed again, he said, "I'll stop tormenting you on one condition."

"I don't think—" Jay began before his curiosity got the best of him. "What condition?"

"When I finish the project I'm working on, I want to paint you."

"You're an artist?" Jay asked in an admiring tone. "What are you working on now?"

"I'm painting a house."

"Oh. You're a housepainter?"

Phillip laughed and said, "Language barriers. I'm not painting a house. I'm painting the likeness of a house on canvas. Yes, I'm an artist."

"And you want to paint me?"

"I want to paint your likeness on canvas," Phillip recited.

"I don't know," Jay said. "I'm still nervous about that 'naked truth' comment."

He was so adorable that Phillip wanted to hug him, but he fought the impulse and held up the obsidian, saying, "Truthfully, I'd never make you uncomfortable while I was painting you."

Jay cut off whatever he was about to say when the phone rang. He picked it up and said, "Stone Love. This is Jay." He gave Phillip a guilty look and turned around, lowering his voice. "No. It's really slow today. Only a few women this morning. I think they were mostly getting out of the rain."

Travis, Phillip thought, and walked to a display case a few feet away, pretending not to listen.

"I remember. I won't be late.... The same time I always close. It may take me a little longer if it's still raining. I'm not stopping anywhere.... I'm coming straight home."

Ew, they live together? Phillip wondered. *Poor Dennis. Poor Jay.*

"Yes, I have it.... Yes, it'll be turned on.... I have to go. I'm getting a delivery. FedEx.... The bald guy with three kids. I'll *be* there. Bye." He turned back to Phillip. "Sorry."

"You ought to be. I still have all my hair."

Jay's shoulders slumped, and he said, "So does the FedEx guy."

"It's a good thing you weren't holding the stone of truth," Phillip said.

"I shouldn't have lied," Jay agreed. "Sometimes I just...it's just..."

Phillip knew better than to get in the middle of a couple's conflict, so he merely said, "I'll come in occasionally. If you change your mind about being painted, we'll work something out."

"Okay," Jay said. The succinct reply made Phillip feel as if a transaction had just closed, so he smiled politely and turned on his heel to leave. He stopped when Jay cried out, "Hey, wait!"

"Yes?"

Jay pointed at Phillip's hand and said, "Are you going to pay for that?"

Phillip blushed as he held out his hand, the obsidian balanced in his sweaty palm, and said, "I swear I'm not a kleptomaniac."

Jay arched an eyebrow but said nothing as he walked behind the cash register and punched some buttons. Phillip leaned on the counter, watching Jay's hands, until a display of jars on a nearby table caught his eye. He opened a lid and inhaled deeply. "This is great. It smells like a garden."

"You like tea?" Jay asked. "We just started selling it. I think that's chamomile, peppermint, and lemongrass."

Phillip felt transported for a moment, remembering steaming mugs of tea with Kieran—sipping, talking, sharing. "Do you have black tea?"

Jay frowned, spun one of the jars around, consulted a label on the back, and said, "Uh-huh. English breakfast."

"Do you have Irish breakfast?" Phillip asked, smiling at his private joke.

Jay tapped another lid, saying, "Right here."

"Could I have two ounces of that, please?"

After weighing and bagging the loose leaves, Jay said, "The tea comes to five dollars."

"And the stone?"

"Since you were willing to go to jail for it, it's on the house," Jay said.

"You wouldn't have called the cops on me," Phillip observed. Jay merely shrugged, saying nothing, so Phillip handed him the money. "When can I paint you?"

"We're back to that again? You don't give up, do you?" Jay said, handing over his bag.

"Nope. You said you're off on Thursdays, right? How about then?"

"Let me think about it."

"All you have to do is sit there. How hard is that?" Phillip pressed.

"Stop," Jay pleaded.

"No," Phillip replied.

Jay laughed and said, "We'll see."

"'We'll see?'" Phillip mimicked. "What kind of answer is that? What does it mean?"

"It means 'I'll think about it and call you,'" Jay said, "if you give me your number."

"Are you brushing me off, or is that the truth?"

"Yes!" Jay exclaimed ambiguously.

Phillip scribbled his number on the back of his receipt and gave it to Jay, saying, "Truth is beauty."

"Great. That's settled," Jay said, pushing Phillip toward the door. "Now go."

Phillip dug in his heels and refused to budge. "Nothing's settled. I still don't know if I'm painting you. Say yes, and I'll go." Phillip managed to hold his ground when Jay tried to propel him forward.

"I already gave you an answer," Jay grunted. "Get!"

The door to the shop opened and Travis stepped in. Jay, his view blocked, laughingly shoved Phillip harder, expecting him to resist. Caught off-guard by Travis's scowl, Phillip pitched forward. He tried to grab Travis for support, but Travis fell backward, dragging Phillip to the floor. Once they landed, Phillip immediately rolled off Travis, feeling disgusted and embarrassed.

"Are you okay?" Jay asked Phillip.

"Fine," Phillip said. Jay offered his hand and pulled Phillip to his feet.

"I'm fine too, if you give a shit," Travis said bitchily. When Jay moved to help him, he said, "Don't bother. What did I walk in on?"

"What are you doing here?" Jay asked. "I said I'd be home right after I closed."

"I was nearby, so I thought I'd keep you company and help you close up." Travis looked at Phillip disdainfully and said, "I see I needn't have bothered. You already have company."

"I was on my way out," Phillip said. "It was nice to see you again, Jay." Before he closed the door behind him, Phillip couldn't resist adding, "Great running into you, Travis."

Chapter 13

Shanon looked at Phillip and said, "We don't have to do this."

Phillip felt her hand on his knee, which comforted him, but he didn't stop staring through the car window at his Aunt Andi's house. The lawn was freshly cut, the shrubbery was trimmed, and the flowers were blooming brightly and perfectly spaced in their beds. The house was gleaming white, which Phillip knew was due to Andi's obsession with having it repainted yearly. It was a perfect plot of paradise, and Phillip hated it.

"Look at it," Phillip said, nodding toward the house. "I love good landscaping, but those bushes look like they've been beaten into submission."

"The trees don't dare grow too much," Shanon chimed in, "lest they be sent to the corner of the lot."

Phillip looked at her and grinned, saying, "You get it. None of it's real. It doesn't mean anything. It's like painting over mold. It looks pretty, but there's still mold underneath."

"That's a terrible analogy. Gross, in fact." She looked out the window and said, "It does resemble Belfast House. However, I'd like to go on record as saying that Belfast House has more character."

"I agree. I'm glad you're here," Phillip said. "It's nice knowing there's somebody watching my back."

"You look good from the back," Shanon said. "But you're making me nervous. Like I said, if you think this is going to be awful, let's just do something else."

"I could make up some excuse. I've done it before," Phillip mused. He shook his head and said, "No. I'd never hear the end of it. Let's make an appearance, then we'll go to the coffeehouse or something." As they walked up the drive, Phillip muttered, "I'll bet there are fifty people in there staring out the windows at us."

"Would you stop?" Shanon urged. "You're being ridiculous."

Chagrined, Phillip ducked his head and they walked onward. He remembered Julianna reprimanding him for not being more sensitive around Shanon with regard to his family. Even if they were a flock of lunatics, busybodies, and control freaks, they were still his family, and Phillip made a silent vow not to disparage them in front of Shanon. He tried to put himself in her place, wondering what it would've been like to grow up without a family. He knew what not having a father was like, and there were countless times he'd wished his mother would vanish. Regardless, he couldn't imagine not having people he could count on, like his aunts, who always looked out for him, no matter how annoying they could be.

They bypassed the front door, and Phillip led Shanon to the backyard. Before they rounded the corner to the flagstone patio, where he could already hear the buzz of conversations, Phillip pulled Shanon aside and said, "When I was six, I ate crayons."

"I preferred paste at that age," Shanon said. She linked her arm in his and said, "Come on."

Phillip saw a swarm of guests milling on the patio. There were a lot of people his age, several of Aunt Andi's friends as well as a handful of men who stood around the grill talking to his Uncle Geoffrey. Nobody seemed to notice them as they approached, and Shanon whispered, "Who should we talk to first?"

"With all these people around? Aunt Andi's head is probably spinning like a radar dish, waiting for someone to break something or—"

"Phillip, you're finally here!" Andi exclaimed, moving toward him with open arms. Her head was cocked to one side, and Phillip noticed that she bore the fixed smile of a politician's wife. In seconds her arms were around him, and he was enveloped in a floral-scented haze, her pearl earring digging into his cheek. Andi pulled back, still holding his arms, her eyes cutting up and down, assessing his khaki cargo pants and blue plaid shirt. When her gaze fell on Shanon, Phillip noticed that her smile faltered momentarily, like an actress consulting a cue card, before she said, "You must be Phillip's friend."

As Phillip introduced the two women, he was pleased when Shanon complimented Andi's home, then immediately said, "I smell hamburgers."

"We've got burgers, hot dogs, beans, slaw, potato salad," Andi replied as she led them to a table laden with food. "Everything a cookout needs. Except ants. You two fix yourselves a plate—there are Cokes in that cooler—and Phillip can introduce you around. I have to fetch more napkins. Excuse me."

"Smooth move," Phillip said softly as he heaped Doritos onto a plate, "mentioning food like that."

"I'm not even hungry," Shanon admitted. Phillip watched as she dabbed tiny spoonfuls of everything around the perimeter of her plate, like paint on a new palette. She grabbed a fork and moved some of the food around, then dropped a few Ruffles into the center, effectively creating the illusion of a nearly consumed meal. "Do you see anyone you know?"

"I don't think so," Phillip said, scanning the backyard. "It's been more than five years since I was here, and back then I was never very social—certainly not with this crowd."

"I've never seen so many twinsets in my life," Shanon said.

"Where are all the guys?"

"Over there," Shanon said, nodding toward the grill.

"I meant our age."

"Maybe they're in the kitchen spiking the Kool-Aid."

"Phillip! Is that you, boy?" a booming voice called. "Don't take any of those burgers on the table. Come get one hot off the grill!"

"That would be Uncle Geoffrey," Phillip murmured as they moved toward the sound of sizzling meat. "Ten more minutes and we're out of here."

"It's not so bad," Shanon said. "I've been to worse functions, believe me."

"For work?"

"Mm-hmm."

"Phillip, it's good to see you again," Geoffrey said, pumping his hand.

"You too, Uncle Geoffrey. This is my friend Shanon."

His uncle's mouth opened and closed a few times, like a fish out of water, before he said, "I'm glad you both could make it. If you hadn't, I'd have heard about it all night."

"Why was Aunt Andi so insistent that I come?" Phillip asked.

"She's got it in her head that you need more friends your own age." He extracted a hamburger bun, put it on Phillip's plate, then added a burger on top of it. "Respectable friends."

"I have respectable friends," Phillip said in a low voice.

Geoffrey glanced at Shanon and said, "Of course you do. But your aunt remembers you as a loner."

"Before I went to New York," Phillip said. "For Christ's sake, Uncle Geoffrey, I was a kid then. I'm an adult. I can choose my own friends."

Andi appeared in front of them with a bowl in her hands. "Banana pudding?"

"No, thank you," Shanon said. She gestured to her plate. "I couldn't eat another bite."

"I know Phillip won't refuse," Andi said, slopping a spoonful of pudding on his plate. "When he was a boy, he couldn't resist my 'nanner puddin'."

"He's not a boy anymore, Andi," Geoffrey said. "We were just talking about that."

Phillip blushed, embarrassed to have become the center of attention. He almost choked when Andi said, "I used to change Phillip's diapers. He'll always be a little boy to me."

"You didn't!" Phillip snapped.

Luckily Andi laughed and said, "As if you'd remember." Then she changed tack, saying, "Phillip, we're so glad you came home."

"Yes," Geoffrey agreed.

Since Andi had practically shoved him out the door of his grandfather's house when he'd arrived from New York, it was all Phillip could do not to gape at her. He chalked it up to more Godbee revisionism.

"Away from that awful city," Andi continued, shaking her head. "It's far too dangerous there. I'm glad the dear Lord saw fit to protect you during that awful time when our country was attacked by heathens."

Geoffrey nodded solemnly. Phillip didn't know what to say. He could remember September 11 vividly: where he was when the World Trade Center was attacked, how scared he felt, and how worried he had been for his friends in the city. He wanted to keep those feelings to himself and not give his aunt's fanaticism any credence, so he simply said, "I wasn't in any danger."

"Satan has many faces," Andi said sternly. Phillip was spared having to come up with a response when she went on. "I think it would be a good idea, Phillip, if you join us next Sunday at Redemption Center so that you can learn about Satan and the ways he tries to capture your soul and deny you entry into heaven."

"Phillip," Shanon said, gently touching his arm. "Would you show me where the bathroom is?"

"Excuse me," Phillip said to his aunt and uncle. He escorted Shanon to the house, where they dropped off their plates in the kitchen before Phillip led her to a powder room off the foyer. "In here."

"Thanks, but I don't have to go," Shanon said.

"Then why did you—"

Shanon shrugged and said, "I could tell they were getting to you."

"Phillip? Are you in here?" a voice called.

Phillip turned and saw a girl entering the hall. "Linda? Linda Bishop?" he asked.

"I was right!" Linda exclaimed. She skipped forward and threw her arms around him, ignoring the fact that he made no move to hug her back. "Your aunt told me you were in here. Look at you! You look just as handsome as the last time I saw you. Better, in fact."

When Phillip was released, he felt woozy as his past and present collided. He craved a cigarette. He stared at Linda, who was smiling expectantly. "You look great too. Linda, this is my friend Shanon."

"It's wonderful to meet you, Shanon," Linda said. "How long have you been invisible?" Phillip whipped around and saw that Shanon was gone. "It's nice to see you picked up a sense of humor while you were in New York. What are you doing back? I thought I'd never see you again—maybe in a magazine after you became a famous artist. I intended to cut out your picture to show all my friends and tell them I knew you way back when."

"Yeah, well, someone forgot to tell that to the rest of the universe," Phillip said. "It didn't exactly work out that way."

"The universe?" Linda asked blankly. Then she laughed and said, "Oh, you mean God hasn't revealed His plan for you yet."

"What have you been doing?" Phillip asked weakly, vowing that the next time he came to a party at his aunt's, he was bringing Dash instead of Shanon. A cigarette wasn't enough; he wanted a joint.

"Things couldn't be more terrific," Linda gushed. "I graduated from USM, got my teaching certificate, and now I'm practically running Redemption Center's day-care program."

"Why aren't you teaching?" Phillip asked.

"I am!" Linda exclaimed. "I'm helping children learn about Jesus. The kids are wonderful too—so precious. You should see them. Hey, why don't you come down and help me out some day? What are you doing tomorrow?"

Phillip had flashbacks of Anna, his flirtatious coworker at Barnes & Noble. Linda used to be the same way when they were in school together. She always managed to sit next to him in class and find ways to flirt. Phillip remembered her reading aloud from passages in *Romeo and Juliet* in English class and directing the lines toward him.

"Oh, man," Phillip said, trying to sound disappointed. "I have to work tomorrow—all day. Darn."

Linda pouted and said, "We'll work it out. Maybe we'll get together after work sometime. Or next Sunday! Anyway, now that you're back, we can do stuff together all the time. I'm going to get some lemonade. Can I get you a glass too?"

"Uh, sure," Phillip said. As she walked away, he tried to think of something to do all day the following Sunday.

The door to the powder room opened and Shanon poked her head out. "Is she gone?"

"Yes, but she might be back. With lemonade," Phillip said. "Where were you when I needed you?"

"I decided I had to pee after all," she said. "What do we have to do to get out of here?"

"I'd kill for a cigarette," Phillip muttered. "And Andi will kill me if I smoke."

"I'm not going back out there," Shanon said, gesturing toward the back of the house. "Is there somewhere we can talk? I don't want to go home in case Julianna's there. She won't give us privacy."

"Let's go get some real food," Phillip said. They ducked out the front door and drove to Pass Christian in silence. After a few wrong turns, he finally found the Burning Phoenix and parked, saying, "I've heard this place is really good."

"It is," Shanon agreed.

"You've been here?" Phillip asked. "We can go somewhere else if you want."

"No. It's fine," Shanon said. "They have incredible quesadillas here."

The Burning Phoenix was near the heart of historic Pass Christian in a renovated home. The interior reflected a Southwestern theme: white stucco walls, dark wood accents, and candles perched on wrought iron fixtures. Taryn looked up from the reservation book and said, "Welcome to the Burning Phoenix. Do you have a reservation?"

"No, but I do have some pocket lint and a receipt from Gas'N'Go," Phillip said.

"In that case," Taryn said, picking up two menus, "right this way." She seated them at a table near the fireplace, which was illuminated by several white pillar candles. Windows on either side afforded a beach view. "The best table for my favorite customer. Our specials tonight are churrasco-grilled swordfish or pan-seared yucca-crusted tuna, which is served with a pineapple pico."

"That sounds incredible," Phillip said. "I'm not sure if we're that hungry, though. We were just at a barbecue at my Aunt Andi's."

Taryn frowned and said, "And you came here?"

"We were looking for a quiet place to talk," Phillip said.

"Look, pal, if that's a slam on my business, it's still early. This place will pick up in no time," Taryn joked.

"I didn't eat much," Shanon offered. "I'd love a blue crab quesadilla. They're fabulous."

Taryn studied Shanon for a moment, then said, "Tell you what. We're experimenting with the menu, and we've got a bunch of stuff in the kitchen. I'll bring you samples, and you let me know what you think. I'll be right back."

After Taryn left, Shanon said, "I got the idea you'd never been here."

"Taryn is Chad's mom," Phillip explained. "If you want to go somewhere else to talk, that's fine. Taryn's cool; she'll understand."

"No. Really, it's fine," Shanon said as she opened her napkin and placed it on her lap. "There's hardly anyone here right now anyway."

"You should see how it is in New York," Phillip said. "People do everything in public. They have arguments right next to you in restaurants or on the sidewalks. They don't care. Actually, I'm guilty of it too. I once had a raging fight with a guy and got dumped in the Ziegfeld Theater—in front of hundreds of people. Nobody batted an eyelash."

"Maybe they were watching the movie."

"It hadn't even started," Phillip replied.

"Funny how that works," Shanon said. "Sometimes being in public is the most private place of all."

"Yes," Phillip agreed.

After their server had brought them water and bread, Shanon said, "I want to ask you a question, but I have to preface it with a disclaimer."

"Okay," Phillip said warily.

"Sometimes when people talk about their families, I can seem unsympathetic. I'm not, but I can't jump in with those affirming comments like, 'Yeah, my mother does this,' 'My father says that,' 'My older brother…,' blah blah blah."

"You grew up in a sort-of family, didn't you?" Phillip asked.

"Yes. Part of it's my personality. I've always felt like there's just me. The only family I've ever had is whatever I create from my friends."

"I understand that," Phillip said. "As a gay man, I mean. I'm starting to realize I do that too."

"I know," Shanon said. "It's one reason I'm comfortable with you—we have that in common. But you do have a family, and now that I've met your Aunt Andi, I'm trying to figure them out. I'm not anti-religion or anything. I grew up in a place that existed because of a Presbyterian orphanage and college. But your aunt is a little over-the-top."

"She's a freak," Phillip said bluntly. "Nobody else in the family is like her."

"Oh. I was thinking that might be one reason why you don't talk about them."

"I've got lots more reasons than that," Phillip said. She gave him her green-eyed gaze, but he obstinately decided to outwait her.

Their server brought several plates of food. As they began to dig in, Shanon surprised him by saying, "Mitch ended our friendship."

"Why? Don't tell me it was because you wouldn't go out with him."

"It was the same reason Lowell moved out." She looked sad as she picked at a plate of enchiladas. "I guess I'm trying to do some emotional banking. Like, if you invest in me, you won't find it so easy to walk away."

"I don't walk away from my friends," Phillip said. He thought a few minutes before saying, "Okay. I'll treat this like one of those retirement accounts. I'll make a deposit that I can't withdraw without paying a penalty."

She smiled and listened intently as he described his aunts and grandfather and, finally, how it felt to grow up with a crazy mother who was the reason he'd come back to Mississippi. By the time he stopped talking, the sun had almost set and the tables around them were all occupied.

"Did you ever do your laundry in one of those places where the driers have glass doors?" Shanon asked. When he whipped his head up to look at her, she laughed and said, "I guess that was random. Sorry."

"I'd accuse you of reading my journal, but I don't keep one," Phillip said. "I do a lot of thinking in front of those driers. I pick out a T-shirt or a bandanna or something and watch for it. I *relate* to it—like I'm being tossed around, and everything is beyond my control. When will I see me again? Who will I be clinging to?"

"It's nice that you get me," she said. "I was going to ask if you ever used one of those driers as an analogy for your life."

"Totally," he said. "The drier was steamy Mississippi. My grandfather dropped the coins in. My family was tangled together, all of us bumping into each other. And I was waiting for the right man to come along, open the door, and dress himself in me. You?"

"I wanted to be the drier sheet," Shanon said. "In there, not wearable but with a purpose."

"I think of you more like the little girl with her nose against the drier window, staring in at all the action but detached from it," Phillip said, remembering his assumption about how Shanon used her telescope.

Shanon turned bright red, confirming his suspicion, and said, "It's a good thing I don't keep a journal either."

"I know what that feels like," Phillip said. "Everything in the South is based on family—not money—and my grandfather was an outsider. He uprooted my poor grandmother from Alabama and plunked her down here, where they gave birth to a bunch more outsiders. My mother made it worse for her and me when she randomly decided to be Catholic. My classmates knew my mother was nuts, so they avoided me. I went to Manhattan and got treated like I came from another planet. Then there's the big one: I'm gay. But I made friends, and so have you."

"They're dropping like lost socks," Shanon said. "I wouldn't say Julianna is really a friend, although I enjoy her. She's funny. That's how I got to know her in the first place. I went into Faulkner's on a slow night, and Julianna was telling stories at the bar. She's good at storytelling."

"I know," Phillip said.

"Too good," Shanon said. "It makes me not trust her. Or else I'm one of those horrible women who doesn't get along with other women."

"You get along with Jess," Phillip pointed out.

"Who doesn't? Jess is great," Shanon said. "I think she's the reason I hold on to Julianna. Anyway, I don't seem to be that good at picking male friends either. That would mean I'm the one with the problem, I guess."

Phillip leaned forward, put his hand over hers, and said, "Go ahead. Throw your dirty laundry at me. You can't shock me."

Shanon glanced at the nearby tables before she drew her hand away and said, "I'm a whore."

"You don't even date," Phillip said.

"No, I mean I'm a whore. Prostitute. Hooker. Call girl. Whatever label you want to put on it." She returned Phillip's stare and said, "Not so unshockable after all, are you?"

"I'm ashamed to admit it, but my first reaction is a kind of sick delight that I took you to Aunt Andi's church party," Phillip said. "Consulting, huh?"

"It's one of those vague terms no one can refute," Shanon said.

"How did this come about?"

"When I moved to Biloxi just after high school, I didn't know anyone. I was working my ass off as a waitress, looking for something else, when I saw this ad for a lingerie model. I'm not exactly a skinny girl so I never thought of anything like modeling. But I do have a nice rack."

Phillip laughed and said, "You're shapely. Lots of straight men like that."

"You're telling me," Shanon said with a roll of her eyes. "The more I thought about it, the more I figured they'd rather have a curvy girl modeling lingerie. So I answered the ad, and it wasn't about lingerie at all. The man who interviewed me wasn't what you'd expect: sleazy, with gold chains and slicked-back hair. Clark is all business. He looks like someone who could be on Wall Street. Of course, I was appalled at the concept and told him no thanks. He gave me his card and said, 'You'll call.' Two weeks later, half the wait staff was fired because...basically because the manager was an asshole. I called the number on the card, went in to talk to Clark again, and undressed so he could check me out and get a picture—without my face—for their Web site."

"They have a Web site?"

"Uh-huh. It's subtle, but if a man already knows about these places, he knows how to find us. We're not an escort service. Or streetwalkers. We're listed in a professional building as providing 'spa services.' If vice were to come in, it looks like a spa. But that's not quite the service we give our clients."

"'These places,'" Phillip repeated her words.

"Like the credit card. We're everywhere you want to be. Well, not you personally, but you know what I mean. Clark even flies girls here from other cities if they have special skills that a client wants."

Phillip wasn't sure he wanted to know what kind of special skills she meant. "What about—I don't know the etiquette for nailing somebody with questions about this." He considered his words and winced.

"Ask me whatever you want to know."

"Isn't it dangerous?"

"No. It's not like we're isolated. Plus it's expensive. Not that having money keeps a man from being a jerk, but we're not pulling in strangers from the street. We service an exclusive network of men—usually quite prominent men."

"I was thinking more about diseases," Phillip said.

"Oh. Condoms are mandatory. Also, the men get a rubdown before we meet them in our rooms, which serves as an inspection."

"Uh-huh," Phillip said. "Don't you ever get undercover police?"

Shanon laughed and said, "Occasionally. But they're not working when they visit us. Besides, the girls never touch the money. We don't even use the word *money*. And if anyone busted us...some of our most loyal clients are judges.

Politicians. I'm not trying to paint a rosy picture. I know I'm in the flesh trade. A few of the girls have boyfriends that push them into it because the money is incredible. Some of the girls do drugs, but not me. Nobody makes me do anything I don't want to do, and I don't have a family or a boyfriend who would freak out about it."

"Lowell and Mitch," Phillip said, remembering how their conversation had started.

"I don't know how Lowell figured it out," Shanon said with a frown. "He didn't seem put off by the moral aspect of it, but he was sure it was all going to blow up on me somehow, and he didn't want to get caught in the fallout. As for Mitch, I finally told him why I don't date. There's no way I can have a man in my life while I'm doing this."

"What if it does blow up?" Phillip asked. "You said the money is incredible. How do you get away with not paying taxes?"

"I pay taxes," Shanon said. "As a self-employed consultant, I pay more taxes than someone who gets wages from a regular job. I get great financial advice from one of my clients who's an accountant, but not as good as the information I get from my client who works for the IRS. If anything goes wrong, I've got at least six attorneys I can call."

"Jesus," Phillip said. "Where can I sign up?"

Shanon laughed. "I know I can't do it forever. I wonder about the girls who get used to the money and spend it as fast as they make it. I try to be smarter. I paid cash for my car and the house, but I save most of it."

"Wait, you *own* Belfast House?"

"I thought you'd figured that out by now." When he shook his head, she went on. "I don't give out a lot of information because it's awkward to answer questions. Julianna and Jess don't know. I put the cash in a safety deposit box and move it to my bank account a little at a time—so as not to raise any red flags. When I stop doing this, I'll keep making deposits until it's all legally accounted for, taxes paid up, the whole thing. It'll pay my way for whatever comes next."

"Which is?"

"I don't know." She shrugged. "Starting my own business. College. Business classes. Whatever. I'm investing in me."

"It sounds sensible," Phillip said. "But don't you…"

When he trailed off, she said, "Worry about getting jaded? Coarse? That's why I say I can't do it forever. I don't have a lot of guilt about it, but it does affect how I see people. Not much surprises me anymore."

Taryn suddenly appeared at their table and asked, "How is everything?"

"This is delicious," Shanon said, gesturing to her plate with her fork. "What is it?"

"Shepherd's Pie de Phoenix. Chili, corn, and jack." Taryn looked at Phillip and said, "She picked my recipe. You've got good taste in friends, Phillip. She can stay."

"Everything's great," Phillip said.

"I'm not sure if you mean the food or your friends," Taryn said. "But either way, I'm glad." The front door opened, capturing Taryn's attention. "I see people that need seating. Excuse me."

Phillip thought for a moment, then said, "What did you mean, nobody makes you do anything you don't want to do?"

"Most of the girls have developed a certain persona. The Dominatrix. The Rich Bitch. The Good Girl. The Girlfriend. The Cheerleader. Mommie Dearest. The Executive Assistant. The Librarian."

"Who are you?"

"Girl Next Door. Guys who choose me want a kind of sexy pal. Nothing too extreme—no lesbian scenes, no whips and chains, no anal. In fact, a lot of them don't even want sex. My room is set up to look like there's a window."

"They're watching Girl Next Door through her bedroom window?"

"Exactly. Except I have this one client, a judge from Mobile. Like you, he comes from a rich family, so his fantasy is to do manual labor. He pretends he's a window washer, and I'm supposed to be a businesswoman. While he's watching me, I act like I'm making phone calls. One time he came on the window. I pretended to dial the phone real fast and complain to building maintenance about the lousy job their window washer was doing—how I wanted him fired. That night, he left a thousand-dollar tip."

"Shit," Phillip said.

"I don't do that," Shanon said. "He never touches me, just himself."

"How much do you make?"

"How rude!" Shanon exclaimed.

"You'll tell me you have sex for money but not how much money?"

"A girl has to have her scruples," Shanon said primly, then burst out laughing. "A good six months can net me about one hundred fifty."

"*Thousand?*"

"More or less."

"I'm not that great at math, but isn't that—"

"Over six thousand a week."

"That's amazing."

"It's easy to get addicted to the money. That's one reason I figure I'd better get out soon. Plus I worry about what happens when I fall for someone. It's not like I can tell him what I've been doing all these years."

"Do you ever run into any of your clients outside of work?"

Shanon bit her lip and looked away before she said, "Sometimes. Remember that day I saw you in the post office and was rude to you? I thought maybe you were a client—not mine because I'd have recognized my own client. But I thought you might have seen me at work, and it's a bad idea to take that into the outside world. If I see a client in public, I act like I don't know him. So anyway—"

"Whoa," he said, struck by a realization. "Back up. I noticed my uncle's reaction when he saw you today. Please tell me he's not one of your clients."

"Not *mine*," she said.

"But you've seen him at the, er, spa."

"Yes."

"You thought you should tell me before he does?"

"Are you kidding?" Shanon asked incredulously. "Risk his family finding out? Or his reputation? He would *never* tell you."

"Aunt Andi looked at you strangely too. Do you think she knows?"

Shanon shook her head and said, "I doubt it. Your aunt seems like the kind of woman who sees everyone as 'less than.' Unless I start showing up to Redemption Center, I'm nothing to her. Like that's ever going to happen."

"Like we care about that," Phillip said.

"Amen," Shanon agreed.

"So why did you decide to tell me?"

"I wanted to be honest because if it makes you run away, I'd rather know sooner than later. You and I are different, Phillip. You're a person who has things done to you. I'm a person who does things. I'd rather make you leave than get dumped by you later."

"I'm not going anywhere," Phillip said. He considered her words. "You think I have things done to me?"

"Sort of. You let other people make your decisions."

"Really," he said, feeling somewhat annoyed. "Examples?"

She sighed and said, "Alyssa decided when to be roommates and when to stop. I found you a place to live; you weren't even seriously looking. Other people decide what your jobs will be. Other men are the aggressors in your relationships, either when they choose to be with you or when they leave. Life is what happens to you, not what you make it. Now I've pissed you off."

"Only because I'm afraid you're right," he admitted, "and I'm eternally stuck in the cooldown cycle."

"Better than being sucked into the lint trap," she said.

"Hey, guys." Taryn sat down with them. "I'm pooped. Anyone care for dessert?"

"I'm stuffed," Shanon said. "Everything you gave us tonight should be on the menu."

"Did I tell you that I like this girl?"

"I think you mentioned it," Phillip said, grinning.

"Are you sure I can't tempt you? Sorbet with fruit? Crème brûlée? Cheesecake with guava sauce?"

"Maybe we could have something to go? For later?" Phillip suggested.

"I'll put something together," Taryn said. She stood, and when Phillip offered a credit card, she waved it away, saying, "You don't pay when you come to my house for dinner. You don't pay here either." She turned to leave but stopped and said, "On second thought, you can pay me. What do you think about that space above the fireplace?"

Phillip looked where she indicated and said, "The cow skull is a little maudlin."

"Bull skull," Taryn corrected. "Yeah, I agree. I'd like to commission a painting from you to put there."

"Oh, jeez," Phillip stammered. "I don't know."

Taryn crossed her arms and asked, "Why not?"

"I don't think—" Phillip was about to refuse, then he saw the plea in Taryn's eyes. He sighed and said, "I don't think I could possibly refuse."

"Excellent," Taryn said. "I thought you might say that. Whatever you want to do will be fine, I'm sure. I'll have your dessert ready and waiting up front when you leave."

"She's great," Shanon said after Taryn walked away.

"She is. Taryn's always been there for me, in my corner. She's like my other mom." As an afterthought, he added, "A mom in reserve. A backup, just in case."

"I want to meet your mother," Shanon said.

"Trust me, no, you don't," Phillip declared. "It's a good idea to keep the different parts of my life separate too."

"I don't agree, but it's your call," she said, standing and dropping her napkin on the table. "Have you been to Singing River Casino yet?"

"No."

"You'll like it," Shanon said. "Let's go."

He followed her like an obedient puppy, saying, "I guess you're right; other people do make my decisions. The only things missing are my leash and collar."

"I told you," she said. "I'm the Girl Next Door, not the Dominatrix."

Chapter 14

Phillip watched heads turn as Florence and Sam followed the host through the Glass Menagerie to the table where he was waiting to have Sunday brunch with them. He wasn't sure if people recognized Florence from the days when her face graced magazine covers, or if they were just struck, as he was, by what a stunning couple she and Sam made. He was grateful that they'd agreed to meet him, giving him a legitimate reason to dodge invitations from his Aunt Andi and Linda Bishop to attend services at Redemption Center.

"Good morning," Florence said, kissing Phillip's cheek when he stood to greet them. "What a great idea to meet here. Sam and I haven't been to Singing River before. At least I haven't. Have you, Sam?"

"Never," Sam said with a wink at Phillip. As they all sat down, he asked, "Have you touched the goat yet?"

"I have," Phillip said. "But I still didn't win at the slots."

"The goat?" Florence asked.

Phillip gestured for her to wait while the server took their drink orders and told them about the specials. After he was gone, Phillip said, "I got a grand tour of Singing River the other night. I can answer all your questions. The casino gets its name from the legend of the peace-loving Pascagoula Indians, who walked into the Pascagoula River singing their death song rather than go to war with the Biloxi Indians. The river still makes a mysterious sound—"

"I know all that," Florence interrupted. "Tell me about the goat."

"Good things come to those who wait," Phillip chided. "Look at your menu like a good girl before our server comes back."

"He's cute," Florence said. "Maybe if you asked him out he'd give us a discount."

Phillip rolled his eyes at Sam and said, "I can't believe she's pimping me out. Be quiet; here he comes." After they'd ordered, Phillip settled back and in his best tour-guide voice said, "Today we're dining in the Glass Menagerie, named after the play written by Mississippi's own Tennessee Williams. If you look at the east wall," he pointed, and Sam and Florence obediently turned their heads, "you'll see the restaurant's collection of hundreds of crystal animals. These are taken down one by one and meticulously dusted by Mose Taylor." He paused so they could watch Mose, a wizened black man wearing a crisp white shirt over black slacks held up by suspenders, pose for a picture with two elderly ladies. "Mose, along with the restaurant's excellent cuisine, makes the Glass Menagerie a favorite of tourists. It's traditional to tip him if he poses for a picture with you."

"They should give you a job here," Florence said.

"I'm just getting warmed up," Phillip said. "For guests who want more bang for their dining buck, the casino puts out a lavish spread in the Black Creek Buffet, where for one low price, snowbirds and locals alike can stuff themselves on traditional Southern fare, including the best fried chicken on the Gulf Coast."

"Odell might argue with that fried chicken claim," Sam said.

"Odell would be right, because their fried chicken doesn't hold a candle to hers," Phillip said. "However, since Papa doesn't allow flocks of tourists into the Godbee kitchen, Odell will have to live with this injustice."

"Does Black Creek Buffet serve Southern fried goat?" Florence asked.

"Let go of the goat!" Phillip implored. "The casino also has another restaurant, Miss Welty's Porch, named, of course, for writer Eudora Welty of Jackson. The restaurant is designed to look like the veranda of an antebellum mansion and even boasts a porch swing, a favorite spot for couples to get their pictures taken while they sip Miss Welty's Delta Juleps, a concoction with a mysterious ingredient known only to the restaurant's owner. For an extra thirty dollars, patrons who purchase a Delta Julep can take home the pewter cup it's served in."

"We have to go there," Florence said. "I don't have any julep cups in my collection."

The server came with their food, and Phillip dropped his tour-guide schtick for a few minutes as they dug in with appreciative murmurs, then Sam said, "Do we get the rest of the casino's Mississippi lore?"

"Of course," Phillip said. "The upper-level bar, designed to resemble a planter's library, including shelves of leather-bound classics, is named Faulkner's Library."

"William Faulkner, Oxford," Florence said with exasperation. "Is there a goat head on the wall or something?"

"No," Phillip said. "Faulkner's Library is one of the few attractions in the casino that isn't just a stop on the way to the tables or the slots. It's a favorite meeting place for local Southern gentlemen to gather and talk about literature, politics, and hunting—or whatever Southern gentlemen talk about."

Sam grinned and said, "Your grandfather often goes there when he's back home."

"So I've heard," Phillip said. "I also heard he doesn't tip well. One of my roommates, Julianna, is a cocktail waitress there."

"I can guess why," Sam said. "By the time he leaves, he's probably about to have a coronary. He's one of the few Democrats among his cronies, and I've heard the discussions can get heated. Tell Julianna to cozy up to him and mention that FDR is her favorite president of all time."

"Pretty?" Florence asked.

"Roosevelt? Not so much," Phillip said.

Florence glared at him. "Julianna."

"Very," Phillip said.

"Then tell her to cozy up to him, period. Daddy's not immune to the charms of pretty girls."

Phillip laughed and said, "I'll tell her. For guests who like show tunes, the Live Oaks Lounge is a piano bar where husband-and-wife duo Rank and Phila perform five nights a week."

"Now them I've heard of," Florence said. "As a matter of fact, they figure into your life too, Phillip."

"How so?"

"Rankin Clark is the last of an old Southern family. The Clarks once owned Whittier Plantation, where you're working five days a week for Selma."

"Three days a week," Phillip corrected her. When Florence gave him a quizzical look, he said, "My choice. I asked for Thursdays and Fridays off so I could have long weekends to paint."

"That's wonderful!" Florence said.

"Selma was actually pretty nice about it," Phillip said. "She says it's okay since the job will wrap up soon, and she'll still use me Monday through Wednesday on other jobs. She even gave me a raise."

"She's been very complimentary of you," Sam said. "You know how she values hard work."

"I've learned a lot too," Phillip said. "It's coming in handy at Belfast House. I'm redoing our flower beds."

"I want to see your yard when it's finished," Florence said.

"Sure." He paused, wondering if it would be rude to excuse himself so he could grab a cigarette. But he'd been coughing a lot over the past week, which he blamed on smoking too much during his visits to the casino, so he resisted the impulse. "Where was I?"

"The goat?" Florence asked hopefully.

"High rollers like to gamble in the room called Dr. Nash's Table," Phillip said, pretending he hadn't heard her. "It's named for a Tupelo ghost who supposedly still haunts his favorite restaurant in that city." He didn't add that the room was popular among affluent gay men, which made it a great cruising spot.

"I wish Daddy's house had a ghost," Florence said wistfully.

"There's always my mother," Phillip said. When Florence frowned at him, he quickly said, "Goat Castle is favored for slots. The room took the nickname of the old Glenwood mansion in Natchez. When the Dockery family fell into poverty, they eked out a living by raising and selling goats, chickens, pigs, and cows, all of which were allowed to wander around inside the filthy mansion. The slot room has a real goat, stuffed of course, whose front hooves rest on the bar. Although some patrons are put off by the goat's unwavering stare, many gamblers swear that touching the goat brings them luck. Touching the goat, however, is strictly forbidden and must be done surreptitiously."

"Are you pulling my leg?" Florence asked.

"No. It's true. That poor goat is like a statue in a Catholic church. The foot, or hoof, or whatever, that's most accessible has been worn down by gambling devotees on a pilgrimage to the big payoff."

"I have to touch that goat," Florence said.

"Whoever came up with the theme for this casino was brilliant," Sam said.

Phillip flinched inwardly at the sound of Kieran's favorite adjective but kept his face pleasant while he said, "I agree. Singing River reminds me of things I enjoy about Mississippi—our stories and legends, Southern humor. The appeal of the casino's retail stores is lost on me, but I'm sure you two don't shop anywhere except Garrett's."

"Well," Florence drawled in a guilty tone, but Sam was too busy wrangling with Phillip over the check to reproach her, so she said, "Don't pay that yet. Let's get another round of drinks and talk. We never see you, Phillip. Tell us about your work."

"Our section of Mississippi is in gardening zone 8B, which makes it the ideal location for growing—"

"Not that work, you brat," Florence said, slapping his arm. "Your art."

"It's going well," Phillip said. "I'm working on a painting now of the Whittier house. And," he paused for dramatic effect, "I just received my first commission."

"Congratulations!" Sam said while Florence beamed at him.

"Taryn Cunningham asked me to do a painting for her to hang in the Burning Phoenix," Phillip said.

"I'm so proud of you," Florence said. "I could burst into tears."

"Funny, that's how I felt last Sunday," Phillip said. "Does anyone have suggestions on how to handle Andi's attempts to save my soul?"

Florence pressed her lips together and met Sam's eyes. Phillip knew she'd never liked discussing her sisters' flaws. She took a deep breath and said, "You could always do what your mother does."

"I'm afraid to ask," Phillip said.

"Ellan goes to mass."

"That's not an option," Phillip said. "I'm quite clear on the concept that a practicing homosexual can't be a practicing Catholic. I intend to keep practicing sex until I get it right. That's another thing. I think Andi's trying to set me up with one of my old classmates."

"Linda?" Florence guessed. When Phillip nodded, she sighed. "You know I don't gossip about the family, but Andi's had some disappointments with her children. I think Linda is a surrogate daughter to her."

"Good. That makes her my surrogate first cousin. That is illegal in Mississippi, isn't it?"

"Not for adoptive cousins," Florence said.

"Damn. So what have my real cousins done to put them on the outs with their mother?" When Florence merely shook her head, he gave up. "I guess butting heads with Aunt Andi isn't that surprising. I'm just grateful that Aunt Selma has started being more like you and Aunt Fala. It's been nice, not fighting with her."

Florence drummed her fingernails on the table, exchanged another look with Sam, and said, "Have you seen your mother again?"

"No. I don't think that's a good idea. Do you?"

"I don't know," Florence said. "She's mad at all of us right now."

"Because of me?"

Florence shrugged and again said, "I don't know. As far as I'm concerned, she's been doing fine without a nurse. Fala agrees with me. But since your visit, Selma and Andi are even more convinced that she needs professional help."

"You don't?"

"Why don't you talk to Odell?" Sam interjected. "She's with your mother every day."

"I'll think about it," Phillip said. "Are you ready to check out that goat?"

"Absolutely," Florence said, looking relieved.

By the time he got home that night, Phillip's head was throbbing too badly to power on his new computer and check his e-mail. He aimed all the fans at the bed, turned off the lights, and crawled between the sheets, trying to decide why he felt more overwhelmed after a day with Florence and Sam, who so openly loved him, than he had the Sunday before, when he'd not only endured Andi and Linda but had learned Shanon's secret. Shanon had been lying low ever since, which worried him. He wasn't sure what he could do about it other than be around if she wanted his company.

He got up to take some aspirin, then grabbed his phone and dialed Alyssa's number. When she answered, he said, "Is this a bad time? Can you talk?"

"For you, mister, there is no bad time," Alyssa said. "You sound subdued. I knew your e-mails were a little too relentlessly cheerful. What's up?"

"I don't know where to begin," he said. "When we lived together, did I cry a lot?"

"The only time I remember seeing you cry was when Claude moved away," Alyssa said. "And when Julia Roberts died."

"You're still not off the hook for eating popcorn all the way through Shelby's death and funeral," Phillip said.

"I eat when I'm sad," Alyssa reminded him. "I guess if you're in a crying mood, it's not a good time to tell you that I now fit into my skinny jeans. What's going on?"

"I'm not in a crying mood," Phillip said. "But I think I've cried more over the past three or four months than in the last five years." She was quiet while he talked about his mother, his aunts, Dash, Jay, and Shanon. When he finally wound down, he said, "I'm sorry."

"For what?"

"For whining your ear off. I didn't even ask how you are. Or about Eric."

Alyssa laughed and said, "I send you daily e-mails about Alyssa's and Eric's excellent northwestern adventure. It makes me feel good that you still confide in me and want my perspective. You do, don't you?"

"Of course."

"Can I just point out all the things you're doing right? You're facing things from your past. You're being a good friend to Shanon and trying to befriend Jay. You're working hard at your landscaping job. And you're painting again, which is amazing and wonderful. Maybe all this feels overwhelming, but think of what you've been through. I moved away. You had a falling out with Bunny. You broke up with Eddie after eight months, which was like a silver anniversary for you. You're hurt over Kieran. You had to move back to Mississippi. But you're not moping around doing nothing, living off some Godbee trust fund. Don't beat yourself up for things you can't control."

"My mother?"

"And Shanon's career choice. Kieran's silence. Or Jay's 'como' relationship."

"His *what*?"

"My term for a codependent gay couple," Alyssa said.

Phillip cracked up. "Thanks for always making me laugh."

His headache seemed to have spread to the rest of his muscles when he woke up the next morning. He considered calling in sick but dragged himself out of bed, took more aspirin, made his lunch, and drove to the nursery.

"You don't look so good," Goldie said when Phillip climbed into the truck's bed. "You sick, Cop?"

"I'm just getting a cold or something."

"Gonna be hot today," Cheech warned.

By the time they stopped for lunch a few hours later, Phillip felt feverish. Roy made him stay in the shade of a live oak with plenty of water after Phillip adamantly refused to let himself be driven back to his car.

He was almost asleep when Booty took a break and checked on him. "Head still hurt?"

"Uh-huh," Phillip said.

Booty squatted down and felt his forehead, saying, "It's so hot out here I don't know if you got a fever or not."

When Goldie wandered up, Phillip squinted at him and said, "Y'all stop fussing over me. I'm fine." He tried to stand up as Roy joined them. When he swayed on his feet, Roy caught him.

"I'm sending you home," Roy insisted. It was the longest sentence Phillip had ever heard from him.

"I'm all right," he mumbled, but when Evita swam into his vision, he felt nauseated.

He dimly heard Evita say, "Ain't nobody driving him home but me."

Roy picked him up like a little kid and took him to the truck. When Evita got into the driver's seat and asked for his address, Phillip mumbled it, then closed his eyes, leaning against the window. He was dimly aware of Evita singing. It was strange how much like a lullaby "American Life" sounded when it was sung in Spanish.

When the truck finally lurched to a stop, Phillip opened his eyes and groaned, realizing that he'd automatically given his grandfather's address to Evita. Before he could correct his mistake, Evita had gotten out of the truck and motioned for one of the gardeners in the familiar Godbee Nursery shirt to come help him. Together they hefted a protesting Phillip up the steps. When the front door opened, he pitched toward the worried faces of his mother and Odell.

The next time he opened his eyes, he looked around, trying to get his bearings. He was on a narrow bed in a small room with shuttered windows that partially blocked out what seemed to be a sunset. He stared at the brilliant white ceiling and pale yellow walls and finally realized that he was in what his mother called the "spillover room." Tucked behind his grandfather's study, it had always been the place where anything broken or useless ended up. Somehow that seemed an appropriate destination for him. He had no idea when the room had been cleaned out, repainted, and made into a small bedroom. But the bed was comfortable, the sheets felt wonderful, and he turned his face into the pillow and went back to sleep.

It was dark when he heard his mother's voice saying, "Phillip, sugar, wake up. I have to ask you something important."

He turned to look at her in the soft glow cast by a small lamp next to the bed. "What?"

"Are you lucid?"

"Yes, ma'am."

"I think you have the flu, but Andi is sending Geoffrey over to check on you. He's bringing a lab tech with him to draw blood. With me so far?"

"Yes, ma'am."

"I don't trust Geoffrey not to—Phillip, I'll drive you to New Orleans myself before I let Geoffrey report you to the health department for HIV and bring down the state of Mississippi on you. Tell me the truth. Is there any chance of that happening?"

"No, ma'am."

"You're sure?"

"Yes, ma'am."

His mother bent over and pressed her lips against his forehead, then said, "I'm sorry I had to ask. It's none of their business, and I care about your privacy."

"I understand," he said. "Thank you."

He lost track of how many days he was there. Sometimes he woke up when his mother pressed cold washcloths against his face or the back of his neck. Other times when he opened his eyes, Odell was sitting next to the bed doing needlework. His mother's diagnosis had been inaccurate. Apparently, he had pneumonia. All he knew was that he felt like he was dying, and he didn't much care. His life was a confusing mixture of having bad dreams and being forced awake to drink water, take medicine, or hobble to the bathroom, always returning to clean sheets, where he collapsed, exhausted.

The haze finally lifted, however, and one morning when his mother came in with his pill and a glass of water, he asked, "What day is it?"

"Saturday."

He thought for a moment and said, "I've been here six days?" She nodded and waited while he took his pill. "How come you put me in here instead of my own bedroom?"

"You must be feeling better if you're complaining about the accommodations," she said. "Odell shouldn't be climbing up and down stairs."

"Odell shouldn't be near me," he said. "Didn't she have pneumonia last year?"

"She's had a pneumonia shot," Ellan said. "If you're feeling good enough to move, we'll get you upstairs."

"No," he said indifferently. "It doesn't matter."

He turned away from her and heard her leave the room. A few minutes later, the door opened again. Feeling like he was trapped in one of Edvard Munch's sickroom-and-death paintings, he turned over, breaking off his protest that he wanted to be alone when he saw Chad standing there. "What are you doing here?"

"Taking you upstairs," Chad said. "I'm under orders to get you into a cool bath, dress you—do you still have those Ninja Turtle pajamas? And put you in your own bed. You're a lot of trouble, aren't you?"

"I don't need a nurse," Phillip objected. But when he tried to sit up, his head swam and Chad laughed at him.

"Pussy," Chad said.

"Asshole."

"If you give me a hard time, I'm sending your Aunt Andi in to pray over you," Chad warned, helping him to his feet.

"God. Is she here?"

"No, but Shanon is. I wonder if I could get her to pray over me."

"Leave my friend alone," Phillip said. "Wait, Shanon's here?"

"She's been here every day to check on you," Chad said.

"Great," Phillip said. Shanon had gotten her wish to meet his mother after all.

"It's fine," Chad said. "She and Ellan seem to get along. Apparently they've bonded over a mutual dislike of Linda Bishop."

"She's been here too?" Phillip exploded.

"Shh. She's here now. That's why I'm sneaking you up the back stairs. You look like shit. We can't let all your girlfriends see you like this."

"Is there any chance of dying from pneumonia?"

"With all of Redemption Central—"

"Center."

"Calling for Jesus to heal you? 'Fraid not," Chad said cheerfully.

"Jesus should have gotten an unlisted number," Phillip muttered.

Chapter 15

The two weeks Phillip spent recovering in his grandfather's house should have been reassuring since he was bombarded with evidence of how many people wished him well. Apparently, Julianna was answering his phone at Belfast House and spreading the word. Phillip received cards and notes from Alyssa, Carlos, Claude, and Dash. The cards were funny. The notes were sweet. Under other circumstances, Phillip would have felt touched by their concern.

Instead, he grappled with the sense that his illness had dropped him into a Robert Altman film. Too many people from disparate places were coming together, and he felt as if catastrophe were looming just when he lacked the energy to deal with it. Every time he thought he was feeling well enough to go back to Ocean Springs, his fever would return, leaving him at the mercy of other people.

Spring semester was over; his Uncle Harold had accompanied a group of students to England, leaving Aunt Fala free to come to Pass Christian for a prolonged stay. That meant that his mother didn't have to deal with drop-ins by Chad, Taryn, and Jess, all of whom Phillip was willing to see briefly. Being sick provided a convenient excuse to avoid other people. These included Selma, who'd brought his car and said he absolutely couldn't return to work in the heat until he was fully recovered. And his Aunt Andi, who dropped by in the evenings with Linda, usually with casseroles that Phillip suspected were thrown out by Odell.

Shanon came every day, bringing flowers from the beds at Belfast House, and sometimes books or magazines that she thought might divert him. She chatted about inconsequential things. She was getting the central heat and air installed so that he'd be a lot more comfortable when he came home. She thought Jess and Julianna were having problems, and she wished Jess, not Julianna, was their roommate. She got a kick out of his Aunt Fala, a fellow redhead, and she'd met and liked Florence, Sam, and their daughters. Odell was teaching her to make biscuits for Phillip when he came back to Ocean Springs.

He knew she was looking for reassurance that he was going back to Belfast House, and he tried to give it to her, because there was nothing he wanted more. But their conversations were a little strained because both of them avoided discussing his mother, who checked on Phillip a couple of times a day but beyond that left him alone. Bored, Phillip had started moving between his bedroom on the second floor to his old studio on the third. He ignored his art supplies—he was too listless to take advantage of the idle hours to begin his painting for the Burning Phoenix. Instead, he stared from the studio windows at his mother and Shanon, who spent hours under the live oaks behind the house. Sometimes they had prolonged conversations; other times, they sat in silence like comfortable old friends. It was unsettling.

His curiosity finally got the best of him. One day as Shanon prepared to leave his room, he said, "What do you and my mother talk about?"

"Not you," she said in a tone that he thought was meant to mollify him.

"Is that an answer?"

"You're awfully cranky when you're sick."

"Wanting a straight answer doesn't equate to being cranky."

"We talk a lot about our childhoods, okay? She understands why I want to know what it was like to have four older sisters. She's just as curious about me. We laugh because we have silly things in common." She pointed to a faint scar on her leg and said, "I got that when I fell off my bike. Ellan has one on her shin from when she fell off her bike. I had chicken pox and measles at the same time when I was seven. So did she, when she was six. We both fell in love with Mr. Darcy in *Pride and Prejudice* when we were twelve."

Phillip narrowed his eyes and said, "How do you know she's not making up those things just to have something in common with you?"

"How do you know I'm not?" Shanon asked. "I love to watch her eyes when she's talking. They're so blue and clear. Your mother is really beautiful, but I guess you can't see that."

Phillip frowned at her and said, "I'll tell you a story. When I was sixteen, my mother decided she wanted to plant a flower bed in the back corner of our yard. You have no idea how that disrupted the order of things. The grounds were Selma's domain, and from the moment my mother had a birdbath delivered, the family was at war. Andi said she didn't need to be outside in the heat; she'd make herself sick. Fala said it seemed a harmless-enough pastime. But Selma was offended beyond belief. Every choice my mother made—about flowers, soil, fertilizer, whatever—was held up for criticism and debate. Papa, as usual, was on Selma's side. Gardening was her livelihood, after all, and while he didn't disapprove of my mother's hobby, he thought she and Selma should do it together. But my mother was stubborn. This was *her* baby.

"It bothered me to see her dragging forty-pound bags of soil across the yard, so I bought a wheelbarrow, since Selma wouldn't provide one, and offered my help. My mother begged me to just let her be, so in the early mornings while she worked, I'd settle into one of the live oaks and keep an eye on her. I always had my sketchbook with me. One day she'd been going at it for a couple of hours when she took a break. Birds were preening themselves in the birdbath, and my mother sat on the ground and watched them intently, as if they could give her the meaning of life. She was wearing a pair of my old cutoffs. The waist was too big for her, and they slid down on her hips, but I was still a scrawny boy, so they hugged her ass. Her hair was pulled back in a ponytail, and she was wearing a white cotton tank top. She was soaking wet with sweat, which left little to the imagination, especially since she wasn't wearing a bra.

"So I was sitting there, watching her watch the birds, and I suddenly thought, *My God, she's as beautiful as a girl.* Mind you, girls held no appeal for me, so my admiration didn't have a trace of sexual awareness. I was looking at her with an artist's eye. I flipped open my sketchbook and drew her exactly as I saw her.

"A couple of weeks later, my aunts were here on a Sunday afternoon. I was sitting in the sunroom, talking to Fala, when Andi walked in with my mother. Andi picked up my sketchbook and started flipping through it, which pissed me off. She's so nosy. I stood up, intending to take it away from her, and that's when she got to the sketch of my mother. She sort of gasped and said, 'Ellan, have you seen this?'

"I stood there, feeling uncomfortable, although I wasn't sure why. My mother stared at the sketch, her eyes filled with tears, and she threw her arms around me, saying, 'Thank you, sugar, for seeing *me*.' She emphasized the *me*, and it made me feel good, like I'd done something right.

"Then Andi said, 'Ellan, this isn't healthy. A boy shouldn't be drawing his mother like she's some kind of femme fatale. It's inappropriate.'

"The next thing I knew, my mother had wrested the sketchbook from Andi's hands and was hitting her with it, screaming, 'You vile, evil woman! How like you to imply something so filthy!' It took Fala, me, and my grandfather to pull her off Andi, who was raging back at her. I don't even remember what all Andi said, but my mother ran out of the room crying, still holding the sketchbook. Andi said she needed to be medicated and told my grandfather that I should be sent away to school before my mother made me unfit for a *normal* life. Somehow Fala calmed them down, and the subject was dropped.

"The problem was, Mama didn't go back to the garden. She slept the summer mornings away, emerging well after lunch to sit with Odell in the kitchen and drink coffee. There were pots of flowers out there dying in the sun, everything was a mess, and I was racked with guilt. I'd ruined this thing that was giving her pleasure. I started going out by myself in the mornings and watering things or trying to plant them, hoping I could lure her outside. Make it right. Instead, one day after I came home after spending the night at Chad's, everything was gone, even the birdbath. It was never spoken of again.

"So you're wrong; I do see my mother as beautiful. But thanks to Andi, I learned not to put my opinion out there for the world's judgment."

"That's an awful story," Shanon said.

"Yeah? Well, stick around. I've got a million of them. Most of them begin and end with her irrational behavior." He watched Shanon as her face reddened and her mouth became a tight line. "If I'm pissing you off, tell me so."

"Your mother's not as crazy as you think."

"Don't explain her to me, okay? I've known her for twenty-three years. You've known her for twenty-three minutes."

"I'm not trying to explain her to you. You're the one who brought it up. An artist should have a better understanding of perspective. If you're painting her as crazy, you brush off everything she does as proof of that. I don't see her through your eyes. When something about her doesn't make sense to me, I just ask her."

"What doesn't make sense is the two of you," Phillip said. "It bothers me."

"I'm telling myself the reason you sound so selfish is because you're sick," Shanon said. "I have to leave."

"Going to work? I'll bet that's one thing you don't talk to her about," Phillip said. Shanon turned from the door and stared at him with hurt eyes. "I'm sorry. That was a bad attempt at a joke. Shanon, my mother can seem fine, then it changes in a second, and she does something that defies reason."

"Or she has reasons you don't know—like being Catholic. Try asking her. I did." She walked out.

Phillip's fist struck the mattress with such force it bounced, momentarily hovering in the air before he regained the strength to move his arm again to snatch the pillow from behind his head. He pummeled the pillow with his fists, feeling his anger flowing through him, exhausting him and making him sweat.

He was tired of everyone thinking they had all the answers. It was his life, not theirs—wasn't it? He knew why his mother had raised him Catholic. It was so he could get into a good parochial high school: a decision his grandfather had approved wholeheartedly, even if he didn't like the Catholic part. Like everything else, nobody had ever bothered to consider Phillip's feelings. He was expected to tolerate it, no questions asked, just like his mother's dramatic outbursts and delusions.

Phillip stopped punching the pillow and laughed bitterly while considering the story he'd just told Shanon. Like his aunts, she'd overlooked him in that story and focused only on his mother. It had been *his* sketch that started the whole incident, after all. He'd had to help pry his own mother off his aunt. He'd felt like it was his fault, and nobody had even asked if he was okay. It had been like that for years.

He looked down and realized his hands were clenched around the center of the pillow, twisting it. The door opened and he looked up hopefully, then saw his mother and audibly sighed. "What?"

"What did you say to Shanon?" Ellan asked.

"Why?"

"Because she looked angry and barely said two words before she left." Ellan looked at the pillow in Phillip's hands. "Don't think the symbolism of that pillow is lost on me."

Phillip laughed derisively and said, "Believe me, I don't." He tossed the pillow back to the head of the bed and fell back on it. "It's not going to work, Mother. I don't know what you're planning for Shanon, but just lay off. Okay?"

Ellan pinched the bridge of her nose and said, "Does your son give you pounding headaches?"

"Stop it," Phillip said in a low voice.

"Tension headaches are caused by stress," Ellan said, staring at the window. "Advil relieves tension headaches. That's why I take Advil when my son comes to visit."

"Too bad Advil won't make your son straight, isn't it?" Phillip said sharply. Ellan froze, her mouth hanging open. "If you're planning on Shanon becoming your daughter-in-law, I'd give up that little delusion if I were you."

"Phillip—"

"What happened to sugar?"

"You're not exactly being sweet," his mother replied, folding her arms.

"No. I'm being real. I think it's about time."

"Really?"

"Yes," Phillip said. He waited for her to fly off the handle, start screaming, or launch into more advertising jingles. Anything to signal that things were back to normal, whatever that was.

But Ellan stood still, staring, then simply shrugged and left the room.

Phillip's tears left cool trails on his hot cheeks. He stared at the ceiling, not wanting to admit that it was Chad he'd hoped to see in his room, not Shanon, and certainly not his mother. Once again, he felt bitterly disappointed and let down. He'd been feeling it for years; for so long that it was a part of him, like the color of his eyes or his talent for painting.

When they were seventeen and driving to the Daytona 500, Chad told him that he'd been accepted to the University of Texas. Phillip was dumbstruck, since they'd talked about going to the same college. Phillip had been accepted to Texas A&M, the University of Alabama, and—like Chad—USM in Hattiesburg. Phillip had assumed they'd both to go to USM. His uncle and aunt taught there, and he already loved the college, but Chad thought Taryn would make him live at home if he went to USM.

"Hattiesburg is too close to the Pass, man," Chad said. "Besides, UT is offering me a full ride. I can't pass that up."

"Right," Phillip said, sliding down in his seat and resting his knees on the dashboard of Chad's Mustang. He glanced at Chad's hands on the steering wheel, then reached into his pocket for his cigarettes. "Maybe there's still time for me to apply to UT."

"Maybe," Chad said. Phillip eyed him coolly, searching his face for clues. "Austin and College Station are pretty close. If you went to Texas A&M, we could still hang out on the weekends, or yeah, I guess you could apply for late admission to UT. No college is going to turn down Exton Godbee's grandson."

"Right," Phillip said again. He wasn't sure he should move too far away from his mother. Her behavior had only gotten stranger during his senior year. He was afraid it was because she couldn't cope with his moving away.

By the time they got to the track in Daytona, they'd agreed to shelve the topic. They parked the car and managed to get admission to the infield, which was party central and packed with RVs, vans, and campers full of half-crazed NASCAR fans. Nobody cared that they were underage. Women thought they were adorable, men were constantly opening their coolers to them, and girls flirted with them.

"We are so gonna get laid this weekend," Chad said. He threw all his energy into finding a girl.

Phillip didn't care about that. He'd long ago decided that his fucked-up family was the reason he wasn't as obsessed with sex as every other boy his age. What Phillip wanted was to get so numb that he could forget for a few days who he was and where he came from. He threw his energy into getting drunk and staying that way.

By their second night there, Chad had been working on a pair of girls who were at the races with their parents. They'd come in two RVs, and the parents put the girls in one while they partied to unconsciousness in the other.

Around midnight, the two couples left Tent City after a prolonged make-out session, and the girls sneaked Chad and Phillip into the RV. They locked the doors, kept only one dim light on, passed a joint around, and did tequila shots.

The girls had been sharing a queen-size bed, and all four of them ended up there, piling a mountain of pillows between them. Phillip could hear that things were progressing well for Chad and Cheryl. He wasn't having as much luck with Brandi. His senses were dulled by alcohol, and Brandi got impatient with him while she listened to her friend getting lucky. She finally rolled him onto his back and straddled him so she could look over the pillows.

Phillip closed his eyes and tried to concentrate. When he heard Chad moan with pleasure, his cock finally came to life—to his relief as well as Brandi's. Brandi figured things out before he did. She slyly moved pillows aside one by one, then nudged Phillip's head so that he was facing Chad and Cheryl. He opened his eyes, too drunk to care that he was watching his best friend have sex. When Chad saw that Brandi and Phillip were looking, he didn't seem to care either. He gave Phillip a stupid grin. Ultimately, all four of them started pushing the pillows aside and getting tangled up with each other. Phillip and Brandi came at the same time, with Phillip's hand gripping Chad's arm so tightly that he bruised it. Cheryl was next, then Chad gave them a big finish.

All four of them passed out. Phillip awoke first, with the beginnings of a killer hangover. He managed to wake Chad without rousing the girls, and the two of them dressed and sneaked out of the RV just before daybreak.

"I'm still drunk," Chad said.

"Me too. Let's get the hell out of here before somebody sees us."

Somehow they managed to stagger from the infield to Chad's Mustang, where they argued for a while about whether to leave or stay and watch the race.

"I can't stand any more of that fucking noise," Phillip pleaded. "Let's just get away from here. We don't have to drive home. We can go to the beach."

"I don't have enough money left," Chad mumbled.

"I've got my emergency credit card," Phillip said. "This is an emergency. I'm too tired and fucked up to drive far."

Chad finally agreed just to shut Phillip up. Phillip knew he shouldn't be driving, but he desperately wanted to get out of there. Chad slept in the passenger seat, and Phillip drove north on 95, stopping at every cheap motel he saw. Because it was race week, he couldn't find a room until he got to Jacksonville. By then, he felt like he was dying, but he managed to call home and make up some lie about having to wait until the next morning to get Chad's carburetor fixed. He wasn't even sure what a carburetor was, but his grandfather seemed to buy Phillip's story. Phillip then managed to get a very fucked-up Chad into the motel room, and they both passed out on the king-size bed.

When he woke up, completely sober, the room was dark except for a light from the bathroom, and he was freezing. He moved closer to Chad, seeking warmth, and suddenly felt Chad turn his head. Phillip opened his eyes and saw Chad looking at him.

"You're always so sad," Chad murmured. Phillip didn't understand until he realized a tear was sliding down his face. He didn't know why he was crying. He felt scared of what he was feeling—alone, abandoned, angry—and worse, he wanted to kiss his best friend. He inhaled sharply with surprise when Chad raised his hand from under the covers to wipe the tear from Phillip's face with his thumb. He brushed the same thumb lightly over Phillip's lips, then moved forward and kissed Phillip's cheek, saying, "You're gonna be fine."

Phillip couldn't remember who kissed whom first, but it was amazing to kiss Chad and feel a hard body against his. The only reason he could quit kissing him was because he wanted to taste all of him. He kept waiting for Chad to stop him, but Chad was as into it as he was. Nothing Phillip had ever done by himself—and certainly not his experience with Brandi—prepared him for the incredible rush of getting blown by Chad. He lost track of how many hours passed, or how many times they both came, before he finally fell asleep again.

When he woke up, he was alone. It freaked him out until he found Chad's note.

> *I've got to get something to eat. I'll bring food for you. There's ice on the desk. Drink water. I think we're both dehydrated.*

Phillip had to turn on the TV to find out what day it was and make sure they'd only stayed there one night. By the time Chad got back, he'd drunk several glasses of water and taken a shower. When he heard the door to the room open, he stepped out with a towel around his waist. "Feel better?"

"Hell, yeah," Chad said. "I just needed food. I brought breakfast for you."

"Thanks," Phillip said, wondering if Chad was avoiding his eyes.

"God, this was so extreme," Chad said.

Phillip's anxiety evaporated and he said, "Last night? It was—"

"It wasn't last night," Chad said with a laugh. "We did those chicks two nights ago. How the hell did we get here? The last thing I remember is passing out with…"

"Cheryl," Phillip said. "Would you mind bringing me some clean clothes from the car?"

"No problem," Chad said.

Phillip knew Chad was lying. There was no way in hell he hadn't been fully aware of what they'd done the night before. Maybe he was just nervous about how Phillip was going to react. Phillip decided to give him some space. They still had hours ahead of them in the car. As Chad relaxed, Phillip was sure they'd end up talking about it.

He ate his breakfast, then they hit the road. Chad found a station he liked and kept the radio loud. Phillip endured it a while before he turned it down and said, "About the college thing."

"I don't want to argue about that again," Chad said. "You do what you have to do."

"Okay," Phillip said, feeling his stomach lurch and hoping he wouldn't throw up. "What should we talk about?"

"I'd rather crash," Chad said. "If you're okay to drive. I'm dead. Mind if I pull over so we can switch?"

"No problem," Phillip said. Even after he took the wheel and Chad was passed out in the passenger seat, he knew Chad was still driving.

Nothing that happened later was a surprise to him. He'd predicted it all on that long, silent ride home. Chad was busy with school. Student council. Planning prom. He accepted the UT offer. He returned Phillip's calls, but he was always in a hurry. They'd get together in a few days. Next week. Or two weeks. Or never.

Phillip had been sick with misery and regret. He couldn't sleep. He didn't care about school. He listened to his grandfather's plans for him with disinterest. He thought he might be having a nervous breakdown.

And he avoided his mother, who always seemed to be watching him, waiting for something. One night he was lying in bed, reliving everything that had happened, when she came in and shut the door behind her, then turned on the light.

"No more," she said.

"What?" he asked. "What's wrong? Are you sick?"

She sat on the bed and said, "Tell me the truth—all of it. If you tell me one lie, I'll know. Just let it out."

He didn't know where his rage came from, but he directed it at her, knowing the one thing he couldn't do was tell her the truth. He detailed all the ways she'd fucked him up since he was born. He said things he didn't even know he thought and wasn't sure he believed. She listened to it all without reacting.

When he finally wound down, horrified by the things he'd said, she stared at him for a few minutes before saying, "That wasn't what I expected. Do you feel better?"

"No."

"Sugar, everybody hates their parents. You're going to think about this conversation a million times in the future and have a lot of feelings about it. When you do, I want you to remember one thing: You're the best thing that ever happened to me."

Phillip wiped his face on his pillow, remembering how much he'd needed to believe his mother then and how much he longed to believe it now. Although he'd wanted to, he'd never come out to his mother, never told her about what happened in Daytona. He'd told himself that it would be too much for her to handle, push her farther over the edge. After he went to New York, he assumed that Florence would take care of it for him.

He rolled over in the bed, thinking about what he'd just said to her. He was barely breathing, listening for chaos, but the house was quiet. He wanted to be worried, but he didn't care anymore. So what if she kicked him out? He'd been on his own before. If Shanon wanted to evict him, he'd land on his feet somehow. There were any number of options available to him.

He realized that his hand was wrapped around his penis, which was thickening and becoming hard. He closed his eyes, remembering Chad's hands running through his hair while Phillip blew him in Daytona. As he slowly stroked himself, he thought about Chad's lips, chest, legs, and ass. Chad's face turned into Claude's, and then it was Claude kissing him, begging Phillip to put on a condom, begging Phillip to fuck him.

Phillip's hand moved faster and he threw off the covers. He bit his lip, remembering Claude's penchant for nipple play. After a session with Claude, Phillip's nipples felt bruised for days. Kieran was more gentle and liked to run his tongue lightly over Phillip's nipple and blow on it lightly, teasingly. Thinking about Kieran made Phillip moan. He remembered Kieran's lips on his ear, describing everything he was feeling in detail, coaxing him, cheering him on.

Phillip's orgasm was intense, and he didn't care about being silent. His head pushed into the pillow and one hand grabbed the edge of the mattress, sweat running off his forehead and into his eyes. He lay panting for a few minutes, then pulled off his T-shirt to wipe off his stomach and cock.

He'd just pulled the sheet over himself when there was a knock on the door and Odell poked her head in, asking, "You okay, Phillip?" She stepped into the room. "I heard moaning. Look at you. You're soaked. I think your fever's broken."

"Yeah, I think so. I'm feeling much better, thank you."

"I've got my chicken soup simmering on the stove," Odell said. "I'll bring you some."

"That's okay, Odell," Phillip said. "I'm really not that hungry."

"You're awake. You're sick. You should eat," she said, and before he could protest again, she went through the door, leaving it open.

Phillip lay back on the pillow. Kieran's face was still fresh in his memory. He recalled the way Kieran would light his cigarettes for him and smiled. But his smile faltered and the memory faded when he heard Odell holler, "Mercy! What's that doing in here?"

He pulled the sheet tightly around himself and hurried down to the kitchen, saying, "Odell? Are you okay?"

"I'm fine. But now there are two things that don't belong in my kitchen. You in a sheet, and that thing," she said, pointing to the Rothko, which was hanging from the pulls of the cabinets.

"Mother strikes again," Phillip muttered.

Chapter 16

Oddly enough, it was Phillip's grandfather who gave him the incentive to get out of bed and try to get his life back, although probably not in the way that the old man had intended. Phillip was in his room sketching late one night when Fala tapped on the door. She held out the phone, whispering, "It's Daddy. He wants to talk to you."

He took the phone and waited until she was gone before he said, "Hi, Papa. Are you still in China?"

"Where else?" Papa barked. Then he softened his tone when he said, "I hear you've been having a rough time."

"I'm okay," Phillip said.

"I've talked to Selma. What the hell were you doing working for her?"

"A good job," Phillip said. "At least that's what my boss said."

"You're supposed to be taking care of your mother. Wasn't that our deal?"

Phillip kept himself from spitting out a rude answer. After his last altercation with his mother, he'd decided that the only way to get through this ordeal was to revert to his best manners.

His grandfather apparently got tired of waiting and said, "A messenger from Godbee will bring you a check tomorrow. It should cover any expenses you have. I don't want you going back to that job."

"Is that because you're worried about my health or so I'll supervise Mother?" Phillip asked.

"I think I've already made that clear. It's not like you get nothing from the arrangement. You wanted to paint. I'm making it possible."

The line went dead. Phillip stared at the phone a few seconds, then gently placed it on his nightstand and picked up his sketchbook.

The next morning he got up, showered and dressed, and went downstairs. Odell grinned when she saw him and said, "Feeling better?"

"Could you make me breakfast?" he asked. "Biscuits and grits?"

"That's what I like to hear."

While she cooked, she talked about her two sons. She spared him any commentary on how successful they were at Godbee Energy, instead telling him about their wives and the grandchildren they'd given her. It was comforting to hear that her family, like Florence's, seemed to have emerged from Godbee drama and madness to have placid, happy lives.

He intended to do the same. Once his check arrived, he left his mother a note thanking her for taking care of him, hugged Odell goodbye, and drove the Volvo to Ocean Springs. It surprised him how weak just that little effort left him, so he went right to bed, grateful for the cool room provided by the new central air.

He was aware that Shanon came upstairs during the night to check on him, but the next morning the house was quiet and empty. He felt like something was different, but he couldn't put his finger on it.

After making coffee, he sat at his computer, automatically reaching for a cigarette while he listened to the comforting sound of his modem dialing up. He lit the Marlboro, coughed, stared at it, and put it out, realizing that he'd gone nearly three weeks without smoking. He wasn't committed to quitting, but he thought it might be a good idea to give his lungs more time to heal.

It took him two hours to read and answer all his e-mail—letting everyone know he was back and feeling better, thanking them for their cards, and encouraging them to call, since he intended to spend the rest of summer painting in his lonely garret. As soon as he signed off, his phone rang.

"Hey, young'un."

"Hey, Dash. You got my e-mail?"

"Yep. Welcome back to the land of the living. I was worried about you."

"What's going on with you?" Phillip asked. "Divert me from my new health obsession, please."

Dash provided a raunchy account of a trip he'd made to New Orleans and told him that Dennis was officially separated from the Navy and living in a Biloxi apartment. Phillip wondered if Jay knew, but of course he couldn't ask Dash that. As soon as he was feeling better, he'd drop into Stone Love to find out if Jay was still with that loser Travis.

"It'll be a while before you go back to the landscaping business, huh?"

"If ever," Phillip said. "I really want to focus on my art. Plus, I can't believe how weak I am. It's ridiculous."

"Probably from being bedridden as much as from pneumonia," Dash said. "You know, my house is empty all day, unless the housekeeper's there. Why don't I drop off a key for you? Swimming's an easy way to build yourself back up."

"Thanks," Phillip said, touched by the offer.

After they hung up, Phillip frowned, realizing that he hadn't heard from Bunny the whole time he'd been sick. Nor had he received the promised box of hand-me-downs. Carlos hadn't mentioned him either. Bunny was always too busy to talk at work, so Phillip dialed his home number and left a message.

He stripped to his shorts and sat on the deck for a while, ruing the loss of his tan. A little time in the sun every day might help him get rid of his sickroom pallor until he could start swimming at Dash's.

The heat finally drove him back inside, where he poured a tall glass of water and studied his painting of the Whittier house. He'd thought it was unfinished, but now that the paint was dry, he liked the soft edges that he'd intended to fill in later. He took a deep breath, mixed some pigment, and with a small brush delicately painted POWELL in the corner.

He wasn't sure yet what he wanted to do with the painting. He would definitely take it by the work site so the men who'd provided its flowers, budding trees, and lush lawns could see it. After that, he might make a gift of it to Mr. and Mrs. Banks, who owned Whittier Plantation. That way everyone who took a home tour would see it, and the Bankses might even use it to make souvenir postcards.

"Are you awake?" Jess called. "May I come up?"

"Yes," Phillip said, grinning as her head appeared over the half wall.

"I'm *so* glad you're here," Jess said. "I missed you." Then she shocked him by covering her face with her hands and sobbing. He gently propelled her to the table and made her sit down. When she stopped crying, he grabbed some McDonald's napkins so she could blow her nose. At least they made her smile. "Classy," she said.

"That's me. A class act."

"You are," she agreed, dabbing at her face.

"Are these tears of joy because I didn't die of pneumonia?" he asked, opening a Barq's root beer—her favorite—and sliding it across the table to her before he sat down.

"Julianna's gone," she said.

"Gone..."

"Moved—lock, stock, and head shot. Left nothing but nail holes in the walls."

"When did this happen?"

"About a week ago." He waited for a fresh flood of tears to subside. "I blame that stupid margarita night we had."

"Why? What happened? Did you have a fight?"

"No. I think talking about that woman from the Atlanta modeling agency made her miss her old life."

"She's gone back to pageants? Or she wants to model?"

"Who knows? The thing is, she called the woman, who remembered her. I guess they started talking on the phone a lot. Then they met in Mobile. Julianna slept with her! She cheated on me! Then she dumped me. She moved to Atlanta."

"I'm sorry," Phillip said, trying to sound like he meant it. He'd always agreed with Shanon that Jess was too good for Julianna. But that wasn't the kind of thing you could say to someone with a broken heart.

"I'm never dating anyone younger than me again. People in their early twenties are self-absorbed brats."

"Can we talk about me?" Phillip asked.

She looked stunned for a few seconds, then she burst out laughing. "Sorry. You are light-years away from Julianna."

"I can't believe she didn't even say goodbye—leave me a Miss Possum Holler sash or something. I guess I'll have to go downstairs and touch those nail holes to get closure."

"You can't. I already filled them." She blew her nose. "Shanon wants me to move in. I told her I'd have to ask you first."

"If it won't bother you to be in Julianna's old bedroom, I'm all for it," Phillip assured her.

"I felt so guilty when you got sick."

"Why?"

"It happened after you went to Singing River all those nights. Maybe you picked up a bug there."

"That's ridiculous," he said. "I didn't pick up *anything* there, but I still love the casino."

"Don't love it too much," she warned. "At least while you're not working." She stood up. "Okay. I guess I'll start packing my stuff. Thanks for letting me move in."

"No sweat." He hugged her and managed to wait until she was down the stairs and had closed the door behind her before he did a little celebratory dance. It sucked that she'd been hurt, but he didn't feel a bit of regret that Julianna was out of their lives.

He took the Whittier house canvas off his easel and put an empty one in its place. He stared at it a while, then closed his eyes, thinking of a photograph of Taryn in the desert that he'd seen long ago. He lost himself, feeling the dry wind on his face and waves of heat rising from cracked sand. When he opened his eyes and stared at the canvas, all he could see were the warm tones of Evita's skin, his glossy black hair, deep-brown eyes, and gleaming white smile. He let the colors mix and swirl in his mind, hit the CD button on his computer, and reached for his palette and some tubes of pigment.

When U2 blared from his speakers, he looked back at the canvas and saw Kieran.

"No," he moaned. "Southwestern, not Irish." It was too late. The canvas was imprinted as indelibly as the Shroud of Turin.

He surrendered and spent the next few days painting Kieran between bouts of sleeping and eating soup or oatmeal. Whenever he lost his light, he sat at his computer, either reading e-mail or playing endless games of solitaire. He left three more messages on Bunny's machine, warning him that if he'd taken that trip to Ibiza without him, he'd be sorry. Shanon was never home until late at night, after Phillip had gone to bed, and Jess wasn't moved in and was rarely there, so he usually didn't bother to get dressed unless he went outside to get the mail.

He sat at the kitchen table one afternoon to read a letter from Claude, which left him contemplative.

Blossom,

Brace yourself. I'm feeling nostalgic, and I've been thinking about the Irishman. You've told me a lot more than you think you have.

I've decided that Kieran and I are the bookends for your life in New York. I don't know all the chapters in between, and I'm not sure the story's over, but I figured I'd give you my thoughts on the beginning.

Do you remember when we met? I thought you were about the sweetest thing I'd ever seen, and I knew I had to get me some of that. I liked the way things started for us. The sex—that goes without saying. It worked. Living in the same building, getting together when we were in the mood. You never spent the night or made boyfriend noises. I never went to your place because that was when you were just getting to know Alyssa, and you didn't want to inflict our rampant gayness on her. There were times that I wondered if maybe we were heading toward more. If you recall, there were even a couple of occasions when I tried to get you to fall asleep in my bed, but you were having none of it. I told myself: The boy is eighteen. This wanton city is all new to him, and he needs to enjoy every second of it unencumbered.

One night I suggested staying at your place, thinking maybe you just couldn't sleep in a strange bed. You turned me down, and I was baffled. "What is it you DO in bed," I asked. "I read before I fall asleep," you said. "I can sleep with the light on," I answered. "I read ART books," you said. "They take up half the bed. I need space." I don't think you ever knew why that made me laugh so hard. The vision of you in bed, all owlish, was so different from the action I thought your mattress was getting.

Eventually, as happens, our sex tapered off. You didn't want to fuck me anymore—just draw me. That was fine. Having you as a friend was as gratifying, in a different way, as having you for a lover. Those were good times, and I welcomed all of them.

I guess we went through two or three birthdays together, and it finally penetrated my lazy brain that nothing much really changed for you in the romance department. Men and boys came and went, but your heart stayed right where it was: locked up in your chest. We never talked about your sexual past, but I knew there was something back there that fucked you up. No surprise, really. Again, I'd remind myself that even though you were smart and clever, and in spite of the experiences you were racking up, you were young. I admired you for learning to be Phillip before you tried to be half of someone else's life.

After I moved away, I found out that you were just as engrossing as a letter writer. I got a real sense of your life without being there to see it. The sketches helped too. Enter Eddie. Unlike other men, he wasn't a passing thing. You told me a lot about the stuff you and Eddie did. Things Eddie said. Ways Eddie was trying to make you be more responsible. But you never told me that you loved Eddie. You never said that he was the one. There didn't seem to be a lot of YOU in you and Eddie. I have to tell you, I didn't like old Eddie much.

You wrote me a letter one night when you were pissed off. I think Eddie was annoyed because you and Alyssa went to see an exhibit on a night that Eddie wanted you to go to a work party with him. You probably don't even remember it, but you said what I'd been expecting to hear: something along the lines of, "I'm tired of feeling guilty because I never measure up to Eddie's expectations. I don't have the right job. I don't know the right people. I don't make enough money. I don't like his friends. I don't want to move in with him. I can't even spend the night; how could I live there?"

I knew the relationship was doomed—even more so when Alyssa moved away. She was the one who met your need for intimacy. Eddie was a man, and he could appease your sexual hunger, but once Alyssa was gone, you'd see all the ways he didn't satisfy the needs of your heart. You'd never cry in Eddie's company. You'd never sleep in Eddie's arms. You'd never tell him your deepest secrets in the dark of night. Any more than you did those things with me.

You see where I'm going with this, don't you? The other bookend. Phillip, I don't care how things ended with you and Kieran, and maybe you'll never see him again. But what you had with him—those things you never had with any other man—don't write those off too quickly. Don't close yourself off again. You're not so young any-

more. I don't mean that like, "Hey, grab it because it may be your last chance." I mean that you need to see that something in you has changed. You're ready for someone beyond Eddie, or tricks, or Dash. As someone who loves you, I hope that when the right man comes along, you'll remember the depth and trust you shared with Kieran, and let that man feed your hungry heart.

Love and hope that I didn't offend,
Claude, Guru of Ghosts

When Jess walked in, dressed for work, Phillip said, "Do you think sometimes our friends know us better than we know ourselves?"

"Probably a lot of times," Jess said, looking at the letter in his hand. "Did someone tell you something you didn't want to hear?"

"No. I'm starting to think that we should let our friends pick our lovers though. Maybe that would work out better for us."

"Would you have picked Julianna for me?"

"Ask me that in a few months," Phillip said.

"I already know the answer. I swear, I'm never falling in love again. In fact, I don't even want to look. The next woman who wants me will have to show up at my door, because—" She broke off, staring out the window with a frown. "That was fast."

Phillip stood up to see what she was looking at. "Oh, fuck. Trust me, she's not right for you. Please hide me."

"Who is she?" Jess asked as the doorbell rang.

"Her name's Linda. She thinks she's going to be my first girlfriend."

"Ew," Jess said, turning to go answer the door.

"Tell her I'm not here!" Phillip hissed.

He cowered in the kitchen, hoping Jess believed that the last thing in the world he wanted was to see Linda Bishop. When she came back, she looked out the window and said, "You're safe. She's driving away." She tossed a manila envelope on the table. "She left you this."

Phillip opened it and pulled out a packet of papers. "Oh, for God's sake. Or somebody's sake."

Jess started reading titles aloud as he passed the pamphlets to her. "'*You Don't Have to Stay Gay.*' '*Stories of Ex-Gays Give Hope.*' '*God Loves You, and So Do We!*' '*Change Yourself, Not Marriage Laws!*' '*Former Homosexuals Offer God-Inspired Solutions: Let Our Lord Cure You.*'" She looked at him. "Is this shit for real?"

"Don't be so cynical," Phillip said. "After all, God made Adam and—"

"Shut up, Anita," she said, pinching his arm.

"Ouch!"

"Smart off at me again, and next time I let 'Linda With an Agenda' see you."

"She's just a hapless tool. It's really my Aunt Andi who's trying to change me." He frowned. "I wonder if there's a way to calm her down?"

"Tranquilizer dart?"

"That might work, but it's temporary."

"Does Linda have a brother? You could ask for his number."

"She does have a brother, but I think he got married and moved to Vicksburg."

Jess sighed and stretched her arms. "I have to go to work," she said. "I'll lock the door behind me so you'll be safe in case any Mormons show up."

"Thanks," he said and took Claude's letter upstairs. He stared at Kieran a minute, then searched the room for his phone book.

The next day, he did all he could to make himself look like the picture of health and went to Pass Christian, driving past his grandfather's house on Scenic Drive to turn into a blindingly white Mediterranean villa. The doorbell resounded through the cavernous house, and he was about to think he'd been stood up when the door opened.

"My word, look at you. All grown up," Paula Bishop said, pulling him into an embrace. "Are you feeling better?"

"Is nothing private?" Phillip asked.

"Not here, honey. Come on in. I just started a pot of coffee for us. Do you drink coffee?"

"I'm surprised you don't know how I take it," Phillip said, checking her out as they walked into the kitchen.

Paula was the same age as his mother, forty-three, but beyond that, the resemblance ended. Too many years on the water had aged Paula. Like his mother, she'd kept her hair long, but hers had been bleached so often that it looked coarse. She was wearing a pair of white jeans and a T-shirt that was emblazoned *Pass Christian Yacht Club.* Her figure was still, as Chad might have said, bangin'. Her feet were bare and her toenails were painted a shocking pink, just like her fingernails. She looked like an aging starlet.

After Paula poured their coffee, she sat at the table across from him and said, "As much as I'd like to think this is a social call, I have a feeling it has something to do with my daughter." She reached into a cigarette case and took out a joint. "Mind if I light up? It takes the edge off Linda turmoil."

"Be my guest," he said, trying to imagine his mother getting high and talking about their troublesome offspring with Paula. "Those rolling papers match your fingernails."

"We have to be stylish or die trying," Paula said when she allowed herself to exhale. "I'd offer you a hit, but I don't want to drive you back to your sickbed. So…Linda. Do you know about my divorce?"

"No, ma'am."

"Don't call me ma'am, okay? I'm clinging to my youth. When Buddy left me for a girl who's younger than Linda, it sent our daughter into a tailspin. Probably my fault as much as Buddy's." There wasn't a wisp of guilt in her expression. "I was furious, Phillip, and I took that bastard to the cleaners. I got the house—even though it was *his* parents' house—the boat, and a good portion of his monthly income. It was one of the most bitter divorces the Redneck Riviera has ever seen. I thought Linda was old enough not to get caught up in it, but I was wrong."

She sighed and finished the joint. Phillip glanced up as a woman in a gray uniform came into the kitchen. She didn't even blink at the sight of her employer smoking pot with a man half her age.

"Maria, hon, go take a load off in the den, okay? I'm entertaining." When the housekeeper left, Paula said, "Did you know your mother was my best friend in school?"

"No," Phillip said.

"Life screwed us. Ellan and I were sandwiched between two generations. We missed out on the whole hippie thing, and we were just ahead of the cocaine and consumption decade. I guess we were supposed to be part of women's lib, but that would have required more backbone than we had. Ellan and I were virtuous girls. We did everything by the book. Good grades. Intact virginity.

"Exton intended for Ellan to go northeast to college. I don't know what my parents wanted for me, but I strayed from the program one time, just *once*, and found myself married and pregnant with Brooks at eighteen. Ellan was the only girl in our group who didn't snub me. When she found out I was pregnant, she bought me a three-piece christening layette. I loved that girl. She also invited Buddy and me to her graduation party when everyone else was treating us like pariahs.

"That's where fate stepped in. Exton had sent some of his men to put up a party tent on the Godbee lawn. I don't know if my situation influenced her, but I do know she took one look at Mike Powell, and that was it. All she wanted in the world was to marry that man. It's to your grandfather's credit that he didn't fight her. Or maybe he knew he couldn't win."

Phillip was riveted and said, "Tell me about my father."

"He was hot," Paula said. "He wasn't tall, but he had some shoulders on him—and a gorgeous ass. Sexy as hell. He was also funny. He could have had any woman he wanted. Including the daughter of his boss. Those two were crazy in love. Buddy and I didn't see them often after they moved to New Orleans. Then Ellan and I got pregnant at the same time, with you and Linda, and she called me like clockwork every other Sunday night so we could compare stories. Sunday was her lonely night, because that's when Mike went back out to his rig. After you were born, the calls weren't as regular. You can't imagine how busy new mothers are. But sometimes when she was back at the Pass, she'd visit, and we'd make up a future for you and Linda while you played together as toddlers.

"After Mike's accident, she brought you home. They couldn't do anything with her for those two weeks while they looked for his body. When they found him, something just died in her."

Paula paused, and tears spilled from her eyes.

"Your mother called and asked me to come over. It was the last time I ever saw Ellan cry. 'Remember that layette I gave you?' she asked. When I told her yes, she said, 'Buy my boy a suit for his father's funeral, Paula. You're the only one I trust.' After that, the Ellan I knew was gone. She held it together for a few years, until you were already in school. Maybe first or second grade? Then I think she had a breakdown. They should have gotten her help, but I guess Exton thought those things were best kept inside the family."

She unrolled a linen napkin from a ring and patted her cheeks, then handed it to him to do the same.

"I didn't mean to upset you. I don't know why I'm telling you all this anyway. You want to know about Linda. I did my duty. I raised my children and tried to be the perfect wife to Buddy. The kids grew up, and I was bored shitless. I got a tummy tuck and an eye lift. Then the bastard left me for that child. I stopped being a good girl." One long fingernail toyed with the roach in the ashtray. "I used to grow great orchids in my greenhouse. Now I grow marijuana."

"To take the edge off," Phillip said.

"I figure, why not? I raise a good crop too," she said with a grin. "Your friend Chad Cunningham buys from me. There's nothing like sitting down on a breezy day and having a joint with Chad. He keeps me apprised of what's going on. That's how I knew you'd been sick—and about you and Linda."

"There is no me and Linda," Phillip said, "in spite of whatever future you and my mother planned for us."

"Linda was a mess during the divorce. What Buddy and I did devastated her, and she won't have anything to do with either of us now. She hates him for marrying that infant. She hates me for going after him with such a vengeance. I should have been paying attention, but since I wasn't, she was ripe picking for that cult your aunt calls a church. Andi with her tidy little life: Linda took to that like white on rice. She doesn't want any more mess, and she's decided that pleasing God—or maybe pleasing Andi—will bring order to her life. She's got the zeal of a missionary. I did hope maybe a boy would come along and snap her out of it. Trust her to let Andi pick one who'd be more attracted to my son."

"How is Brooks?" Phillip asked.

"Sane, thank goodness, unlike Linda."

"Or my mother."

"Don't you believe it." She narrowed her eyes at him. "Pardon me for insulting your family, but don't let that sour old bitch Andi or your Aunt Selma make you judge your mother. They've got their secrets too."

"I know."

"Fala is sweet, but she's a little dizzy. I think the best thing that happened to Ellan in a long time was Florence coming home. Florence and Sam are like the fulfillment of the dreams Ellan had for herself with Mike. Florence is a capable woman, but she turns to Ellan for advice about her girls. That makes Ellan feel needed. I still love her. I always will. She's got the same good heart she had when we were eighteen. Two lovely people made you, Phillip. They're worth a dozen of me."

"I don't think so," Phillip said.

"Now see? You get that kindness from her." She sighed again. "Don't you know any boys as appealing as you to throw at Linda?"

"They'd all rather have Brooks too," Phillip said. "I'm not sure what I expected you to do about Linda, but I guess I at least understand the situation now. Thanks for explaining."

Paula followed him to the door and hugged him again before he left. He'd started down the walk when she called his name. He turned around.

"Your mother's got the same problem as me. We're just two good girls who ended up lonely in these big, empty mansions. It wasn't supposed to turn out this way. We want more for our babies."

Phillip nodded thoughtfully and went to his car.

When he got to Godbee Lane, he stopped the car and stared at the house, thinking of his mother and Paula. He felt guilty when it struck him that in some ways Shanon was the lucky one. She didn't have to carry all the baggage of her parents into adulthood. Even Chad wasn't exempt, although he didn't realize it. He would freak out if he knew that Taryn was a lesbian.

He remembered Taryn's words. *You look at your children when they're babies, and you imagine their future. You can map out a million different scenarios, but they'll always surprise you.*

And Paula's: *We want more for our babies.*

He thought of his mother's broken heart, which made him remember Claude's letter and his advice that Phillip not close himself off.

"Okay," he said. "I get it."

Chapter 17

Phillip signed his painting of Kieran and crossed the room to lie on his bed and stare at it. With any luck, he'd exorcised his Irish demon so he could move on to the painting he was supposed to do for Taryn.

"May I come up?" Shanon called. "Are you dressed?"

"Yes. And yes."

He saw her head come over the half wall, then she stopped, staring at the painting. "That's really good. You're a zillion times better than Lowell."

When she walked to the easel to study the painting, he watched her. Things hadn't been right between them since their argument at his grandfather's house. They were civil to each other, but something was off, and he wished he could fix it.

"What was all that banging I heard earlier? Is Jess tearing down the walls?" he asked.

Shanon kept staring at the painting and said, "No. I had new furniture delivered. Well, not new furniture. Antiques. I'm furnishing the other rooms on the second floor."

"What'd you get?"

"A couple of beds, a wardrobe, a rolltop desk. I'm still looking for stuff."

"I should take you to Hattiesburg and let you plunder Aunt Fala's attic." Her lack of an answer, and the way she kept her eyes fixed on the painting, were clear signals that she wasn't going to risk another argument by appearing too eager for more contact with his family. "I need your help," he said.

She turned around. "What's up?"

"There's this guy."

"I'm the last person to give you pointers on how to get a man," she said.

"No, Jess is probably the last person. But I'm not trying to get a man—not in the way you think. There's a beautiful boy named Jay that I want to paint. But he won't let me. He has an insecure boyfriend—Travis—who won't let Jay out of his sight. Travis would probably think it's all a ruse to get Jay into bed."

"Are you sure it's not?"

"He's tempting, but there are other considerations besides Travis. I only want him in my bedroom so I can paint him. I just don't know how to get around Travis."

"You have to befriend him," she said. "Make him know that you're safe."

"But I don't like Travis," he whined.

"Sometimes we have to do things we don't like to get what we want," Shanon said. "*That* I'm an expert on."

"Please don't make it sound like I have to do Travis," Phillip begged. He thought it over, then said, "Will you help me?"

"What is it you want me to do?"

"Give me a night of your time. Wednesday night. Hold on. Let me make a call." She sat on the bed while he dialed the number at Stone Love. When a woman answered the phone, he asked for Jay.

Shanon picked up a book on Keith Haring and flipped through it while he and Jay caught up. When Phillip got to the point of his call, she glanced up from the book to listen.

"Wednesday night, some friends and I are going to Singing River Casino," Phillip said. "I've got all these comps. I thought maybe you and Travis might like to go with us."

"That could be fun," Jay said. "I'll have to ask Travis, though."

"Why don't you call him, then call me back? Do you still have my number?"

"You better hope Travis doesn't," Shanon whispered.

"Yes. I'll call you back in a few minutes," Jay said.

When Phillip dropped the phone between them, Shanon said, "You're practically living at that casino. What's up with that?"

"Thanks to Jess, I can eat and drink for nothing there. Everything's free except gambling."

"Are you winning?"

"Breaking even," he lied, thinking how quickly his grandfather's money was dwindling. Not that it mattered. He'd saved nearly everything from his landscaping job to pay his rent, and if he needed more art supplies, he could get his stuff from Pass Christian. When the weather cooled off, he could always go back to work for Selma if he needed money.

"How do you think Jess is doing?" Shanon asked.

"She seems okay. She says her tips dipped for a while after Julianna left. I guess she was sort of moody. But lately she's been more upbeat."

"Probably because she's finally getting some rest," Shanon said. She noticed his curious expression. "Think about it; she's been doing three jobs. She worked on the house renovations and at the casino. Then when she got home, she had to cater to the whims and sexual demands of Julianna, the do-me princess."

"Too much information," Phillip said.

Shanon looked again at the painting. "Is that Kieran?"

The phone rang, and he grabbed it.

"Hey," Jay said. "Travis wants to know who else is going."

Phillip improvised, "My friend Chad. He has a couple of roommates, all straight. My roommate Shanon, maybe a few other friends."

"Okay, hold on."

Phillip listened to the hold music and shrugged at Shanon. "I guess he has Travis on the other line."

"Is that Enya I hear? Where does Jay work?"

"A New Age shop. Stone Love."

"Mitch shops there," she said. "I've never been."

Jay came back on. "Travis says okay. Should we just meet you there?"

"Yeah. Say nine o'clock? At the bar in Goat Castle?"

"See you there," Jay said.

Phillip hung up and said, "That was relatively painless."

"Do you need me to round up anyone else so it looks innocent?"

"It *is* innocent," Phillip swore. "I only want to paint him."

"I believe you," Shanon said, though she obviously didn't.

"Yes," he said.

"Yes?"

"That's Kieran."

"Is he as beautiful as you painted him, or is that just how you see him?"

"He might not be everyone's cup of tea, but I think how I see him and paint him is accurate."

"Lord," she said, then left him alone.

He crossed the room to the painting and took it off the easel, saying, "You're done. No, really. I have to get on with my life."

Crap, he thought. *I'm starting to act like my mother.*

He put an empty canvas on the easel and stared at it, but nothing happened, either Southwestern or Jay-like. He went back to the phone and called Chad at the paper. Chad was too busy to talk but agreed that he was game for a night of drinking and gambling and would try to round up a few other people.

After they hung up, Phillip briefly considered calling Dash. Then he remembered that Dash and Travis didn't get along. It was tempting to invite Dash anyway, but that would definitely be an impediment to winning Travis's trust.

Shanon was willing to go early Wednesday night, so they arrived at Singing River long before the others. Shanon, with more income at her disposal, headed for the blackjack tables. After getting a drink at the Goat Castle bar, Phillip sat at his favorite slot machine and began losing his grandfather's money. He glanced enviously at the machine next to him as coins clattered into its tray.

"Don't matter," his elderly neighbor said, a cigarette hanging from the corner of her mouth. "I'm down too much now to quit."

"Sounds like me and men," Phillip said without thinking.

She turned her face toward him, one inexpertly penciled eyebrow raised, and said, "Men? That's a gamble that never pays off, honey."

He nodded and turned his attention back to his machine, grateful that she hadn't started spouting Leviticus at him.

Getting occasional bonuses allowed him to keep playing, and when the woman next to him finally scooped her remaining coins into a cup and walked away, he reminded himself not to lose his sense of time. He'd found that playing the slots was just like playing solitaire on his computer; hours could pass before he knew it.

He glanced around. Shanon was sitting alone at a table close to the bar. He stood up then, on a whim, put three coins in the machine next to him and hit BET MAX and SPIN. As bells sounded and lights flashed, he stared dumbly at the machine.

"I'm right here," a floor attendant said from beside him. "I'll have to do a hand payout and fill out a tax form."

"How much did I win?" he asked.

She grinned and said, "Eight thousand."

"Crap." He looked frantically around and spotted his former neighbor at a distant slot machine. "I need to talk to that woman over there."

His attendant signaled to another, who tapped the woman on the shoulder. She looked at Phillip with confusion, and he motioned her over.

It took him a while to make her understand that he wanted to halve his payout with her. By the time Phillip had convinced her—and endured several grateful hugs, finished his paperwork, got his money, and tipped the two attendants—Shanon, Chad, Chad's roommate Pete, and a woman whom Phillip didn't know were all staring at him as he walked toward their table.

"I sort of won," he said humbly, still a little dazed.

"How do you sort of win?" Chad asked. "And why was that grandma hugging you?"

Phillip shrugged and said, "I guess she was happy for me." He didn't feel like explaining his generous impulse toward a crusty old Southern woman who didn't react in horror upon hearing that he was gay. "Hi, I'm Phillip," he said to the stranger at their table. "Drinks are on me."

She smiled and said, "I'm Melissa, and you can buy me drinks all night." Since she was sitting between Chad and Pete, Phillip wasn't sure whose date she was.

"I guess you're feeling better," Chad said.

"Much," Phillip said.

"Yeah, I heard you'd been sick," Pete said. "Pneumonia, right? Pneumocystis?"

Phillip felt a flush of anger, then realized by the blank expressions on everyone's faces that they didn't understand Pete's implication that since Phillip was gay he must have an HIV-related illness. His mother had been so much more tactful and respectful of his privacy. "No, it wasn't PCP. It was pneumococcal pneumonia."

"Ah," Pete said. "I see that more often in children. Penicillin?"

"Yes," Phillip said curtly.

"You finished your full dose, right?"

"Are you going to bill me for this consultation, Doc?" Phillip asked.

Before Pete could answer, Phillip heard a low voice behind him say, "Hey, Cop. Good to see you're still alive."

Phillip turned around, checked out the smile, and said, "Booty! What's up?"

"Me and Shawnee," Booty nodded toward a woman at the bar, "are out celebrating my twenty-first."

"By drinking and gambling?" Phillip asked, laughing. "You don't waste any time." He introduced everyone and explained that he'd worked with Booty and his twin at the nursery. "How's Goldie celebrating?"

"He's around here somewhere."

Shawnee came up with a drink for Booty. Phillip checked her out while Booty introduced her to everyone. She was a full-figured knockout, with braided extensions, long red fingernails, and what he was sure was a genuine Fendi handbag.

"Y'all want to join us?" Phillip asked.

"Sure," Booty said happily.

Shawnee frowned and said, "You can, baby, but I want to gamble."

"Did you touch the goat for luck?" Phillip asked as Booty took some bills from his wallet and handed them to Shawnee.

She looked askance at him and said, "That ratty-ass thing? It gives me the willies. Always staring with those glassy eyes."

"Aw, I love the goat," Melissa said with a pout.

"I ain't touching no dead goat," Shawnee said firmly. She got a kiss from Booty for luck and walked away.

"This your girlfriend?" Booty asked, looking from Shanon to Phillip as he sat down.

Phillip noticed that with the exception of Melissa, the others seemed to be holding their breath. "No, Booty. I'm gay."

Booty blinked a couple of times and said, "Gay? You?" When Phillip nodded he said, "Huh. So's my brother."

"Goldie?" Phillip asked, startled.

"Not Goldie. My other brother, Clarence. He's here too, wherever Goldie is."

"Is your brother single? Maybe you should introduce him to Phillip," Chad said with fake enthusiasm.

"Clarence won't date white men," Booty said. "He says they're fine alone, but when they go to bars, they pretend they're not with him."

"Phillip wouldn't do that, would you, Phillip?" Chad said.

"Phillip wishes you'd fuck off," Phillip said in the same falsely cheerful tone.

Except for Shanon and Chad, everyone laughed as if he was joking.

"I think we should order appetizers," Shanon said. "I'm hungry."

Pete waved for menus while Booty told a story about Phillip and the other men they worked with. The atmosphere settled into something approaching normal as the conversation flowed from one topic to another.

Phillip was wishing he'd brought his cigarettes and wondering if Jay and Travis were going to show up when Booty directed attention back at him by asking if he was planning to work for Selma again.

"I'm not sure," Phillip said.

"Maybe he's going to live off his gambling winnings," Melissa said, using her thumb to clean barbecue sauce from Chad's chin.

"Yes, I'm lucky," Phillip said.

"Thanks, Missy," Chad said, then looked at Phillip. "Maybe we should rub you instead of the goat."

"Yeah, maybe you should," Phillip said.

"Shawnee might go for that," Booty said.

"Unless she thought he was ratty-ass too," Chad said, taking a potato skin from Melissa's plate and laughing as she slapped his arm.

"Actually, Phillip's art is keeping him pretty busy these days," Shanon said.

Chad's head whipped toward Phillip and he said, "You're painting?"

"Yes."

"I had no idea."

"Did you finish the one you were doing of the Whittier house?" Booty asked.

"You've seen his work?" Chad asked, sounding jealous.

"Hi, Travis, Jay," Phillip said brightly as the two men walked up.

Everyone began introducing themselves and chairs were shifted around. When they all settled, somehow Chad and Melissa were no longer sitting next to each other. She was practically in Pete's lap; Chad was between Shanon and Booty; and Phillip's bad mood was fading.

The waitress came over with appetizer menus for Jay and Travis. Travis discussed ordering options with Pete while Melissa, upon discovering where Jay worked, starting quizzing him about Stone Love.

Booty took advantage of their distraction to say, "How's your mother?"

"*My* mother?" Phillip asked, surprised, and Shanon and Chad broke off a conversation about Chad's job at the *Sun Herald* to listen. "You know my mother?"

"I never met her, but my Grandma Ruby lives in Taller Pines Trailer Court."

"I don't get the connection," Phillip said, bracing himself for another tale of Mad Ellan Powell.

"Everybody there knows Ms. Powell," Booty said. "It all started when Grandma Ruby told Odell Cannon some problems she was having with her Medicare bills. Grandma won't let us do anything for her; she's afraid we'll make her come live with us if we think she's feeble-minded. When Odell told your mother, Ms. Powell came and looked through all the bills, made some calls, and got it straightened out. Ever since then, all the old ladies at the trailer court call her when they have problems."

Phillip vaguely remembered his aunts telling him that his mother had disguised herself to interview people in a trailer park. He wondered how they'd gotten the story wrong. He saw a smug look flicker over Shanon's face and said, "That's nice."

"Sometimes," Booty went on, "I think they make up problems just so she'll come visit. She entertains them."

"I'm sure," Phillip said, exchanging a wary glance with Chad.

"Does anyone know where the restroom is?" Jay asked.

"Why?" Travis barked.

All conversation ceased as everyone stared at Travis.

"Because I have to pee," Jay said, blinking at Travis.

Phillip pointed in the direction of the men's room, noticing that Travis watched Jay until he was out of sight.

"Are we going to gamble tonight or what?" Melissa asked Pete.

"Sure," he said. "If y'all can do without us for a while."

"We'll manage," Phillip said.

"What do you do?" Shanon asked Travis.

"I'm an insurance claims adjuster," Travis said, staring in the direction of the restroom.

"How did you guys meet?" Chad asked, looking from Phillip to Travis.

"Party," Travis said shortly. Then he looked at Phillip. "Phillip likes to hang out with Jay at his shop. How often do you do that?"

Forgetting that he was supposed to be winning Travis over, Phillip said, "Not as often as I want to. But I'm not working now, so maybe that will change."

Travis scowled, but before he could answer he saw the same thing Phillip did. Jay was on his way back from the restroom when he took out his cell phone and answered it, stopping about twenty feet from their table.

"Who's he talking to?" Travis asked.

Booty and Shanon rolled their eyes at each other. Chad looked at Phillip and mouthed "freak." Travis took out his own cell phone, punched in a number, and waited. Phillip saw Jay pull his phone away to look at the display before he glanced at Travis, shook his head, and put his phone back to his ear to keep talking. Travis angrily snapped his phone shut and without a word, left their table, heading toward Jay.

"Did he really just try to break into his boyfriend's phone conversation?" Chad asked.

"That's crazy," Booty said.

"You weren't joking about the possessive thing," Shanon said to Phillip.

They all watched as Travis fumed next to Jay until he finished his call.

"Uh-oh," Booty said as the two began to argue.

"I think your friends are about to get bounced from Singing River," Chad said.

"Shit," Phillip said, leaving the table as he saw Jay shove Travis out of his face.

He realized that Chad was moving next to him like they were a well-rehearsed dance team. They got to Travis and Jay just as it looked like Travis was about to hit him. Chad pulled Travis back, and Phillip stepped in front of Jay.

"You two want to take it down a notch?" Chad suggested.

"Stay out of it," Travis snarled.

"I can't deal with this anymore," Jay said, looking humiliated. "It was my father. He just wanted to know if I'd take our dog to the vet tomorrow."

"That's bullshit," Travis said. "Who were you talking to?"

"Do you want to call him?" Jay asked, holding out his phone.

"Let's go," Travis said. "We'll talk about this outside."

"No," Jay said. "I'm not leaving."

"The hell you aren't," Travis said.

When he tried to push past Chad, Booty and Shanon blocked his way.

"He said he's not leaving," Shanon said. "Why doesn't everyone come back to the table and sit down before they kick us all out?"

"You either leave with me now, or you can get your shit out of the house tomorrow," Travis said.

"I'm not leaving," Jay repeated.

Travis glowered at him a minute, then looked at Phillip. "I know you're behind this. He's all yours."

They watched as Travis shoved past a couple of security guards on his way out.

"What's the problem?" one of the guards asked Chad.

"No problem," Chad said.

Shanon led a tearful Jay away from them to the table, and Booty said, "Y'all gonna be okay? Do you think he'll wait on you outside?"

"We've got it covered," Phillip said. "You find Shawnee and enjoy your night. Tell Goldie happy birthday from me."

"Okay," Booty said, looking a little doubtful. "You know, if you need any help, Cop, me and Goldie got your back."

"Thanks," Phillip said.

Booty left and Phillip looked at Chad, who said, "You've got your own posse."

"Apparently," Phillip said.

They walked back to the table, where Shanon was making soothing comments to Jay as he recited a woeful tale of Travis's irrational jealousy. "Can somebody give me a ride to my parents' house later?" Jay finally asked. "They live in Pascagoula; I'll pay for the gas."

"Don't be silly," Shanon said. "You can stay with Phillip and me."

Phillip tried not to look startled, reminding himself that it was her house.

"Really?" Jay asked, his eyes as hopeful as a puppy's. When she nodded, he said, "Thanks. Thanks, Phillip. I'll be back. I need to wash my face."

As soon as he was gone, Phillip said, "What are you thinking? You don't even know him."

Shanon smiled and said, "I didn't know you either, did I, when I invited you to move in?"

"You're going to let him move in?" Chad asked, sounding so appalled that Shanon and Phillip both turned to stare at him. "I mean, like Phillip said, if you don't know him…"

"I'm an excellent judge of character," Shanon said. "He has a job. He needs a place to chill out. If he's stuck at his parents' house, it'll be too much of a temptation to go back to Travis."

"It's really not a good idea to interfere with a relationship," Phillip warned.

"Oh, look on the bright side," Shanon said. "He'll be right under your nose. You'll have him in your bedroom in no time."

"I think I'll try my luck at the slots," Chad muttered and walked away.

Phillip watched him leave, then turned to Shanon. "Thanks."

"I'm always happy to help out a friend," she said cheerfully, pretending to believe he was sincere.

He bit off his retort as Jay came back to the table.

Chapter 18

Phillip sat at the end of the pier, staring at the water in the moonlight and listening to the slap of the waves mixing with the distant sounds of cars on the highway and people laughing on the beach. It was almost midnight, and even though he felt the comfort of being on *his* pier, he was tense and ready to spring if a stranger walked up behind him. When he finally did hear footfalls on the planks, he was already turned and ready to run or yell if need be.

"Oh, it's just you," he said when Chad came into view through the dim light.

"Just me? Who were you expecting? Jay?" Chad said. He passed Phillip a beer. "There's more in the truck if we need them."

"Thanks," Phillip mumbled. He popped open the can, took a sip, and set it beside him on the pier. "No. Jay is the last person I was expecting. I wasn't expecting anyone. Maybe the bogeyman."

"It is a little freaky out here at night," Chad agreed.

Phillip was quiet, sipping his beer, until he said, "I need…something."

"Okay," Chad said slowly, staring out over the whitecaps. "What's up?"

"Give me a sec." Phillip tried to pull together everything that he'd been feeling since he'd returned to Mississippi, wanting to sum it up into one request, which seemed impossible. He finally said, "This may sound strange, but I'm trying to move forward. I'm trying to create some sort of life for myself, and I feel like I can't do that because I keep thinking about stuff that's in the past."

"You just need to let it go and move on," Chad said.

Annoyed, Phillip said, "Yeah, it sounds that easy, but it's not. I need to know why my mother's nuts. Will it happen to me too? Has it already?"

"I seriously doubt it," Chad said. "You seem fine to me."

Phillip looked up and saw Chad assessing him. He blushed but didn't look away. It was too dark for Chad to notice. Phillip was flooded by memories of Daytona and everything that happened between them afterward. He tentatively asked, "Do I still seem sad to you?"

Chad looked puzzled. "How do you mean?"

"You used to say that about me."

"I used to say a lot of things," Chad said, shrugging.

"That's not helpful."

"What do you want from me?" Chad asked.

"Nothing!" Phillip exclaimed. He rethought his answer and said, "I want my friend back. Why did you fuck me?"

Chad didn't move. Phillip felt his stomach churn as he waited for a response. Chad finally lifted his beer and took a long pull. Then he asked, "What are you talking about?"

"Daytona." In the dim moonlight, Phillip could see Chad's forehead wrinkle and his mouth become a straight line as he seemed to think about it. Phillip knew that he was going to get evasive again, so he added, "After Daytona. In the motel room."

"That was a long time ago," Chad said. "I don't remember much after we had sex with those two girls in their camper."

"This is a familiar song and dance."

"It's the truth," Chad barked. "I don't."

"Fuck you," Phillip said.

"Hey. Watch it."

"No, really. Fuck off," Phillip said. "I know you remember everything that happened. You kissed me—"

"Stop it," Chad warned.

"You begged me to suck your cock—"

"I mean it, Phillip. Stop it."

"You fucked me. You started it too. You loved it."

Chad's body hit him with such force that he fell sideways before he realized what was happening. Chad pinned him, screaming, "Shut up!" Phillip wriggled free but then realized that they were dangerously close to the pier's edge. Before he could warn him, Chad flipped him, obviously intending to pin him on his back. Instead, they both toppled over the edge of the pier and into the Gulf.

Phillip immediately kicked upward, fighting the water's pull. When he broke the surface, he realized he was still close to the pier. He managed to paddle to one of the pylons and held onto it.

"Chad! Where are you?" he called, frantically trying to spot Chad in the dark. The water was cold and slimy. He hung on to the pylon but kept kicking to stay warm, listening. He thought he heard Chad splashing behind him, but it was the waves lapping against the pier. He called again, "Chad! Where are you?"

He turned, thinking he'd heard Chad's voice, and saw something moving toward him. His fear that it was a shark did battle with his common sense, then he saw Chad's head struggling toward him. Phillip pulled him toward the pylon, and they both clung to it. Once Chad caught his breath, they swam inland, helping each other, moving from pylon to pylon, until they could touch bottom again. Shivering, they fell side by side on the beach.

After a few minutes, Chad leaned over him and said, "That was scary."

"Yeah," Phillip agreed, panting. "I thought I'd lost you. Are you okay?"

"I'm fine," Chad answered.

Phillip sat up. "Good," he said. He helped Chad up, asking, "Sure you're fine?"

"Yeah."

Phillip drew his right fist back and brought it forward, feeling a quiver of satisfaction when it connected with Chad's nose. Chad yelped, and when he covered his face with his hands, Phillip's left fist sank into his stomach. Chad doubled over and sank to his knees. He looked up and asked, "Are you happy now?" He stood and spread his arms, saying, "Go ahead. Hit me again. I deserve it."

"Why?" Phillip asked. "Why do you deserve it?"

Phillip was caught off-guard when Chad started crying. He stared at him, watching Chad's tears mix with the blood running from his nose. Phillip sighed and pulled Chad to him, running a hand over his back. They stood like that a while, until Phillip pulled him toward the parking lot and said, "Come on."

Phillip parked his car next to Jess's Jeep and led Chad up the outside stairs to the third floor of Belfast House. Once inside, he shucked off his shirt and said, "Get out of those wet clothes. I'll find something for you to wear." Chad nodded in reply and began undressing. Phillip found clothes for each of them and put them in two piles on the bed. He turned around and saw Chad standing somberly in the middle of the room in a pair of gray boxer-briefs. Trying not to stare, Phillip walked to the bathroom, saying, "Let's clean up that ugly mug of yours."

He motioned for Chad to sit on the edge of the tub, then wet a washcloth in cold water. Gingerly, he brought the cloth to Chad's nose and wiped away the dried blood.

"Does that hurt?" he asked.

"Not really," Chad replied. "Who taught you to throw a punch like that?"

Phillip rinsed the washcloth and returned to his ministrations, saying, "My friend Carlos in New York City. He said if I was going to run around the city late at night, drunk, I should know how to protect myself."

"He taught you well," Chad muttered. "But I wasn't defending myself. If I was, you wouldn't have been able to sucker-punch me like that."

"Right," Phillip said. "Whatever it takes to save your ego. I won't tell anyone that you got beat up by a fag."

"You didn't beat me up," Chad said. "And you're not a fag."

"Whatever." Phillip dropped the washcloth in the sink and said, "I don't know about you, but all I want to do is get that nasty Gulf water off me. Do you want the shower first?"

"You go right ahead," Chad said, getting up to leave.

Phillip turned on the water and took off his jeans and underwear. He stepped into the tub and closed the curtain, sighing as the water hit his chest. While he was lathering up, the curtain parted and Chad stepped in, saying, "A shower sounds like a good idea."

"Hey!" Phillip exclaimed. The soap slipped from his hands and plummeted, skittering around the bottom of the tub and hitting their ankles. "What are you doing?"

Chad's face was inches from Phillip's. He grinned and said, "Uh-oh. You dropped the soap." He bent over to pick it up, grazing his cheek over Phillip's thigh. He held Phillip's waist with one hand for balance as he stood up again. Chad rubbed the bar of soap over Phillip's chest and said, "I don't know what I'm doing."

"I don't believe you," Phillip said. He tentatively kissed Chad's cheek and said, "Not one bit."

Chad pressed his body against Phillip's and kissed his neck. "Are you calling me a liar?"

Phillip ran his hand over Chad's ass and asked, "Are you going to defend yourself?"

Chad kissed Phillip, then said, "Nope."

Phillip woke at dawn and wondered if everything that had happened was a wild dream. He rolled over, expecting to find a note from Chad on his pillow. Instead, he saw Chad with his arm tucked behind his head, asleep. Phillip grinned, remembering how great it had been to let his eyes, mouth, and hands explore the familiar territory of Chad's body. He pulled back the covers a bit to get another eyeful of Chad's chest and the downy trail of hair that led to his abs.

He was startled when Chad stirred and mumbled, "Cold," then laughed when Chad's arm pulled him down and threw the covers over their heads. "Too early. What are you doing up?"

"It's the lingering curse of the landscaping business," Phillip answered. "It's too late for me. I'm doomed. Save yourself. Go back to sleep."

"Nah." Chad sighed and threw off the covers, squinting against the daylight. "I'm up."

Before he realized what he was saying, Phillip said, "Is this where you throw on your clothes and burn rubber on the driveway?"

"Aren't you funny?"

Phillip yelped when Chad rolled over on top of him, pinning him to the mattress, and tickled his ribs. He remembered his roommates and tried not to be too loud as he laughed uncontrollably. Chad finally rolled off him and lay back on the pillows. "I thought I'd leave a twenty on the dresser," he said.

"Classy." Phillip leaned over and implored, "Would you kiss me?"

Looking quizzical, Chad sat up and leisurely kissed Phillip, taking his time as he ran his hand over the back of Phillip's head. Afterward, he asked, "What was that for?"

"This is where it stops. I wanted one last—" Phillip broke off, searching for the right word. "Good thing. Before it all goes to shit."

"What are you talking about?"

"I want to know," Phillip said. "I want to know everything. What's going on between us? Is this Daytona all over again? Are you going to leave and not speak to me for five years? What happens now?"

Chad groaned and rubbed his eyes. "Jesus. You're like a woman."

"If you start comparing me to some girlfriend of yours, I'll hit you again."

Chad laughed. "Actually, I was thinking that you give better head than any girl I've ever been with."

"Thanks. Let's save that for my epitaph," Phillip said drily.

Chad rolled over and stared at Phillip as he said, "Seriously. I don't know what's going on. With me, anyway. You got in that shower last night, and I stood there and thought about how much I wanted to be in there with you. I thought it would be sexy."

"It was," Phillip whispered.

Chad nodded in agreement. "Part of me thought it was wrong. The other part—well, let's just say that the other part had a woody. You know which side won."

"Me," Phillip said. "I scored—big time."

"I remember everything about Daytona," Chad said. "If you hate me because of that, I don't blame you. I was young and scared. That's the only excuse I can offer for what I did afterward."

"So was I," Phillip said. "You really hurt me."

"I'm sorry," Chad said. "I'd never intentionally hurt you. You've always been like—"

"Don't say it," Phillip exclaimed, interrupting him. "Don't say the brother thing."

"It's true," Chad insisted. "You have."

"Great. That's what every boy wants to hear after sex," Phillip said. "It's right up there with 'Let's just be friends.'"

Chad shook his head and said, "I'm not saying I want to stop this. All I'm saying is that I care for you, and that's probably what I'm responding to. I don't think I'm..." he trailed off, then finally said, "Like you."

"So this is like some guy thing? Where you jerk off and mess around with your buddies, but that doesn't mean you're gay?"

"I guess," Chad replied.

Phillip thought about it, then said, "I can live with that. Who knows? Maybe, after a while—"

"You, of all people, should know that people don't turn gay," Chad said, thumping his hand on Phillip's chest for emphasis.

"True. But maybe you have the gene."

"My dad's not gay," Chad said, rolling his eyes.

"No, but your mother is," Phillip said. When Chad stared at him, open-mouthed, Phillip winced and said, "Oh, shit."

"What do you mean? What are you saying about my mom?" Chad demanded.

"Nothing," Phillip said. "I was kidding." Chad got out of bed, bypassed the clothes that Phillip had set aside for him, and began putting on his own. Phillip watched him, horrified and worried. He couldn't think of a way to stop Chad, whose jaw was clenched as he furiously pulled on his sneakers. He feebly said, "Chad, don't. Let me explain."

Chad glanced at him but said nothing. Instead, he pushed through the door and slammed it behind him. Phillip sat still and listened to Chad's feet pound down the stairs. He waited, certain that Chad would come back when he realized that he didn't have a car. After a few minutes, Phillip got up, looked out the window, and spotted the back of Chad's head as he walked down the road.

Minutes later, Phillip was dressed and in his car, a cigarette dangling from his lips. He had no intention of trying to coerce Chad into the Volvo, offer him a ride, or attempt to make up with him. He was worried that Chad was on his way to Taryn's house, and he wanted to get there first so that he could warn her the cat was out of the bag.

He pulled into Taryn's driveway and killed the engine but didn't move. He stared at the house and wondered if she was even awake yet. He didn't like the idea of starting Taryn's day with potentially bad news and worried that she'd be angry with him for outing her to Chad. Taryn had always said he could talk to her about anything. She'd always been supportive, comforting; someone who made him feel safe. The idea of no longer having her to rely on was frightening.

He was about to turn the key and leave when a sudden knock on the window next to him made him jump. He turned and saw Taryn peering into the Volvo. After he lowered the window, she said, "Hi. What are you doing?" He stared blankly. "Is something wrong, Phillip? You look pale. Would you like some breakfast?"

"Tea," he said. "Hot."

He followed her inside, mute while she cooked in silence. He stared at his plate of eggs, bacon, and toast with disinterest but began eating politely. Taryn set a steaming mug of coffee in front of him and said, "Sorry. I was out of tea. When did you start drinking hot tea? Is that some hip New York thing?"

"Not really," Phillip said. He swallowed a bite of toast, which nearly caught in his throat on the way down. "I have unfortunate news."

"How dire. You sound like a loan officer. Spit it out. It can't be that bad."

"Chad knows that you're a lesbian."

Taryn, who'd just swallowed a mouthful of egg, began coughing. She dropped her fork and started beating her chest with one hand, the other pointing toward the sink. Phillip jumped up and brought her some water. She gulped from the glass, then took a few deep breaths.

"How did this happen?" she finally asked.

Phillip nervously twisted his hands. "I accidentally told him."

"When?" she blurted. "How does one accidentally say something like that? Were you guys drunk?"

"No."

Taryn stared at him, and Phillip felt as though her eyes were laser beams, scanning him for information, like something out of one of the *Terminator* movies. Finally, she closed her eyes and said, "You had sex with my son?"

"I didn't mean to—"

"Fuck him?" she interrupted. She stood up and dumped her plate of food into the sink, then stared out the window with a pained expression. "I watched the two of you for years, thinking how wonderful it was that you boys had each other. Neither of you had fathers in your lives. You barely had a mother. And I tried so hard, Phillip, to be everything for both of you: mother, father, friend. Mostly, I thought it was so sweet that you two were always there for each other, like brothers." She turned to face him. "Like lovers."

Phillip stared uneasily at the table, not daring to move. He felt as if he were on trial but didn't know what crime he'd committed.

"I knew something happened on that trip to Daytona," Taryn said. She sounded tired, like someone who'd been fighting something and had given up. "He never told me, but I figured it out. I wanted to talk to him about it, but how? I was wrestling with my own self-awareness, self-discovery. I didn't know how to talk to him about sexuality. I didn't know how it all works, back then."

She stepped to Phillip and pointed at his plate. "Are you done with that?"

"Yes, ma'am."

"We all grew up thinking that homosexuality was something evil," she continued. Without bothering to scrape the uneaten food into the trash, she dropped his plate into the sink on top of hers. She walked by him and took a cigarette from his pack. She grabbed his lighter before he could light it for her and started coughing as soon as she inhaled.

"Give me that. You don't even smoke."

She handed over the cigarette and said, "A lot of people around here still feel that way and fear us, Phillip. They don't understand us and don't want to. This isn't New York City; there's no gay ghetto."

"This ain't no disco," Phillip muttered.

"That's for sure," Taryn said. "Back in 2000, a boy was abducted and killed after leaving a gay bar in Biloxi. Did you hear about it?"

"No," Phillip said.

"He was about your age now. His killers were convicted and tried in Alabama, where his body was found. They got life in prison, but the district attorney said it wasn't a hate crime. They just wanted his car. The boy's family still maintains that he wasn't gay." She absently emptied the ashtray after he stubbed out his cigarette. "Even after death, people are still worried about perception. That's what it's like here, Phillip. You know that. This isn't the safest place in the world to be gay. After I heard about that boy, I thought of you and Chad and was so glad you both got out. I imagine Ellan felt the same."

"Chad's not gay," Phillip said.

"But I am," Taryn snapped. "I have a business. I have a boy who's obviously confused. I'm not sure how I feel about any of this."

"Maybe I should go," Phillip said.

"Maybe you should," Chad said.

Phillip and Taryn looked up to see Chad standing in the doorway to the kitchen.

"How did you—"

"I hitched to my truck," Chad said, interrupting Phillip. He looked at Taryn and asked, "Is what he told me true?"

"Honey," Taryn said, "sit down. We need to talk."

"Not until he leaves." Chad glared at Phillip and demanded, "Get out. You've got your own mother. Stop ruining mine too."

"Chad!" Taryn exclaimed. "I know you're upset, but that's not fair."

"Thanks for breakfast, Taryn. I'm sorry for putting you in this position," Phillip said.

He pushed past Chad, left their home, and drove the short distance to his grandfather's. He went inside, expecting to see Odell in the kitchen, but the house was quiet. He called out, "Mom?"

He found her in the parlor, sitting in a chair with her back to him, staring out the window. She was wearing a lavender chenille robe, and her feet were bare.

"What are you looking at?" he asked. She didn't answer or turn around. He stood behind her and placed his hands on her shoulders. Through the trees, beyond the lawn and the gate, he could see the beach and almost make out the waves lapping against the sand. Phillip knelt beside the chair, stared imploringly at his mother, and said, "Mom? Look at me."

Ellan's eyes stayed fixed on the window, blinking periodically. She was rigid, like a statue or a warm waxen figure.

Phillip rested his head on her lap, the chenille soft against his cheek, and said, "You never *see* me."

Chapter 19

Phillip awoke on the parlor sofa and tried to remember how he'd ended up there. It all came rushing back to him. The night with Chad. The confrontation with Taryn. His feeling that things were spinning out of control. The hunger he'd felt for his mother to be sane, just for a little while, and falling asleep with his head on her lap, worn out from it all.

He went to the bathroom, then looked for his mother, finding her in the living room. Her unkempt hair had been pulled up into a haphazard tangle. She'd propped the Rothko against the sofa and knelt in front of it. Several candles flickered on a marble-topped table next to her. Phillip made a decision. The painting needed to be loaned to a museum. As if frequent moves and salty air weren't damaging enough, his mother was likely to set it on fire.

She turned her head to look at him and said, "You've caught me in prayer. Would you like to hear my rosary?"

"All right," he said tentatively and sat on the piano bench, thinking that whatever this new game was, at least she wasn't doing commercials or pretending to be catatonic.

"Bless me, Father, for my family has sinned," Ellan began.

"Mom, that's confession, not the rosary."

"Excuse me," she said. "Did I ask if you wanted to hear *the* rosary? Don't you already know it?"

"I probably remember it."

"I asked if you wanted to hear *my* rosary. Are you done interrupting me?"

"Go on," he said, raising his hands in a gesture of resignation.

"My family," Ellan repeated firmly, fingering her beads. "Exton Godbee had an affair with Lorna Timmons."

Phillip rolled his eyes. Lorna Timmons had died of cancer the year after she taught him second grade. He'd been forced to go to the funeral home for the viewing. Instead of feeling grief, he remembered his twinge of triumph that he'd outlived the woman who told his class that his mother was crazy as a Bessie bug. He doubted that his grandfather had even known Miss Timmons, much less shared a bed with her.

His mother's fingers slipped toward another bead as she said, "My sister Eufala questions God's existence because He didn't give her children. She breaks the Tenth Commandment every time she covets my son." She paused to glance at Phillip as if daring him to refute her, but he gave her a level stare and kept his mouth shut. "My sister Florence is guilty of vanity, although she *is* beautiful," Ellan conceded.

"I think I've heard enough of your rosary," Phillip said.

She ignored him and moved to the next bead, saying, "My sister Andalusia violates the First Commandment with her false gods of money and possessions. Plus, she's a hypocrite. As for her children, Allen has twice eluded prosecution for drunk driving after his father bribed judges. Her youngest, Jack, carries on a dissolute life of gambling and womanizing."

Phillip perked up, somewhat enjoying this litany of familial sins.

"Then there's her daughter, Bethany. Her father has repeatedly kept her from running afoul of the law after she *borrowed* items of apparel from department stores in Jackson. Eighth Commandment."

"Ninth Commandment," Phillip said.

"No, the Eighth Commandment is stealing."

"I wasn't talking about Bethany," Phillip said pointedly.

"I'm not bearing false witness," Ellan said. "I'm telling the truth. And you'd be well advised to heed the *Fifth* Commandment."

"I honor you," Phillip said. "I'm listening to this crap, after all." His mother's mouth twitched, but she managed not to smile. When she stared at the Rothko as if she really was praying, he couldn't stop himself from saying, "You forgot Selma."

"Heavens, what sin has Selma ever committed?" Ellan asked. "She's perfect. If you don't believe me, you can ask her. Or Daddy."

"She gave me a job," Phillip said, defending his aunt.

Ellan cast her eyes heavenward and said, "Keeping you under the family's greenest thumb when you should be living your own life somewhere else, instead of lurking around here with your hand hovering over my commitment papers."

"Selma tried to get me to go back to New York. I chose to stay here. It doesn't matter where I am; I'm living my own life."

"Then let me give you a great big congratulations," Ellan said, flinging the rosary at his feet.

"What is it about my being here that bugs you so much?" Phillip asked. "God knows you don't alter your behavior one bit on my behalf, even if you do think I want to commit you, which I don't."

"You have no idea what God knows—or what I know, for that matter." She paused and played with her hair, handling it much the way she had the rosary. "I hear you went to see Paula Bishop. If Linda would loosen up, she and Paula would like each other more. Maybe Shanon could get Linda a job at the fake spa."

"Shanon told you what she does?"

"Why wouldn't she?" Ellan asked.

"What did you say?"

"I told her to stop, of course," Ellan said. "What kind of life is that for a young woman with Shanon's potential?"

"At least you're mothering someone," Phillip muttered resentfully.

"She told me she'd already quit her job," Ellan said. "Do you know why she quit?"

"How would I know her reason when I didn't even know she had quit?"

"Because of you," Ellan said.

"Why? I didn't tell her to stop."

"She told you her secrets, and you didn't judge her. You saw things about her that she doesn't let people see, and you didn't abandon her. Abandonment is her worst fear. She's a complex girl. If I could have a daughter-in-law, I'd much prefer Shanon to Linda." Phillip glared at her, and she went on. "However, if I could pick a son-in-law, it wouldn't be Chad Cunningham."

"That's enough," he said, standing. "I apologize for anything I said about you and Shanon. Thank you for being nice to her. I'll get my paintings and leave." He frowned when his mother followed him up the stairs.

"I'm surprised you didn't pick up your paintings sooner. You came to the house several times before I knew you were back, didn't you? I should have been able to feel the disruption in the air."

"Is that what I am? A disruption?" Phillip asked angrily. "What about my sins? You didn't count me on your rosary."

She started humming a Billy Joel song and drifted past him. After a few seconds, he heard her open her bedroom door.

"Sometimes I hate you," he said, not bothering to lower his voice.

"You need new material," she called out.

Changing his mind about the paintings, he turned to go back downstairs. Odell was waiting for him at the foot of the stairs with an irate expression. "That's no way to talk to the woman who brought you into this world."

"She provoked me. Don't worry. I'm leaving. She'll be fine after I'm gone."

"Into the kitchen," Odell ordered, pressing her palms flat against his back. "March."

"There's more than one kind of crazy in this house," Phillip muttered, but he went to the kitchen and sat at the table.

"She doesn't want you to take the paintings," Odell said.

"Why?"

"She likes to sit with them. They keep her company."

"I'm leaving without them," Phillip pointed out. "You should stop speaking for her. Then maybe she'd say something that isn't deranged."

"Everything she said to you was the gospel truth."

"You should also stop eavesdropping."

"You're taking your mother for a drive. She needs trees."

"There are several outside her bedroom window."

"Different trees."

Phillip stared at Odell with exasperation. "She has to be forced to leave the house as it is. How am I supposed to talk her into taking a ride with me?"

Odell was no longer speaking to him, and he watched as she concocted one of her famous iced coffees and set it in front of him. He sipped it and watched her gnarled hands as she wiped down the counters. Then she stopped and leaned against a cabinet. Although she was looking at him, he could tell she wasn't seeing him.

"She was different before it happened," Odell said dreamily. "She laughed all the time and moved through the house light as a feather. We couldn't help but spoil her, but I guess I was the worst. Having her was like having a little bit of Lorraine back. Her eyes were just like her mama's. Lorraine was still looking at the world through Ellan's eyes."

Odell stopped talking, and Phillip finally prodded, "You mean before my father died?"

Odell looked confused for a moment and then said, "No. Before Camille. They said the hurricane would be bad, but no one knew how bad. Maybe Exton. They didn't start evacuating soon enough, but Exton had already sent trucks to drive us north. The older girls didn't want to go. They had friends whose families planned to ride it out in their homes or at the VFW. Not Ellan. She thought it was a big adventure, going to a Jackson hotel.

"But the wind was bad even there. She spent the night with her hands over her ears, not saying a word. When we came back, it was like somebody had dropped an atom bomb—roads torn up, town gone, lumber and cars piled everywhere. Everybody had to work so hard—black and white, rich and poor, side by side, trying to clean up the mess. Nobody thought about how it looked to a nine-year-old. Exton took all the girls to New Orleans to school that fall. She came back at Christmas with bad grades and hollow eyes. Sick. That spring, she stayed home. He had someone come here to teach her, but my little girl was gone, even after she got well."

"I never heard that story," Phillip said when Odell stopped talking.

"She hasn't had an easy life," Odell said. "Remember that before you smart off at her."

"You know what? My life hasn't been a bed of roses either. Nobody stops her from saying hateful things to me. It's always her who has to be taken care of. Nobody protects me. The road I've been on has led me to obsessive-compulsives, slackers, drunks, and cat killers. Not to mention religious fanatics, bigots, kleptomaniacs, voyeurs, and hookers. There *is* a path at the end of my road—a sociopath."

"Who am I hurting?" his mother asked from the doorway, making him jump.

"Me," he said, staring at her. Her hair was wet from being washed, and she was dressed in jeans and a Led Zeppelin T-shirt. "Where'd you get that shirt?"

She looked down and said, "It was Mike's."

"Can I have it?" When she reached for the bottom of the shirt as if to pull it over her head, he said, "Not now! Just sometime. We're going for a drive. Odell too."

His mother walked out the back door, and Phillip and Odell exchanged a look. Odell shrugged, then followed.

He drove randomly, taking back roads away from the coast. No one talked. He occasionally glanced at his mother in the rearview mirror as she looked out at the countryside. He finally headed toward home through De Lisle, and she broke the silence, saying, "Watch your own damn children."

Odell rumbled with laughter. Phillip sighed inwardly, wondering if Odell was getting senile.

"The sign," Odell said.

"What?" Phillip asked.

"The road sign. It said WATCH CHILDREN."

"Oh," Phillip said, finally comprehending that his mother had made a joke. He looked in the rearview mirror again and saw her roll her eyes at his dull-wittedness. "Do either of you need anything? We can go into Gulfport to the grocery store, or the drugstore. Wherever you need to go."

"We aren't shopping in Gulfport anymore," Ellan said.

"But that's where we always ran our errands," Phillip said. "Where do you shop now?"

"Bay St. Louis, Long Beach. Just not Gulfport."

"Did you get mad at someone, like Aunt Andi did with her old church?"

"I don't believe in shopping for religion," Ellan said.

Phillip sighed and said, "We aren't talking about religion. We're talking about buying groceries."

"You're the one who brought up church."

He wanted to scream and changed the subject. "I've decided not to take my paintings yet. I didn't ask Shanon if it was okay to hang them in Belfast House."

His mother stared out the window without comment, but Odell reached over and patted his arm to show her approval. By the time he turned into Godbee Lane, his jaw hurt from being clenched so tightly. He turned off the engine. His mother and Odell waited for him to get out and open their doors, but he didn't move. He couldn't get Shanon's advice out of his head.

"Phillip?" Ellan said.

He turned around and looked at her. "Will you give me a straight answer? Please?"

"About what?"

"Why won't you shop in Gulfport?"

Ellan smiled faintly and said, "I don't know if you could call it a straight answer, but I'm honoring the boycott."

"What boycott?"

"The city council passed an antigay resolution," Ellan said. "Gay and lesbian groups called for a boycott of the town's businesses. Why should I spend Godbee money in a city that questions my son's right to be who he is?"

Their gaze held, and Phillip realized that Shanon was right. His mother's eyes could be brilliant and clear. "Thank you," he said.

She understood that he was thanking her for more than just answering his question, and they smiled grimly at each other.

"Is anybody gonna let me out of this car?" Odell asked.

Both Phillip and his mother got out and helped Odell, then watched as she lumbered through the hedge to her own house.

"Give Shanon my best," Ellan said as she turned to walk toward the kitchen door.

"Mom? When did you know?" He held his breath, knowing she could pretend not to understand his question.

She turned around. "When Chad broke your heart."

Which time? he wondered, but merely asked, "Not before?"

She tilted her head, staring into his eyes. "Phillip, you were never a problem. The difficulties I've had were not caused by you, or anything about you. Ever. Don't let my failures be your burden."

He didn't move after she went inside. He tentatively considered what she'd just said, as if it might evaporate if he thought too hard about it. She'd just managed to communicate twice that she had no problem accepting an essential part of who he was. He wanted to be satisfied. The safe thing would be to go home, savor it, and move on.

He walked inside the house and climbed the stairs, knowing where he'd find her. She was sitting on the studio floor staring at his Cézanne-style painting of their house. She didn't turn her head when she said, "It wasn't enough?"

"I know it should be." He sat on the floor next to her.

"What I was trying to explain to you with the rosary is that no one in this family is perfect, so I don't know why you think you have to be. I've made so many mistakes. I'm sorry," she said.

"I'm not looking for apologies. I just want to understand you. Maybe if we talked like two people, instead of mother and son. Like you and Shanon talk."

She smiled, her eyes still on the painting, and said, "Shanon understands me because I'm *not* her mother. The first day she came here, when you were sick, I didn't intend to see her. It was Odell who took her to look in on you. I went outside and climbed our tree, waiting for her to leave. You must have told her that you and I always take to the trees, because she came right to me and sat on the branch below me. I waited for her to lecture me on what a bad mother I am."

"Did she?"

"No. Shanon's exact words were, 'I grew up in an orphanage. For as long as I can remember, I was afraid my mother died when I was born. That pain and guilt never leaves my heart.' Phillip, that was the earliest reality of my life. The only person who understood it before Shanon was your father. When I was a little girl, I'd look at my sisters and feel like it was my fault we didn't have a mother. If I hadn't been born, she wouldn't have died. I thought I had to be perfect so they'd forgive me." She was quiet for a few minutes. "Odell was right. When I was nine, Hurricane Camille showed me that the whole world can change in a day, and I can't control it. It was too much for me." She turned to stare at him, looking like she was working something out in her head.

"What?" he asked.

"September, nearly two years ago, I was so afraid for you. You swore to Florence that you were okay, but I kept thinking of how much damage something like that can do to us inside."

"We can talk about that sometime, but I am okay," he said. "I wasn't nine years old."

"I don't think it matters how old you are when the world falls apart. I had panic attacks until I met Mike. I'd go to pieces over the most trivial things, and he'd always reassure me. 'Life is messy, El. An overdrawn check or a burned meal or diaper rash isn't the end of the world. We're fine.' No one ever knew me like he did. Little by little, I let go of that guilt and fear." She stopped talking and put her hands over her face.

"Then he got killed," Phillip said.

"I felt cursed. My mother. My husband. I thought if I didn't bring you home and let other people take over, if all you had was me, I'd curse you too. I don't want to talk about those years. They were awful. I'm sorry…I just couldn't…I can't…"

"It's all right," Phillip said, rubbing her back. He could feel every ridge of her spine. She seemed so fragile.

"But it was never you. It was never that I didn't love you or that you disappointed me. You were great. I'd watch you for signs of my weakness or his strength, but you were your own little person."

He stared down at her hand as she folded and unfolded the hem of the T-shirt. He'd never noticed before how similar his hands were to hers. "Artist hands," Claude had always said before he made a sensuous journey of Phillip's fingers with his tongue. Phillip wondered if his father had loved his mother's hands.

"When you were eighteen, Florence told me you had a right to be free of all this. I helped you leave, Phillip. I didn't make you come back. I'm sorry for your terrible childhood. If you're not happy now, you're the one who insists that it's your choice to be here. You have your life; I have mine." She paused. "Do you remember a drawing you did for art class when you were ten?"

"I've done thousands of drawings since then. No."

"Your class took a walk on the beach. Then you went back to school. Your assignment was to draw and color a picture that had something to do with your field trip. Your art teacher hung the pictures in the hall on PTA night. All the boys had drawn water with sharks, jellyfish, or divers fighting sea monsters. All the girls drew little domestic scenes on the beach, and most of them had a big rainbow over the families. Picture after picture of boys seeking adventure and girls making things pretty."

"Please don't tell me I drew a rainbow," Phillip said.

"No. What you drew was what you saw. You didn't use crayons. You used pencils. Your water was shaded in a way that showed movement and power. There were no people on your beach, just white sand and some seaweed that had washed ashore."

"Did you think I lacked imagination?" Phillip asked.

"No. I saw that you look through the eyes of someone who sees what's real and doesn't try to embellish it or otherwise change it. If you knew that at ten, if you can be that way for Shanon, why do you keep trying to fit me into some idealized version of a mother? I'm who I am. I never asked you to fix me. Do I seem that deranged to you right now?"

"No," he said.

"Go and live your life, Phillip. I'm okay."

"Maybe it's not you I'm worried about," he said.

"I used to wonder why you were drawn to artists who committed suicide—Rothko, van Gogh, Gorky, de Staël. But I could see that your work was never a descent into the darkness of depression or madness. Your art transcended your environment. You're not going to lose your mind. Is that what you want to hear?"

"I don't know," he said.

She was still staring at his painting when he left. He drove to Belfast House and looked at the downstairs lights with dismay. This was one night he'd rather be alone. He wasn't in the mood to put on his cheerful face, and he didn't want to talk any of this over with Shanon. He didn't want to hear any Jay and Travis drama. He didn't even want to see Jess. The only person he could imagine expressing his fears to was Chad. Unreliable, confused, angry, absent Chad.

He was skulking toward the side of the house to take the outside stairs when Jess opened the front door, motioned for him to come inside, and said, "Two friends of yours are here."

Phillip groaned and said, "All I want is to go to bed, or maybe sketch a little. I just want some peace and quiet for once. Who is it? Can you give them some excuse?"

Jess fidgeted and tentatively said, "I don't think so. They came all the way from New York. Phillip, wait, you should know that—"

Phillip went to the living room before Jess could finish her sentence and was startled to see Carlos and Kieran stand up as he walked in. Carlos moved toward him first, enveloping him in his strong arms. Phillip looked over his shoulder at Kieran, who hung back, regarding him with a sad expression.

"Hey," Phillip said to Carlos as he extricated himself from the embrace. "It's great to see you." He looked at Kieran and added, "Both of you. Come here." Kieran stepped forward, and Phillip pulled him into his arms. He wanted to cry because of how good it felt to touch him again, to smell him, to feel Kieran's long hair tickle his cheek. "I missed you so much."

Kieran stared Phillip in the eye and said, "Me too, mate. More than you know."

"I don't understand," Phillip said. "Not to be rude, but you two are the last people I expected to see tonight. I guess I'm a little shocked." He laughed, then asked, "Is Bunny hiding around here somewhere too?" Carlos dropped his gaze to the floor, and Kieran's sad expression returned, causing Phillip to ask, "What is it? What's wrong?"

Kieran placed his hands on Phillip's shoulders and said, "I'm afraid Bunny's sailed on, mate."

"What?" Phillip asked, hoping he'd misunderstood.

"Bunny died," Carlos said softly. "We wanted to tell you in person; to be here for you."

Phillip suddenly realized that he was sobbing, and Kieran's arms were around him again.

ONE MUST KNOW THERE IS A PATH
AT THE END OF THE ROAD.

Chapter 20

Phillip sat at his easel, lost in a trance, blending pigments on his palette and daubing the final mixture onto the canvas in tiny hatch-strokes. Every now and then he'd peer around the canvas to look at Kieran, asleep on his stomach in Phillip's bed, twisted in the sheets, hugging the pillow. One leg dangled over the side of the bed, and his big toe grazed the floor. Phillip frowned and bit his lip in concentration, then darkened the color he'd been using to highlight Kieran's hair, which twisted down his shoulders and over his arms.

Phillip had begun the painting at two in the morning, when he'd given up trying to fall asleep after staring at the ceiling for hours. He'd already finished a painting of Bunny that he'd started only hours after Kieran and Carlos told him about Bunny's death. The Bunny in the painting was just as Phillip remembered him: a drink in one hand, a cigarette in the other, holding court in the center of a dance floor with shirtless men all around him. But there was a distant sadness in Bunny's eyes that Phillip hadn't remembered until he looked at the finished painting.

"May I move?"

Phillip looked up and saw that Kieran's eyes were open. "Yeah," he said. "I think I need to stop for a while."

Kieran sat up, stretched, then got out of bed. He sat behind Phillip and began kneading his shoulders. "You've done far too many pictures of me."

Phillip took the paintbrush out of his mouth and said, "Only one painting. The rest are sketches. You're my favorite subject. That feels good. Don't stop."

"You didn't sleep again?" When Phillip shook his head, Kieran said, "We came down here to take care of you. I don't feel I'm doing a good job."

"Maybe I don't need to be taken care of," Phillip said.

"Maybe not," Kieran said. "Did you finish the one of Bunny?"

"The painting? Yeah. In the middle of the night. It's drying on the mantel downstairs."

"I want to see it," Kieran said. He gave Phillip's shoulders a final squeeze and began to dress. Phillip watched him, admiring Kieran's ass in a pair of faded blue jeans while he pulled on a T-shirt and tied back his hair. "Are you coming?" he asked.

Phillip followed him downstairs to the living room, where Shanon, Jess, and Carlos were sprawled over furniture and studying the painting on the mantel.

"Good morning, sleepy boys," Carlos said.

"I'm the sleepy boy." Kieran wrapped an arm around Phillip's chest and said, "This one didn't sleep."

"Again?" Shanon said, sounding worried.

"I'm fine. Stop fussing over me," Phillip said.

"Leave him alone," Jess urged. "I love this painting. This is Bunny?"

"Yeah," Phillip murmured.

"Definitely," Carlos agreed. He echoed Phillip's thoughts when he said, "I never noticed how sad he could look. I wish I'd known what was going through his head. Maybe I could've done something. Maybe if I'd spent more time with him—"

"Stop, please," Phillip said.

Jess put a hand on Carlos's shoulder and said, "Just remember the good stuff. That's the best tribute you can offer Bunny."

"Aye," Kieran agreed softly.

Phillip stared at the portrait, remembering Bunny's best biting comments, his laughter, and his penchant for witty gossip. *Be in the moment,* he mentally repeated in an endless loop. *Be in the moment.*

"Is there breakfast?" he asked. He wasn't hungry, but the painting was making him sad and he was beginning to regret doing it.

Everyone perked up at his suggestion. They were obviously grateful to have something to do, something to provide for him.

Phillip sat at the table in the kitchen, watching them move around him as if they'd been choreographed. Shanon made coffee and directed Carlos to the pots and pans. Kieran passed off ingredients from the refrigerator to Carlos. Jess diced green peppers, onions, and potatoes and marveled aloud to anyone who'd listen about her handiwork in the newly refurbished kitchen.

There was a familiarity about it all that Phillip easily identified. They were treating him the way people treated his mother when she was in one of her blue moods—talking around him, faking a cheer they didn't feel, keeping up a pretense of normalcy. He understood why she often threw a bit of craziness into the mix. It would be like blowing a whistle in the middle of a game to stop everything for a minute. But he wasn't crazy, and they were doing their best for him.

"Your tea, monsieur." Shanon placed a steaming mug in front of Phillip and sat down beside him. She followed Phillip's gaze. Carlos had commandeered Jess's knife and was tossing mushrooms into the air and trying to slice them, shrieking like a Ginsu warrior, while Kieran and Jess laughed. "Aren't we a motley crew?"

"The best part of my time in New York followed me. Although I still think it's stupid that Carlos quit his job to be here."

"I heard that," Carlos said. "Don't call me stupid."

"I didn't. I said what you did was stupid. What are you going to do when you go back?"

Carlos shrugged as he passed a bowl of diced vegetables to Jess. "I don't know. Maybe I won't go back."

"And maybe I'll run for president next year," Phillip said.

"You're too young," Jess said.

"Why wouldn't I want to stay here? It's beautiful," Carlos said.

"You've been here three days," Phillip stated, "and you haven't even left the house."

"I've left the house. I've walked around the neighborhood. There's so much space. Sky. Air. Trees. No noise. No litter. You can actually see the sidewalk when you look ahead, instead of just hundreds of people's heads."

"You don't move a thousand miles for sidewalks," Phillip said.

"I'm giving Carlos and Kieran a tour today," Shanon said. "Ocean Springs to Bay St. Louis. Want to come?"

"I don't think so. I've got things to do," he said cryptically.

"Then we're going to Singing River Casino tonight. Would you be up for that?"

"Maybe," Phillip said. "Did Jay leave for work already?" Even without looking up from his tea, he could feel the tension in the air. He glanced at their faces. "What?"

"Jay left early to meet Travis for breakfast before work," Jess said rapidly.

Phillip reached for a cigarette and said, "It's his life."

"I don't think he's getting back with Travis," Shanon said. "It was either see him or get a new cell phone number. Travis is calling relentlessly."

"Whatever," Phillip said. "Do you need help finishing the omelets?"

"I've got it covered," Jess said.

Phillip realized that Kieran was watching him. He smiled and quietly said, "I'm glad you're here."

"I am too," Kieran said.

After breakfast, they left Phillip alone with Jess to do the dishes while they got ready for their day of sightseeing. He hoped Shanon didn't intend to include the Madwoman of Godbee Manor on their tour.

"If you want to talk," Jess said as an opening.

"Not really. I need some alone time, you know?"

"I do know," Jess said. "I can run errands so you'll have the house to yourself."

When they were finally all gone, Phillip took the portrait of Bunny upstairs and put it on the easel in place of the one he'd started of Kieran. Then he picked up his phone, knowing he couldn't put off this call any longer.

"Did I wake you?" he asked when Alyssa answered the phone.

"No. We've been up for a while," Alyssa said. "Have you been out of town or something? I've sent several e-mails."

"Is Eric around?" Phillip asked casually.

"He's right here. Why?"

"Brace yourself. It's bad."

"Is it your mother?" Alyssa asked.

He took a deep breath and said, "Bunny."

"No," Alyssa said in the tone of a child who was being accused of something.

"'Lyss, Bunny's dead." He could hear her breathing, but she didn't say anything. "I'm sorry. I'm sorry I have to tell you over the phone. If you want me to call back later—"

"Was he sick? What happened?"

Phillip stared at the painting and said, "He hung himself. Alone. In his apartment."

She started sobbing, and he could hear Eric asking her questions.

"Phillip? She's right here, but she can't talk. Tell me," Eric said. "She can hear you."

"I don't know much," Phillip said. "It happened a couple of weeks ago. None of his friends knew. Bunny's family…you know how they are. They didn't tell anyone. They handled Bunny's death with the efficiency of a NASCAR pit crew. Somebody found him, the Wallaces were contacted, and he was cremated as soon as his body was released to them. There was no funeral, no service, no obituary that we know of. A lawyer contacted Renata because of the lease. She called Carlos in a fit of despair. Any attempt to contact Bunny's family has been intercepted by a lawyer, a secretary, or a maid, all of whom give the same perfunctory response: 'We'll convey your respects to the family. Good day.'"

"Jesus," Eric said.

"It never crossed my mind that Bunny would do anything like this," Phillip said. "I still can't grasp it."

"Phillip, are you okay?" Alyssa asked, sounding like she'd been kicked in the stomach.

"Not really. Carlos came down to tell me in person. He brought Kieran."

"It's good you're not alone," Alyssa said. "I can't...it doesn't seem real. Are you home now?"

"You can call me back," Phillip said. "I'll be right here."

He looked around the room after he hung up, fighting the same thing that Alyssa was feeling. Nothing had seemed real since the night he'd come home to find Kieran and Carlos in the living room. Jess had left him alone with them. Phillip had made Carlos tell him over and over what details he knew, until he finally noticed that Carlos was exhausted and sent him to bed. It was only then that Phillip realized they were out of beds, since Jay was in one guest room and Carlos had been put in the other one. He'd looked helplessly at Kieran, who said, "I left my things in your room—if that's okay."

Phillip had nodded mutely, and they went upstairs together. It was apparent that Shanon or Jess had been there before him. Kieran's portrait was back on the easel, and the sheets he'd slept on the night before with Chad had been replaced with clean ones.

Phillip had been numb and silent. Chad, Taryn, his mother, Bunny, Kieran—it was all too much. He and Kieran hadn't talked about their misunderstanding, nor had either of them made any kind of sexual overture toward the other. They'd held each other until Kieran fell asleep, which was when Phillip got up and put a clean canvas on the easel to paint Bunny. While he worked, he kept mentally replaying his mother's observation: *I used to wonder why you were drawn to artists who committed suicide.... I could see that your work was never a descent into the darkness of depression or madness. Your art transcended your environment.*

Painting provided his only relief from the news of Bunny's death. Phillip would lie down until Kieran's breathing deepened, then he'd get up to paint, comforted by Kieran's presence. He caught a few naps during the day, in any room where someone else was. He hadn't wanted the house to be empty until today, and somehow the others had known it.

He was staring at Bunny's portrait when the phone rang.

"I can talk now," Alyssa said. "Does anyone know why? Did he leave a note?"

"I don't know," Phillip said, "since his family won't talk to his friends—at least his friends that I know. You've heard Bunny talk about his parents. You know how they are."

"When was the last time you talked to him?" Alyssa asked.

"Before I was sick," Phillip said. "In fact, I know exactly when it was: Mother's Day. He said he was sending me a new lease to sign, one that has Carlos on it, and some clothes because he was cleaning out his closets."

"Do you think he was planning it that long ago?" Alyssa asked. "That's been over two months."

"He didn't sound depressed. He sounded like Bunny. It was weird, though, because I never got the box. So I never signed the new lease. Which means our apartment is still in my name—and Bunny's."

"What are you going to do?"

"I don't know," Phillip said. "I guess I need to call Renata."

"If you need money—"

"No, I have money, and I can always get more from my family. I can help Carlos with the apartment. I can go back. I just haven't thought about it."

"When does Carlos have to go back?"

"He doesn't. He asked for time off so he could come down here and tell me, and Stewart wouldn't give it to him. Did you know Stewart was manager now?"

"No. What an asshole."

"I know. Carlos lost his temper in the Science Fiction department, yelled at Stewart, and quit on the spot."

"I'd have paid to see that," Alyssa said. "I just wish…"

"I know. It's unreal, isn't it?"

"Have you told Claude?" she asked.

"Carlos called him. They decided together that Carlos should tell me in person, and I should tell you. I hated having to tell you on the phone."

"It couldn't be helped. I just feel like we should *do* something," Alyssa said. "Get together. Have some kind of service. But we're scattered all over the country now."

"I know. Maybe if I go back to New York, we can find a time when you and Claude can both come there. Do it when we're all together."

"In a nightclub," Alyssa said. "Get drunk on foo-foo drinks, read sad poetry…"

"Pick up hot men," Phillip said with a faint smile. "It'll be a Bunny night."

"Then I guess I should forget the poetry," Alyssa said. "We'll all have to wear Bunny's favorite designers."

"And do his favorite designer drugs."

"Phillip, I love you so much."

"I love you too."

Phillip heard Alyssa's breathing change as she shifted the phone from one ear to the other. "Tell me about Kieran," she said.

"Nothing to tell. He's here. I'm sure Carlos already explained how I came to be lying in his arms on my last morning in New York."

"How did those two hook up?"

"Carlos had actually tried to find Kieran right after I moved. He knew what he looked like because of the mural I did on the wall. He went to Posh and other bars in the neighborhood, hoping he'd run into him. He never did. But I'd told Claude—in a letter—Kieran's last name and where he worked. When Carlos got in touch with Claude about Bunny, Claude told Carlos. Carlos left a message at

Kieran's company, Kieran called him back, and they flew down together."

"Carlos is an angel," Alyssa said.

"Yeah, he is."

"How long is Kieran staying?"

"I have no idea. 'Lyss, I've sort of been in a fog."

"I understand. But you and Kieran need to talk."

"I know."

After his conversation with Alyssa, Phillip wandered through the rooms of Belfast House, finally returning to his bed to stare at the ceiling. His eyes unfocused and he saw shapes forming on the stark white ceiling: Bull skulls morphed into eagles flying against a desert sky, which morphed into seagulls diving into an ocean and snatching fish for their dinner. The scene changed, and Phillip saw rats scurrying down a narrow alley, where a young man ahead of him took on Chad's appearance, then Jay's, then Kieran's, as he ran down the alley and glanced over his shoulder like someone was chasing him. It occurred to Phillip that he too was running, desperately trying to reach Kieran, who had become Bunny. He tried to call out to Bunny, but no sound came. He watched as Bunny reached the end of the alley and ran into the street in front of an oncoming bus. Phillip found his voice and screamed, which made Bunny stop in his tracks and turn around, smiling just before the bus hit him.

"Phillip? Was that you? What's wrong?" Jess asked, reaching the top of the stairs just as Phillip sat up. "I heard you scream."

"Where is he?"

"Who?"

"Bunny. I saw him," Phillip said, looking wildly around his room. "He was here a minute ago. I swear."

"It was a dream," Jess said. She used the sheet to wipe the sweat from Phillip's forehead. "You were dreaming."

Phillip looked up and saw nothing but a bare ceiling. He was in his room. There were no skulls, no eagles, no rats, and definitely no Bunny. He sighed and gave Jess a helpless look, feeling foolish. "I feel like I'm going crazy."

"Then you aren't," she said. "You're just tired. You haven't been sleeping."

"I suppose."

After a long silence, Jess asked, "Should I leave? Do you want to try to sleep again?"

"No. Stay, please. What time is it? I thought you were out doing errands."

"I was. It's almost five. The others will probably be back soon for dinner."

Phillip counted back, figuring that he'd been asleep for about six hours. He leaned against the headboard and said, "Why am I so angry? I thought I was sad, but I'm not."

Jess softly asked, "Who are you angry with?"

"I'm angry at Bunny for being so fucking stupid—for killing himself, for not asking for help." Phillip thought about that for a moment and added, "I'm angry at myself for not realizing that my friend was so desperate, that I was so wrapped up in my own problems I couldn't see what anyone else was going through." Phillip waited for Jess's objection, but it didn't come. She looked at him blankly and seemed to be waiting for more, so he said, "I'm angry at my grandfather for making me come down here, apparently for no reason, since the rest of my family never lets my mother out of their sight. I'm angry at my mother for being so nuts, for her moods that were so erratic when I was younger that I barely trust anyone today. I'm pissed off that I'm in a place where I can't be myself, that I can't hold hands with my boyfriend when we walk down the beach without feeling like I'm going to be killed."

"What boyfriend?" Jess asked, startling Phillip.

"I don't know," he said. "If I had one, I mean. Which is another reason I'm angry. I seem to drive away anyone who loves me, and I don't know why."

"There's way too much anger in this room," Jess said. "Are you mad at me?"

"No."

"Not yet," Jess said, which made Phillip smile. "You need to let go, Phillip. You can't control everything in your life. Or everyone."

"What control? I don't have control over anything," he said. "Shanon says I let everyone make decisions for me."

"For that theory to be true, you'd have to have had a lobotomy at some point. From what I've seen, you've made your own decisions. People make suggestions. Life gives you choices. But ultimately, you make the decisions."

"I guess you're right," Phillip said.

Jess slapped his knee playfully and said, "Of course I am. The other thing to remember is that you can't control what other people think about you—or what they do. Like Bunny. From what I've heard, he was wrestling with those issues too. Probably for a long time. It's really hard to think that you're alone in life, that the people you love don't love you or accept you. I hope you don't feel that way."

Phillip shook his head. "No."

"Hang on a second." Jess went down the stairs, then came back with a brown cardboard box. "This came in the mail from Julianna. She accidentally mixed it up with her things when she moved out. I wasn't sure when I should give it to you. It's from Bunny for you."

Phillip stared at the box, afraid to touch it, as if it might blow up in his hands. He realized it was the box he'd told Alyssa that Bunny never sent, but he couldn't help feeling that it was a message from the great beyond, or that Bunny was pulling one last prank on him. He found a knife in his box of art supplies and delicately cut the tape that sealed the box, parted the flaps, and peered inside.

He pulled out several articles of clothing: pants, shirts, T-shirts—all of which he'd seen on Bunny at some point in the past. He unfolded a pair of vinyl pants decorated with zippers and a complicated series of straps and laughed. "Where did he think I'd wear these in Mississippi?"

"To church?" Jess suggested.

"Only if you go with me. To Redemption Center."

"In a word, no," Jess said.

"None of this stuff is me." He sighed and pushed the box toward Jess. "Here. Sell them on eBay. Give them away or something. I can't deal with it."

"Are you sure?" When Phillip nodded, she shrugged and pawed through the box. She pulled out a black leather jacket and thrust it at him, saying, "This is too nice not to hold onto. Keep it."

"This was his favorite." He rubbed the soft, supple leather and remembered times that Bunny had worn it: breakfast at three in the morning after clubbing, drinks at Xth Ave. Lounge, trips to the museum. Phillip slipped into the jacket, expecting a bolt of lightning to crash through the roof and strike him. Instead, he felt warm and comforted. "I guess it's good to have something to remember him by."

"Exactly," Jess said.

"Wait. What's this?" Phillip had put his hand in one of the inside pockets and brought out an envelope. He opened it, found a note, and read it to Jess:

> *Hope you like the clothes. They'll be just what you need to shake things up in Buttville, Mississippi. Remember that no matter where you go, there you are. You're great, Phillip. Be proud. Be fabulous. Be you. You'll go far. And I've enclosed a ticket to help you get there. Love, Bunny.*

Other than the note, the envelope was empty. Phillip searched the jacket and found a series of open-ended airline tickets. "Round-trip tickets to Ibiza."

"Wow. For two?"

"Nope. First class for one. I guess this was his way of telling me to go without him."

"You should go," Jess urged. "It would be fun."

"There's no way I can go now." He stuffed the tickets into a pocket of his cargo shorts and carefully hung the leather jacket in his closet. "Maybe when my grandfather comes home. We'll see."

Jess held out a sheaf of papers and said, "Here. This was at the bottom. Looks like a lease."

Phillip looked at the lease and shook his head. "His name's on it. Just like Bunny to keep things unclear. Giving up his clothes, sending me a trip for one, makes it seem like he was already planning his exit. So why send me a lease with his name on it?"

"I wish I could tell you," Jess said.

"I have to call Renata, my old landlady."

"Just don't call her old when you talk to her." Jess picked up the box of clothes and asked, "Are you sure you don't want these?"

"You do what you want with them," Phillip insisted. "Don't worry about me. I feel better now."

Phillip looked at the painting of Bunny again. He wasn't as angry as he'd been earlier. Although he felt sad, he smiled wanly and tried to think of Bunny in a happier place—perhaps organizing disco parties on a billowy cloud or chairing the membership committee at heaven's gates. Phillip pulled the airline tickets from his pocket and carefully tucked them behind the painting.

When the others returned from their outing, they found Phillip kneeling in one of his flower beds, weeding and loosening the soil with a trowel. He stopped his work and listened as Carlos and Kieran recounted their journey through the coastal towns, describing everything they'd seen and done with the exuberance and awe typical of strangers in a strange land.

After Carlos and Shanon went inside to start supper, Kieran sat on the lawn next to Phillip and said, "You look better."

"I feel better," Phillip said. "Being in fresh air and sunlight feels good. I talked to Alyssa, then had a good talk with Jess." He pulled up a long blade of grass and began winding it around his ring finger. "I don't know. Things are looking up."

"Good to know," Kieran said. "I've been wanting to ask you a question."

"Okay."

"How long should I stay around?" When Phillip didn't answer, Kieran said, "I was wondering, because my next stop after this is Belfast."

"You're going home?" Phillip asked. The blade of grass split and fell from his finger. "When?"

"Whenever I see fit to leave, I suppose," Kieran answered. "I've been sacked. It's happening everywhere. A lot of computer companies are downsizing, outsourcing jobs. It's terrible. My mates have all moved on; some stayed, some went home. A few weeks ago I sent my things home. Carlos caught me before I left. And here I am."

"You can stay here as long as you want," Phillip said.

"Unfortunately, that's not the way it works," Kieran said. "I'm not a citizen. My visa expires in a month."

"Then I guess we have a month," Phillip said. "That sounds familiar, doesn't it?" He leaned over and tentatively kissed Kieran on the cheek.

"Come here," Kieran said. He lay back on the grass, pulling Phillip with him. He wrapped his arms around Phillip's chest and held him tight. "I've missed you madly."

"Me too," Phillip whispered.

Chapter 21

"Kieran and I were talking about muses on the drive here," Phillip said.

They were sitting at the dining room table with his Aunt Fala and Uncle Harold. Persia had long since cleared their dessert dishes and left them to their coffee and conversation, and Phillip was thinking that Kieran by candlelight could be anyone's inspiration.

"Phillip loaned me a book of your poetry," Kieran said. "I enjoyed it, especially the one about the muse."

"Thank you, but I stole the idea from your own Yeats," Harold said. "Yeats said that when he was young his muse was old, but when he was old his muse was young."

"I'd think any Irish writer would need only Ireland itself as a muse," Fala said.

"You've been?" Kieran asked.

"When I was in college," Fala said. She looked almost girlish when she added, "And a second time, on our honeymoon."

"I didn't know that," Phillip said. He settled back, listening as the three of them discussed Ireland until Kieran, looking ashamed, said that they'd seen more of his country than he had.

"Maybe none of us appreciates the magic of our home the way visitors do," Fala said. "But I think an artist, even if he's unaware of it, absorbs it into himself and uses it in his work." She turned to Phillip. "Do you have a muse?"

"I never thought so," Phillip said. "Until I moved into Belfast House. It unlocked something inside me." He looked at Kieran a few seconds. "Or maybe it was a person who unlocked it, then Belfast House made me feel brave enough to open the door."

Fala smiled indulgently and said, "Even when he was a little boy, Phillip was susceptible to houses. I used to get so frustrated with him whenever he went anywhere. I'd ask who he met, what they were like, but the only thing he'd really describe was the house he'd been in. As a linguist, I should have understood him better. For Phillip, people were inseparable from where they lived. He was answering my questions, but in his own language of houses."

Phillip winced. "Don't tell him that. He saw the chaos of my New York apartment."

"Aye," Kieran said. "It was a tip."

Fala noticed Phillip's confusion and said, "A mess."

"I need you around to translate for me all the time," Phillip said. "He's right. It was a mess, like me. Whereas in his apartment, there was a place for everything, and everything in its place: a manifestation of his orderly mind."

"Oh, dear," Fala said, looking toward the living room. "You must think this house is a disaster."

"It's lovely," Kieran said. "Do you have any snaps of Phillip as a muzzy?"

Fala burst out laughing at Phillip's expression and said, "Pictures of you as a little one."

"A little brat," Kieran corrected her with a grin at Phillip.

"No, she doesn't," Phillip said emphatically.

"I do," Fala disagreed.

"Hundreds," Harold added. "We didn't have children of our own, so Phillip had to endure being documented by us."

"Please," Kieran begged Phillip.

"No!" Phillip said, knowing his refusal was futile. "Would you like to join me outside for a smoke?" Kieran shook his head, and Phillip walked toward the door saying, "Just please don't show him the bad ones from puberty."

He smiled as he stood on the porch, listening to his aunt dig through drawers like an archaeologist trying to excavate his past. He'd spent days avoiding opening up his history to Kieran. Instead, he'd taken him to Whittier Plantation to introduce Kieran to his old work crew and show off the landscaping they'd done for Godbee Nursery. The Bankses were out of town, so Phillip had left the painting of the house and a note with their housekeeper.

They'd gone to Singing River Casino and gambled. They'd gone swimming at Dash's. They'd gone out to eat with Shanon and Carlos, visited the Hurricane Camille Memorial with Jess and Carlos, and walked on the beach with Jay at night. Phillip wondered if Jay's incessant dissection of his relationship with Travis annoyed Kieran as much as it did him. If it did, Kieran didn't complain. Nor did he ever question why Phillip didn't show him where he'd grown up, gone to school, hung out as a teenager. He seemed to be willing to let Phillip call the shots, never asking about his mother or the rest of his family. Phillip had finally decided that Fala and Florence were the safest Godbees to inflict on Kieran. Since Florence and Sam were on one of their twice-yearly trips to New York, Fala and Harold had won the first introduction to Kieran.

He walked back into the dining room just as Fala set an album on the table and opened it for Kieran. Phillip looked over Kieran's shoulder, quiet as his aunt and uncle talked about outings and family gatherings where some of the pictures had been taken. He'd seen the photos many times, and his mind wandered.

"Still no muzzy snaps," Kieran said.

"That sounds like a dog treat," Phillip said. He'd never really noticed that the Phillip in Fala's photos was between the ages of three and eighteen.

"There aren't many pictures of Phillip from New Orleans," Fala said. "Ellan never had film in her camera, and when we were all together, it was Andi who took pictures of him with her children. She has all those."

"This is your mother?" Kieran asked, pointing to a picture. When Phillip nodded, he said, "She resembles that singer."

"Judy Collins," Harold said. "We always told her that."

"She does have lovely eyes," Fala said. "Phillip got his brown eyes from his father."

"I wish you had pictures of him," Phillip said absently, his eyes on Kieran's hands as they turned pages in the album. He was suddenly acutely aware of Kieran's shoulder against his groin, and the sheen and scent of his hair. It seemed insane that they hadn't made love since Kieran's arrival. But once again Kieran seemed to be holding back, letting Phillip decide.

"Who's this?" Kieran asked. "He keeps showing up."

Phillip looked at the picture of Chad and him when they were about ten years old. They were behind his grandfather's house, and Phillip was sitting on an old ice-cream maker as Chad cranked it. He remembered fighting about who had to sit on the ice-filled bucket and who got to turn the crank. He could almost taste the homemade ice cream—vanilla flavored with peppermint and sprinkled with chocolate chips.

"Chad Cunningham," Fala said when Phillip didn't answer Kieran. "Wherever you saw one, you saw the other. I didn't know you two were still in touch until he came to Daddy's house when you were sick. He's a good friend."

"Yes," Phillip said, noticing that as Kieran turned pages, he seemed to linger on any that included pictures of Chad.

He kept thinking about that later while he tried to get comfortable in the yellow room, and about Kieran finding him in bed with Carlos and storming out. He finally got up, put on his shorts, and slipped down the hall to the blue room. He went in without knocking and found Kieran staring up at the ceiling.

"Can't sleep?" Phillip asked. When Kieran shook his head, he said, "Me either." Kieran pulled back the sheets and Phillip climbed in next to him. "I've gotten used to sharing a bed with you."

"Shh," Kieran said, pulling Phillip close.

"They don't care," Phillip said, although he lowered his voice. "They put us in separate rooms for comfort and privacy, not because they have a problem with us sleeping together."

"Have you stayed here with a man before?" Kieran asked.

"No," Phillip said. He waited out the silence that followed. He was sure he knew what Kieran was thinking but thought it best to let Kieran broach the subject in his own way.

"I showed you my Achilles heel," Kieran finally said.

Phillip smiled and said, "That you can be jealous?"

"Not like your man Travis," Kieran said. "More like a bit of insecurity."

"Yes, I remember how insecure you sounded when you told me what I could do with my keys at the crack of dawn one morning," Phillip said. "You know nothing was going on between Carlos and me."

"Carlos." Kieran's tone made it sound like he'd never heard of Carlos in his life.

Taking a deep breath, Phillip said, "Chad was my best friend from eight to eighteen."

"Your mate, like."

"Yes."

"You're still in touch, but I haven't met him. Yet you introduced me to Dash."

"What does one have to do with the other?" Phillip asked.

"I could see Dash had a go at you and it was nothing for me to worry about. But you've never mentioned this best friend." Kieran turned his head to meet Phillip's eyes. "Let's drop it. None of my business."

"It's complicated," Phillip said. "I'm not sure I understand it myself. But if you want to hear it, I'd rather we didn't drop it."

"Start talking," Kieran said, sitting up against the pillows.

Phillip reached over to take a pen from Kieran's nightstand and said, "I'll give you a story if you let me tattoo your arm while I talk."

"What kind of tattoo?" Kieran asked suspiciously.

"Does it matter? It's only a pen. The ink will wash off." Kieran nodded, and Phillip began talking as he drew. He told Kieran about becoming friends with Chad in elementary school, how they stayed friends even when they went to different high schools, how they worked part time at the same bookstore after school, or hung out at Smith's Diner together.

"Did you date girls?" Kieran asked.

"I never dated. I told myself it was because my mother's behavior made my life too complicated. Chad dated. But on the weekends after his dates, somehow we always ended up together—hanging out, sleeping over at each other's houses. I have to backtrack. When we played together as kids, we had a lot of buddy fantasies. We were Butch and Sundance in the Old West. Batman and Robin. Confederate soldiers going after Yankees. James Bond–type spies. Chad was always the main man, and I was his devoted sidekick. I guess it didn't seem weird to me when I started having masturbation fantasies and they were just an extension of that—me and Chad. I didn't get it, until a trip we took to Florida."

Kieran listened silently while Phillip told him what had happened in Daytona and about the misery afterward, when Chad shut him out. Phillip kept his eyes locked on the drawing he was doing on Kieran's arm. It was easier to tell the story with something else to focus on.

"What happened with Chad, as much as my problems with my family, made me go to New York. I didn't want to stay around here, unhappy and haunted by regrets about the end of our friendship. We didn't talk the entire five years I was gone."

"Was he one of the reasons you came back?"

"I didn't let myself think about it at the time. I mean, after five years in Manhattan, I'd managed to bury it pretty well. I thought I was over it. Then I saw him again. I'm all done here," Phillip said, tapping Kieran's arm.

Kieran didn't look down at the drawing when he said, "And?"

"Chad was a little freaked out to hear that I'm gay. He dealt with it, but not comfortably. He acted like Daytona never happened. I wanted to let it go. I almost succeeded."

Phillip stared at the drawing until Kieran reached over and turned his face up, saying, "This self-professed straight man had sex with you again?"

Phillip nodded and said, "It was just like Daytona—amazing. Only the next morning, he didn't run out on me, at least not because of the sex. We argued about something else, and just like before, he shut me out. I haven't heard from him since."

"How do you feel?"

"Confused. Helpless. Resigned, I guess."

"Not about the outcome. About him."

"The same. Confused."

"Are you in love with him?"

"I don't...think so. I don't know. I don't want to bury my feelings again. I want it resolved, one way or another, for good. I can't force Chad to deal with it together, though. He has his own crap he's working through anyway." He gave Kieran a rueful smile. "Come look at this in the mirror so you can get the full effect."

"Phillip—"

"Please," Phillip begged gently.

Kieran allowed himself to be pulled from the bed to the mirror. He was silent as he assessed Phillip's rendition of the Celtic Tree of Life. In the drawing, Kieran and Phillip were wrapped in a tight embrace and formed the trunk of the tree. Kieran's hair flowed out and became the branches over their heads, then wound down to become the tree's roots so that Kieran and Phillip were within a circle.

"I feel strong with you," Phillip said. "You make me feel alive and grounded. You are everything that's good about what men share with men. I love being in this house with you, because this was the home where I was happiest."

"I wish it weren't temporary," Kieran whispered, meeting Phillip's eyes in the mirror.

"I can draw it on paper for you," Phillip said.

"You know I didn't mean the tattoo," Kieran said.

"I know," Phillip said. He ran his fingers over the back of Kieran's arm, –feeling the softness of his pale skin and the firm muscle underneath. He wrapped his hands around Kieran's biceps and rested his chin on his shoulder, staring at their reflection in the mirror. "Trust me. You don't want to stay here. The locals do nothing but talk about fishing or catching shrimp. It's like living in the movie *Forrest Gump*. Nothing ever happens. You can't be gay here without living under a rock. I'm sure it's much nicer in Ireland."

Kieran shook free of Phillip's grasp and said, "I don't want a scrap, so do me a favor. Don't tell me what I want." Hurt and confused, Phillip stared balefully as Kieran sat on the bed. "What did you learn about New York?"

"Are you mad at me?"

"No. Just tell me. Did it solve everything for you?"

Phillip stared at Kieran, wondering where the question was leading. Was Kieran breaking up with him? Again? He almost laughed at the thought, since they weren't really together anymore. He thought about the time they'd spent together in Manhattan and how happy he'd felt in spite of the looming expiration date on their romance. He remembered that for a fleeting moment, before he learned about Bunny's death, he'd felt that happiness again when he saw Kieran standing in Belfast House. With that in mind, he answered, "Yes. I was happy there."

"Why?" Kieran asked.

"Because I met you," Phillip admitted bashfully.

Kieran grinned and briefly looked up at the ceiling before saying, "That wasn't the answer I was expecting. You got me, mate. Come over here."

Phillip crossed the room and climbed onto the bed. Before Kieran snuggled against him and pulled the covers over their heads, Phillip remembered being six years old and tiptoeing into his mother's room at midnight, feeling frightened and unsure if seeking comfort was right or wrong. He could still feel the apprehension of that moment, as if it was a wound that was never allowed to heal because he kept picking at the scab. When Kieran held him and eventually fell asleep with his nose buried in his hair, Phillip felt the same soft calm he'd experienced when his mother had accepted his presence and held him tightly, running her fingers through his hair while her steady breathing warmed his neck. His worry would evaporate, and for the rest of the night he felt safe.

Phillip lay in Kieran's arms and soaked in the safety, absorbing it like rays of sunlight on his skin. He stared at the ceiling, and his mind reeled through the years. He remembered sitting on his grandfather's porch, wondering when his father was going to come back. The unpleasant moments when his mother would cry and scream for no apparent reason and how he'd run down the road to Taryn and Chad. A problem at school and the principal's frustration at trying to find a member of his family who'd take responsibility. The fight with his grandfather that drove him north to New York City. The loneliness he felt on the flight back to Mississippi.

With all those moments colliding in his head, Phillip realized that fear was his muse. Fear had always driven him, lurking, waiting to jump out at him. He was afraid of his mother. Her outbursts and chaotic emotions always threw him off balance. He felt similarly about his grandfather. Even though he could usually anticipate how his grandfather would react to certain situations, he was still a controlling and gruff man. Just thinking about him made Phillip's stomach tighten.

Mississippi held a different kind of fear for Phillip: hatred. Not his own. He thought the Gulf Coast was aesthetically stimulating: the beaches, the trees, the light, the air—it all made him feel alive. But the mindset of the South frightened him: the closed-minded people, the bigotry, the hatred thinly veiled by religious fervor. Phillip was aware that people were often afraid of what was different, and that those people were everywhere, but he felt it most strongly when he was home in Mississippi. In Manhattan, there was safety in numbers.

Bunny had put that theory to rest for Phillip. Even with a million other gay people around him, Bunny had obviously felt alone and different. Phillip thought about all the times he'd felt that way. How he'd sit at the end of his pier and stare at the murky water, wondering what it would be like to sink to the bottom of the Gulf, consumed by the blackness. There was always a reason not to: the trees, Fala's laughter, Odell's biscuits, his art. Something always made him walk back down the pier to the shore.

Kieran shifted in his sleep, moving a hand over Phillip's side and tickling him. Phillip took Kieran's hand, moved it to his lips, and kissed his lover's salty palm. He thought about how odd it was that their situations were reversed. Now it was Kieran who would be leaving.

Phillip felt fear creep out from its hiding place under the bed and begin to play with his mind. He didn't want to be left with drawings and paintings—

mere imprints of Kieran. He wanted the real deal. What would he do after Kieran left? Would he be alone again?

He shook away the dread, knowing it was useless to think that way. He had to be hopeful. After all, Kieran had found his way back to him. Maybe it could happen again sometime in the future. Phillip wanted to enjoy their time together and not worry about things that were beyond his control.

A thought occurred to him and he shook Kieran's shoulder, whispering, "Are you awake? Kieran?"

Kieran rolled away from Phillip and pulled the covers tighter, groaning, "Lay off."

"I just thought of something," Phillip said. "I want to share it with you."

"I'm knackered, mate. Can it wait until morning?"

"Neither of us has a job," Phillip said. "We're men of leisure. We can sleep anytime."

Kieran sighed and said, "Go on, then. What is it?"

"When I moved to New York, I was running away. No, it didn't really solve anything. But I did learn that I'm going to be okay. It gave me confidence. Maybe I didn't fully understand that until I came back here." Kieran sat up against the pillow. While he brushed his hair from his face, tucking it behind his ears, Phillip lay his head in Kieran's lap. "I wanted to tell you something Jess said to me the other day. She said I should stop worrying about things that are beyond my control. She's right."

"I think so too," Kieran said.

"Said the control freak," Phillip joked.

"I can't argue with that. I made it rather difficult for you to fit into my neat and orderly life, didn't I?"

"In your apartment, yes," Phillip agreed. "But when it was just the two of us exploring the city and each other, we were a good fit."

"You have to understand," Kieran implored, "I'm the product of a very strict upbringing. Everything my sisters and I did—read, listened to, watched on telly—was regulated by my parents. They even decided my mates for me. They were prominent in the community, so I always felt like I was being watched. Someone would always tell them what I did after school, who I was mucking around with, that sort of thing. So after a while of it, I just fell in and was the perfect son."

"Perfect—except that you're gay," Phillip surmised.

"Let me tell you a joke I learned in school," Kieran said. "What should you do if your daddy's gay?"

"I'm afraid to guess."

"Kill him."

"That's awful."

"That's life. But it's like that anywhere you go, isn't it?"

"That's what you were getting at earlier, right? You can't run away from your problems because every place is basically the same."

"Bang on," Kieran replied. "Ireland, Mississippi—it's six of one, half-dozen of another. There are foolish people everywhere. Whatever issues you have with life don't get left behind. You always take them with you. Listen to me talk. Smack me a good one if I'm getting preachy, would you?"

"You're not," Phillip assured him. "Even if you are, I don't care. I've wanted to hear more about this part of you."

"It's what gay guys do when they get together, isn't it? Compare notes, share coming-out stories, critique their last boyfriends. I try not to do all that. It gets really boring, and my story is quite typical, I'm afraid." Kieran stopped talking, but Phillip gazed at him, urging him to continue. Kieran relented. "Fine. My parents found out I was gay and went ballistic because they expected me to become a priest." Phillip sniggered, and Kieran said, "Don't laugh. They had no reason to believe I wouldn't. I was the perfect altar boy—went to Catholic school, catechism classes—I knew it all backward and forward. It never occurred to me that I didn't want to do it."

"What happened? What changed your mind?"

"Father McCarthy sucked my knob, and I saw the light." When Phillip's eyes nearly popped out of his head, Kieran laughed and said, "I'm yanking your chain, mate! Naw, nothing like that happened. At least not to me it didn't. But the scandals of the Church were hard to ignore. It all seemed so dodgy and banjaxed. Corrupt. Hypocritical. Did you know that a person with an allergy to wheat is basically screwed? There are some orders that will make gluten-free sacraments, but the Vatican rejects the practice. It's better to receive the sacrament and die, apparently. They're not evolving with the rest of the world, and it just got to me. When it came time to choose University or Seminary, I finally put my foot down and told my parents I wasn't going to be a priest."

"How'd they take it?" Phillip asked, even though he felt he knew the answer.

"They kicked me out of the house, swore I wasn't their son any longer. Since they went that far, I drove the nail in the coffin even farther and told them I'm queer. I lived with Katherine—my eldest sister—got a job, and finished Uni on my own. Eventually moved to New York, and then I met you."

"Do you ever talk to them?"

"I haven't, no. Not for ages. My sisters keep me up-to-date." He tapped Phillip's forehead with his index finger and said, "Count yourself lucky, you. Your mother may be nutters, but at least she still talks to you."

"I suppose," Phillip said. "What our parents think and do is beyond our control."

"Right," Kieran agreed. "That's quite Zen of you. A terribly twelve-step mindset, isn't it?"

"Hey, if it works, why fight it? Jess is right. Just thinking that makes me feel like a weight has been lifted," Phillip admitted.

"Thank you for sharing it with me, then. I'll try to adopt it for my own situation." Kieran kissed Phillip and said, "Shall we try to get some zeds?" Phillip grinned slyly and pulled Kieran's mouth to his again and kissed him deeply. Between kisses, Kieran murmured, "Right. Sleep is highly overrated anyway. Try not to smudge my tattoo, okay?"

Phillip was still smiling the next day on the ride back to Belfast House, remembering how nice it was just to hold Kieran and make out for hours, like desperate teenagers. Even though they didn't have sex, he still felt satisfied. Kieran was like a drug—a powerful, mind-altering substance that enabled him to momentarily forget all his troubles. "Like ecstasy with lips."

"What?"

"Nothing," Phillip said, blushing.

"Weren't we supposed to turn back there?" Kieran asked, pointing to the left.

"Ever drive a car and suddenly realize you haven't been paying attention at all to what you're doing?" Phillip glanced over and realized Kieran was staring at him with a peculiar expression. "We're taking a small detour. I want to show you something." After he parked the car in the beach lot, Phillip pointed and said, "That's my pier."

"Your grandfather bought you a pier?"

"No. It's owned by the town." When he realized that Kieran was joking, Phillip smacked him on the leg, "Bastard. Come on."

It was almost suppertime, but there were still people on the pier. Phillip was used to having it to himself, but he didn't mind. He watched a small boy casting a line over the side of the railing while his father praised him for a good cast. Farther down, a man and woman were staring at the horizon. As they walked past, the man put his arm around the woman's waist, and she rested her head on his shoulder. The end of the pier was crowded with people holding fishing poles, so they stopped and leaned against the rail.

"This is where I come to be alone," Phillip explained.

"With all these people?" Kieran asked.

"I usually come late at night when there's hardly anyone here."

"I'll bet it's peaceful," Kieran said. "Back in Belfast I used to spend hours at St. Patrick's. There's something about the quiet in a church that puts things in perspective. I can't really explain it properly."

"Try," Phillip urged. He liked to listen to Kieran talk.

Kieran paused for thought, then said, "The votives by the altar always reminded me that other people had far grander needs and hopes than my own. Everything about the church itself—the hugeness of it, the vast space, the stained-glass windows—made me feel small. One person in a sea of hundreds. It's humbling to kneel in a church and feel how small your problems really are in the grand scheme of things. It always made me feel better about my lot in life."

"What about your parents?"

"What about them?" Kieran said. "They're a different lot, aren't they? They come from a different time. They may never understand me. I can accept that. I may not like it, but I can still honor them."

"You're a far better man than I can ever hope to be," Phillip said, shaking his head in amazement.

"Ah, Phillip," Kieran said, slapping him on the back, "there's hope for you yet, mate. Learn from me." Kieran spread his arms in front of him, as if to part the Gulf waters. "Let me teach you the way."

"You know what they say. Once a heathen…"

"Always a Sodomite?" Kieran said hopefully.

"We'll see. Hey, speaking of places of worship and sinning, let's go to the casino."

"Casinos and churches. Either way, you're giving away all your money." Kieran shrugged and added, "Sure. Why not?"

As they walked back down the pier, Phillip suddenly felt a hand on his ankle. He stopped, looking down to see Chad sitting with his legs dangling over the edge and staring up at him.

"What are you doing?" Phillip asked. He looked to his left and saw that Kieran was still ambling down the pier. "You scared me."

Chad shrugged dismissively and stood up. "Whatever."

"Was that an apology?"

"I don't think I have anything to apologize for," Chad said.

"Okay. See ya later." Phillip turned, but Chad grabbed his shoulder. "Was there something else?" Phillip asked.

"I just want you to know that things are fine with my mother and I," Chad said.

"And me," Phillip corrected. "That's great, Chad. I'm thrilled for you. Can I go now?"

"I'm going to California."

"To see your father?" Chad nodded, and Phillip asked, "Is that a good idea? When was the last time you saw him? Do you even know where he is?"

Chad flushed and said, "Of course I know where he is. We talk all the time. Just because we don't see each other doesn't mean he doesn't care about me, Phillip."

"Fine," Phillip said. "You're right. My bad. When are you going?"

"Tomorrow. For a week."

There was an awkward silence between them, until Phillip weakly said, "That's great. I hope you two have a good time together."

"Right."

"I mean it!"

"Fine!" Chad exclaimed.

Kieran approached them cautiously and asked, "Phillip, you all right?"

"I'm fine." He looked down, noticed empty beer cans where Chad had been sitting, and muttered, "Oh, crap."

"Who the fuck is this?" Chad asked, gesturing to Kieran.

"Kieran, this is Chad."

"I'm well aware," Kieran said, putting his hands in his pockets.

"You got a problem with me, Leprechaun?"

"Shut up, Chad," Phillip warned.

"He's langers," Kieran observed.

"He's got problems," Phillip said. "Chad, we'll drive you home."

"I'm not drunk," Chad argued. "And you're one to talk about problems. My mother may be a dyke, but at least she's not fucking nuts."

"I think you need to shut your cake-hole, dry your arse, and go home, then," Kieran growled. "Some friend you are."

Phillip was aware that people were staring. He was torn. He felt compelled to walk away, but he also wanted to resolve things with Chad. He obviously couldn't do that with Kieran there. Nor could he do it when Chad was drunk. However, he found it interesting that Chad and Kieran were so adversarial without really knowing each other. Kieran at least had a reason to be jealous. But Chad was acting like an old hound dog that had peed on Phillip's leg to claim him. Now he was warding off another male who'd come sniffing around.

"You're acting like a jealous schoolgirl," Chad said to Kieran. "This isn't any of your business. Why don't you leave us alone?"

"I'm not going anywhere," Kieran said, folding his arms.

Chad looked at Phillip with sudden realization and asked, "Are you fucking this faggot?"

Kieran's fist moved so quickly that Phillip barely saw it connect with Chad's face. All he really noticed was Chad suddenly pitching to the left, falling to his knees, and shouting obscenities. A mother grabbed her kids and hurried down the pier. Other people stood by and openly stared.

Phillip squatted next to Chad. "Are you okay?"

"Fuck off," Chad moaned, wrenching away from him.

"You heard him. Leave him be, Phillip. He's not worth your pity," Kieran said.

Phillip ignored Kieran and assessed the damage. Chad's lip was split and swelling rapidly. "This is bad. Does anyone have ice?"

Chad looked at Kieran and said, "I'm gonna kick your ass."

"You want to have a go?" Kieran asked, raising his fists again.

"Nobody's having a go," Phillip stated. He threw his keys at Kieran and said, "Except for you. Take my car back to Belfast House."

"But—"

"Just do it, Kieran!"

Kieran looked stunned for a moment but smiled with resignation before he walked away. Phillip sighed, feeling the tension of the moment ebb away like the tide beneath the pier. A man handed him a T-shirt wrapped around a hard clump of ice cubes, and Phillip thanked him. He gently pressed it against Chad's mouth and said, "Hold this and keep your mouth closed for once so it will heal."

Chad rolled his eyes but kept his mouth shut and handed Phillip his keys. They maintained a stony silence as they walked down the pier together and climbed into Chad's truck. Phillip pulled out of the parking lot and drove toward Biloxi.

"You never answered my question," Chad mumbled.

"Which one?"

"Are you fucking the Irishman?"

"Do you care?"

Chad looked out the passenger window without answering, which Phillip took for a yes. He stopped at a light and tapped the wheel with nervous agitation. He looked at the car next to them and nearly laughed when he saw Kieran in the Volvo. Kieran pointed at Phillip, then himself, and gazed questioningly. Phillip grinned and blew him a kiss, laughing when Kieran pantomimed grabbing the kiss out of the air and eating it.

"What's so hilarious?" Chad asked.

"Nothing."

The light changed, and Kieran tapped the horn before speeding down Beach Boulevard. Phillip drove on and occasionally glanced at Chad, who sulked with the ice pressed to his lip and melting down his arm.

When Phillip parked the truck in front of Chad's house and got out, he left the key in the ignition. "Why don't you come inside?" Chad asked.

"Because I'm mad at you," Phillip replied. "Have fun in California. See you later."

"Wait," Chad said. "I don't know what got into me back there, but will you let me explain?"

"You're a horse's ass. I think that about covers it, don't you?"

"If it makes you feel better to insult me, go right ahead," Chad said. "I deserve it."

Phillip frowned. "I can't. You're taking all the fun out of it."

Chad cast his eyes downward, looking forlorn. Phillip stared at him and remembered the boy he'd met many years ago. The one who always showed up at school with scrapes and bruises. Badges of honor and ciphers of pain. Phillip had learned long ago that Chad loved getting hurt. He was purposely reckless, attempting dangerous jumps with his skateboard or climbing trees with hazardously rotten branches. Every wound won him more attention from his mother.

Chad hadn't changed much over the years. Phillip didn't want to indulge him, but he couldn't help feeling that it was his fault that Kieran had hit Chad. He'd liked the idea of Chad and Kieran fighting over him. The pier was their sacred spot, and he obviously shouldn't have taken Kieran there. Chad's fat, bleeding lip was like an affliction—a punishment from God for Phillip's every selfish and vengeful thought.

Phillip took the soggy T-shirt from Chad's hand and propelled him toward the house. "Let's see if your roommates remembered to fill the ice trays," he said.

Chapter 22

Phillip woke because he was so hot he couldn't breathe. He hadn't meant to fall asleep on Chad's couch. The fabric was scratchy and felt like a heater. He got up, found the thermostat, and slid it down until he heard the air conditioner kick on. He supposed they turned it up when they were out of the house, but he didn't care if he was acting like a spoiled Godbee. He wasn't going to be hot and miserable so they could save a few pennies on their power bill.

He went into the kitchen to get some water, which is where he saw the clock. Eleven. He groaned, knowing Kieran was probably furious with him. Hadn't they agreed to go to the casino tonight?

He dialed his number, but naturally it was the one time none of his roommates answered, and he knew Kieran wouldn't. For a brief moment he hated Chad. He called Shanon's cell phone and felt tremendous relief when she answered.

"Where are you? Where's Kieran?" he asked.

"Hello to you too. I'm at home. Kieran's asleep on the sofa in the living room. Should I wake him?"

"Yes," Phillip said.

"Hold on."

Phillip lit a cigarette while he waited and looked around at the disaster that was Chad's kitchen. The whole house was worse than his apartment in New York had ever been. He didn't understand how people could live that way.

"I'm here," Kieran said, sounding out of it.

"I put Chad to bed with his face against a bag of frozen peas," Phillip said. "Then I fell asleep on his couch. I just woke up."

"It's okay," Kieran said. "The last thing I remember, Carlos was talking to me. Then I did the same here. You kept us up all night with your blathering, remember?"

"No. I remember being kissed a lot. Anyway, I don't know what to do. Chad's passed out. I saw his ticket. He's supposed to fly to L.A. at seven in the morning. Which I guess means he should be at the airport by six. Up no later than five. If I set his alarm clock and leave, I don't know if he'll wake up."

"You don't have a car," Kieran reminded him. "If you take his truck, he can't get to the airport."

"Somebody could pick me up." Phillip paused, thinking. "If one of his roommates comes in, I'll get a ride home. If I'm sure someone will wake him up in time to make his flight. Otherwise, I guess I'm stuck here until I drive him to the airport. I'm sorry. I know we had plans tonight."

"I'm wall-falling tired," Kieran said. "I'll go drool on my pillow and see you tomorrow."

"You can drool on my pillow," Phillip offered.

"That's thoughtful of you, mate."

"You're pretty wonderful," Phillip said, grinning.

"Yeah? Well, you're a wanker. But for some reason, I seem to like it."

They hung up, and Phillip went to Chad's bedroom. Chad was lying exactly as he'd left him—his face resting against the bag of peas, which had to be mush by now. Phillip didn't intend to wake him to find out. There was nothing more boring to him than a drunk friend when he himself was sober.

He looked around the room for something to read, but all he found were automotive magazines and an ancient *People* with Tipper Gore on the cover. He wondered if Chad thought her ass was bangin'. He also found three glasses, four coffee cups, and two empty Tupperware containers that he knew were Taryn's. He took the dirty dishes to the kitchen and looked around with a sigh. He was awake. He was gay. He had to improve things.

It took him two hours to retrieve dirty dishes from all over the house, run the dishwasher twice, and bring order and cleanliness to the kitchen. He wondered if these pigs would even notice. His snooping paid off, however, when he found a carton of Benson & Hedges in Roger's bedroom. He'd smoked all his Marlboros and figured a pack of cigarettes was a small price to pay for a typhoid-free kitchen.

Chad had turned over, and Phillip threw the package of peas away. Then he took a wadded quilt from the foot of Chad's bed along with a pillow and made himself a pallet on the floor. He set the alarm clock for four, turned off the lamp, and lay down.

He dozed for a bit, then woke with a start when he felt a hand graze his ass. *Kieran,* he thought. Then he remembered where he was and said, "Chad?"

"I want to know," Chad whispered. He rested his chest against Phillip's back. "I want to know what it feels like."

Phillip tried to figure out what the hell he was talking about, since this wasn't exactly their first time. "Are you asking me to fuck you?" Phillip asked and pulled away. "No."

"You don't do that?"

"Not to you. Especially not when you're about to fly two thousand miles and you're drunk."

"I'm not drunk."

"No," Phillip said again. "How's your face?"

"It hurts. What is it with gay men? You're always whaling on somebody."

"You're always provoking us," Phillip said. "Go back to sleep, Chad. I'll get you up in time to catch your flight."

"Why's it so cold in here?" Chad said, again pressing himself against Phillip for warmth.

Phillip felt Chad's hard cock against his thigh and repeated, "Go to sleep, okay?"

"Uh-huh," Chad said agreeably. He kept hugging Phillip, but at least he was quiet, and Phillip started to relax again. "It's not like I want to love you—not that way. I just do. I'm sorry."

Phillip turned over and held him. "Don't be sorry," he said. "I love you too. You're just confusing—"

"Don't tell me how I feel, okay?"

Don't tell me what I want, Kieran had said.

"All right," Phillip said. "I won't."

He didn't resist when Chad unzipped and unbuttoned his shorts. Nor did he pretend that this was one of those times when he was letting someone else make his decision. He loved Chad. It was as simple and as complicated as that.

Chad's hand was around Phillip's penis, and he said, "Your fucking boyfriend made sure I couldn't blow you." He waited a beat, as if he were expecting Phillip to deny that Kieran was his boyfriend.

"Who's talking too much now?" Phillip asked. He was willing to fool around with Chad, but only to a point. Actually fucking him would take their relationship somewhere Phillip wasn't sure either of them was ready to be.

After he dropped Chad at the airport later, Phillip wasn't ready to go home and face Kieran. He drove Chad's truck to Dash's, and it wasn't until he got there that he remembered Kieran had his keys. Of course nobody was home. Phillip looked around, hoping no one was watching him, and climbed the gate to get to Dash's pool. He stripped to his underwear and dived in. He stayed under water as long as his lungs would allow, then he surfaced and started swimming laps to clear his head of everything except the need to push himself as hard as he could.

He was lying on the concrete, letting the sun bake him, when he heard Dash say, "So you're the criminal my neighbor called me about. You're lucky she didn't call the police."

"You'd bail me out, wouldn't you?" Phillip asked, squinting up at Dash, who was wearing a suit and tie.

"Always," Dash said.

"Could you do that now? I'm making a huge mess of my life."

"I've got nothing else on the docket," Dash said. "Have you eaten anything?"

"No."

"Come inside, young'un. Let's take care of your creature comforts first."

Phillip picked up his clothes and took a hot shower while Dash made him breakfast. He did feel better once he'd had food and coffee. Then he sat in the kitchen, smoking the rest of Roger's cigarettes while he made a full confession about Kieran and Chad. Dash listened, smiling occasionally or shaking his head.

"I'm worse than Jay," Phillip finally said. "Tell me to shut up and kick me out."

"I'd tell you that your twenties are hell, but you seem to have figured it out on your own," Dash said. "So I'll just advise you to decide what you want and go after it. You may not get it, and Chad and Kieran get to make choices too. But at least you won't be making things worse for everybody."

"Do you think I'm a complete asshole?"

"You're too young to be complete," Dash said, reaching over to ruffle Phillip's hair. "You're human, Phillip."

"Kieran told me that once too," Phillip said.

"You seem to think Kieran's put up with a lot from you," Dash said. "He must think you're worth it. What really matters is that you get some faith in yourself."

"I want to apologize for all the snotty things I've said about Mississippi—not knowing why anyone would stay here. It doesn't really matter where you are, does it?"

"It matters *who* you are," Dash replied. "That you have the guts to be yourself wherever you find yourself."

No matter where you go, there you are, Bunny had written.

"I've kept you away from the office long enough," Phillip said, getting up.

Dash stood and put his arms around Phillip. "You've got a hell of a lot, Phillip: good friends who love you, a family who'll look out for you, your whole future. It's all good even when it sucks. You're alive, and that's the best thing of all."

"I know," Phillip said, thinking again of Bunny. "Thank you, Dash, for being one of those good friends."

"Like Kieran, I think you're worth it," Dash said, releasing him.

Phillip drove Chad's truck to Belfast House, which was empty. Kieran had left a note to let him know that he'd gone exploring with Shanon and Carlos. Phillip wasn't sure where Jess was, but he assumed Jay was at work. He changed clothes and looked through his mail. There was a card from Alyssa and a letter from Claude. He opened Alyssa's card.

> *Ibiza is a great idea. If you decide to go, I'll go with you. And you don't have to buy my ticket. Eric thinks it's good for you and me to do this together. Just let me know when the time is right for you, and I'll make it work. I love you.*

Ibiza was the last thing on Phillip's mind, but he was happy at the prospect of seeing Alyssa again. He put the card aside and opened Claude's letter.

> *Phillip,*
>
> *Thanks for the letter and for reminding me of some of our better Bunny moments. I confess that the news laid me low(er than usual). Like you, I started wondering if there was something I could have done to make a difference. Should I not have moved away? Written him more? Bent my "I don't talk on the phone" rule? Read more between the lines of his letters?*
>
> *After many days of beating myself up, I've reached one conclusion: This was Bunny's show, start to finish. We stumbled in as players, some of us with bigger parts than others. But we didn't kill Bunny, and we couldn't have kept him alive. I know Bunny would never have killed himself over a love affair gone sour, a friend gone missing, or even a family…just…gone. Whatever rabbit hole he fell down, he chose not to take his friends with him. This is what we all have to accept. Not easy, but what choice do we have? All we can do is love him. And love each other—*

Phillip dropped the letter and picked up the phone, hoping Claude would break his rule and take a call.

"Hello."

"I love you," Phillip said.

"Oh, crap, what did I say in my letter? I swear I only had a couple of shots of Maker's before I wrote it."

"It's not bad," Phillip said. "I haven't finished it yet. For all I know, you ended it with upbeat quotes from *The Sound of Music.*"

"Somehow I doubt that. What's the verdict? Are you going to Ibiza?"

"Don't you start," Phillip warned. "I didn't call to talk about me, or even Bunny. I want to talk about you."

"You've thanked me many times for my part in your introduction to New York. I know you value me as a friend. You don't have to—"

"Would you shut up a minute?" Phillip asked. "What I have to say doesn't involve how I feel about you. It's just you. Hear me out."

"I'm listening."

"Don't spend another winter in that graveyard. There's no way you can be anything but melancholy—"

"I'm not Bunny," Claude said. "I'm sorry if I worried you."

"You're talking again," Phillip said. He sighed. "Listen, I don't know what I'm going to do. I'll keep paying rent on that apartment, but I get the idea Carlos isn't going back. If you want it, it's yours."

"Thanks for the offer, but I've done New York. I'm better suited for a slower life. Sometimes I just get fucking lonely, and Bisquick is bored listening to me."

"Come here," Phillip said. "I've got a job for you."

"Again, thanks for the offer, but I'm way too lazy to landscape for your aunt."

Phillip laughed and said, "Not that job. I'm not the crazy one in my family. That's my mother. Who I've been told is also fucking lonely. Ever thought of living in a mansion overlooking the water? Keeping a madwoman company? Being spoiled by a few meddlesome aunts and one mouthy old woman who can cook like you wouldn't believe?"

"You don't even know if you're staying in Mississippi," Claude said. "Why would I come there?"

"I have a friend who can introduce you to all the men you've never loved before," Phillip said. "Whether I'm here or not, you could have a good life. Will you at least think about it?"

"Let me make sure I've got this right. You want me to move there and live at your grandfather's to keep an eye on your mother?"

"Although I've honestly started thinking she doesn't need that, my grandfather is going to insist on paying someone to do it. Why not you?"

"I'll think about it," Claude said.

"Really?" Phillip asked, shocked. He'd had no idea Claude would do anything but turn him down.

"Yes. Could Bisquick come?"

"Absolutely. I haven't talked this over with my mother. But even if she says no, there's always room for you at Belfast House. And Bisquick."

"Not that you've talked it over with Shanon," Claude said, laughing at him. "You're just offering other people's homes right and left, aren't you?"

"Yes," Phillip said. "That's how it is with family. You get to take advantage of them."

"Sounds like my kind of gig," Claude said.

By the time they said goodbye two hours later, Claude noted that they'd used up his annual quota of phone time, but he said it without rancor. He also promised to answer when Phillip called him back after talking to his mother.

Phillip liked driving Chad's truck so he used it to go to Pass Christian. His grandfather's house was empty. He went next door to find Odell. She told him that his mother was across the road at the beach with Samantha and Susan, who'd come back from New York with their parents the day before. He drove over, left his shoes in the truck, and crossed the sand toward the huge beach umbrella that Odell had told him to look for. As he reached it, he could hear his mother telling his cousins a story, so he sat behind the umbrella to listen.

"They got back home with their chests full of the pirates' treasure, and that was the end of their great adventure," Ellan said.

"What did they do with the treasure?" Samantha asked.

"They bought anything they wanted," Ellan said.

"Elmo?"

"Maybe."

"Care Bears?"

"Most definitely."

"PlayStation?"

"Is this your Christmas list?" Ellan asked.

"Why did Daddy say we can't go to the pirate movie?" Samantha asked in a joke-telling voice.

"I don't know; why?" Ellan asked.

"Because it's rated arrrrr," Samantha said.

Phillip bit down on his hand to stop himself from laughing as loudly as his mother, who finally said, "Do you even know what that means?"

"No," Samantha said. "Daddy said it. What do they do next?"

"In their next adventure, King Michael gives Prince Phillip a magic brush so he can paint the face of his true love, whom he'll meet when he's grown up."

"A beautiful princess?" Samantha asked.

Phillip smiled, wondering how his mother was going to field that one.

"You'll have to wait and see," Ellan said. "But whoever it is, they'll have lots of adventures too."

"Can I make a sand castle now?"

"Yes, but you'll have to use the water in your bucket. I can't help you get more until Susan wakes up."

Samantha slipped from behind the umbrella, spotted her cousin, and said, "Hey, Phillip!"

"Hi," Phillip said. Since he'd been discovered, he moved around the umbrella and smiled at his mother, who was propped on pillows with Susan's head in her lap. After a minute, he took off his shirt, and his mother handed him a bottle of suntan lotion.

"Put this on if you're going to sit in the sun."

"Why is everyone in this family obsessed with my skin?" Phillip muttered, but he did as she'd ordered. "I caught the end of your story. I hope some of those pirates looked like Johnny Depp."

"Most definitely," she said in the same tone she'd used with Samantha.

Phillip hoped her stories had improved since the ones she'd scarred him with as a child. "I guess with four sisters, you heard a lot of stories when you were growing up."

"Why does everyone forget that I also have two brothers?" Ellan asked.

And we're off to Crazy Land, Phillip thought, saying nothing.

"You can wipe that long-suffering expression off your face," Ellan said. "I'm talking about James and Rodney."

"Odell's sons?"

"Do we know anyone else named James and Rodney?" Ellan asked. "Of course Odell's sons. They were my playmates while I was growing up. They taught me to climb trees, shoot marbles, bait my own hook, put gas in the car, and fend off boys."

"Sorry," Phillip said, properly chastised.

"They used to play cards with your father and me whenever we were all in New Orleans at the same time. We helped Rodney court his wife. Since James and Tracey now live in New Orleans, and Rodney and Amelie are in Houston, I don't see them often, but they're still my dear friends. You don't know everything about my life, Phillip."

"I guess not," he said.

His mother stared at the horizon, then she smiled and said, "Remember what I told you about Daddy and Lorna Timmons? Your second-grade teacher?"

"Yes."

"It was true. He did have a relationship with her when I was a teenager. You want to know what stopped it?"

"What?"

"My wedding. My attendants were Fala and Paula. It was a little scandalous of me to make Paula wear a dress that clearly showed she was pregnant with Brooks, but she and I didn't give a hoot what people thought. For God's sake, it was 1978. What really made a few tongues wag, including Lorna's, was that James and Rodney were Mike's groomsmen. It never occurred to us to ask anyone else. They were my brothers and Mike's friends. Miss Lorna exposed herself for the racist she was to your grandfather, and that was the end of that. I guess she blamed me, although Daddy never asked for my opinion about anything he did. That's when she started telling people I was crazy."

"Including my second grade class a few years later," Phillip said.

"I tried to get you out of her class, but Daddy said you had to grow up knowing everything about the South, good and bad. I really wasn't in any condition to fight him. I'm sorry."

"I survived my Humpty Dumpty year," Phillip said. His mother grimaced. "I shouldn't have said that. I'm sorry."

"We can sorry each other into old age, I guess," Ellan said.

They were both quiet and watched Samantha fuss over her sandcastle, until Phillip said, "There's something I've been wanting to tell you. I had a friend in New York: Bunny. He came from what most people would call the perfect home. His parents are both successful. Bunny went to good schools, including college. From the outside, everything looked ideal. But his parents refused to accept the fact that he was gay. Bunny brushed it off like it didn't matter. He made jokes about it—right up until he hung himself this summer."

Ellan's hand flew to her heart. "Oh, Phillip," she said. "I had no idea. You must be devastated."

"It's awful," Phillip acknowledged. "But as much as it hurts to lose Bunny, especially that way, all I can think about is him—how hopeless he must have felt. He had friends, people who loved him. I don't know why he did it. Maybe it wasn't because of his family. But their love, their acceptance, could have given him whatever strength he needed not to do it." He met her eyes. "I was always too cowardly to tell you the truth about myself. I knew Florence would do it. Or Selma. I wasn't sure how you'd react to having a gay son."

"Phillip—"

"You've helped me realize it wasn't a problem for you. I think I may have already known that deep inside, because I never had to endure from you or the rest of the family, even Andi, what Bunny did. I wanted to thank you for that—for accepting me—and also for never being as hopeless as Bunny was and hurting yourself the way he did."

Susan sat up, looking cranky, and said, "Hungry."

"I guess it's time to go home," Ellan said.

"You take them," Phillip said. "I'll bring all this stuff over. I need to talk to you. I need a favor."

"That's interesting," she said. When he remained silent, she shrugged, stuffed a few things in her beach bag, and made the girls tell him goodbye before she led them away.

Phillip stared out at the water for a while, then gathered up the rest of their things and took them to the truck. He found Florence making sandwiches for her daughters in his grandfather's kitchen.

"How was New York?" he asked.

"Wonderful, as usual."

"Where's Mom?"

"Taking a shower. How are you doing?"

Phillip looked at Florence and saw sympathy on her face. "Oh, my God," he said. "She already told you about Bunny?" Florence nodded. "Has it always been this way? Have you always told each other everything?"

"Not everything," Florence said. "Just what needs to be told. Would you like a sandwich? Peanut butter and jelly?"

"No, thanks," he said.

"I'm sorry about your friend," Florence said. "How old was he?"

"A year older than me," Phillip said.

"God. That's awful anytime, but even worse when someone's so young."

"Could I ask you a question? Before Papa came to New York and badgered me into moving back, were you all freaking out about my age? Thinking, *This is the year Mike died; this is the year Ellan lost her mind:* Were you doing that?"

"I wasn't," Florence said. "In all honesty, because I didn't live here then, it's not a connection I make. Do you?"

"Sometimes," Phillip admitted. "I've only got a few weeks left before I turn twenty-four. Maybe everyone will heave a collective sigh of relief and let me get on with my life."

Florence struggled to clean Susan's face with a wet paper towel, then turned to look at him. "I think you've been living your life all along. Even in Mississippi."

"I have. But—"

"Just like Samantha and me, you want to know what happens next," Ellan said, running her fingers through the tips of her hair to shake off water drops as she walked into the kitchen. "Florence, you'll have to excuse us. Phillip and I need to talk privately."

Florence's eyebrows shot up with amused curiosity, but all she said was, "Go. Leave me with the jelly monsters."

Phillip heard Susan giggling in response to being swept into her mother's arms while he followed his mother to the library.

"Smoke," she said. "I hate it when you get that crazy look in your eyes."

"That's the pot calling—"

"Don't speak to me in clichés. You said you need a favor."

Phillip lit a cigarette. "Before he died, Bunny sent me an airline ticket—to Ibiza. I have been nagged, ordered, and begged to go. My friend Alyssa wants to go with me, sort of as a Bunny send-off. I'm getting a passport, but I don't know if or when I'll go."

"What's stopping you?"

"You, among other things."

"You don't have to stay here for me."

"I told you there are other things. I'll get them all sorted out eventually. What I'm about to say isn't easy, so hear me out, okay?"

"Do *I* need a cigarette?" Ellan asked.

"No. Let me have one vice that sets me apart from the rest of our family," he said. She settled on the sofa, tucked her feet under her, and waited until he'd composed his thoughts. "It's an unpleasant surprise for me to realize how much I'm like Papa: stubborn, sometimes stupidly independent in ways that don't really matter. One other thing we have in common is worrying about you. I know that you have Odell's family and ours. In spite of that, and however wrongheaded it is, I understand why Papa wouldn't leave the country without knowing you had someone here who'd make sure you're okay. Admit it: You've never done a lot to reassure us that you'd be fine on your own."

"Sometimes I'm not fine on my own."

"I know," Phillip said gently. "Neither am I. When I went to New York, just a dumb Mississippi boy with a lot of anger and hurt, I found a new family. We loved each other, took care of each other, fought and made up, had love affairs and survived them. Even when we moved away from each other, the relationships lasted. Now all the people in my life are overlapping, and I'm beginning to think it's meant to be this way."

His mother nodded, her eyes intense as she listened to him. "What's the favor?"

"My friend Claude is in need of a change. I'd like him to come here."

"Here? As in this house?"

"Yes," Phillip said. "I'm not trying to dodge my responsibilities as a son. I know that's how it will look to Papa. But sometimes you and I get locked in these patterns that aren't all that healthy for either of us. You told me I want to make you into my idealized version of a mother, but I admit that you never tried to turn me into the ideal son. I'm starting to think my biggest hang-up about coming back wasn't you, or Papa, or the South. I was afraid I'd turn back into someone I've outgrown."

Ellan regarded him thoughtfully. "Have you?" she asked.

"I haven't figured that out yet," Phillip said. He was quiet a moment. "Is life really about stepping back and letting things happen? Am I trying to control people the way Papa does?"

"That you can even ask yourself the question should reassure you," Ellan said. "Anyway, control is an illusion. People generally do exactly what they want, even if they say otherwise."

"So what do you think? About Claude?"

His mother stared at the floor a few minutes, then said, "Could I call him myself? Talk to him without you?"

"Sure," Phillip replied. "I'll keep out of it."

On his way back to Belfast House later, Phillip pulled the truck over. He watched Jet Skiers skim across the gentle Gulf waves as he replayed the conversation he and his mother had on the night he found out Bunny was dead.

It was never that I didn't love you or that you disappointed me.... I helped you leave.... I didn't make you come back... You're the one who insists that it's your choice to be here. You have your life; I have mine.... Go and live your life...

"She may be crazy, but she's not stupid," Phillip said.

He was no longer the scared kid from Pass Christian or the young man sleepwalking his way through Manhattan. At least he knew that wherever he was, he was going to paint. But he was still daunted by the rest of it. Ibiza. Mississippi. New York. Chad. Kieran.

His gaze drifted from the water to a distant billboard advertising a restaurant. The all-you-can-eat oyster bar made him remember Carlos's wisdom before he'd left New York: *Your family needs you. But once that's settled, the world is your oyster.*

"I still have no idea what that means," Phillip said aloud as he pulled back onto Beach Boulevard.

Chapter 23

"Phillip, I'm getting a crick in my neck," Jess said. "Can I please move?"

Phillip checked the canvas to make sure he had enough guide lines to work with. He closed his eyes and allowed the completed vision of the painting to form once again in his mind. Then he looked at the canvas to match the image in his head to the incomplete painting. "Sure. We can take a break."

"Thank you," Jess said, relieved. It had been hours since Phillip saw her coming up the walk, begged her not to move, and ran to fetch his supplies. She'd protested, insisting that he find someone else, but Phillip eventually wore her down. His instincts told him that she was the perfect subject, and nothing was going to stop him from capturing her spirit. "Can I see?" she asked.

When she took a step toward him, Phillip nearly flung himself over the canvas to hide it from view. Fortunately, he remembered that the paint was still wet and held up his hand, saying, "Please, no. You'll be the first to see it when it's finished, I promise."

"Artists." She folded her arms and arched an eyebrow, an expression that made Phillip laugh. "I should be replacing the window in Jay's room, not standing around out here. Why are you torturing me? What did I ever do to you?"

"Whiner. I've been stuck on this painting for ages. You inspired me. Is that so awful?"

"Is this the painting for Taryn's restaurant? The one you've been bitching and whining about not being able to do?"

"I don't whine, but yes."

"No way. I didn't know people were going to see this. I don't know," she said, looking uneasy.

"It's too late now."

Jess ran her fingers through her hair and said, "But I look like crap."

"This isn't photography," Phillip said, laughing. "I'll paint you beautiful. I promise. Not that it's going to take much effort on my part."

"Charmer."

"What did you think would happen? It's pretty obvious that I'm painting you. Did you think I'd paint you, then whitewash over the finished product?"

"I don't know! I didn't realize that people would see it, or that it would wind up being hung in a local restaurant." Jess wiped sweat off her forehead. "Can we go inside? It's really hot out here."

"Huh. I didn't even notice," Phillip said with remorse.

"I'm sweating like a construction worker," Jess said. "I'll make margaritas."

"Is it cocktail hour?"

"I don't care," Jess said, tromping up the steps to the house with Phillip on her heels. "It's my day off. I can do whatever I want."

Like a surgical team in an operating room, Phillip passed Jess the ingredients while she crushed, blended, mixed, then poured.

"This painting you're doing for Taryn is a commission, right?" Jess asked. "It's not just a tool to land that hunky son of hers, is it?"

Phillip pulled a face, as if there were too much salt on the rim of his glass. "No! Been there, done him." He couldn't believe how easily he confessed what had been his darkest secret for so many years. But that was the effect Jess always had on him; he could tell her anything.

"What?" she exclaimed. "Did I know that? I've been so wrapped up in my empty love life that I couldn't possibly keep up with yours." She saw Phillip's expression and said, "Stop that. No sympathy from you. You're hoarding. You've got one man too many."

"Then I won't mention Dash," Phillip said.

"That's so unfair. Why do women go through courtship rituals and toe the line of monogamy, when gay men get to have rampant sex?"

"That's so untrue," Phillip said. "There must be some women who have rampant sex. It's your own damn fault for having morals."

"I suppose." She sighed. "It's just difficult to find someone."

"You want me to introduce you to my Aunt Selma?" Phillip asked. "I think she's single."

"Fix-ups never work. Whatever. I'm done whining. I thought Chad was supposed to be straight."

"He is straight."

"Call me crazy, but in my book, if a guy screws another guy, he's not straight."

"I'm not sure sexuality is that black-and-white."

"So he's bisexual?"

"I don't think he knows." Phillip patted Jess's hand and said, "When he figures it out, you'll be the first to know."

Jess affected a hurt attitude and said, "Okay, I get it, bitch. None of my business." She rolled her eyes when he laughed, then adopted a serious demeanor. "I don't want you to get hurt."

"I'll be fine. Maybe. I'm more worried about Chad at this point. Not only is he trying to sort himself out, but he just found out his mother is a lesbian."

"She is? Is she hot?" Jess asked hopefully.

"Suddenly, you sound a lot like Chad," Phillip said, laughing. "All you'd have to say is, 'Dude, is she a MILF?' "

Jess wrinkled her nose but asked, "Um, is she?"

"I think she's beautiful," Phillip answered.

"How's Chad dealing with it?"

"He's gone to California to visit his father. Which baffles me, because I didn't think they ever talked. As far as I know, they haven't seen each other since Chad was sixteen. His father was passing through when some band he worked for played at the coliseum. Chad went to the concert expecting a backstage pass, which never materialized. The whole scene sucked."

"That's sad," Jess said, frowning into her margarita.

"Luckily some groupies told him where the band and crew were staying."

"That's good."

"But security wouldn't let him in."

"That's sad."

"He didn't get to see his dad until the next day—for an hour. It was typical. His dad was always like that; I think Chad got more visits from the flu bug than his own father." Phillip paused to sip his margarita and remember how upset Chad would get when they were younger. Phillip would tell him that he was lucky to have a father, which would send Chad into tailspins of anger and depression. "He always told me that I was the lucky one because my father was dead."

"Jesus," Jess said dully. She emptied her glass and refilled it, then pointed the pitcher toward Phillip, who nodded. As she topped off his glass, she said, "I can see why his trip to California has you concerned. But is it concern for a good friend or for a potential lover?"

"You're kidding me, right?"

"Yes," Jess said between barks of laughter. "I'm just trying to lighten the mood. Speaking of lovers—"

"We're not lovers," Phillip interrupted.

She continued, "Carlos and Shanon make an interesting pair." Phillip stared at her blankly, not comprehending. "Oh, come on. Surely you've noticed how they do everything together. They're like a matched set these days."

Phillip thought about it. In the wake of recent events, it had seemed to him that everyone was giving him breathing room, letting him sort out his feelings about Bunny's death, figure out his future, and deal with his family situations. He was grateful for their support and patience, but he felt a little selfish. "Do you really think they're together?"

"Would that be bad?" Jess asked.

"No!" Phillip said adamantly. "I'm just surprised. I'm not an observant person."

"That's not true," Jess said, filling her glass again. "I'm willing to bet that, as an artist, you see things other people don't even notice."

"Objects, yes," Phillip agreed, "but when it comes to people, sometimes I don't see what's right in front of me."

"You see the important things. You saw Kieran."

Phillip smiled. He wanted to argue that Kieran had actually seen him first. But the truth was, he saw something new to appreciate in Kieran every day. Kieran also made him view the world in a different way, often pointing out objects that interested him—computers, architecture, an apple on a clean surface—and explaining to Phillip why they caught his eye, what they made him feel. Phillip liked that. It made him feel important. It made him feel like he mattered to someone.

"Kieran's great," he said. "But we were talking about Carlos and Shanon. I knew he wanted to stay here, but I didn't know why."

Jess cocked her index finger at him and said, "Now you know."

"You're getting sloshed," Phillip said, mimicking her gesture.

"I am not," Jess argued.

"If you're right—about Shanon and Carlos—I think it's great. Good for them."

"Oh, sure. Yay for them. Yay for you and every man in Mississippi. But what about me?"

"I'm guessing you're over Julianna now?"

Jess sat up straight and pointedly asked, "Who?"

Phillip grinned. "Don't worry. You'll meet someone when you least expect it," he said. Jess stood and lurched away from the table. She pivoted, picked up her glass, then walked toward the door. Phillip laughed and asked, "Where are you going?"

She turned, pointed upstairs, and said, "After that last cliché, I'm going to my bathroom to throw up. Then I'm going to sand the baseboards in the upstairs hallway. No sense letting the entire day go to waste." She turned around, ricocheted off the doorframe, and muttered "damn" under her breath before stumbling out of the kitchen.

Phillip sat at the table, making circles of moisture on the table with his margarita glass while he thought about Carlos and Shanon. Upon reflection, he realized they'd been instantly playful—teasing, making jokes, flirting with each other. Carlos was always tagging along with her on the most inane errands, ostensibly to explore the coast. Now Phillip understood that he'd been witnessing Carlos with a crush.

Carlos with a crush was only slightly different from Carlos without a crush. The variation was subtle because Carlos was normally charming, polite, witty, and helpful. The only difference was that Carlos with a crush would do anything to be constantly around the object of his affection. Sometimes this was his downfall. While his behavior was cute at the onset of a relationship, some women saw Carlos's eternal presence as clingy, or they misinterpreted it as untrusting and controlling.

But Carlos was none of those things. When he liked someone, Carlos wanted to immerse himself in her. Like an addict, he couldn't get enough. But Carlos was also unpretentious, patient, and mellow. It took a lot to rile him. Phillip knew that when the right woman came along—someone who would appreciate everything Carlos had to offer—she'd be cared for and deeply loved.

However, Phillip hadn't thought of Shanon as a Carlos crush candidate. Fiercely independent, solitary, and wary, Shanon didn't seem like the kind of woman who would put up with Carlos's shadow technique. Then there was her profession. Even if his mother was telling the truth and Shanon had given up prostitution, he wasn't sure if Carlos could deal with that, however mellow and understanding he was.

Phillip finished his margarita and set the glass on the table with firm resolve. He would stay out of it. He knew from experience that third parties often did more harm than good, so the wisest thing was to let them figure it out on their own.

On the tail end of that thought, he heard the front door open on Shanon's voice saying, "...them down. I'll take them upstairs later."

Whatever Carlos was doing left his answer hard for Phillip to hear. Something about "a fun time" and "still burning." Phillip's curiosity was piqued, and he crept quietly to the kitchen door to hear more clearly.

"I've got an ointment for that," Shanon was saying. "It might tingle a lot at first, but the burning sensation fades quickly."

"Cool. It was worth it. What a great day!"

"I had a lot of fun. Thanks for doing it with me. I'm not sure I would've done something like that on my own."

"Really? You seem pretty adventurous," Carlos said. "I'm glad you talked me into it."

"I'm excited about doing it again," Shanon said, "but next time on our own."

"No doubt. All those people watching made me nervous. It's bad enough that *you* were watching."

Shanon laughed. "The book I found will definitely help us. There are a lot of step-by-step instructions and pictures."

"If you say so. I mean, you're a natural," Carlos crowed. "You could teach a class."

"Maybe," Shanon mused. "If we do go into business on our own, it might be something to consider."

Either Jess's margaritas were too strong, or Carlos is far more accepting than I gave him credit for, Phillip thought.

He heard them walking toward the kitchen and dashed back to the table. As he sat down, Shanon walked in, followed by Carlos. Phillip tried to look nonchalant as he gestured toward the pitcher and said, "Jess made margaritas. Want some?"

Shanon looked at Carlos, who shook his head as he took a banana from the counter. "No, thanks," she said. "We saw your easel outside. Whatever you're painting, I can already tell it's going to look great."

"It's a bunch of lines," Phillip protested.

"Bro, listen to me," Carlos said, the banana in his hand cutting through the air like a knife while he spoke. "Even back in New York, when you weren't painting, I knew you weren't bullshitting anyone. Art is in your blood. Now that we're here, I've seen what you can do, and you're great." When Phillip's mouth opened, Carlos quickly added, "If you say one negative word about yourself, I'll shove this banana up your nose. You seriously need to start taking your stuff to galleries or something. You're that good."

Shanon pointedly glared at Phillip, so he meekly said, "Thank you, Carlos," although he hadn't been about to make any self-deprecating remarks. After five years of tormenting himself with doubts, he was the first to appreciate his unblocked creativity. He just needed time to develop and build his body of work.

"He's right. You *are* good," Shanon said. She seemed to read his mind when she added, "I understand your need to move at your own pace. You'll share your art when the time is right. In the meantime, feel free to cover my walls with your work."

"Shanon's House of Budding Artists," Carlos said grandly.

"Shanon's House of Transient Lunatics," Phillip said drily. "Speaking of, Jay's at work. Where's Kieran? Wasn't he out with you guys?"

"Some of the time," Shanon said cryptically. "He went off on his own for the most part."

"He said he had a few things to do," Carlos added. "He dropped us off and went out to get some wine. He'll be right back."

"We got movies." Shanon waved a package of microwave popcorn seductively. "Care to join us?"

Phillip tried to get Jess to come downstairs for a movie, but—from behind a dust mask and goggles coated in a light film of grime—she insisted that she was behind in her list of chores. As Phillip passed through the entry hall on his way to the living room, he nearly collided with Kieran. Phillip stared at him in surprise and said, "Your hair."

Kieran looked bashful and said, "It was a bit impulsive but something that needed doing. Do you like it?"

His long dark hair was gone, cut short in a more contemporary style, which emphasized every angle and feature of his face. Phillip found his voice and said, "I love it. You look amazing."

"I'm glad you think so. I hate it. At least I don't have to look at me," Kieran said. "Can you get the door, mate? My hands are full."

"Sure." He shut the door and followed Kieran into the kitchen. "If you hate the haircut, why'd you do it?"

Kieran removed bottles of wine from the bags, then paused, pointing to various drawers while biting his lip. He snapped his fingers, opened one of them, and withdrew a corkscrew. "Ha!" he exclaimed. "Found it on the first try. Not bad. Right, the hair. It was time. When I go back to Belfast, I'll need to find a new job. Can't go in looking like a dodgy midden, can I?"

"I suppose not," Phillip said, though he had no idea what a dodgy midden might be. "I probably should've offered sooner, but you could get a job at my grandfather's company. I'm sure there's something computer-related that you could do. If not, my uncle would help. His store must—"

"Phillip," Kieran interrupted, "that's bleedin' deadly of you to offer. I want to take you up on it more than you know, but I can't. I have to go home."

"I understand," Phillip said.

Kieran smiled, shook his head sadly, and stepped around the butcher-block island to embrace Phillip. "No, you don't. But it's grand of you to say so."

Phillip kissed him and said, "I meant what I said about your hair. It's smashing!"

Kieran winced, patted Phillip on the head, and replied, "Remember what we agreed? No accents but our own. You sound like Madonna when you do that. Now grab some glasses and let's join the others."

Once everyone was settled and the coffee table was covered with bowls of popcorn, bottles of wine, glasses, and ashtrays, Phillip asked, "What are we watching?"

Carlos held up a DVD case and said, *"Michael Collins."*

"Not one I'd pick but okay," Kieran groaned.

"Have you seen it?" Carlos asked while he tried to figure out Shanon's DVD player and various remotes.

"Aye. A few times," Kieran answered. "Depending on where you live in Ireland, Michael Collins is either a legend or a complete bastard. I prefer to think of him as a controversial hero and patriot of Ireland."

"Sort of like Sinead O'Connor?" Phillip asked playfully.

"Nothin' like!" Kieran said, swatting at Phillip's head.

"I wish we'd found something you hadn't seen," Shanon said.

"Naw, it's fine. It's good cinema," Kieran insisted.

Even before the movie started, Phillip was content to sink deep into the sofa and lean against Kieran with a bowl of popcorn in his lap. The wine flowed while the gunfire roared and a two-hour movie doubled in length when Kieran kept insisting on pausing to point out factual errors in the script and explain what really happened. The history lesson continued through dinner when Shanon and Kieran compared and contrasted the civil wars of Ireland and America.

After dinner, Carlos, Shanon, and Jess insisted on cleaning up and pushed Kieran and Phillip out of the kitchen. "They're sick of listening to me talk," Kieran said.

"They aren't," Phillip insisted. "Oh, shit. I left my stuff outside."

"I'll help," Kieran offered.

They carried Phillip's easel, canvas, and paints up to his room. Afterward, Kieran paused, as if unsure of himself. Phillip pulled him down so they were sitting together on the bed and said, "Today was great. Thanks for the European history lesson. They never taught us that stuff in school."

"In that case, let me tell you about when the Irish House of Commons condemned the tithe of agistment on pasturage for dry and barren cattle."

"Maybe not," Phillip said.

Kieran laughed and said, "It's just as well. I feel like I've nattered on all night."

"I love it when you natter," Phillip said. He kissed Kieran's neck and murmured, "Natter some more for me."

"Natter," Kieran said, kissing Phillip's face. He pulled off his shirt. "Natter." After he kicked off his shoes, he looked at Phillip, and they both said, "Natter." Phillip unbuttoned Kieran's jeans and slid them down his legs, pausing at the sight of a small scar on his thigh, just above the knee.

"What's that?" he asked.

"Remember my telling you how I like to spend time at St. Patrick's?" Kieran asked, and Phillip nodded. "When I was fourteen, I was standing on the steps of the church, staring at the statue of the Virgin Mary. The next thing I knew, I was down on the steps, clutching my leg. I'd been shot."

"That's terrible."

"It happens," Kieran said offhandedly, lightly touching the scar as if he'd forgotten it was there. "All I knew was that someone driving by in a car shot at me, and that's only because someone told me later. I passed out."

"I would've too, I'm sure," Phillip said.

"That's my 'I got shot' story," Kieran said.

Phillip stared at him with amazement and said, "I can't believe you're so blasé about it."

"What's the use?" Kieran asked. "Okay, right. I could get angry, I suppose. But I'm fine. I'm alive. A lot of people aren't. It doesn't matter to me if it was an IRA gunman that shot me—a Loyalist, a Unionist, whatever. Whoever it was believed in something, you know? I don't condone violence, but I can't condemn a man's passion. God will judge him. That's not my job."

Phillip was in awe of Kieran's ability to forgive and to look for the good in people. When Kieran gently pushed him back onto the bed and kissed him, Phillip was in awe once again of Kieran's passion for passion.

Later, when Kieran whispered in his ear, praising Phillip for the gentle way he entered him, Phillip thought that if he looked out the window, he'd be back in Manhattan. It was as if there was no time lost between them. "I wish I could paint this feeling," he said.

"I'm seeing fireworks, mate," Kieran gasped. "Surely you know how to paint that."

Phillip pondered that afterward as he and Kieran passed a cigarette between them. He looked out the window, seeing Shanon's telescope instead of the New York City skyline. "At least when you're back in Belfast, we'll still share the same stars," Phillip said, instantly regretting the corny sentiment.

Kieran lay with one hand between his head and the pillow as he drew a thoughtful pull from the Marlboro. He exhaled and said, "I have to tell you something."

Several responses flashed through Phillip's brain: *He's not leaving. He's staying. He's straight. He wants to try a threesome with Chad. The condom broke. He faked that orgasm.* Instead of voicing any of them, he said, "Oh?"

"I've wanted to tell you for ages but couldn't, for many reasons. First, I thought there was no use, since you were leaving New York and I'd probably never see you again. Then I thought you were screwing Carlos behind my back and you weren't worth telling. I have apologized for being a complete eejit, right?"

Phillip smiled and said, "Yes. Go on."

"Then I came here and wanted to tell you, but you had so much to deal with—your friend's death, your own family problems. This time I'll be leaving. So again, what's the use?"

Phillip swallowed and asked, "And now?"

Kieran rolled onto his stomach, looked directly at Phillip, and said softly, "I've got a baby to go back to, Phillip."

When Phillip realized that his mouth was hanging open, he instantly shut it and tried to think of something sensible to say. "That's—wow! Really?" He held up a hand to stop Kieran from replying and said, "Wait. That's not what I wanted to say at all. Obviously this has been weighing on you for a long time. I'm glad you told me. A baby? How old?"

"He's fourteen months," Kieran said, smiling bashfully.

"What's his name?"

"Derry," Kieran answered. "Dermot, actually. Dermot McClosky Sheehan."

"Wow." Phillip rolled his eyes and said, "I promise, I'll stop saying wow any minute now. How did this happen?"

"I had sex with a woman," Kieran said, grinning.

"I figured that much."

"Kyla Sheehan is an old friend. I hadn't seen her for years, but when I went to University, there she was." Kieran stared at the wall as if watching a movie of his past. "She had always fancied me, and I was still feeling insecure about being a poof. We went out on a tear, I got twisted, and the next thing I knew, I was shagging Kyla—hating it, I might add! It was as if I came to in the middle of the act and thought, *What the feckin' hell am I doing?* But being a gentleman, I finished what I'd started."

"Of course," Phillip said.

"A few weeks later, Kyla informed me that the condom must have been defective and she was pregnant. I thought my balls were in beef and I'd have to marry her, but she wanted no part of that. She said whatever I did was fine by her. So there I was: gay, ostracized by my family, and now a daddy yet *not* a daddy. What's a guy to do? Move to America, of course." Kieran sighed, looking pensive.

Phillip patted Kieran's stomach and asked, "Do you have a picture of Derry?"

"Aye." Kieran sprang from the bed, fumbled through his clothes, and pulled his wallet from his pants. He unfolded a worn piece of paper and passed it to Phillip. "Kyla sent it before I left Manhattan."

It was a printout of a computer file—a laughing, pleasantly pudgy baby comprised of millions of tiny dots. "He's got your eyes."

"You think?" Kieran said, sitting beside Phillip and looking at the picture. "He'll have my nose, poor babby. Don't you think his ears are kind of like mine? See how they do that, right there?"

Phillip laughed and said, "He's the spitting image of you and only you."

"He's got Kyla's chin. I'll give her the chin."

Phillip kissed Kieran and said, "He'll be lucky to get your mouth. I love your mouth."

Kieran folded the picture and tucked it into his wallet, saying, "The wee one shouldn't see what's about to happen, should he?"

"No," Phillip agreed.

Chapter 24

Kieran was still sleeping when Phillip left the house. Phillip knew he didn't have to leave a note. As soon as Kieran noticed that the painting of Jess was missing, he'd realize that Phillip had wanted to go somewhere alone to work. Of the many things about Kieran that Phillip appreciated, he was especially grateful for Kieran's understanding and respect for his creative needs. Any other man might have complained, pointing out that their time together was rapidly approaching an end. Kieran would simply find ways to occupy himself until Phillip came back.

When he got home that afternoon, pleased with his progress on the painting, the driveway was empty. He wondered if Kieran had gone out with Carlos and Shanon, but when he went upstairs, Kieran was napping on his bed. Phillip assumed he'd been out, because he was wearing jeans and Phillip's Zooropa T-shirt.

He quietly put away his art supplies, returned the canvas to the easel, then lay on the bed, his back to Kieran. He closed his eyes and thought about Derry, as he had over the three days since Kieran had told him about his son. He wished he had a clearer picture of Belfast as he tried to envision Kieran living there with Derry. Kieran walking down the street, holding Derry's hand, matching his stride to his son's. Taking him to a park, helping him up a slide, pushing him in a swing. Riding a bus with Derry on his lap, both of them looking out a window clouded by their warm breath. Phillip's mental images made Kieran seem stronger, sexier.

"What are you thinking?" Kieran asked as he turned over and tucked Phillip beneath an arm.

"When I came back here," Phillip said slowly, "I lived with Florence and Sam for a while. Sometimes at night, before their daughters went to bed, one or both of them would climb into Sam's lap to watch something on TV or be read to. I envied them those moments."

Please don't make a joke about me wanting to be in Sam's lap, Phillip silently begged.

Kieran pulled him closer. He hadn't shaved for a few days, and his whiskers were soft against the back of Phillip's neck. "As the youngest, I got a lot of babying," Kieran said, his voice soft. "Being held close against Da's chest. Being cuddled by Ma or my sisters. I know these things happened not because I remember them, but because I've been teased about them: 'Kieran walked late because we never let his feet touch the ground.' Or I've seen snaps of myself being held. Having no memories doesn't mean they didn't happen. You probably don't remember spitting out your strained peas or every time you got your shoes tied for you either."

"You can be so comforting," Phillip said, staring at the wall.

Kieran's arms tightened, and he said, "Even when I'm not here, I'll always be holding you in my heart."

"I know," Phillip whispered. They lay quietly for a while, then he pulled away and reached for the phone. When Florence answered, he said, "I need a favor."

"Name it," Florence said.

"I'd like to take my friend Kieran to meet my mother. Can you be at the Pass for breakfast tomorrow morning and make sure all the other aunts stay away? I don't want tension and drama. This is important to me."

"Be there around ten," Florence said. "It'll be just the four of us and Odell."

"Thank you," Phillip said. After they hung up, he turned over to look at Kieran. "Maybe I should have asked you first."

"Naw, it's a smashing idea," Kieran assured him.

"I can't promise how it will be. She always keeps me off balance. Lately, she's seemed unusually normal, which probably means we're heading into disaster."

"We Irish are at our best during the worst," Kieran said. "Come here. I didn't get to give you a proper good morning."

"Proper wasn't what I had in mind," Phillip said.

"I'm your man, then."

When Phillip lit his third cigarette on their drive to Pass Christian the next morning, Kieran reached over and took it from him.

"I can't help it," Phillip said. "It either has to be a cigarette or a pencil, and I can't sketch while I drive."

"You worry too much, mate."

But even Kieran looked nonplussed when Phillip stopped just inside the gate of Godbee Lane, and Phillip said, "You mean Shanon never pointed out the house to you?"

"No," Kieran said. "It's stunning." As Phillip tried unsuccessfully to regard the house through unfamiliar eyes, Kieran said, "Who's that waving so frantically?"

"Crap," Phillip said. "Aunt Florence. She wants us to come in the side entrance. This can't be a good omen."

They got out of the car, and Phillip realized that his aunt looked less upset than excited. "I didn't want you to go through the front door and interrupt," she said. "Is this your young man?"

"Kieran McClosky," Phillip said. "My aunt, Florence Gar—" He broke off to listen. "Is that the stereo? It sounds like someone's playing the piano."

"Come inside; just be quiet," Florence said. "My last name is Garrett, Kieran. But please call me Florence." She gave them a conspiratorial look and led them into the kitchen, where she introduced Kieran and Odell while Phillip cocked his head in bewilderment. The piano stopped, started again, stopped, and he heard the sound of laughter.

"Is that my mother playing?"

Florence nodded happily and said, "She hasn't played for years."

"She plays all the time," Odell disagreed. "Just not when anyone can hear."

"I've never heard her play," Phillip said. "I didn't even know she could." He heard her say something, then laugh again. "Who's with her?" he asked.

"No one," Florence said.

"Great," Phillip muttered nervously. "Is she doing Salieri in the asylum?"

"What's that?" Odell asked.

"It's from a movie," Florence explained, frowning at Phillip. "She's on the phone. She's playing for someone, then picking up the phone to talk."

"On the phone with—"

"Claude," Ellan said as she came through the door.

Phillip blinked at her and said, "*My* Claude? He hates to talk on the—"

"You must be Kieran," Ellan said, noticing the way Kieran's eyes were going back and forth between them. She held out her hand and said, "I'm Ellan Powell. I'm so glad you could join us for breakfast."

Kieran took her hand, and Phillip saw his mother's appearance register on his face. He had to admit that she'd made an effort. She was dressed the way he liked her best, casually in jeans and a sleeveless white linen shirt. Her only jewelry was a pair of tiny silver earrings and the silver wedding band that she rarely took off, although she did sometimes wear her diamond with it when she went to mass. Her brown hair shone from the sunlight spilling through the windows. She'd pulled it up into a loose knot, letting wisps fall down the back of her neck. She'd never needed makeup, but she was wearing mascara, which emphasized her light-blue eyes. She looked more like Phillip's older sister than his mother, and her smile and body language conveyed warmth and sincerity as she offered to give Kieran a tour of the house after breakfast.

"You two go sit down," Florence said. "Phillip, you can help Odell and me take the food in."

Kieran let himself be guided away without a backward look, concentrating on Ellan's comments about the history of the house.

"How does she do that?" Phillip asked as the swinging door closed behind them. "It's like she casts some kind of spell on my friends."

"I'd think you'd be glad," Florence said as Odell pressed a platter of bacon and sausage into his hands. "She's having a wonderful morning, mostly because of you."

"Yeah, it's great," Phillip said, thinking that this must have been just the way it was with Shanon. He would end up having to explain one more time why growing up as Ellan's son had been a cross between a nightmare and a fairy tale.

He walked into the dining room and put the platter on the table, then went to the coffee urn on the sideboard to pour himself a cup. His mother and Kieran were still talking about the house, and he made Kieran a cup of tea and set it next to his plate.

When Odell came in with the eggs, she gave him a look and nodded toward his grandfather's chair at the head of the table.

"No," Phillip said. "I'm sitting next to Kieran. You can sit there."

"I had my breakfast hours ago," Odell said.

"Then you can watch us eat your cooking," Ellan said, and Odell shifted the place setting over to Phillip. His mother eyed the bowl of scrambled eggs with a faint look of revulsion. As Phillip sat down and reached for his napkin, she said, "Florence, could you move those eggs closer to the boys, please? I don't… like…eggs."

Phillip felt the pressure of Kieran's leg against his. When he smoothed the linen napkin over his lap, Kieran quickly reached down and squeezed his hand.

He remembers, Phillip thought. *No matter how she acts, he doesn't just write off my memories and fears. He believes me.*

"Kieran, I hope you're not a vegetarian," Florence said. "Take some of that sausage. Daddy has one of his employees ship it here from Chapel Hill, Texas. He swears there's no sausage like it on earth."

"I'm not a vegetarian," Kieran said and obediently speared a piece of sausage.

"Biscuit?" Ellan asked, pushing the bread basket his way. "We butter them all. It's not a Mississippi breakfast unless you leave the table with hardened arteries."

"I ate this way all my life," Odell said. "I'm seventy years old, and there's nothing wrong with my heart."

"Grits!" Kieran said happily and reached for the bowl.

"You like grits?" Florence sounded shocked.

"Love them," Kieran said. "Phillip had to coax me to eat them the first time, but now I'm an addict."

Ellan smiled and said, "Grits are hard-core. What gateway food did you use, Phillip? Fried squash?"

"Hush puppies," Phillip said.

Odell's face radiated approval as Kieran took a generous dollop of butter from the crystal dish next to his plate and dropped it on his grits before he salted and peppered them. It was one of the family scandals that the only way his Yankee grandfather would eat grits was after drowning them with butter, sugar, and milk.

Phillip made himself relax while Florence and his mother kept the conversation light, without pestering Kieran with questions, although they had to be dying of curiosity since this was the first time he'd ever brought a man to meet them. As much as he wanted to know about his mother's phone conversation with Claude, he had no intention of disrupting a morning that was proving to be much easier than he'd anticipated.

"How long have you been here?" Florence finally asked.

"Nearly a month," Kieran said. "In Mississippi. I lived in New York for a year."

"You met Phillip there?" Ellan asked.

"Aye," Kieran said. Phillip hoped he wasn't about to tell them about seeing him first with his grandfather, but Kieran adroitly said, "It's such a beautiful state, Mississippi. The light is amazing—and the warmth: the weather and the people."

"Stay around for hurricane season," Florence said. "That's a different ball of wax."

Phillip looked nervously at his mother, who met his eyes and smiled faintly before saying, "It's just a fact of life. You know, a lot of early Irish immigrants settled in the Southern states. You are Irish?"

Kieran nodded, swallowed his last bite of biscuit, and said, "Much of what I knew about America came from films. When I told a coworker about Phillip, she teased me that I thought all the houses in the South were like *Gone With The Wind*." He looked around. "Yet here I sit in one where Scarlett would feel at home."

"Are you ready for your tour?" Ellan asked.

"Let him finish eating," Phillip said.

"I'm done," Kieran said and looked at Odell. "It was wonderful, thank you. I'd grow quite stout if I ate like this all the time."

"I used to, and look at me," Phillip said. When everyone stared at him, he said, "Okay, stop looking at me. But I have kept my boyish figure. Let's take that tour."

"You help Florence clear the table," Ellan said as she stood up. "I can show Kieran the house."

Kieran grinned at Phillip as he followed Ellan from the dining room. When they were gone, Florence said, "Relax. Without Selma or Andi here, she won't put on a show. I thought you'd figured that out. Isn't that why you made sure I'd keep them away?"

"She never restrained herself when Chad came over," Phillip said.

"That was years ago."

He and Florence began picking up dishes, and Odell said, "I'll put coffee and more hot water for tea in the sunroom."

"Could you put some ashtrays in there, please?" Phillip asked. "Kieran smokes too." While he and Florence loaded the dishwasher, he said, "Was that her first phone conversation with Claude?"

"You'll have to ask her. Kieran is so handsome and likable. It must be serious if he followed you here."

"Why should I give you information when you won't give me any?" Phillip asked.

Florence laughed and said, "You can be so ornery."

"This was just an extended stopover," Phillip said. "He's leaving for Ireland in a few days. For good."

"That's too bad," Florence said.

Odell had gone home, and Phillip and Florence were settled in the sunroom, Phillip with his second cigarette, when Ellan and Kieran found their way back to the living room. Phillip watched them through the open French doors between the two rooms as they paused so she could point out the Rothko to Kieran.

"Phillip, did you tell Kieran the story of this painting?" Ellan asked, glancing into the sunroom.

"I didn't know there was a story," Phillip said, wondering if she was going to explain why it seemed to travel through the house or sometimes hung upside down.

"I'd love to hear it," Kieran said.

"Me too," Phillip said under his breath.

"After Phillip's father died, I wasn't very…this was a sad house, and it affected Phillip. He was only three, but he knew things weren't right. He stopped laughing, or even smiling. His grandfather began taking him places so he could—well, honestly, so he could get away from me. Daddy's company has offices in several cities, but he knew I didn't want Phillip to fly. So now and then, when there was time, he'd make his trips by car and take Phillip with him."

"Is this true?" Phillip whispered to Florence, who nodded.

"Just after Phillip's fifth birthday, they went to Godbee's Houston office. Daddy wanted to make sure Phillip behaved himself, so he told him that he could have anything in the office he wanted. Phillip loved to draw and color. Daddy thought he'd ask for markers and paper. But they walked into the lobby, where solemn little Phillip saw this painting. Mark Rothko is a big deal in Houston;

that's why Daddy kept the painting there. Anyway, Daddy said Phillip's face lit up. He crossed the lobby and stared up at the painting. He clasped his little hands behind his back, looking for all the world as if he knew how one should appreciate great art. Daddy was tickled to death and watched him for several minutes before Phillip turned around and said, 'I want that, Papa.' The painting was crated and on its way here before the end of the day."

Florence jumped up to get a cup of coffee for Phillip and to give herself a reason to stand between him and the others. She held out a napkin and softly said, "Just take a deep breath."

He nodded, unable to speak, and wiped his eyes with the napkin. He was dimly aware that his mother and Kieran moved to the other side of the living room so she could show him something else. By the time they came back, he'd gotten control of himself.

"I didn't take Kieran up to your studio, sugar," Ellan said. "I thought you might like to show him that yourself."

"Yes," Phillip said. "If you don't mind postponing your cigarette and tea?"

"Bang on," Kieran said.

Neither of them spoke as they took the stairs to the third floor, but once they were inside the room, Kieran put his arms around him.

"You told me. Just because I don't remember doesn't mean..." Phillip couldn't finish.

"I think you've been loved all your life, lad."

"It kills me that you're going back," Phillip spoke into Kieran's shoulder. "I just keep telling myself that Derry needs his father. He deserves to have you in his life."

"I've got a chance to do better. I can be the kind of father to Derry that I wish I had. He's halfway round the world, and I've only seen pictures, but I love that boy with all my heart, Phillip. Just think how it's going to be once I hold him."

Phillip wiped his nose on his forearm and said, "Derry's going to be lucky to have you back."

Kieran put his hands on Phillip's shoulders and said, "No. You don't get it. You're just as lucky. I chose to miss Derry's first year. Your mother didn't wake up one day and decide to be nuts. She may be nuts, but she's still your mother, and a parent loves their child no matter what. I can vouch for that." Phillip was silent, taking it all in and trying to think of what to say. "You've got to forgive her, Phillip."

"For what?" he asked. "If she didn't choose to be crazy, then what do I have to forgive her for?"

"For not living up to your expectations. It seems to me that she's done that for you. After all, how many parents would have breakfast with their son's lover? Mine certainly wouldn't! But I forgive them for that. And hopefully, when I do get back home, they'll forgive me for not living up to their expectations too."

"Do you think that's possible?" Phillip asked.

"I'll never know unless I give them the chance," Kieran said. He smiled and added, "I won't lie to you. I'm nervous. I might be less nervous if you were there with me."

Phillip's eyes widened. "I can't," he said.

"Take all the time you need to think about it," Kieran said sarcastically.

Phillip smiled and took Kieran's hand. "I've thought about it ever since you told me that you were planning to go back to Belfast. I hoped you'd ask me. I'd love to see your homeland. And now I'd love to meet Derry. But there's too much holding me here right now."

Kieran released a long sigh. "I understand," he said.

"I can't leave my mother yet," Phillip continued, "and I couldn't go away without my grandfather's permission. It wouldn't be right."

"Calm your jets, Phillip. I agree with you," Kieran insisted. "You've a lot to work out with your family and yourself before you go anywhere."

"Ain't that the truth," Phillip muttered.

Kieran kissed him lightly and said, "The only place you're going with me is back to Belfast House."

"Oh?" After Kieran nuzzled his neck and nibbled his earlobe, Phillip said, "That's a convincing argument. Okay, let's go."

They thanked their hostesses for breakfast and just before they turned to leave, Ellan blurted, "Kieran, do you get restless on long flights? Agitated? Cramps in your legs?"

Phillip, fearing she was about to launch into another commercial-themed diatribe, groaned and said, "I knew this went too perfectly. Mother, please."

"I was only going to offer him some Valium," Ellan said innocently.

"I'll be fine, Mrs. Powell, but thanks for offering," Kieran said.

"I don't think it's a good idea to dole out Valium as a parting gift," Florence softly commented, placing a cautionary hand on Ellan's arm.

Ellan shook free and said, "I know what I'm doing!" She turned to Kieran and added, "And you should call me Ellan. Please."

"If I were mad, I would," Kieran said. He seemed to regret his choice of words, because he hastily added, "Your son and I get on like a house on fire, and I've grown fond of him. The way I feel for him is quite powerful. I'm not sure if it's love, but I know that whatever it is can't be half of what you feel for him. So to honor the person who brought the object of my affections into this world, I feel obligated to be a little formal with you, if you don't mind, ma'am."

"Thank you for being so wonderful to my son," Ellan said. She stepped forward and enveloped Kieran in her arms, kissed him on the cheek, and said, "Have a safe journey home. You better come back to see us."

"I will," Kieran promised.

Phillip was touched. He was also impressed by Kieran's ability to charm and soothe the savage mother.

When Phillip related these feelings later, Kieran sat up in bed and said, "I was being honest with her, not to mention to you. I don't think I've ever told you how I feel about you."

"I think you've managed quite well," Phillip assured him.

"I mean with words."

"You don't have to." Phillip placed Kieran's hand on his chest. "Feel that?"

"Aye."

"The music's never stopped."

They kept their conversation light on the day that Phillip drove Kieran to New Orleans for his flight out of Armstrong International. They mostly rehashed the events of the preceding days—a picnic on the beach, a tour of historic homes in Pass Christian, a jazz concert, and a lot of sex. When the signs leading to the airport became more frequent, Phillip felt the knot in his throat grow larger and tighter. He parked the Volvo behind a row of other cars in front of the terminal and realized that his hands were sweating despite the air conditioner's best efforts.

"Here we are," he said lamely.

"Aye," Kieran said. He put on a game face and said, "Let's get this over with."

Phillip popped the trunk and helped Kieran with his baggage. Once the trunk was closed, they stood awkwardly, staring at each other until Phillip said, "I hate this part."

"Me too," Kieran said. "You'd better send lots of e-mails."

"I will," Phillip promised. "Isn't this the moment where you realize that you forgot your passport?"

Kieran brought his passport from his pocket and flashed it at Phillip. "Sorry, mate. Besides, I'm unemployed. I can't afford to miss my flights now."

An airport security officer stopped nearby and said, "You can't park here. Move it along, gentlemen."

Kieran turned to him and exclaimed, "Wind your neck in, Blue Shirt. I'm trying to say goodbye to the man I love, if that's all right?"

"We'll be out of here before you know it," Phillip said, not wanting an incident.

The officer glared at Kieran and said, "Be quick about it."

Phillip grinned. "I want you to stay longer, but not in a prison." He pulled Kieran into his arms and said, "I'm so glad I met you. I'm going to miss you so much."

"I do love you," Kieran whispered into his ear.

Phillip felt himself edge toward the verge of tears. "I'd buy a ticket in a second to go with you, but—"

"That again?" Kieran looked him in the eye and said, "We covered that. I understand. Got it?" Phillip nodded. "Do me a favor? I've been talking to Shanon about your mother. She's quite keen on her, and it sounds like they get along well."

"This is a goodbye scene?" Phillip asked incredulously.

"Just listen to me, mate. The both of us have some repair work to do with our parents, right? If you can't forgive, the first step is to at least honor them. Respect them. If your mother wants to be friends with Shanon, let her. What's the worst that can happen?" Phillip couldn't think of anything to say, so he simply nodded. Kieran said, "Exactly. It's gonna be fine, mate. You'll see. Honor and respect, right?"

"Aye," Phillip said and felt a tear escape. He quickly wiped it away. "When you fly over Manhattan, wave for me."

Rather than answer, Kieran kissed him long and hard. Before Phillip realized what was happening, Kieran was walking toward the terminal, bags in hand. He turned and shouted, "I nicked your Zooropa shirt!"

"Bastard!" Phillip called after him. Kieran grinned and waved one last time before walking through the terminal doors.

Phillip drove home on autopilot, replaying their last conversation over and over in his head, committing it to memory. He savored the feeling of emptiness and assigned it colors: blues, reds, and shades of gray. He wanted to paint through the pain of losing a dear friend and lover, but when he got home and picked up a brush, it didn't move. The colors he'd thought about earlier didn't seem right somehow, so he gave up.

He went to the kitchen and spent long moments opening cabinet doors and staring blankly at their contents. After opening the refrigerator for the third time, he stomped out of the kitchen, feeling like a caged beast. When Jay walked through the front door on his way in from work, Phillip pushed him toward the stairs and barked, "You. Go to my room."

Jay hurried up the stairs, asking, "What did I do wrong?"

"It's not a punishment. I'm going to draw you," Phillip said. "Sorry. I didn't mean to be so brutal about it."

"I thought you wanted to paint me," Jay said.

"I don't want to start another painting until I've finished the one of Jess. Sketching you is my way of working out how I'll paint you." He looked at Jay. "You don't really have a bad angle. But I want to find the one that most captures you—your personality, who you are on the inside."

Jay blushed, just as Phillip had known he would. When Phillip began sketching, Jay said, "Who do you think I am on the inside?"

Self: everyone's favorite topic, Phillip thought—including his own, so he knew he couldn't hold it against Jay.

"You're a very gentle soul," Phillip said. He thought about Dash's brother, Dennis, who was willing to offer his heart to Jay. He couldn't ask Jay about him, since he wasn't supposed to know—if there was anything to know. "You deserve someone who adores you for the sweetness of your nature, someone who doesn't try to control you."

Jay grimaced and said, "Please don't start talking about Travis. He's not a bad person."

Phillip dropped his eyes to the sketch and made a note about how Jay's fair skin colored to indicate strong emotion. "Changing his locks so you couldn't get your stuff, then putting some of it on the curb?"

"I know," Jay said. "I think he keyed my car too. And he still won't give me my Rollerblades."

"I've had a few bad breakups," Phillip said. "But I never lived with anyone, so I didn't have to endure that kind of drama. I guess I should be glad Travis didn't key *my* car. My grandfather wouldn't be amused. Does he still think I took you away from him?"

"I don't even know your grandfather," Jay said.

Phillip grinned and said, "At least you're making jokes."

"I think he started believing me when I told him about Kieran. Though for a while he thought we had some kind of three-way going."

"Good grief," Phillip said.

"I've lived with Travis since I was nineteen. Two years is a long time. Even if I do deserve somebody better, I'm not jumping into another relationship. I want to be free for a while—have fun and not worry about making someone else happy."

"Want some advice?"

"Could I stop you?"

"No. It's a human right that anyone older gets to dole out wisdom. It's not possible to make someone happy. We can be happy *with* someone." He thought of Kieran and Chad. "And maybe unhappy away from them. But real happiness is something we have to do for ourselves."

"Do you think you're a happy person, Phillip?"

Phillip looked up from the sketch and said, "It's against the rules to question your elders."

"Be serious."

"I wasn't happy," Phillip admitted. "You sure you want to hear this?"

"Yes."

"There was a time when I thought if I could just get away from here, I'd be happy. It did solve a few problems, and I met people I love who are still part of my life. Even so, it was a kind of artificial happiness because I hadn't dealt with what I'd left behind. I wasn't being truthful with myself. That fucked with my art, which has always been honest. I couldn't be happy because I wasn't painting. And I couldn't paint because I wasn't happy. I don't mean happy like jumping up every day in a good mood or always being ready for fun. Or having a lot of friends or living in the right place. All those things are fine. They can get you through a lot." He paused as he thought about his mother and Bunny. "I guess what I'm trying to say is that real happiness comes from believing I can take even the bad things and be okay with who I am."

"So you'd say you're happy now."

I knew I was my own favorite topic, Phillip thought. He sighed and said, "I'm happier than I was. It's kind of a road I have to travel without knowing what's around the next curve."

One must know there is a path at the end of the road.

Jolted, Phillip looked up at Jay and said, "I know how I'm going to paint you."

"How?"

"Sitting at a table with a broken fortune cookie. Only instead of one fortune, there are three. And your face is going to convey a little hope, a little confusion, and a little fear. You know something's going to happen, but you're not sure what."

"Cool," Jay said and was quiet for a while. "Will you be able to do this from your sketches? Because you just helped me make a decision."

"I did?"

"My friend Greg lives in New Orleans. His roommate moved out, and he wants me to share his apartment. My parents are okay with it. I was afraid to do it—give up my job and leave you, Shanon, Carlos, and Jess. Y'all have been taking good care of me, and I'm grateful. But in a way, I want to make a leap into the unknown."

So much for Dennis, Phillip thought. Then again, maybe not. People had a way of finding each other again when they needed to. As he'd learned with Kieran. And with Chad.

"It's like you said. Fear can cripple you, or you can use it constructively," Jay added.

Phillip nodded, sent a silent apology to Dennis and a thank-you to his mother, and said, "Do it. People who love you unselfishly won't hold you back."

"That's right." Jay gestured to the unfinished painting of Jess, which rested against a wall across the room. "Don't hold yourself back either."

At the end of a week of painting away his lonesomeness for Kieran, Phillip carefully transported the canvas to Taryn's house. He'd finished the painting a day earlier, but he couldn't wait for it to dry, because he was proud of the result and eager for her reaction. When Taryn came to the door, she looked tired and distracted.

"Phillip! I'm glad you're here. Come in, please."

"Wait, no," he said, beaming. "Thanks, but I brought your painting."

"My what?"

"You commissioned a painting from me, remember? It's leaning against my car. It's still wet, but I want you to see it. Come on," he urged, leading her to the car.

Phillip stood next to Taryn, trying to see his work as if for the first time. He'd wanted to be cheeky and simply paint a bull's skull on canvas to replace the real one that hung over the fireplace in Taryn's restaurant. But when he'd seen Jess coming up the walk toward Belfast House, he was inspired to paint her into a desert scene: Jess dancing by a burning fire in the desert night, as a phoenix rose into the sky, clutching the moon in his beak.

"It's too literal, isn't it?" Phillip suddenly said, frowning at the painting and taking her silence as disapproval. "The desert, the phoenix, the name of the restaurant—it's all too much, right?"

Taryn put a hand on his arm and said, "Oh, Phillip."

"You're crying," Phillip observed. "It is too literal. I knew it."

"No," she said, slapping his shoulder and sniffling. "It's beautiful. Don't touch it—unless you want to take it inside for me."

"What's wrong?"

"It's Chad," she said. "Roger finally heard from him today."

Phillip mentally grasped at the name for a moment, then said, "His roommate? Your cook."

Taryn nodded. "Chad's still in California. The visit with his father was a bust. I don't know the details, but apparently Chad took it really hard. He's been holed up in his hotel all this time."

"Doing what?"

"Drinking. Drugs. I don't know. He quit his job at the paper—or lost it. I don't know what's going on, and that's the worst part." Phillip put an arm around her shoulders, and she said, "I know I have to let my kid live his own life, make his own mistakes, and all that bullshit. But I don't have to like it."

"He'll be back," Phillip said, almost believing himself.

"He'd better not," Taryn said, trying to smile, "or I'll kill him for putting me through this—and for losing that job! You don't lose a job in today's market."

"But you'll forgive him," Phillip said, thinking of Kieran.

Taryn shrugged and said, "Of course I will. When he comes back, will you—"

Phillip interrupted her with a hug. "Of course I will."

Chapter 25

Even before he opened his eyes, Phillip knew he was waking up in a foul mood. He sat up and stared around him. The room reeked of cigarette smoke. He'd pulled his little table over to his easel, and it was covered with paints, rags, and an overflowing ashtray. Clothes and shoes were strewn everywhere. Dirty laundry loomed menacingly from the floor next to him, as if it might rise up to smother him in his bed. His sink was jammed with coffee cups, and his garbage can was overrun with takeout containers.

"All I need is a phone call from Renata telling me I'm late with my rent," he said to the empty room. He sighed, remembering his phone conversation with his former landlady. He'd felt like he was losing another friend when he gave up the apartment, but since Carlos wasn't going back, and Phillip wasn't sure when he could, it would have been impractical to keep it. Renata had told him to come to her first if he moved back to Manhattan, so at least she didn't think he was a bad risk as a tenant.

He continued to survey the room. The canvas on his easel was painted black. Not with Rothko's subtle nuances of underlying color and texture. Just flat black. Like his state of mind.

He forced himself from the bed to the bathroom to do the drill: *pee, brush teeth, stare at bad hair, shave, shower.* At least he could multitask in the shower. He masturbated, then scrubbed the tub with Comet, which he assured himself also exfoliated his feet.

He missed Kieran. He was worried about Chad. To divert himself the day before, he'd helped Jay pack his car and waved him off to New Orleans. Then he'd tried to call Claude to hammer him with questions, but Claude hadn't answered. He'd wanted to call Bunny, who would never answer again.

It took him a couple of hours to return order and sanity to his space. He shoved his dirty clothes in pillowcases and took them down to the Volvo, intending to use laundry as an excuse to go to Pass Christian, as if Shanon didn't have a washer and drier. Then he went back inside and found Carlos, Shanon, and Jess at the kitchen table, looking as bleary-eyed as he felt. They all watched in silence as he poured himself a cup of coffee, turned around, and leaned against the counter to stare back at them.

"Is there an agenda?" he asked.

"I'm working later," Jess said.

"No," Shanon said.

"Good," Phillip said. "I have a demon to face."

"Another one?" Shanon asked.

"Maybe you should go to services at Redemption Center," Jess said.

"You've got more demons than a *Buffy* episode," Carlos added with a nod.

"Yeah? Well, you're facing this one with me."

"I left my wooden stake in New York," Carlos said.

"You won't need it. Be dressed and in the Volvo in a half hour."

He took his coffee upstairs to the sounds of Carlos's mumbled objections. He tried again without success to call Claude. Then he checked his e-mail, hoping for something from Kieran, but all he had was a note from Alyssa letting him know that her passport was in order. Apparently, she was still suffering from the illusion that he'd actually get to use that ticket to Ibiza.

Carlos was silently suspicious as Phillip drove them to Gulfport before he headed north toward I-10. When he pulled into the parking lot of Barnes & Noble, Carlos started laughing and said, "This is your demon?"

"Yes. And yours."

"I never hated the bookstore," Carlos disagreed.

"I didn't either. Just Stewart. And sometimes the customers."

"And poor Anna."

"It's a good thing you don't have that wooden stake, or I'd use it on you for invoking her memory," Phillip said. "Cover me, Brie. I'm going in."

"Why does it always have to be Sabrina?" Carlos asked.

"She was Charlie's smart angel."

"I'd rather be the cute one," Carlos said, following him inside.

"I'll be in Art," Phillip said.

The store actually felt comfortingly familiar, although the employees had Southern accents and were nicer than he'd ever been when they asked if they could help him find anything. He waved them away and studied the shelves, unsure what he was looking for.

Unfortunately, it found him, just as Anna always had. He turned around when he heard a soft female voice saying, "Hi, Phillip."

"Hello, Linda," he said.

"You never returned my calls. I wanted to—"

"Stop," Phillip said, holding up a hand. "Let's clear this up once and for all. I'm happy with being gay. I like men—spending time with them, having sex with them, sharing all my hopes and dreams with them. Even if that could be changed—and it can't, no matter what your pamphlets say—I don't want to change. I don't want a girlfriend or a wife and house with two kids and a picket fence. I'm not going to your church. I'm not going to teach finger painting to your little captives, and I'm not going out with you."

He'd kept his rant quiet, but it had drawn the attention of a man who came down the aisle. He stopped next to Linda and said, "Good thing. She's my girlfriend."

"Oh," Phillip said, feeling stupid. "I'm sorry."

"That she's my girlfriend?"

"That I'm a jerk," Phillip said.

Linda laughed and said, "You are not. Ryan, this is Phillip Powell. We went to school together."

"Ryan Harper," the man said, extending his hand.

Phillip shook it, thinking that Linda had done well for herself as he noted Ryan's blond hair, perfect teeth, and smooth skin. Her mother would be pleased.

"We met at church," Linda said.

Or maybe her mother wouldn't be pleased, but Phillip smiled and said, "I'm happy for you."

"What I was going to say was that I tried to see you when you were at your mother's house, but you were too sick to have visitors."

"Thank you for coming by," Phillip said. "And for the casseroles."

"You're welcome. You're still invited to church."

Phillip sighed and said, "Linda, I know you mean well. Just let me be, okay?"

"I'll pray for you," Linda said.

Phillip sighed again.

"Nice to meet you," Ryan said as he pulled Linda away.

Yet another person moves on from me into a relationship, Phillip thought.

"I guess he's afraid your tainted soul might be infectious," Carlos commented from behind him.

"Why you want to live down here is beyond me," Phillip said.

"I like your tainted soul. Did you find what you were looking for?" Carlos chirped in his best Barnes & Noble voice.

"And more," Phillip said. He closed his eyes, ran his fingers along book spines, paused on one, and opened his eyes. "Oh, fuck it. I'm not buying a Warhol book. Anna's evil influence strikes again."

Carlos paid for his books, then they left the store and walked to the car. "Want to go to my mother's with me?" Phillip asked. "I'm going to do some laundry there."

"No," Carlos said. "You'll make me fold or something."

"Why'd you buy a book on mosaics?"

"Remember when Jess took us to the Hurricane Camille Memorial?"

"Yeah. You said that you'd always been interested in that kind of work."

"Shanon found someone in Bay St. Louis who's giving classes—teaching us to set broken tile, glass, mirrors in designs we create. We're going to start small and see how it goes—wall hangings, plaques, flowerpots, bowls. If we have any real talent for it, we'll move to bigger projects like tables, then look for shop space in Ocean Springs to start our own business. Eventually, we want to do large-scale projects like walls in bars and restaurants."

"That's great!" Phillip said. "I had no idea you two were so creative. Here I thought you were just falling in love."

"That too," Carlos said with a grin. "You seem to always lose your roommates to entrepreneurs."

Phillip gave him a sideways glance and said, "I didn't lose Alyssa." He thought about it a few minutes. "When I came back, I kept trying to fill what I thought were empty spaces in my life. Sex with Claude: sex with Dash. Best friend Alyssa: best friend Jess. Loyal straight friend Carlos: loyal straight friend Chad. Free spirit Bunny: free spirit Shanon. It was stupid. There were no empty spaces. Distance didn't mean the people I loved weren't still there. I just found room for new ones."

"You left out a name."

"Okay, predator Anna; predator Linda."

"You know that's not who—"

"There's never been anyone before, and there could never be anyone again, like Kieran," Phillip said. "I'll be in your debt forever for bringing us back together when Bunny died."

"You owe me nothing," Carlos insisted. "Without you, I wouldn't have met Shanon." They were quiet until Carlos said, "If you're brooding over what to say about Shanon's past, I already know."

"That she grew up in an orphanage?" Phillip asked.

"I know how she made the money that's financing our joint venture. Her honesty is one of the things I love best about her."

"What did you say when she told you?" Phillip asked, even though it was none of his business.

"I told her I used to work as a male escort." When Phillip darted a shocked glance his way, Carlos burst out laughing. "You're so easy. At least *she* knew I was joking."

"I was just thinking how pissed Bunny would be to know you held out on him," Phillip said.

"Are you sure I did?"

"I'm not falling for it again," Phillip said.

Phillip dropped Carlos in Ocean Springs and drove by Chad's house in Biloxi. Phillip had parked Chad's truck on the street when he'd returned it. It didn't look like it had been moved, so Phillip assumed Chad was still gone. When he got to his grandfather's house, no one was home. Nor did anyone come to the door at Odell's. He chose to take that as a good sign. Chad was enough to worry about.

After he started a load of laundry, he wandered through the house and finally went to his bedroom to lie down and stare at the ceiling. He dozed until a fly crawled on his cheek. He brushed it aside and turned his head. When it came back, he swatted at it again and opened his eyes.

Claude was kneeling next to the bed with the pine needle he'd been using to torment Phillip. Unsure whether what he was seeing was real, Phillip stared at Claude for a moment, then opened his arms. Claude grinned and got on the bed. Both of them were quiet as they held each other.

"This feels familiar," Phillip said, breaking the silence. "Do I know you?"

"Biblically," Claude said. "You're in my room."

"Finally found a way to spend the night in my bed, did you?"

"I'm resourceful."

"Yeah, taking advantage of an old widow to subsidize your laziness."

Claude laughed and said, "Your idea."

"I have one now and then."

They held each other for a couple of minutes, each listening to the other's breathing.

"I miss Bunny," Claude said finally.

"Me too." Again they were quiet for a while. "Tell me how you came to be in my bed."

"*My* bed. You know I don't like talking on the phone, and Ellan and I were doing it two or three times a day. I figured the only way to put a stop to it was to continue our dialogue in person."

"Do you two talk about me?"

"Only at first. You were what we had in common, and she was curious about our relationship."

"What'd you tell her?"

"I told her that when you say a man's name during sex, it sounds like a prayer."

Phillip felt his face turn bright red and he said, "Shut up! What did she say?"

"She said Kieran is a more musical name than Claude." Claude started laughing. "You'll fall for anything, won't you? Like your mother would talk about your sex life."

"You're as bad as Carlos. I'm going to stop believing either of you. What do you really talk about with my mother?"

"Whatever random topic might occur to her. I tell her a lot of Bisquick stories."

"Did that mongrel come with you? Will he be sleeping in my bed too?"

"He did come, but he prefers the floor."

"So what's the arrangement? Or is there an arrangement?"

"Phillip," Claude said in a reproving tone, "that's between Ellan and me."

"She's not going to fall in love with you, is she? There's not that much of an age difference, and you're an extremely appealing man."

"If such a thing happened, I'd know how to handle it," Claude said. "She has no illusions about who I am." When Phillip gave a doubtful grunt, Claude smiled. "Ellan doesn't seem more or less crazy than anyone else I know. However," he gave Phillip's shoulder a little shake, "I'm not saying it's not difficult to be her son, or that you didn't pay a price for her emotional instability."

"You don't have to add the next part," Phillip said. "If I could let that go, it'd be better for me. I think I have let a lot of it go. Our history just makes me leery of her. The thing is…" He paused to think about his situation. "She's not asking me to pretend like everything's okay. She's not asking for anything except maybe a little forgiveness. I'm the one who puts all this pressure on us. Or I let her relationships with other people, like Florence or Shanon, make me feel guilty for expecting more than she can give me. I don't want you to become one of those people."

"That's for you to deal with," Claude said. He kissed Phillip's forehead. "Go downstairs. Do that pile of laundry we spotted next to the washing machine. I'll come down after I unpack."

On his way downstairs Phillip paused on the landing to glance through the window that overlooked the vast backyard. His mother was throwing a stick for a large dog that resembled Florence's golden retrievers, except for its white-tipped coat. Every time Bisquick picked up the stick, Ellan would lean over, laughing and calling him while she slapped her knees. Bisquick would lope back, tail wagging, to do it all again. Phillip watched for several minutes before he ran upstairs to his studio to grab a sketchbook and some graphite pencils. Then he went to the laundry room to start another load.

He pushed himself up to sit on the drier and draw and was overwhelmed by a sense memory. He'd done it before—sketching while he sat on the drier, enjoying the white noise; the warm, moist air; the smell of soap and wet fabric. He recalled feeling as if he and Odell were in collusion to keep him from being disturbed; only rarely did anyone else have a reason to come into the laundry room. It had given him a secret vantage point to observe the moods of the house and decide whether he wanted to sneak away to the beach or to Chad's house.

He rapidly drew his mother the way she'd looked outside and surprised himself when his pencil moved away from her to create a little boy instead of a dog. The boy wasn't him. It was Derry.

"...can't just move people in and out of here like we're running a boarding house."

He looked up with a frown when he heard Selma's voice. She was with his mother in the kitchen; he had a feeling that neither knew he could see and hear them. He wondered if the strange little thrill he felt was what Shanon experienced when she watched people through her telescope.

His mother took out one of the Meissen bowls, filled it with water, and set it on the floor for Bisquick, who looked done in.

"Ellan! There are a hundred other bowls you could use."

"Are there?" Ellan asked with a vague expression as she stared at the dog lapping up his water. She sighed and turned her gaze on her sister. "But you see, these are my bowls. And it's my house."

"They're Mama's bowls, and it's Daddy's house."

"I don't think Mama has any need of bowls. And you know as well as I do whose name is on the deed of this house."

"Let's not get into that again. I'm simply saying that before Phillip moves his boyfriends in, you might want to clear it with Daddy."

Ellan raised her eyebrows and said, "Boyfriends?"

"Don't be coy. It's no secret that Phillip is gay."

Ellan smiled and said, "It wasn't the gender I questioned. It was the plural. If you know something I don't, maybe we'd better air out more bedrooms."

"You're not funny."

"I have a suggestion for you, Selma. If the things that go on in this house are so irksome, why don't you give me the privacy you have? After all, I don't traipse into your home whenever I take a notion to. Or snoop into your business."

"You don't even know this Claude."

"That's debatable, but 'this Claude' is Phillip's friend. That's all I need to know." Ellan looked thoughtful for a moment. "For years, you've been tossing your inexpert diagnoses my way—chronic depression, bipolar syndrome, agoraphobia, panic disorder. Phillip has never treated me like whatever disease he might find in *Reader's Digest*. He just wanted a mother who didn't scare him and a home where he didn't have to be the parent. I failed him. But he's never let me down, and he's never brought a single thing into my life that wasn't good. If he wants to fill every room in this house with men and dogs, it's got nothing to do with you."

"You'll regret this day," Selma said before she stomped out the back door.

Phillip jumped as the drier turned off and he heard Selma's truck roar to life. His mother jumped too when he stepped into the kitchen from the laundry room.

"Don't do that," she yelped. "I hate surprises."

He hugged her and said, "Thank you for what you said. What do you think she'll do?"

"She can't do a damn thing," Ellan said as she pulled away to look at him. "None of them can." She stared into his eyes and frowned. "I didn't want to bother you with this, but it might explain a few things about your aunts. It goes back a few years, when Daddy made some changes to his estate."

"Do I want to hear this? Or need to? I'm sure Papa cut me out of the will when I left Mississippi."

"You watch too much television."

"I don't even own a TV."

"I don't deny that he was angry when you defied him—and disappointed that you had no interest in Godbee Energy. But I don't think that ever affected his plans for the business. If Daddy dies, James and Rodney Cannon will still run things, but we'll all keep getting money from Godbee. That's not what set Fala and Florence against Andi and Selma. It was this house."

"Oh," Phillip said, remembering her comment to Selma about the deed. "They have their own houses. It would only be right for him to give it to you."

"He can't give it to me," she said. She looked away as Claude came in.

Claude let Bisquick out, then turned around and noted their silence. "Am I interrupting?"

"I don't mind if you hear this, as long as it doesn't bother Phillip."

"I don't care," Phillip said, reaching into the refrigerator to take out two beers. He handed one to Claude and looked at his mother. "Do you want one? Or anything else?"

"No, thank you, sugar, but it's sweet of you to ask."

"Why can't he give the house to you?"

"Because he no longer owns it," Ellan said. "The deed to our house is in your name."

Phillip gaped at her, sure that he hadn't heard her correctly. "How did that happen?"

"We'd better sit down. This may take a while." They sat on opposite sides of the kitchen table, with Claude between them. "When he redid his estate planning, he met with the girls—without me. What I know is secondhand."

"From Florence, I'm sure."

She smiled and said, "You'd be surprised what all of my sisters will give away when they're stirred up. He wanted to make sure that if something happened to him, I could stay here, with nurses, if necessary." She rolled her eyes. "Or housekeepers, as he likes to call them, thinking I don't know what's going on. I've become friends with some of them. Especially the avid card players. Which reminds me; Claude says he plays a variation of our card game. We should find a fourth person and—"

"Mom."

"Oh, right. The house. He wanted to deed it over to me, which didn't sit well with Florence. She knew he wouldn't be cold in his grave before Andi or Selma would have me declared unfit—"

"Incompetent," Claude said.

"And take over. Florence told Daddy to put the house in your name. Fala, of course, supported that wholeheartedly."

"But not Andi and Selma? They don't think I should inherit the house?"

His mother gave him an exasperated look. "Aren't you listening? You don't have to inherit it; it's already yours. They didn't think you cared about the house and that given the chance, you'd sell it to some stranger—the way it was once sold to Daddy—just to be free of it and the family."

"That's not fair. I'd never sell our house."

"Daddy did what Florence and Fala wanted as soon as you turned twenty-one. They've all been fighting about it since, with me in the middle."

He frowned at her. "How could you be in the middle? Did you disagree with his decision?"

She was quiet for a while, then said, "When Mike died, this is where I *wanted* to be. No matter how sick I was, I remembered that the wind in our trees and the water lapping our beach was the first music I ever knew. These walls had always sheltered me. I wanted to give you that when you lost your father, but instead this became the place where you were afraid and lonely. I worried that Daddy would somehow use the house as a trap—to force you to come back to a place you didn't want to be."

"He didn't," Phillip said.

"No, he used your near destitution and your concern for my health to get you out of New York. He paid your bills and promised you a place to paint if you'd look after me."

Phillip drummed his fingers on the table and said, "I see Florence has been forthcoming, as usual. Mom, I don't deny that I was broke, and things weren't likely to get better in New York unless I found a roommate. But I could have picked up the phone and asked you to have someone at Godbee write me a check. I could have asked Fala or Florence for money. I didn't have to come home to keep from starving to death. I came home because I needed to. I just couldn't admit that—even to myself."

"Now that you're painting, it seems like it was a good decision," Claude said.

"It was," Phillip agreed. He looked back at his mother. "Thanks for clearing up why the aunts acted so weird when I got home. They made it sound like it was all about your health. But about Papa… *Is* putting the house in my name a way to make me do what he wants?"

"I don't know. From the time we moved back here from New Orleans, he always acted like the house would be yours eventually."

"Why me? There are other Godbee grandchildren. Even if Andi's kids displease him more than I do, there's still hope that Florence's daughters could end up okay."

"Phillip, I think the house is meant to be an atonement," Ellan said in the careful tone of someone who wanted to be understood. "You and I weren't the only ones who lost something when your father died. Daddy loved Mike like a son. Do you ever think of how he must have suffered because he also lost someone he loved?"

"No," Phillip said. "I guess all I ever think about is how everything affects me."

You're human, Phillip, Kieran's Irish brogue and Dash's Southern drawl reminded him.

Ellan's hand came down on his in a soothing gesture. "Claude is going to teach me to cook Italian food," she said. "Are you staying for dinner?"

"When did *you* learn to cook?"

"Enh, we'll teach other," Claude said.

"No, thanks," Phillip said. "I have places to go, things to do. Crap, I've still got laundry to finish."

"I'm not doing it," Claude said.

"Like that surprises me."

"I'll finish it," Ellan said. She laughed at his dubious look. "I can be a mother."

"If I won't wash my own clothes, I guess I have to wash my hands of the consequences," Phillip said, standing up to let Bisquick inside. He patted the dog's head, then went to hug Claude goodbye. Claude's arms were strong and reassuring.

As he headed out the door, Ellan said, "Phillip?"

"Yes, ma'am?"

"When you see them, tell them we need keys to at least one of the cars."

He nodded. She knew him too well, because he intended to visit Andi first. Then he'd have a talk with Selma.

When he got out of his car at the Beasley house, he noted with satisfaction that some negligent neighbor had allowed a dog to leave a huge memento next to the driveway. His Aunt Andi would be horrified.

She answered the door, looked past him as if to make sure he was alone, hugged him in the aloof way she usually did, and led him to the kitchen, where she'd been ladling homemade soup into plastic containers.

"For our church's soup kitchen," she explained. She declined his offer of help, put a glass of iced tea in front of him, and went back to her task. "It's been quite a while since I saw you."

"I wanted to ask you in person to please remove my name from Redemption Center's mailing list," Phillip said as politely as he could. "Linda already gave me a packet of your materials. In fact, I saw Linda earlier and told her the same thing I'm telling you. I couldn't change if I wanted to, and I don't want to. I don't need to be reminded on a weekly basis that there are people who believe I'm going to hell. I'm sure you think your intentions are good. But if you're serving up guilt and damnation with your soup, it's not charity. It's small and mean, and I want no part of it."

Andi stopped ladling to stare at him. "How can you call any act of kindness mean?"

"It's not an act of kindness. It's an attempt to control the way people live or what they believe. You don't have that right. No one does. I'm not broken. I don't need to be fixed."

"We're all sinners," Andi said. "Some of us are trying to do good."

"This isn't a blanket condemnation of religious people—people of faith, whatever you want to call them. My mother, as crazy as you think she is, has an uncanny ability to see people for who they are. And I know that when she's kneeling in church, she doesn't pray that I'll change. If my own mother can see me as a man who's just being who he's supposed to be, then it's no concern of yours."

Andi let out a snort and said, "Your mother became Catholic and raised you that way for one reason, and it had nothing to do with faith."

"Maybe not, but—"

"She was being a good wife because your father was Catholic. But he's been dead twenty years. Now she does it to annoy our family."

They maintained a tense silence while Phillip considered her words. No one had ever told him his father was Catholic. He'd always thought his mother's religion was a random choice. When Shanon had suggested there was some reason behind it, he'd figured it was to get him into a good school. But if Andi was right, maybe his mother had been giving both of them a connection to his father.

"Nobody's annoyed but you," he finally said. "Because you can't mind your own business. Her faith comforts her. Stop harassing her, or me, or inciting Linda or anyone else in your church to harass me."

Andi's mouth hung open in shock. Then she sputtered, "Harassing you? By trying to help you turn from a life of sin?"

"I never asked for your help."

"You're my family. What kind of person would I be if I didn't want you to achieve eternal life?"

"I just want to live *this* life," Phillip said. "With some humor and love. How I do that is my business."

"And how I love you is my business," Andi said. "Do you think I don't care that you're living a shameful lifestyle that could cost you your soul?"

"You know next to nothing about my life," Phillip said. "You religious extremists whip yourselves into a froth of fear, lies, and suspicion. If it wasn't gay people, it'd be somebody else. You need a devil to scare yourselves into righteousness."

He jumped as Andi dropped her ladle on the stove.

"From the time you were a little boy," Andi said, her voice shaking, "I watched over you when Ellan was too wrapped up in grief to properly mother you. I have always cared about your well-being."

"Is it concern for me that makes you torment my mother about her sanity and about Papa's decision to give me the house?"

"Your mother is sick," Andi said. "Something you didn't really care about over the last five years, when you abandoned your family. So you found out about the house? I guess now I understand why you came home—greed."

"That's not true. I'd never sell Papa's house."

"What if your mother wasn't there? Would you live in it?"

"I don't know," he said irritably. "It's not something I have to decide for a long time." He stood up. "Do you have a plastic bag?" When she nodded, he said, "May I have it?"

She reached into a drawer, gave it to him, then followed him through the house. He went outside, cleaned up the dog droppings next to the driveway, and put the bag into her trash container.

"Thank you," she said, watching from the doorway.

He went back to where she stood. "I know you'll never approve of me, Aunt Andi, and we'll never agree about religion, but at least realize one thing about your church. If it separates people like Linda from their families, it can't be good. Even if you don't think Paula Bishop is the ideal mother, she's the one Linda's got."

Andi's shoulders slumped, and she covered her eyes with her hand. "Maybe I need Linda more than she needs me, but she does need me."

"That's fine. But if you keep making her choose, one day it might not be you she chooses. Blood is thicker than grape Kool-Aid."

"Redemption Center isn't a cult," Andi said, frowning.

"There's no reason why she can't have both of you in her life, just like I had Mom and Taryn Cunningham—or Mom and all of my aunts."

Andi appeared to consider his words. Finally, she said, "Do you have even one happy memory of me from your childhood?"

Phillip grinned and said, "Definitely. You and Selma took me to Mobile. Some gardens."

"Bellingrath Gardens," Andi said with a nod.

"You were wearing a white shell and a long black skirt. And you had on black strappy sandals."

"That's the best memory you have?"

"I wasn't finished. We were walking back to the car, and the wind whipped your skirt up. You were mortified. You were trying to hold it down and hold on to your purse, and as you reached for the car door, another gust of wind blew your skirt up again. That time, I was ready for it, and I gave you a wolf whistle. You blushed, then you said, 'Oh, the heck with it. I always had good legs.' You let your skirt go and started spinning, then you grabbed my hands. We whirled around until we were dizzy and laughing so hard we could barely stand up."

"That is nice," Andi said with a smile. She had a dreamy look in her eyes as she remembered.

"The thing is, any other thirteen-year-old would have died of embarrassment to be manhandled like that by his aunt. But you were lucky enough to have a gay nephew who was willing to dance with you. We're still having our own little dance, aren't we?"

"I guess we are," she said, giving him a look of grim agreement. "I don't know what you're planning to do with your life, Phillip. I'm sure you won't stay in Mississippi. But no matter where you go, you're like the prodigal son. When you come home, we'll rejoice and kill the fatted calf for you."

"Uncle Geoffrey will need a bigger grill," Phillip said. When she smiled, he said, "Truce?" She nodded, and he walked to his grandfather's car.

Phillip pulled into Godbee's Gulf Coast Nursery when he saw that Selma's truck was still there. She was alone when he walked inside the office. "I need the keys to all the cars at Papa's house, please," he said. "Claude will be using them to do Mom's errands, take her to the doctor, whatever."

Selma leaned back in her chair and stared at him. "Do you honestly think the rest of us are going to hand over your mother's care to this stranger?"

"Claude's not a stranger to me," Phillip said. "I have no idea where Papa is or what time it is in China, but call him. The three of us can straighten this out. Bringing me home was the best thing he ever did for my mother and me, and I'll be happy to tell him so. You'll have to decide for yourself whether you want to be at odds with us. But if you try to have her declared incompetent or to take the house from me, I can give you the name of my lawyer. Dash will help me fight you every step of the way."

Selma narrowed her eyes at him. When he refused to look away, she turned to unlock a drawer in her credenza and tossed a ring of keys on the desk. "You think you're winning, but you're not. Your mother does need help."

Phillip sat, propped his elbows on his legs, and rested his chin on his hand while he looked at her. "Have you ever loved anyone so much, so desperately, that even the idea of losing her could make you come unglued? I've never loved anyone that way. I'm not sure I'm strong enough. That's the only way she knows how to love. Maybe that means she's stronger than the rest of us. Uncle Harold says she copes in her own way. Uncle Sam says we're all a little crazy. Taryn Cunningham made me see how intensely a mother fears for her child." He dropped his gaze to the keys. "But it was Paula Bishop and Odell who helped me understand that someone who's all heart has no defenses against getting it broken. Since she's not going to change, maybe all we can do is help her through her bad moments."

"*We?* Seems like you want Claude to do that for you."

Phillip sighed. "I have the same problem you do. We let our memories color how we see her. Like Paula, you and the other aunts remember her before my father died, when she at least gave the impression of stability. You want her to be that person again, but she never will be. What I remember are her weird mood shifts and hysterics. That's not who she is now."

"What about the day she found out you were home? You think she was faking that fit?"

"Of course not. She was furious. That was between her and me, and we worked it out. She's a lot better than the way I remember her. So what if she's never like everybody else? She's who she is. I think she needs people in her life who'll just let her be. Maybe some of my friends can make her life happier. I'm sorry if you don't understand or approve. But she's *my* mother. It's *our* home. We'll do what we want, and if the rest of you don't like it—"

"Sometimes you sound just like your grandfather," Selma interrupted.

"Coming from you, that's a compliment," Phillip said with a grin. "Since you're like him too. There's something else I've been meaning to say to you. Thank you for giving me a job. That work helped bring me back to myself. I'm sure with your love of the soil and your passion for growing things, you understand that better than I do. I finally saw your offer as an act of love, and it meant a lot to me that it came from you. I know you've been disappointed in me for a long time. I'm sorry if truths about my life made yours harder. I don't judge you for guarding your privacy. I just hope you've found some happiness along the way."

She stared hard at him for a minute. Then, unexpectedly, she smiled. "Phillip, you still have a lot to learn. Just because I don't march in parades or slap rainbow decals on my truck doesn't mean I don't have a full life. I'll stop pestering your mother if you stop pestering me. No matter what you think, I'm too busy to worry myself over every detail of Ellan's life. Let's hope your little arrangement works out."

"It will," he said, standing. "Thank you."

"Did you get the note I left at your house earlier?"

"No."

"Billy Banks at Whittier Plantation wants you to get in touch with him. He wasn't sure how to reach you to talk about the painting you gave them. Call him. Or go by. The place is looking great."

Chapter 26

Phillip removed his keys from the ignition but didn't get out of the car. He stared at Belfast House, lost in reflection as he idly thumbed the miniature disco ball on his key ring. He'd dreamed of his big break for so long. From the day he'd left for New York City over five years before, he'd worked out every possible scenario in his mind, but as time went by he'd felt his dream fade. He'd been to parties in every borough of Manhattan, crashed gallery openings, submitted his portfolio to agents, worked the club scene, slept with all the wrong people, visualized success daily—all to no avail. He'd assumed that he had to live in a thriving city to be a working artist and never imagined that moving home would further his career. Billy Banks had proved him wrong on a morning that hadn't begun auspiciously.

He'd taken his portraits of Kieran and Bunny to Pass Christian to show them to Claude, who rested them one at a time on the mantel in the living room to study them. Phillip wasn't comfortable with the way the Rothko loomed above them. He didn't need to be reminded of the creative distance he still needed to travel.

Claude, however, shook his head at Phillip's insecurity and said, "First of all, you're painting. Second, your paintings are brimming with emotion: sadness, longing, love. Which tells me that you've found your vision and your heart. If you paint over these canvases with Rothko darkness, I'll have to hurt you."

Phillip grinned and said, "Please don't hurt me. And thank you for not saying that Kieran is hot."

"That too," Claude said, taking everything off the mantel so he could put the paintings side by side to study them.

Phillip wasn't aware that his mother had come into the living room until she said, "Is Taryn Cunningham still doing photographs?"

Startled, he whipped around and said, "I don't know. She's probably too busy with the restaurant. Why do you ask?"

"Just curious," Ellan said, staring at Phillip's paintings.

He wondered briefly if she thought Taryn should photograph his paintings, then an uneasy suspicion injected hostility into his thoughts. "Are you calling me a photographer?" he asked. "You don't like the paintings?"

Since that was usually the moment that an aunt or Odell would have interceded, he glanced at Claude, who backed up to rest his hands behind him on the grand piano, as if to remove himself from whatever was playing out between Phillip and Ellan.

His mother walked to him and said, "The paintings are beautiful." She lifted her hand and lightly brushed a finger over his eyelashes. "Paint what you see—what *you* see." She turned around and left the room.

Phillip turned toward Claude and said, "Whether or not she's crazy, she'll make me that way."

"Only if you let her," Claude said. He turned to look at the paintings again.

His mother's reaction made Phillip reluctant to follow up on the message that Selma had given him. But after putting the portraits in the trunk of the Volvo, he went back inside and called Billy Banks, who thanked him profusely for his painting of the Whittier house, praised his talent, and asked if they could meet for lunch. Phillip was grinning by the time they hung up and sketched a mental image of what Billy Banks might look like: late twenties, curly dark hair, preppy, with a faithful golden Lab at his side.

The Billy Banks who answered the door was hardly the suave heartthrob that Phillip had envisioned. He was stocky with prematurely graying temples and bushy eyebrows, and he wore a tracksuit. Mr. Banks greeted him warmly, reminding Phillip that anyone who appreciated his art was someone to be treated kindly.

"It's a pleasure to meet you, sir," Phillip said.

"Sir?" Billy Banks looked stricken. "Call me Billy, please. Only guys in handcuffs call me Sir. Although it's hard to say anything with a ball gag in your mouth, don't you think? Come on in."

Phillip hesitated, considering Billy's last statement before he took a cautious step into the house and said, "If I'm late, it's because I was nosing around the grounds before I rang your doorbell. Everything turned out great."

"Isn't it wonderful?" Billy said, leading him into a parlor off the entry hall. "Your aunt is simply amazing. Didn't you work for her? Isn't that what led you to do a painting of our house?"

"Yes," Phillip answered. "But I had to quit the job halfway through the project. I got sick—blah blah blah. That's boring."

"Certainly not. You're a fascinating young man," Billy stated. "It's beastly hot today. Iced tea?"

"Please."

Billy poured two glasses of tea from a pitcher sweating on an antique push-cart in the corner of the room. He set the glasses on a coffee table, carefully nestling them on top of coasters, and gestured toward a settee. Phillip sat and tried not to look uncomfortable when Billy sat next to him rather than on one of the nearby armchairs. There was a strained silence while Billy smiled like an idiot and stared at Phillip, who was desperately trying to think of something to say.

"You're obviously interested in restoring houses, but other than that I know little about you. What do you do?" Phillip asked. When he saw Billy smirk, Phillip hastily clarified, "For a living, I mean."

Billy's expression turned bland, and he said, "Oh, that. Thanks for reminding me of the grim reality that is my life. Let's not talk about such mundane things. Let's talk about you."

"Okay," Phillip said. He answered Billy's questions as cordially as possible, wondering why he was so uncomfortable. He wanted to be true to his Southern upbringing and be polite to his host, but in the back of his mind he heard a strong New York accent saying, *This guy is crazy, man! Get the fuck out of there and let's go get a beer, dude.*

"Are you okay?" Billy suddenly asked.

"What?" Phillip responded, snapping out of his reverie. "Yes. I'm fine."

Billy placed a hand on Phillip's leg and said, "Am I making you uncomfortable?"

Phillip realized that the arm of the settee was digging into his back. "No. Not at all. When are we eating? I'm starving."

Billy opened his mouth to say something, but just as he licked his lips and smiled lasciviously, a woman in a gray suit burst into the room and said, "Hello there. You must be Phillip, yes? I apologize for keeping you waiting. I hope Billy's been entertaining you."

Relieved, Phillip jumped to his feet and said, "Yes, he has. It's a pleasure to see you."

Billy looked defeated for a moment, but he polished off his iced tea, bussed his wife on the cheek, and said, "Now that you're here, darling, and Phillip is in good hands, I've a meeting tonight in New Orleans. I'll see you on Monday. Phillip, it was lovely meeting a talented young man such as yourself."

"Thank you," Phillip said, trying not to wince when Billy placed a hand on his cheek before he left the room.

"You'll have to excuse my husband. He can be a bit forward."

"Was he? I didn't notice."

"It's sweet of you to lie. My name is Candice, but please call me Candi. All my friends do." They shook hands, and Candi said, "I see Billy stopped flirting with you long enough to offer iced tea. Would you like any more?"

"No, I'm fine," Phillip said.

Candi looked him over and smiled, saying, "Have we shocked you? He's harmless. He just can't resist a lovely young man. But perhaps you're not accustomed to such behavior."

"I…" His curiosity about Candi and Billy's relationship was fierce, but he wasn't sure what to say. He was mesmerized by this tall, cool ash-blonde in a smart suit who exuded confidence and poise. "Is the renovation to the house complete? May I have a tour?"

"Certainly," she said. "We're proud of it."

His compliments were genuine as she guided him through the house. Just as with Belfast House, he felt a deep sense of happiness to see such painstaking restoration to something that could have fallen into ruin. When she showed him the second floor, he kept his face blank in reaction to his awareness that she and Billy kept separate bedrooms.

Candi let his sudden silence stretch out before saying, "You don't remember that you met my husband before, do you?"

"He never visited the job site," Phillip said, confused.

"He met you at a party in Biloxi," Candi said.

The only party Phillip had been to was Dash's. Although Phillip couldn't remember meeting Billy there, it would explain the ball-gag remark.

"Let's have lunch," Candi said. "If you don't mind, we're going out. We'll take my car, unless you'd prefer to follow me. It's up to you."

While Candi drove them to Pass Christian, she explained her marriage to Billy. It was an arrangement that served them both. Billy came from a family with a long and distinguished military background. Billy's father and uncle were heads of a corporation contracted to provide the U.S. armed forces with military vehicles. Billy had chosen to stay in the closet to protect his interests in the family fortune and business. Candi, a friend of Billy's from college, helped Billy by marrying him, which also benefited her, since Billy was willing to help her pursue a passion: owning her own gallery.

"Do you think less of me now?" Candi asked. "If so, I'll understand."

Phillip stared ahead, thinking about the price Bunny had paid because he wasn't willing to live a lie for his family. The Godbees, whatever their flaws, hadn't forced Phillip to sacrifice anything to live openly on his own terms.

"Who am I to judge you and Billy for your arrangement," he finally said. "It's just ironic that Louisiana and Mississippi call it a marriage, since I wouldn't have that right with a man I'd vow to love passionately for a lifetime."

"Point taken. You and I will get along fine, Phillip," Candi said as she parked the car in front of an old home that was undergoing renovation. A crew of men swarmed the building, painting, drilling, hammering, and bringing in materials and various tools from their trucks. "This is it."

"We're eating here?"

"Yes," Candi said. She reached for a basket in the backseat, saying, "I brought sandwiches. Come on."

The contractor handed them hard hats, and Candi led Phillip through the house, pointing out walls that would be removed, explaining how she wanted to add a theatrical lighting grid to the ceiling, and saying that the floors would soon be sanded and stained. She said excitedly, "It's going to be a great space. What do you think?"

"I suppose," Phillip said. Candi stared at him expectantly, so he finally said, "I'm sorry. I don't really understand what this is all about or why you brought me here."

"I thought Billy had explained everything. The minute I saw the painting you did of our home, I got excited. The details were exquisite. The color, the balance—your technique is raw, but it worked with the simplicity of the subject matter. It added something, you know? I own a gallery in New Orleans, and I'm opening a new space here," she said, gesturing around them at the gutted house. "It won't be ready for about six months, but I want you to be part of our grand opening."

"You want to show my art?" Phillip said, finally grasping the situation.

"Yes," Candi said. "If I could see more of your paintings, that would be great. But I already think that your work will mesh well with the other Mississippi artists I've lined up."

Phillip was stunned. He heard himself talking, but it seemed like his voice was thousands of miles away. "I just did a painting for Taryn Cunningham that will be hung in her restaurant, the Burning Phoenix."

"Congratulations," Candi said. "I'll definitely go by to see it. I'll need six or eight paintings for the opening. Pick out the ones you like best. We'll see how they look, then we'll work it out from there."

"I appreciate your offer, and I can't tell you how desperately I want my art shown. But I have to be honest. The painting of your house is the only one I have like that. I've done a few portraits. I was blocked for a long time, and these paintings eased me back into my work. But they aren't the direction I'm going in. If you want pretty Southern landscapes, I may not be the artist you're looking for."

"Tell me what you want to paint," Candi suggested.

He remembered the way his mother's finger had brushed his eyes, took a deep breath, and said, "One of my aunts says that I describe people in the language of houses. For example, my grandfather's home is stately. It's surrounded by live oaks. The house is a shelter much the way he was for me. The trees are not invincible, yet they have his strength and dignity. But unlike Realist painters, I wouldn't stand my grandfather under the trees and paint him in front of the house. It's as if the mental pictures I have—of him, the house, the trees—are cut into little pieces and tossed into the air. However they fall, that's how I paint them, because my grandfather, the house, and the trees are all one thing to me. I can't divide them based on what the human eye sees. Nor would I reproduce a piece of a column, a leaf, and my grandfather's hand in a Cubist effect. I convey what I see through color and light. That may sound crazy, but it's the way I interpret the world. That's how I want to paint."

While he'd talked, Candi's expression became intense, and her eyes were fixed on his. As soon as he stopped, she said, "I'll kill you if you don't have several paintings for me to exhibit in six months—or if you let anyone else have your paintings first. One day I plan to be a chapter in your biography, Phillip Powell."

"I could just be a good bullshitter," he said.

"Honey, I'm a Southern woman. I can look at a pile of manure and tell you the bull's age, what mood he's in, and his mother's maiden name. Do we have a deal?"

"Yes," Phillip said happily.

"Good. Now let's eat those sandwiches and talk about my commission."

Phillip picked up the manila envelope that Candi had given him that contained her card, pamphlets about her New Orleans gallery, and a contract, and got out of the car. It wasn't until he shut the door that he noticed Taryn's red Honda in the driveway. He went inside the house, found her with Jess in the living room, and said, "Hey, guys. What's up?"

"There you are!" Taryn exclaimed. "Chad's back."

"He is? When?" Phillip asked, wondering why Chad hadn't called him.

"Roger told me that he came back last night. It took every ounce of restraint I had not to go over there or call him, but Roger said that Chad's a mess. Strung out and holed up in his room. Would you go over there, Phillip? He'll talk to you."

As much as Phillip wanted to share his good news with them, he didn't feel the time was right—especially if Chad needed him. He'd known all along that Chad's trip was a bad idea.

Before he left, Jess pulled him aside in the front hall and said, "Don't worry about Taryn. I'll keep an eye on her until you call us with news about Chad."

"Why are you so good to me?" Phillip asked.

He'd meant it as a rhetorical question but was pleasantly surprised when Jess answered, "Because you're important to me, and whoever is important to you gets my respect."

He thought about friendship during the drive to Biloxi. Chad had been his first teacher. He'd trusted Chad more than anyone in the world, and when Chad cut things off, it had left Phillip afraid to believe in anyone. Even when he became friends with Alyssa, Claude, and Carlos, he'd always been sure that if he needed to, he could slip away unnoticed and resume a similar life elsewhere. Unlike with Chad, however, being separated from them had only strengthened their bonds, which helped Phillip see how important they were to one another. It reminded him of a song that his mother loved. He couldn't remember the lyrics—something about not knowing what you had until it was gone. It was a concept that was growing more familiar because of Kieran.

And Bunny.

The Volvo lurched when the tires drifted onto the shoulder of the highway, and Phillip jerked the wheel, trying to shake away his grief and concentrate on the road. "Be in the moment. Get a grip. Get a grip," he repeated aloud. "Stop being such a pussy."

He made it safely to Chad's and parked the car on the street in front of the house. As he walked up the driveway, the front door opened. Chad appeared, looking pale and haggard with dark circles under his eyes. "Why am I surprised to see you?" he asked.

"'Cause you're drunk?" Phillip guessed.

Chad lifted a bottle of Jack Daniel's and said, "And stoned."

"How lovely for both of us," Phillip said, frowning.

"You've seen me. Run along and tell Taryn that I'm still alive." When Phillip rolled his eyes, he asked, "Isn't that why you're here?"

"Are your buddies here?"

"They're working."

"Why aren't you?"

Chad groaned. "Is that what this is about? Why can't a man take a shit in this fucking town without everyone knowing about it and judging him for it?" He looked heavenward and hollered, "Get me out of here!"

"That's enough. Why don't you get in the car and we'll go back to my place, okay?"

"No way," Chad said. He folded his arms, knocking the bottle against the doorframe and spilling half its contents down his leg.

"Fine," Phillip muttered, thinking it was probably better to hang at Chad's until he could make sure Taryn had left Belfast House. He stood on the steps for a moment, then said, "Aren't you going to ask me in?"

Chad looked up and down the street and said, "Are you alone?"

"Yeah, why?"

"This is usually the moment when someone punches me in the face," Chad said. "Where's the Irishman?"

"In Ireland," Phillip said.

"Good." Chad stumbled inside, and Phillip followed him. Chad collapsed on his bed and offered the bottle to Phillip. "Drink?"

Phillip took the bottle but didn't partake. "So what's going on, Chad?"

"Is this an intervention?"

"No. I'm just concerned. What happened in Los Angeles?" Chad didn't answer. Instead, he rolled over and put his head under the pillow.

After a few minutes, Phillip left the room. He emptied the Jack Daniel's into the kitchen sink and left the bottle next to a half-dozen empty beer cans and stacks of dirty dishes. He wondered if Taryn knew that her chef lived in squalor, or if anyone at the hospital where Pete worked knew. Had neither of them learned about hygiene?

He watched a rerun of *Roseanne* and kept an ear trained for any sounds of movement from Chad's bedroom. After a while he went back and found Chad passed out. He spotted two duffel bags by the closet with airline tags still attached. He moved them into the living room and shut Chad's bedroom door. With no guilt whatsoever, he unzipped Chad's luggage and pawed through it until he found a film canister stuffed with joints and a baggie filled with withered-looking matter in a toiletry kit.

"'Chad scored 'shrooms in L.A.?" Phillip muttered. "Good grief. He's lucky he's not in jail."

A few hours later, he shook Chad awake and said, "Come on. We're busting out of here."

Chad sat up. "Oh, man. Can't we just stay here?"

"Nope," Phillip said, lifting him to his feet and half dragging him down the hall. "Your bags are in my trunk. Your mother has been notified of your safe return, and I left a note for your roommates letting them know that you're staying with me for a few days." He maneuvered Chad out of the house and locked the door behind them. He poured Chad into the passenger seat and said, "If you puke in my car, I swear I'll dump you into the Gulf."

The next morning, Phillip woke to the sound of his toilet flushing. He sat up, rubbing his eyes, and opened them to see Chad stumble out of the bathroom.

"Don't worry. I cleaned the toilet."

"Good boy," Phillip muttered. "I left your toothbrush and stuff in there. Did you find it?"

"Yeah, about that," Chad said. "There were a few items missing from my shaving kit. Any idea what might've happened to them?"

"I'm sure your roommates will be thrilled by the gifts that you left for them," Phillip replied. "We're drying you out."

"I hate you."

"No, you don't."

Chad sat on the floor and put his head between his knees. "Jesus, my head is killing me. Got any scotch?"

"Perhaps you misunderstand the concept of drying out."

"For fuck's sake, Phillip, would you shut up? You're not my father."

"Like he ever gave you any direction," Phillip said.

Chad's head slowly raised, and his half-lidded eyes bored into Phillip's. "You don't know what you're talking about."

"I don't?" Phillip asked. He swung his legs over the side of the bed and sat up. "Let me see if I can guess how your visit with him went. Stop me if I'm wrong. Your plane touched down in L.A., and he met you at the gate. Wait, no, you can't do that anymore. He met you at baggage claim, and you ran into his open arms."

"Shut up."

"He swung you into the air, just like he did every day when you were a little boy."

"I mean it, Phillip. Shut up."

"Then he let go, ruffled your hair, and remarked on what a fine young man you've become. He took you directly to his house, where steaks were sizzling on the grill. He called all his friends to come over and meet his beloved son. After dinner, he sat down at the piano and you all sang songs together. Later that evening, after everyone went home, he tucked you into bed and promised that he'd take you to a ball game the next day. And you fell asleep, feeling safe, loved, and happy." Phillip stopped, watching as Chad shuddered and sobbed into the palms of his hands. "I guess that's not exactly how it went down."

"Of course not," Chad said. He wiped his nose on his arm and took a deep breath. "I don't know why I expected anything from him."

Phillip moved to the floor and sat behind Chad, holding him against his chest and stroking his hair. "Because in spite of it all, he's your father and you love him."

He listened as Chad described what had really happened. Chad spent his first few days in L.A. leaving messages on his father's voice mail, despite the fact that he'd told him when he was arriving and where he would be staying. Finally, he gave up being polite and showed up at his father's house uninvited. The woman who answered the door regarded him with disdain when he explained why he was there but went inside to fetch his father, leaving Chad on the doorstep.

"The look on his face when he saw me said it all," Chad recalled. "I could tell that he thought I'd be like him and not follow through. He was counting on me not to show up. Can you believe it?"

"Yes," Phillip said bluntly.

"So he shuts the door to the house and makes me go into the garage to talk to him, under the guise of how all his buddies hang out with him there and we're buddies, right?" Chad shook his head and said, "Yeah, right. Anyway, we had a couple of beers—"

"There's beer in the garage?" Phillip asked.

"Of course. There was a refrigerator in there," Chad said. "We drink, we talk, and he acts like he's Father of the Year and tells me about all the cool bands he's worked with. Then he made a mistake by telling me about a gig he'd be working the next night. I jumped on that and invited myself. 'Gee, Dad! Why don't I come along? It would be so rad!' Retch. Like that hasn't blown up in my face before, right? But he was caught off-guard and gave me all the information before he even realized what had happened.

"At that point, these two little brats run into the garage and demand to know who I am. They called him Dad, which totally shocked me. They were probably around five or six years old. Not only do I have a step-bitch, but I have brothers."

"Wow," Phillip said.

"You can say that again. I said, 'I guess I'm your half brother,' and they looked at me like I'm nuts, then ran away screaming. I could totally relate to that. That was the last I saw of them. I have no idea what their names are. Isn't that a pisser?

"Then he said something about them having plans and shooed me away. I went to the gig, and we did hang out that night, but afterward, any time that I called or went by, they weren't home."

"Fucker," Phillip said.

"Yeah. I went back to the club where I thought he was working, and this guy, Felix, told me he went on tour with some band. I fucking broke down on the spot. First, I was pissed off, hitting the walls with my fists and cussing, then I bawled like a baby. Felix was really cool, though. He took me to his office, sat me down, and just listened to everything. Then we went out and got smashed."

"Nice," Phillip remarked. "Then what?"

"Then I woke up puking in your toilet," Chad said. "I don't know. The rest is pretty much a big blur." Chad sprawled out on the floor and put his head in Phillip's lap. "Why is it always like this? When will I wake up and realize he doesn't want me in his life?"

"I don't know." Phillip played with Chad's hair. "This is where I usually tell you that you're lucky to have a father."

"That's bullshit."

"I know." Phillip laughed and said, "Can you believe I used to be jealous of you? Even though he was a fuck-up, you had a father. At least you had the hope that he'd come visit or something. I didn't even have that."

Chad rolled his eyes and said, "He's nothing to be jealous about."

"I know that now," Phillip said. "But back then I thought you had it all—a safe house, a dad, and a mother who didn't talk to imaginary friends. You had the life I wanted."

"My parents grew to hate each other, my father abandoned us, and my mother smothered me and never gave me a moment's peace. We ate food from cans in front of the TV. She always worried about money because that asshole never paid his child support. She started catering because we could eat the extra food someone else had paid for. I had to work my ass off after school to be able to afford a car so she could use hers to run her business. You, on the other hand, had a mother who let you do what you wanted and a rich grandfather. You had a housekeeper who cooked you meals and sat you down with china and linen napkins. You worked at the bookstore with me because you wanted to. And then you had the fucking nerve to whine because I accepted a full scholarship to UT. You snubbed your grandfather's offer to put you through college and ran away to New York. Did I leave anything out? Yes: that *you* lived in a palace."

"The palace was haunted."

"So? I was jealous of you."

"I guess the grass is always AstroTurf on the other side of the fence," Phillip said.

"Why do we always think everyone has it so much better?" Chad wondered.

"It gives us something to strive toward? So we don't give up. I don't know. What I do know is that I wouldn't have made it through my first eighteen years if you hadn't been my friend." They were silent for a moment until Phillip said, "What do you mean Taryn smothered you? You were always killing yourself to get her attention."

"Idiot. I was always trying to impress you."

"Oh," Phillip said, smacking Chad's head.

"Hangover!" Chad whined, suddenly going fetal. "Do you have any aspirin?"

"Yeah." Phillip got up, causing Chad's head to thump against the floor and inciting him to curse. Phillip called from the bathroom, "Two tablets?"

"Four."

"Your jeans are chirping," Phillip said as he handed Chad the pills and a glass of water.

"It's my cell." Chad downed the aspirin and water, then said, "It just means I have a message. I don't give a shit right now."

Phillip returned the glass to the bathroom and brought Chad's jeans back with him. He tossed them at Chad's head and flipped open the cell phone. "It's an L.A. number."

"Then I definitely don't give a shit. Gimme."

Phillip handed him the phone and said, "Call your mother. Let her know you're alive and drug-free."

"Fine," Chad said.

"I'm going downstairs to score some breakfast. Do you want anything?" Chad mimed puking and shook his head. "I'll bring back some orange juice."

As Phillip ate a bowl of cereal, he found a note from Shanon explaining that she and Carlos were taking another mosaic class and would be back later that evening. He washed his bowl, poured two glasses of juice, and just as he put his foot on the stairs, Jess came through the front door.

She looked sheepish for a moment, like a teenager who'd missed curfew, and said, "Good morning. How's Chad? Is he okay?"

"He's had a rough couple of weeks, but I think he'll be fine. Do you mind if he hangs out here for a few days?"

"Of course not."

"Thanks." Phillip took a step up, then stopped again. "How's Taryn?"

"What do you mean?" Jess blurted. "I mean—she's fine."

"I'll bet she is." Jess blushed, and he said, "I knew it! This happens to everybody who meets me."

"Oh, don't jump to conclusions. It wasn't like that."

"What was it like? Ew. Never mind."

"I told you, it wasn't like that," Jess repeated. "We talked—"

"You're lesbians," Phillip interjected. "Of course you did."

"And I mostly comforted her," Jess finished. "She was really worried about him—and you, I might add."

"Huh?"

"She thinks of you as a son," Jess said. "I'm sure that's no surprise to you. She just wants her boys to be happy. Are you happy?"

"Deliriously," Phillip said. Jess looked askance at him, so he added, "I didn't get to tell you my big news yesterday. I'm going to be shown at the Banks Gallery."

"The what?"

"Big gallery in New Orleans. The woman who owns it is opening one at the Pass, and she wants to show my work and sell it for huge amounts of money."

"That's amazing! Congratulations," Jess said.

"So, yes, I am happy," Phillip said.

"Great," Jess said, smiling.

"How about you? You finally got some. Are you happy?"

"I told you—"

"Yeah, yeah," he said, moving up the stairs. "You talked, you held each other, vanilla candles burned, but you didn't. Whatever." Phillip took the stairs to his bedroom and handed Chad his orange juice. "Did you call Taryn?"

"Yes. Damn, you're worse than she is," Chad said. "Although she didn't nag me. She kept apologizing for him, but I made her stop. It's not her fault he's a fuck-up. We're supposed to go to the restaurant for dinner. She said we can bring your friends. It's all a ploy to check up on me, but I'm cool with that."

Phillip drank his orange juice, put down the glass, and saw Chad staring at him. "What?"

Chad smiled and said, "I still get hard when I look at you."

Phillip blushed and suddenly felt naked, even though he was wearing boxers and a T-shirt. "I guess the aspirin is working. I'll choose to be flattered by that."

"You should."

"I didn't realize you suffered from this hardship," Phillip said, trying to look anywhere but at Chad's crotch.

"Oh, yeah," Chad said. He stood up and walked to Phillip. "That night on the pier, for example."

"There have been many nights on the pier," Phillip said, trying not to tremble as Chad put his hands on his waist. "Which time?"

"Almost all of them," Chad said, lightly kissing Phillip's neck.

"Aren't you dating somebody?" Phillip asked nervously. "Whatever happened to her? Glow?"

"Glee. Broke up," Chad said. "Right after you came back."

Chad pulled him closer. Phillip felt Chad's erection press against his, which made him light-headed. He held on to Chad's shoulders and regained his balance. "Why?"

"Why what?" Chad asked. He kissed Phillip hard, opening his mouth and lightly touching his tongue to Phillip's.

When they parted, Phillip gasped for breath and said, "I'm so glad you brushed your teeth."

"When I drank that orange juice, I wasn't."

"Why did you break up with her?" Phillip asked.

"I don't know. Why does it matter?"

"Did you do it for me?" Phillip asked. "So we could be together?"

"Maybe," Chad said.

Phillip kissed Chad again, lightly and sweetly, knowing it would probably be the last time, and asked, "Chad, are you gay?"

Chad was silent. His eyes were closed and his lips were pressed together, as if he was struggling inside. Finally, he said, "I'm not sure."

"Then you aren't," Phillip said. "Unless maybe you're bisexual."

Chad opened his eyes and said, "Can you for one fucking minute stop telling me who I am? Fuck your stupid labels. I love you."

"I know you do," Phillip said, resting his head on Chad's shoulder. "I love you too. It's confusing, isn't it? I've been here before, years ago, wondering about myself and wishing I could turn to you."

"After Daytona," Chad whispered.

"Even before that. Eventually, I figured it out. No, check that. You're right about labels. Who really has sexuality figured out? I think we all go through a period of self-analysis when we figure out what's in our realm of possibilities."

Chad drew back but didn't let go of Phillip. "You do, huh?"

"Yes," Phillip said, smiling. "And not just about our sexuality. I think everyone has moments where they check out all their boundaries."

"Like, should I score some magic mushrooms and take a break from reality, or not?"

"Right! Or, is that person I'm talking to really there or a figment of my imagination?"

"Do I want to fuck Phillip, or just be his friend?" They simultaneously put their fingers on their lips and said, "Hmmm."

"Maybe you should take some time—like I did when I moved to New York—and think about where your sexual boundaries are and whether or not you're gay. Let me ask you this," Phillip said. "Is it just me? Have you ever seen another guy and thought, 'Man, his ass is bangin'!'"

"That Irishman you brought to the pier was pretty hot." Chad yelped as Phillip pushed him to the bed and tried to pin him down. "Okay! He was butt ugly. Let go of my nose!"

"Take it back."

"Which part? Ow! Okay, I don't want to fuck anybody but you."

Phillip let go of Chad's nose and rolled over. "That's not exactly what I meant."

Chad rolled on top of him and surprised Phillip by kissing him and saying, "Me either."

Chapter 27

Phillip spent the morning of his twenty-fourth birthday walking the most deserted beach he could find. The weather wasn't noticeably different, although they were in the last stretch of hurricane season. Except for Pascagoula's heavy rain, Florida and Texas had borne the brunt of the year's Gulf Coast hurricanes, and the air still felt like summer. Nonetheless, he perceived the shifting seasons as an artist who measured time by variations in light. They were definitely into autumn.

He stared at the water and took stock of the changes since his last birthday. People had moved on—Alyssa, Eddie, Julianna, Jay, Kieran, Chad—but only one had broken his heart. He didn't have to be in the church of his mother and Kieran to send up a silent prayer for peace for Bunny.

People had come back to him—Chad, Kieran, Carlos, Claude—and he had come home to others. They'd all given him something. His aunts and uncles. Odell, Taryn, and Paula. The men he'd worked with at Godbee Nursery. New friends like Dash, Shanon, and Jess. He pondered, as he had so often during the past six months, how much his world had expanded emotionally even as it had narrowed to this twenty-mile stretch of coast. It hadn't happened without growing pains—particularly with Chad and Kieran. Nor did he have a clear vision of where he'd be next—either in the geography of heart or land.

It didn't matter. He knew that he was stronger than he'd ever been. His grandfather had given him three gifts: the house, his will to paint again, and his mother. In a way, she was like the South itself: sometimes an uneasy ally, sometimes a force of love, sometimes the cause of anger and fear. And she could be a little crazy, but also a source of wisdom. Only when they'd navigated their way back into each other's life had he been able to see how fiercely their hearts had stayed connected.

All this peace of mind is like the calm before the storm, he thought, but there wasn't a cloud in the sky. He shook off his apprehension. He'd made it through the deadly year—his twenty-third—without falling prey to his parents' catastrophes. He was safe. The path at the end of the road had led him home.

He drove back to Belfast House, knowing he'd find it empty. He wasn't sure what had possessed him to agree to the birthday celebration they were planning: a night in Pass Christian with his mother and the rest of his family, along with many of his Mississippi friends. Maybe he was a little crazier than he wanted to acknowledge. But he'd instinctively known that Claude and his mother would be good for each other. He'd followed his better nature and Kieran's advice and contrived to find ways to bring Shanon and Ellan together, which had brought Carlos and Jess into her life as well. As for Chad...

He relived the days they'd spent together after Chad came back from L.A. They'd never made it to Taryn's restaurant that night. Chad had put himself back in the driver's seat with a simple sentence: "I owe you a road trip and a conversation."

Phillip had left a note for Jess, asking her to tell Taryn that they were leaving for a few days, then they'd hit the road, where Chad made good on his promise. They had a lot to talk about. Phillip's years in New York; Chad's years in Austin. Their lovers. Their friends. How much Chad had hated working at the paper, using his rage at his father as his incentive for quitting. He wasn't sure how he was going to support himself, but he wanted to write.

"I know you think I'm an inarticulate clod," Chad had said. "But just because I don't carry on about my feelings like you do doesn't mean I don't have them. With a keyboard under my hands and a monitor in front of me, I can be expressive."

"Of course you can be," Phillip said. "You honed your skills with all those fantasy games we used to play as kids."

"Clearly, you're trying to grab some of the credit for my creativity," Chad answered.

They were on the beach in Destin, Florida, late one night when Phillip broke down about Bunny. Chad listened and was quiet for a long time afterward, finally saying, "You know, it doesn't matter what's going on between us—sex, love, friendship. It doesn't matter if we live in the same city or a million miles apart. That's one way I'll never leave you. You'd better promise me the same thing."

"Never," Phillip said.

Chad's words about living apart had been prophetic because they came back to Mississippi to find out that his trip to California hadn't been a total washout. The calls Chad had been ignoring were from Felix, the L.A. club owner, who made Chad an interesting offer. Like Chad's father, Felix had worked for years with musicians. He had a thousand stories that some movie-producer friend had been hounding him to write down. Felix wasn't a writer, but Chad was, and the producer was willing to pay him to write a screenplay based on Felix's stories. Chad flew back to L.A. for meetings, unsure whether it would really pan out but feeling like he had nothing to lose.

Phillip opened the e-mail from Chad that he'd already read twice that morning.

Happy birthday from another coast. L.A. scares the shit out of me, and I admire you for being able to live in New York for five years. I could adapt to the urban milieu (that's my pricey writer's word for the day), but why should I? I took some of that obscene amount of money that gets thrown around out here as an act of faith and rented a furnished apartment in less frantic Long Beach. Still a city, but with a name and landscape that's more familiar to me. If you go onto my balcony, climb on the railing, heft yourself up to the roof without sliding down the stucco walls to your death, go to the highest point, and stand on your tiptoes, you can sense there's an ocean out there somewhere. The apartment is two bedrooms. I was going to use the second as my office, but I put my computer in my dining room and haven't moved it yet. You have a standing invitation. For either bedroom. Whenever you want it.

There'd been no new e-mail from Kieran for a couple of days. But Phillip knew it would come. For almost two weeks, Kieran had sent e-cards leading up to Phillip's birthday. It would be so great to have Kieran at the party, but Phillip suppressed his selfishness. Kieran hadn't exactly made peace with his parents, but he'd made overtures. Mostly he and Kyla were finding ways to fit him into Derry's life, and everything Kieran wrote Phillip was confirmation that he'd made the right choice. A boy needed his father.

He leaned back in his chair, staring up at the ceiling and letting that old grief wash over him without a struggle. He would never know life with a father in it. He thought of the fantasies his mother wove for his little cousins about King Michael and his son, Prince Phillip.

"Even when I'm not here, I'll always be holding you in my heart," he said, repeating Kieran's promise aloud. Then silently, he said his second prayer of the day, this one an expression of gratitude to his father for giving him life and his love of making art from that life.

When he heard frantic knocking on the front door, he ran downstairs and opened it to a woman who looked frazzled and upset. His eyes went past her to the taxi waiting at the curb, then his heart froze when she asked, "Are you Phillip Powell, then?"

Her voice had the same Irish music in it as Kieran's, and again he noted her look of obvious discomfort and stress. He didn't want to answer. He didn't want to know what she would say next. He stared at her.

"I have a letter to deliver to Phillip Powell," she said. "Am I at the right address? I'm in the devil of a hurry, and I—"

"I'm Phillip Powell."

"I'm so sorry," she said, thrusting the letter into his hand. "I don't like bringing awful news. I wish I could—I have to go; I can't be missing my flight."

He nodded mutely as she rushed down the brick walkway to the taxi. He watched it pull away, then he looked down at the envelope, which had only his name and address written on it in unfamiliar handwriting. He shut the door and stood motionless, knowing there was no way he could open the envelope, which she so clearly hadn't liked giving him. If he wasn't alone, if any of his friends were there with him, he might have been able to. But in spite of his earlier reassurance to himself that he was strong, he wasn't ready to find out that fate had dealt him catastrophe after all—a day late.

Still holding the letter, he walked outside to the Volvo. He dropped the envelope on the passenger seat, fastened his seat belt, and slowly drove to Pass Christian, ignoring the irate drivers who sped past him with annoyed glances and hand gestures.

He needed Claude. Of all the people at his mother's house who loved him, Claude knew him the most intimately. Claude had shared his body, as Kieran had. Claude knew what it was to laugh with him in bed, as Kieran did. To smoke from a shared cigarette. To run his hands and tongue over skin that was intensely alive with pleasure. To lie still, hiding nothing of body or soul, while Phillip sketched him. Claude was the closest man to Kieran he'd ever known, and the only one who could be there when he endured the contents of the envelope lying like a bomb next to him.

That's my "I got shot" story.... But I'm fine. I'm alive. A lot of people aren't.... I don't condone violence, but I can't condemn a man's passion. God will judge him. That's not my job.... What should you do if your daddy's gay? Kill him.... Ireland, Mississippi...there are foolish people everywhere...

Before he got to the house, he saw him standing in the corner of the front lawn by the azaleas, staring at the stately mansion. He looked peaceful and happy to be where he was. Phillip stopped the car and pulled as far off the road as he could, watching him, willing everything to be okay. Then, instead of driving in, he picked up the envelope and left the car, walking the short stretch of Scenic Drive before going through the front gate. He went straight to him and cleared his throat.

His grandfather whipped around and said, "What's the matter, boy? You look like you've seen a ghost." His half-smile at his grim jest faded when Phillip continued to stare at him, and his wooly eyebrows knitted as he barked, "Phillip?"

"Could you read this, please?" Phillip asked, holding out the envelope.

His grandfather gave him a curious look but took the envelope and opened it. His eyes scanned it, and he finally said, "I can't make sense of this. Who are these people?"

"Kieran?" Phillip asked.

"No. It would sound like a children's story, except you'll get no enjoyment out of it. Some people named Bunny and Bazzer."

Phillip was so weak with relief that his muscles couldn't hold him up. He took the letter from his grandfather and sank to the grass.

Dear Phillip,

I doubt you'll remember me, but if you get this letter from an Irish girl, it means she finally found your address. I'm afraid what I have to tell you isn't good, and it's probably news that's long overdue, but I'll try to explain all that.

You and I had an awkward meeting at a party many months ago, introduced by Bunny Wallace. There's no easy way to tell you that Bunny is dead. He hung himself in his apartment in early July. I'm so sorry.

I know you were a close friend of his, so of course you were aware of the difficulties he had with his family. When it happened, they closed off any access to information about him. Several of his friends got together and tried to find out details. We'd have contacted you, but there were one or two of us who knew from Bunny that you'd moved away.

It was some time before I received a call from one of the Wallaces' maids. That's probably who gave you or sent you this letter. She was quite fond of Bunny, and I hope her employers never find out, but she went through Bunny's effects that were given to the Wallaces. Among those was a note to me. All it said was, "Bazzer, you know why. No one else needs to. Thank you for caring for me. Bunny." She found my name and number on a slip of paper and contacted me to give me a copy she made of the note.

Sadly, I'm really not sure why. Bunny had been drinking a lot; I don't believe he was thinking clearly. The last time I saw him, he talked about his parents' distance; that wasn't new. But he also said, "I'm so fucking tired of being here." I had no idea what he meant until later, when I heard the news. If I'd known, I would have tried to get him through it.

You were the one friend he used to talk about that I couldn't find. I asked my messenger to keep looking in hopes that she could locate your address. I have to go back to England, so I'm giving her this letter with some money and asking her to deliver it in person if she can find you.

We had a service for Bunny, and I'm enclosing my address, number, and e-mail address if you want to ask me about that or talk about anything. If it's any comfort, everything Bunny ever said about you was light and funny, never maudlin, never sentimental. And only slightly bitchy. You were a good friend and he loved you.

God bless you,
Bazzer

Phillip dropped the letter and looked up at his grandfather, tears streaming down his face.

Papa knelt down, his knees creaking, and said, "What the hell kind of family would treat a boy that way?"

Phillip remembered walking through the rain, crying after his grandfather banished him from the house when he was eighteen. But as angry as Papa had been, he'd known that Phillip could go to his aunts for help. "Not ours," he finally said. He couldn't stop crying, and Papa sat all the way down, putting an arm around his shoulders and pulling him close.

"It's okay," Papa said. "I'm sorry about your friend."

"I already knew. I just didn't know these details."

"It's damnable," Papa said. He pulled away to look at Phillip. "Don't you ever go through that kind of misery without turning to your family."

"I'm okay, Papa. I thought the letter was something else. I don't know if I'm crying from relief or grief. I'll stop any minute."

"No tear shed for a friend is wasted," Papa said. They sat quietly together for a while, both of them staring at the house. "I had no idea I'd come back to a home full of people planning a party for you."

"You probably just wanted some rest after your trip," Phillip said. "I'm sorry."

"I wasn't complaining. It's good to come back to a noisy, happy house. It's been a long time."

"Too long," Phillip agreed. "Papa, thank you for being who you are."

"An old bastard?"

"The man who takes care of us all. Thank you for talking me into coming home—for knowing what I needed even if I didn't. From the Rothko to this house, you've been generous." He paused for a moment, then went on. "I'm still going my own way. There's just too much of you in me for me to do anything else."

"Don't blame me for your nonsense," Papa said. He smiled crookedly, as if against his will. "That was some birthday present. It can only get better from here."

"You're right about that. Let's go inside."

"Not yet," Papa said. "Who's this Claude fellow? He seems like a good hand."

"He's as lazy as the day is long," Phillip said. "But he has a way with Mom. Papa, she's going to be fine. She has bad moments, but she doesn't need me—or you, for that matter—to watch her every minute. She knows when she needs help, and she'll ask for it."

"Is this your way of shirking your duty?"

"No. It's my way of repeating what I heard from her a thousand times growing up: 'Let me be, Phillip.' Let her be, okay?"

Phillip's gaze locked on his grandfather's hands. The light that broke through the tops of the live oaks made his skin seem translucent. The backs of his hands were lightly spotted, and his fingers were crooked and shook slightly. They were hands that had worked hard for many years.

As if aware of Phillip's scrutiny, Papa said, "We can shelve this topic for now."

Phillip suppressed his smile, knowing that his grandfather wasn't going to make concessions without further argument. Between Bunny and his birthday, he'd gotten a temporary reprieve. He stood and extended a hand to help the old man up. "You should be enjoying your senior years, not running yourself ragged over us. Why don't you find a nice woman and settle down?"

"That's about as likely to happen to me as it is to you," Papa said acidly.

And thus, Phillip thought, *does the old bastard let me know that he's fully aware of what everyone thinks they've kept from him.*

As they walked together toward the house, Phillip said, "You sure hold your cards close."

"What kind of fool do you take me for, Phillip? Unlike the rest of this family, I live in the real world. I helped shaped the Democratic party platform to be inclusive. I run a business with an equal employment policy that covers all my employees. Do you think I didn't know that you dragged me into a gay bar in New York so you could make calf eyes at every man in there?"

"Just one," Phillip said, smiling at how differently he and his grandfather remembered that night.

They paused inside the front door, and Phillip surveyed the madness. Since everyone seemed to be hard at work, Claude was nowhere to be seen. Selma and Jess were on the landing, winding ribbon through the stair rails. In the living room, several people were gathered around a helium tank. Inflated balloons were allowed to float freely, long ribbons attached to some kind of party favors tied on the ends. A table already contained several brightly wrapped packages.

It was noisy and messy—everything he deplored about birthdays—and it made him happy.

Fala spotted him first and said, "Happy birthday, Phillip!" in a helium-induced squeak.

"Pathetic," his grandfather said.

"What are you doing here?" Shanon demanded. "You're not supposed to see all this until tonight!"

His mother crossed the room, her eyes wide with questions. She lightly touched his face, then stepped between him and his grandfather, keeping her back to Phillip. "Daddy? What did you say to him?"

Phillip reached from behind her and pulled her back against his chest, saying, "It was something else that upset me, Mom. It's okay."

She was rigid at first, then he felt her tension melt as she rested against him. She finally pulled away and called out, "Everyone listen." When the noise stopped and she had their attention, she said, "Phillip doesn't like surprises, and he doesn't want to be on display. So he's going to help prepare for his own party, and rather than make him open gifts tonight in front of everybody, he can just open them throughout the day."

"What gifts?" Carlos asked.

Phillip was in the kitchen later, helping Odell and Andi with the food, when Shanon came in with a box, saying, "I can't stand it any longer. Open this! It's from Carlos and me."

He wiped his hands on his apron and took the box, tearing off the paper and pulling back layers of tissue. He inhaled deeply as he stared at the gift. "Shanon, this is amazing."

They'd taken bits of clear and amber-colored broken glass and arranged a mosaic over reduced reproductions of sketches he'd done of his mother and his aunts.

"It's called *Five Sisters.* I hope you don't mind that we snooped through your stuff to find the sketches. They were able to copy them without removing them."

"I don't mind," he said. "If this is the kind of work you and Carlos are doing, you're going to be really successful." Andi and Odell bent over the piece and made appreciative comments while Phillip hugged Shanon with gratitude. "I absolutely love it."

It was like that throughout the day, with Phillip being presented gifts privately. When Selma cornered him in the parlor, holding out an envelope, he said, "It's nice to have Papa back sticking his nose in everything, isn't it?"

"It's good to have the whole family together," she agreed. "Without tension."

His eyes widened when he opened the card and saw the amount of the check. "Aunt Selma..."

"It's an investment," she said. "Use your time to paint, although you always have a job at Godbee Nursery if you need it."

He went up to his studio later to get a little respite from them, but Fala followed to present him with an impressive collection of books on Italian art. "Hopefully, you'll travel there some day and see all this for yourself," she said.

They looked through the books together for a few minutes. He stopped to compare two paintings of the Madonna, one done by Jacopo Bellini and the other by his son, Giovanni. "Do you think my father would have been proud of my work?" he asked.

"Yes," Fala said without hesitation.

"How do you think he'd have handled having a gay son?"

"The answer to that lies with your mother," Fala said.

"I don't want to ask her. I want to know what *you* think."

"You misunderstood me. Mike's reaction would have been the same as Ellan's. He'd have loved you, accepted you, and protected you from the judgment of others." She noted his skeptical expression and said, "I'm not telling you what I think you want to hear. Those two were of one mind, and I know I'm right."

Phillip was smoking in the backyard later when he said to Florence, "Today, it feels good to be a Godbee."

"We're not perfect," she said. "But so far we've managed not to kill each other."

"If you hadn't met Sam, would you have come back from New York?"

She weighed her answer, then said, "I loved living in New York, but let's just say Sam gave me a way to save face when I came back. I didn't have to admit that I was homesick." She narrowed her eyes when he smirked at her and said, "But you understand that, don't you?"

"Maybe," he said, hating that she was right. "When I came back, why didn't you tell me you were all fighting over whether I should know about the house? You knew I'd never sell it, didn't you?"

"What I knew was that you looked worn down, Phillip. Beaten. I couldn't let your mother see you like that. Plus Fala and I always agreed with Ellan that you shouldn't be forced to live here if it wasn't what you wanted. It all turned out okay, didn't it?"

He nodded, and they went back inside together.

More art books, clothes from Andi—like Bunny, she'd never approved of Phillip's indifference to what he wore—and several other unopened gifts had accumulated by the time he went to Belfast House to shower and change before the official start of his party. He checked his e-mail and found one from Kieran.

Hope you're having a great birthday, mate. I'll message you what will be tomorrow for me, but deep into the night for you, so you can natter about your party. File attached isn't your birthday gift. You'll get that when I find just the right thing. Birthday gifts, like love, should be offered when they're right, not when the time is. We know a bit about that, don't we?

The attached file contained a dozen pictures of Kieran with Derry. They made a happy father-and-son team on the playground, just as Phillip had envisioned. He burned the pictures to a CD and stopped on his way back to Pass Christian to have them printed so he could show everyone else.

The party had started when he got there. He greeted a group of his Godbee Nursery friends who were shyly clustering next to the grand piano. As he talked to them, his eyes traveled to the wall above the mantel, which caused him to give Florence a panicked look. She walked over and said, "What?"

"Where's the Rothko?"

"Daddy moved it to the library," she said. "That's where it stays when he's home. Nothing to worry about."

"Okay," he said, relieved.

By the time he left the group that Chad referred to as his posse, Shanon had joined them and everyone was enjoying listening to Goldie accompany Evita at the piano. He went to Taryn, touched that his mother had invited her. He knew the two of them would never be friends, not only because his mother wasn't overly fond of Chad but also because they had too much uncomfortable history through Phillip.

"I got an e-mail from Chad this morning," he said.

"Good. When you answer it, tell him to call his mother. How does he seem?"

"He's fine. Settling into his new apartment. I think this writing gig is going to work out for him."

"I hope so." She took a deep breath. "I don't want to worry about him. I guess it's just a mother's job."

"It's not like it's the first time he's lived away from you. He was in Austin for four years."

"I know. But it's different this time. Maybe because he's so far away. Maybe because I know he's really growing up now, and each time I see him again, he'll be less like my little boy."

"Please. When we're with our mothers, all of us are five years old again. He'll always bang through the front door, track dirt in the house, and bitch about what's for dinner—except you'll be serving it up at the Burning Phoenix."

Jess walked over and said, "I think Ellan wants you."

Phillip looked around until he saw his mother standing in the doorway to the parlor. "This is just your way of getting rid of me so you two can be alone," he said, leaving them before they could protest.

"Are you having a good time?" he asked his mother.

"It's *your* party," she said.

"If it's my party, where's my present from you?"

"I gave you life."

"Nice try."

"In the library." He followed her there, and his eyes widened at the beautiful set of leather luggage stacked near the fireplace. "You'll be doing some traveling now, right? Your grandfather's back, Claude is here, and the rest of your friends can make sure I'm not scaring the tourists."

"Where do you think I should go?" he asked, thinking, *Belfast and Kieran. L.A. and Chad. Like it's even debatable for her.*

"You could start with Ibiza," she suggested.

"I have a lot of work ahead of me during the next few months," he said. "I can't go anywhere for a while." He watched as she walked to the fireplace and reached above it for the Rothko. "Stop that! What are you doing?" he exclaimed as he dashed over to stop her.

"This is yours. You should take it with you," she said.

"To Ibiza?" he asked, struggling to keep her from moving the canvas.

"No. To Belfast House," she grunted. "Let go."

"It's not going anywhere," he answered. "It belongs here."

"That's your opinion."

"Why do you move this thing every damned day?"

"I'll tell you. But only if you let go," she said cagily.

They both stopped struggling with the painting, but neither let go. Phillip said, "You have to let go too."

"We'll let go together, okay?"

"Fine."

"One, two, three, release," she said. They simultaneously let go and slowly backed away from the fireplace, hands still in the air. As if performing mime, they stopped moving, faced each other, and slowly lowered their hands. They both signed audibly. Then they looked over as the painting slid down the wall to the top of the mantel and began to pitch forward.

"Fuck!" Phillip yelled, running to catch it. "It came unhinged."

"Oh, shit! Catch it!" Ellan cried, running to help him.

Phillip caught it first, ducking under the painting and splaying his hands so that the canvas landed on the pads of his fingertips. Ellan clutched the frame and helped him balance it, and together they maneuvered it back to the wall.

"Is it okay?" worried Ellan.

"I'm not sure," Phillip answered. He examined the bottom first, where the painting might have been scratched by the mantel, but it was intact. He scanned the rest of the paint for damage and saw none. "It looks fine."

"Thank goodness," Ellan said, breathing a sigh of relief. "I thought—"

"You thought!" Phillip growled. "This is exactly why I hate it that you're always carting it around like an Etch A Sketch. It's a great work of art. It can be damaged from the oils on your skin, the salt in the air, not to mention stupid accidents like this one. Don't touch it."

Throughout his diatribe Ellan held up her hand, opening and closing her fingers, as if an imaginary hand puppet was speaking Phillip's dialogue back to him. When Phillip stopped talking and fumed, so did Ellan. The hand puppet remained still until she said, "Fine. It stays."

"Thank you," Phillip said. "Now explain; why are you so fixated on that damn painting?"

Ellan and the hand puppet said, "That damn painting—" She broke off, glared at her hand, and used her other hand to muzzle it and drag it to her side. Satisfied, she continued, "That damn painting reminds me of you. That's why I keep moving it around."

"Because I chose it?" Phillip asked. "Because it's dark and depressing? I don't get it. You won't let go of it, but you keep pushing me out the door."

"I like to try it out in new locations. I like to see how it changes the atmosphere of a different room. What law says that it *has* to be in one spot?" She turned to face the painting. "Look at it. It's beautiful, larger than life, and multilayered. It has more depth and meaning than I could ever perceive. It can inspire people, make them sad or happy, really make them feel something." She turned to him and gently clasped his face. "Just like my boy."

Phillip put his hands over hers. "Thank you," he whispered. "I love you, Mom."

"Oh, sugar," Ellan said, enfolding him in her arms. "All I ever wanted was for you to go into the world and live, love, and thrive. I don't want you rattling around here like poor old me."

"You're not poor or old," Phillip said into her shoulder.

"I've seen what you can do when you let yourself, Phillip. I've seen how you touch people. I've seen how you love. I've seen how people respond in kind." She broke their embrace. "You've got a great gift. And you can paint too!" Phillip laughed. "You can paint anywhere. I want you to live, paint, and leave a meaningful mark behind."

"No pressure," Phillip said, rolling his eyes.

"You'll never fail," Ellan decreed.

"What about you?" he asked.

"I'm like the Rothko too. Unhinged but unscathed."

"Mom—"

"You've brought interesting people to my life. No matter how hard I resist, my sisters will always be around. And Odell will outlive us all. Even if you're halfway around the world, I've always got you."

"Don't ever doubt it," Phillip replied.

"Good. Now let's go back to your party," Ellan said. As she turned to leave, her hand popped up again and said, "You didn't tell him about your appointment next week with that therapist." Ellan looked over her shoulder at Phillip, who was grinning. Then she continued walking, saying, "Why bother? He knows I'll be fine."

Claude followed him later when he sneaked outside to smoke a cigarette. He intended to share the contents of Bazzer's letter with Claude and Carlos as well as Alyssa, but he wasn't sure a party was the appropriate moment. Particularly when every time he talked about Bunny, he ended up crying.

Claude took his cigarette and finished it, then hugged him. "Are you having a good night?"

"I am," Phillip said.

Claude looked thoughtful for a few seconds, then said, "What the hell. It's your birthday," and pulled him closer for a deep, tongue-tangling kiss.

"It appears you have another package for me," Phillip said when his mouth was free.

"I have one, but your box is full," Claude said.

Phillip laughed. "We had good times, didn't we?"

"The best."

They walked inside and were still standing together in the living room when Phillip saw Paula Bishop come through the front door carrying a small gift. "The neighborhood dealer," he said in an undertone to Claude, whose face showed that he thought Phillip was kidding.

"Happy birthday," Paula said. "I'm crashing your party because I wanted to give you this. Maybe now isn't the best time or place to open it."

"See?" Phillip said to Claude. "Is it part of your fall harvest, Paula?"

She laughed and said, "Right. Like I'd do that under your family's nose."

"Then I'm opening it," he said and greedily tore the paper off the gift.

"I got in touch with some of my high school classmates, and everyone went through their old stuff until Gail Finney hit pay dirt," Paula said.

Phillip pulled back the tissue. Without removing his gaze from the framed picture, he said, "Thank you, Paula. So much."

"I told you he was hot," Paula said.

Phillip studied every detail of the picture of his father. He was standing with one hand on the pole of a party tent, an amused look on his face seeming to indicate that he expected it to come down any minute. He wore a chambray shirt with the sleeves rolled up to expose powerful forearms. A breeze blew his dark, shoulder-length hair from his face. In every other picture Phillip had seen, his father's hair had been short. He looked strong, handsome, and heartbreakingly young.

As Phillip stared at the picture, he saw the hand that so much resembled his own reach over to brush fingertips against glass. "Oh, Paula," Ellan said. "That's the day we met."

"All the girls were acting like fools over him," Paula said. "No one had any idea who he was, just that he worked for your father."

"He's a looker," Claude said.

"I look nothing like him," Phillip said.

"Your eyes are just like his," Ellan said. Phillip finally tore his gaze from the picture to make sure his mother was okay. She smiled, seeming composed.

Fala joined them, looking down at the picture as Paula said, "I remember it like it was yesterday—the way he ignored all those giggling schoolgirls. Buddy and I were standing near him when Ellan walked down the stairs from the house."

Phillip looked back at his mother when she said, "My eyes went right to him. He was watching me. It was like nobody else was there. I felt like I was being pulled toward him."

Fala said, "When you got to him, didn't he say—"

"Come to daddy," Claude murmured. The spell was broken as all three women gave him bewildered looks.

"That's not what he said," Fala objected.

Phillip turned his head, wondering who'd caught Claude's eye. He saw that Dash had just come in, looking very manly in jeans, a sport coat, and a white shirt with three buttons undone to show off his chest hair. As Claude brushed by Phillip, it took him a second to remember that he'd introduced Claude and Dash the week before. The sudden attraction didn't make sense, until he realized that Dash hadn't come alone. He'd brought his gorgeous brother, Dennis, with him.

"Ah," Phillip said and rolled his eyes. "In-fucking-credible."

"Phillip," Ellan scolded.

"You should have named me Cupid," Phillip muttered. "Observe: The normally inactive homo erection can demonstrate enormous energy when stalking his prey."

"*Homo erectus,*" Fala corrected, while Paula roared with laughter and his mother shook her head.

Phillip could tell Claude's party story was Kieran's favorite when they messaged each other later. After Phillip had exhausted the subject of the party, and Kieran had talked about his new job and his plans for the next time he saw Derry, Phillip decided to describe his scare that day, when he'd thought someone was delivering tragic news about Kieran.

Poor Phillip. I'm not in danger here. It was never quite as sensational as the news would have you think. And your president helped make it much better, after all.

He did? I thought everybody over there hates him.

Not this president, you dolt. His predecessor.

Oh. Don't I feel stupid. My grandfather has played golf with him. Papa was a big contributor to Clinton's campaigns.

Shut the lights! That's the kind of yarn I expect you to tell Derry some day.

By the time Phillip crawled into bed, he was worn out. He'd left all his gifts in Pass Christian except one. The photograph of his father was next to his bed, with one of the new pictures of Kieran and Derry tucked into the corner of the frame. He kept the light on so he could stare at them all until he fell asleep.

They were still watching over him the next morning, but they'd been joined by Carlos and Claude, who woke him by clambering onto the bed on either side of him.

"I don't know what perversions you two have in mind, but can I pee first?" Phillip asked. When he came out of the bathroom, they were still on his bed, watching wordlessly as he started a pot of coffee. Finally, Phillip walked over, lit a cigarette, and asked Claude, "What's the story on you and Dennis the Sailor Man?"

"They both got laid," Carlos said. "That's not why we're here."

"Okay," Phillip said, dizzy as always from his first cigarette of the day. Or maybe it was the vision of Dennis and Claude fucking.

"Your grandfather told Ellan, who told me, that you got a letter about Bunny," Claude said. "Which you failed to mention to us."

"You're not the only one who lost him," Carlos said.

Phillip put out the Marlboro, found the letter, and crawled on the bed between them. He handed the letter to Carlos, who read it and passed it to Claude.

"It doesn't tell us much more than we knew, does it?" Claude asked.

"We know he left a note," Phillip said.

"What bothers me most," Carlos said, "is that not knowing about his death doesn't seem a lot different from not knowing about his life—like we never really knew him at all—as if a man can be summed up by his love for fashion, partying, and PlayStation."

"Oh, Carlos," Phillip said, wincing. "That's so not true. We knew that his family caused him pain. We knew that he'd do anything to help a friend. We knew that the sight of a beautiful man was like music to him. That anything brutish distressed him. And we all knew that the dancing, the parties, and the drugs were his way of numbing himself to whatever hurt him."

"All of us hurt, don't we?" Claude asked. "At some point, each of us has to decide whether to be ruled by our pain, find a way to express it, or rise above it. Bunny chose to end it."

"I'm so angry with him," Carlos said. "Why wouldn't he let us help him?"

"I don't know," Claude said.

"See? It always comes back to that." Carlos sighed.

"I can't figure out if suicide is selfish or selfless," Phillip said.

"Selfish, because it leaves people behind feeling guilty and helpless," Carlos answered.

"No. I think it's a total negation of the self," Claude replied.

"That clears it up," Phillip said. He nestled into the crook of Claude's arm and stared at Carlos. "Can I ask you a question totally unrelated to Bunny? How is it that a straight man is so comfortable in bed with one or more gay men?"

"Four brothers in a small apartment," Carlos said. "We had to sleep all over each other. At my grandmother's house, when we were little, it was all five of us in one king size bed. It's no big deal." He turned on his side to face Phillip and Claude. "And you, little brother, are about to get some advice."

Phillip tried to get up, but Claude held him down. "I've had no coffee," he moaned.

"I couldn't handle Bunny's death alone in New York. I didn't just come here to tell you and to bring Kieran to you. I needed you."

"Likewise," Claude said. "And you need us. Which is the way it should be."

"But?" Phillip asked.

"But Bunny gave you a ticket out of here for a reason."

"What?"

"That's for you to figure out," Claude said.

"Bunny couldn't understand the way a family can support you. And apparently, he also didn't grasp the sustaining nature of friends. I'm not unhappy here," Phillip insisted.

"Not being unhappy isn't the same thing as being happy," Carlos said.

The phone rang, and Claude picked it up and answered, "Three guys philosophizing—hi, hon. He's right here."

Phillip took the phone. "Hello?"

"Good morning," Alyssa said brightly.

"Right on time to throw your two cents in," Phillip said. "Do you want me to read Bazzer's letter to you?"

"Yes," she said.

When he was finished, Alyssa was quiet for a minute, then said, "Have they pitched the trip to you yet?"

"That's what they were doing when you called. You're like a Greek chorus. My passport came. When do you want to go?"

"In about seven months," Alyssa said in a tiny voice.

"I can pay for your ticket if money's tight," Phillip said.

"Actually, it may be more like seven months and a couple of years."

"Oh," Phillip said, sitting up with excitement. "Are you serious? You're pregnant?"

"Eight weeks," she confirmed. "Happy birthday."

He looked back at Claude and Carlos. They were both grinning at him. "Did these two assholes already know this? I'm your best friend. You were supposed to tell me first—after Eric, of course."

"When they called earlier to tell me it was time for a Phillip talk, I couldn't stop myself. I'm too happy to shut up about it."

"I'm happy too," Phillip said. He took the phone with him to the coffeemaker while Carlos and Claude talked in bed. "I don't want to taint your news, but it feels like you've returned balance to the world."

"It's okay. I thought the same thing. It's an affirmation of life after losing Bunny. It doesn't make the hurt go away, but it tempers it with something good."

"Exactly," Phillip said.

"So you can either get pregnant, or you can take the trip to Ibiza. Because life in this crazy world goes on, Phillip. Grab it. Live it. Paint it."

Chapter 28

The debate in Phillip's head raged on: *Should I go outside and smoke or not?* He'd arrived at the airport two hours early for his flight to Spain, as advised by the airline. The check-in process had been surprisingly quick, which meant he had loads of time to kill before takeoff. Unfortunately, in Phillip's case, idle hands were the devil's nicotine fit. He scanned the waiting area, looking for a clock, but didn't see one.

"For the love of..." he trailed off, looking behind him. Nothing. "The whole point of an airport is getting to where you need to be on time. You'd think there would be clocks everywhere."

"It's almost noon," the woman next to him said, barely looking up from a magazine.

"Thank you," Phillip said.

He hoisted his backpack over his shoulder, snatched up his carry-on bag, and walked quickly toward the exit. As soon as he was outside, he lit up a Marlboro, inhaled deeply, and sighed with relief.

"You can't smoke there!" a security officer bellowed. "Go down past the taxi stand!"

Phillip meandered onward, lazily smoking and savoring the moment, knowing that all too soon he'd be trapped in the belly of an airplane with nowhere to smoke for almost ten hours. When he reached the designated smoking area, Phillip pulled his flight itinerary from his pocket and studied the time between layovers, wondering if he'd have enough time to smoke.

"I'm such a slave," he said to his cigarette butt. He tossed it to the ground and promptly lit another.

He felt jittery despite his nicotine fix. He thought briefly of his mother and hoped she would be okay without him, then forced the worry away. She'd be fine. She'd had her first visit with a therapist and even seemed interested in going again. Phillip's aunts had promised to keep a respectable distance while she adjusted to Claude's presence, and Phillip almost believed them. Most of all, it was the sound of his mother's laughter that he'd heard that morning, just before he entered the kitchen, that made him feel comfortable about leaving. Not to mention the way she smiled as she placed a heaping plate of pancakes on the table and urged him to eat quickly so he wouldn't miss his flight.

Thank you, Claude, he thought, *for being a great lover, a great friend, and someone who's brought joy to my mother's life.*

Phillip crushed out his second cigarette and went back inside the terminal. Somehow the lines at the security stations had gotten longer, and he worried about missing his flight. He couldn't help looking back at the doors and remembering when he'd said goodbye to Kieran. He wondered what had happened after that moment. Did Kieran cry? Did he pee?

Oh, man, I have to pee, Phillip thought. The line was moving painfully slow as people took off their shoes and put their bags and briefcases on the conveyor belts. Every time he saw someone with a laptop computer he screamed at them inside his head to hurry up.

When it was his turn to pass through the metal detector, the security woman said, "Haven't I seen you before?"

"It was so much fun the first time, I had to do it again," Phillip joked. She laughed and waved him through. After Phillip gathered his belongings, he raced through the terminal, looking for a restroom.

While he washed and dried his hands, he was struck by a memory of Bunny bitching about the absence of public restrooms in Manhattan.

"That's something you'll never see on *Sex and the City*." Bunny imitated Carrie Bradshaw's voice-over, saying, "I was suddenly struck with a realization. In a city with nearly eight million people, where does everybody pee?"

"At Barnes & Noble," Carlos had answered. "Trust me. I know."

Phillip emerged from the restroom and was confronted with an advertisement for New York City. He stared at the picture of the Empire State Building and recalled visiting the top of it with his friends—Alyssa fighting her hair in the wind, Bunny continually balking about looking like a tourist, Carlos spitting over the side when he thought nobody was looking. He could distinctly remember wishing that Chad was with them so he could share the wonders of the city with his oldest friend.

Thank you, Alyssa, Carlos, and Bunny, for giving this Mississippi boy a million happy memories of Manhattan.

Phillip walked on, scanning the ads for great destinations: London, Sydney, Athens, and on around the globe. He paused at a picture of the Hollywood sign and tried to remember how far Chad said he lived from the landmark. He smiled, moved to the next picture, and laughed helplessly at a picture of Belfast.

"Of course," he said aloud, looking between the two. "Where's the picture of Ibiza? That's what I want to know."

He pulled the ticket from his pocket and pondered the pictures some more, which launched him into another internal struggle expressed through the voices of his friends. Bunny: *No matter where you go, there you are.... I've enclosed a ticket to help you get there.* Shanon: *You let other people make your decisions....* Jess: *People make suggestions. Life gives you choices. But ultimately you make the decisions....*

He decided to throw caution to the wind and approached a check-in counter. "Excuse me. I was wondering if I could change my flight," he said and named a new destination.

"Let's see what we've got here," the ticket agent said. As he spoke, he typed relentlessly on a keyboard and stared at a screen. "An open-ended ticket, eh? Someone likes you."

"Yes," Phillip said, thinking of Bunny and wondering how the man knew that the ticket was a gift.

"Because of the value of the original ticket, the cost to change it won't be that bad. I'm assuming you want the first possible flight?" When Phillip nodded, the agent said, "I can do that, but it means you'll have more than one layover."

"I'd still like to keep it open-ended," Phillip said, "if that changes things."

It didn't, and after ten more minutes of typing, the agent handed Phillip a ticket and said, "Here's your new boarding pass. You need to be at the gate in fifteen minutes."

"Of course I do."

"Better hurry. Your luggage will probably be a day or two late, though."

"Of course it will. But that's okay," Phillip said, thinking that he could buy whatever he needed after he arrived. "Thanks for your help!"

He barely made it to his gate after a hurried credit card call that ensured he'd be met on arrival. His heart was pounding as much from the call as from his sprint to catch his flight.

Later, Phillip leaned back in his seat, thankful that he was in first class. Bunny had been right; it was four stars all the way. He'd passed on the chocolate chip cookie and other perks but was grateful for the extra leg room and warm face towel. Lulled by white noise, he drifted off to sleep and didn't wake up until it was time to change planes. Once again, he slept until his second quick layover. He was disoriented by the unfamiliar airport but still managed to get in a quick smoke between gates. The nicotine dulled his edginess from a long day of travel.

He reclined in his seat the minute it was deemed safe to do so and stared out the window at the passing landscape, which looked like an endless miniature train set. He fished his Discman—a newly purchased gift for himself—from his backpack and allowed Michael Stipe's voice to lull him into the dreamy half-sleep of the peaceful traveler. As he listened to the lyrics of "Nightswimming," he thought about Chad, who'd included the song on a mix tape he'd made for their journey to Daytona.

But this time Phillip was able to think about that time of his life and smile. He definitely felt a sense of closure on the angst-ridden bitterness of his teenage years, mostly thanks to Chad and their ongoing discussions. Phillip had learned that there was never just one perspective on a situation, and Chad had helped him see that even his own perceptions could change over time.

For the first time in his life, Phillip felt stable. He had a better understanding of the past—his and his family's. He felt closer to all of them than he ever had, and he was sure he could count on them for love and support. He liked knowing that no matter where life took him, he could always go home. His family made him feel grounded but also optimistic that there were smooth skies ahead.

R.E.M. began skipping as the plane shuddered violently, then dropped a few hundred feet, which made Phillip feel as though his stomach had leaped into his throat. The passengers were urged to fasten their seat belts, and Phillip grumbled, "Figures."

When the plane finally landed, Phillip forgot all about the turbulence, his aching limbs, and the baby that had screamed during the final part of the flight. He didn't even think about smoking. His only craving was to see the face that would be waiting for him—to hold him once again and finally express what he'd been thinking ever since he'd decided to change his travel plans.

I'm in love, Phillip thought again and smiled. *I love him.*

With that awareness coursing through him, everybody else on the planet became an annoyance—the people lined up in front of him to deplane, the people who lazily milled about the airport like cattle in a field, not to mention the people crowded around the baggage carousel, which seemed to move inordinately slowly, until he finally remembered that his luggage was on its way to Ibiza without him. He blamed his stupidity on travel fatigue.

When he reached the lobby of the airport—exhausted, nervous, and filled with anticipation—he scanned the crowds. He didn't dare move, worried that they'd miss each other in the throng. Phillip was about to start screaming his name when a sign rose above the heads in the crowd. The sign read: BASTARD.

Phillip laughed and moved toward it, practically pushing people out of his way, until he could fling his arms around the man he loved. "I can't believe I did this," he said.

They finally pulled apart to stare wordlessly at each other for a moment, then Phillip got the kiss he craved. Both of them were oblivious to the stares of the other people around them.

"It was the oddest thing," Phillip said when he was able to speak again. "I had Chinese food the other day and got the craziest fortune."

"Oh? What did it say?"

"Go to Belfast, you idiot, and tell Kieran that you love him."